THE PAPERBACK PLACE
1711 CALUMET AVE
VALPARAISO IN 46383
☎ 219 476 0625

"Sensational Shirl Henke is
one of the top ten authors
of American romance."
—*Affaire de Coeur*

The Endless Sky

Shirl Henke

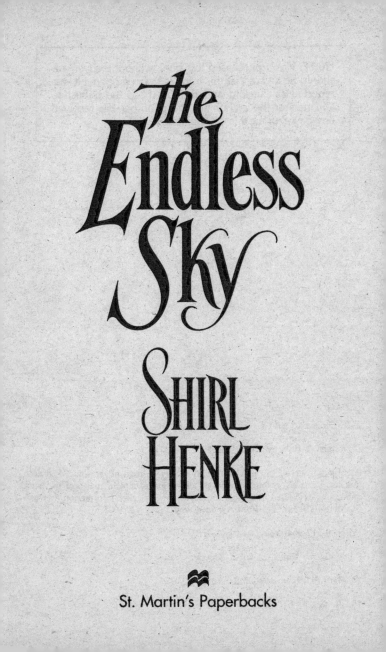

St. Martin's Paperbacks

THE ENDLESS SKY

Copyright © 1998 by Shirl Henke.

All rights reserved. No part of this book may be used or reproduced in any manner whatsoever without written permission except in the case of brief quotations embodied in critical articles or reviews. For information address St. Martin's Press, 175 Fifth Avenue, New York, NY 10010.

ISBN: 0-312-96405-6

Printed in the United States of America

St. Martin's Paperbacks edition/January 1998

10 9 8 7 6 5 4 3 2 1

For Jennifer Enderlin
who believes in the magic

Acknowledgment

My associate, Carol J. Reynard, and I received invaluable assistance in completing this book. Any mistakes in the text are, of course, our own. For their excellent resources on the army, the Indians, and the politics of the era, especially the works cited in the author's note, we once more owe our thanks to the Public Libraries of St. Louis and St. Louis County. In addition, the materials supplied us by the Carbon County Visitor's Council in Rawlins, Wyoming, were most helpful.

As usual my husband, Jim, has read the entire manuscript twice, reworking fight sequences, as well as offering us insights on syntax, plot continuity and even character motivations. Once more, we owe great appreciation to our weapons expert, Dr. Carmine V. DelliQuadri, Jr., D.O., who armed our heroes and our villains.

Only the stones remain on earth forever.

—Old Cheyenne proverb

∽ *Prologue* ∾

1857, Fort Riley, Kansas Territory

The People trudged in resignation, herded between the soldiers' horses in a long straggling line. There were far more women and children left than men. Most of the warriors had been killed. The wives, mothers and sisters had slashed their arms and legs in mourning as was the custom of the Cheyenne. The blood dried and blackened on their skin in the cold November wind that swept across the plains. A thin veneer of ice glittered like scattered diamonds on the desolate earth, a sparkling mockery beneath low pewter clouds. Even the vegetation begged for mercy against the relentless elements, but the People did not. Freezing air seared the brown buffalo grass, striking it down and flattening it all around them.

Soldiers huddled on their horses, drawing heavy overcoats close against the bite of the wind. On foot, the Cheyenne leaned into its teeth, their thin blankets and ragged buffalo hide coverings whipping around their knees. Soon they would reach the white man's fort. None knew what would become of them after that.

The trouble had begun only a few years ago, but it seemed like a lifetime now. For several generations trappers and traders who were friends of the People had come in small numbers, never disturbing the mother earth. But now they were followed by an ever-widening stream of miners and settlers, who scarred the sacred soil with their wagon trails and gouged it with picks and plows. The buffalo herds had begun to shrink and the People learned hunger.

Clashes between emigrant wagon trains and Cheyenne hunters brought the Long Knives who spoke of peace but made war. Treaties were signed and then broken and the vast trackless hunting grounds of the Cheyenne, stretching from the sacred Black Hills in the north to the staked plains of the Comanche in the south, were no longer theirs to roam. The soldiers harried them, and the trails to California and Oregon became safe for the white men but dangerous for the red.

The Blue Coat leader raised his hand and signaled. An ugly adobe fort sat, squat and forbidding, directly ahead of them. Babies wailed and old men sang their death chants while small children clung to their mothers' skirts. They were all herded through the wide stockade gates into the center of a bleak parade ground where the striped flag of the Great White Father snapped in the wind. The Cheyenne stood around it, stoically waiting as the Blue Coat leader greeted another officer.

Freedom Woman watched them, her heart hammering wildly in her chest, her mouth gone dry in spite of the fine sleet that peppered her face. Her arms and legs were crusted with dried blood. *Blood calls to blood, mine to his.*

But Vanishing Grass was dead and she had followed the custom of his people, so wild in her grief that she did not even feel the bite of the knife.

Four days ago the Long Knives had ridden through their village at daybreak, burning the lodges with their dearly garnered winter meat supplies, and killing all the men who resisted. The Pawnee scout who spoke for the Blue Coats had promised them food and medicine from the government. They had seen nothing but bug-ridden hardtack and corn mush thus far. Freedom Woman had heard the Old Ones saying there would be no fresh meat and none of the white man's medicines for starving and sick Cheyenne. In her heart she knew they spoke the truth. The small boy beside her coughed again, his thin face flushed with fever. She had bundled her heavy buffalo robe around him but still he shook with chills.

I will not let you die, no matter what the cost, she thought fiercely, clutching the child by one thin arm. She began to weave her way through the waiting Cheyenne to where the troopers stood in a line, rifles gripped tightly in their hands. Behind them the fort commander and the three leaders started to walk off the parade ground. She had to stop them before it was too late!

Seeing her break free of the group, a blue-eyed soldier lifted the stock of his rifle and shoved it in her face, saying, "You gotta get back. Capt'n'll decide what's to be done here."

Panic clawed at her when she struggled to speak. The words would not come for a moment. They stuck in her dry throat, unfamiliar after so many years. She had wanted to forget, perhaps succeeded all too well! The young trooper's boyish face was wide-eyed with amazement when she flung the heavy woolen scarf away from her head, revealing two thick braids of golden blond hair.

Dumb with shock, he lowered the rifle and she seized her opportunity. Rushing past him, she dragged the child behind her across the icy ground and fell on her knees in front of the post commander.

Brilliant blue eyes stood out in her sun-darkened face as she sobbed, "Please, for the love of God, I cannot let my son die here. You must help us. My name is Anthea Remington. . . ."

1

1871, Boston

"Lord, Ray, she's scarce old enough for corset stays!"
Chase Remington said in amusement as his bored gaze
swept the glittering assembly, scarcely lingering a moment
on the slender young brunette across the room. The Cabots'
Christmas ball was one of the social events of the season.
Everyone of consequence in the city was invited.

His companion Rayburn Lawrence's attention remained
fixed on the girl, who was surrounded by a bevy of young
swains. "Stephanie's seventeen, old enough for courting."

Remington's husky laugh was cynical. "Old enough for
a sizable dowry to present to her husband or else you
wouldn't be interested."

Ray's fair complexion darkened to an unflattering beet
red. "Easy for you to dismiss the issue of money, Chase,
old man, but I must be practical. At least the girl's passable
looking as well as rich. She's old Josiah's only heir."

"And young and gullible enough to be putty in your
hands," Remington said dryly as his eyes once more
alighted on the girl's face when she turned in their direction. Wide-set eyes of some pale color were made dramatic
by dark, winged eyebrows which contrasted with the unusual color of her hair, neither brown nor blond but a rich
bronze color somewhere between. As she shook her head
firmly to something an admirer said, Chase noted the stubborn determination of her chin. "On second thought, for
all her tender years, she might prove more difficult to mold
than putty," he remarked. There was something nigglingly
familiar about the tilt of her jawline and the way her eyes

crinkled when she laughed. Before he could consider it further, Ray distracted him.

"I can handle her even if I'm not the exotic Lothario you are, Chase. That wicked Indian blood combined with the Remington millions makes women drop like ripe fruit just for your taking."

Chase scowled but knew Ray meant no particular offense with the reference to his Cheyenne heritage. Rather it was the mention of Remington wealth that made him uncomfortable. "Women, especially rich Eastern socialites, fickle creatures that they are, love the thrill of the forbidden. Out West I'd be called a half-breed bastard, which technically speaking is true." He shrugged carelessly at Lawrence's embarrassment.

Eager to drop the uncomfortable subject, lest he set off his college companion's volatile temper, Ray seized Chase's arm, saying, "Let me introduce you to Stephanie. Of course, after I do, I shall expect you to act the gentleman and leave the field clear for me." His pale blue eyes were alight with excitement as he started toward the group of men encircling the lady in question.

"Since we both know damn well I'm no gentleman, why don't I retire from the field right now, Ray? The punch bowl beckons and you know how Indians are with liquor." His tone was light but beneath his lazy drawl lay a hard-edged bitterness.

Ray knew the warning signs. Dropping his hand from Chase's arm, he nodded. "Well, I'll see you later then—unless I can convince Stephanie to take a carriage ride with me." He leered nastily as Chase left, heading to the refreshment tables.

After a couple of drinks and a tedious flirtation with the daughter of a prominent congressman, Chase was ready to leave the party, which was crowded with far too many young debutantes and their marriage-minded mamas for his comfort. Agatha Lodge had promised to meet him at midnight if her elderly husband drank himself stuporous as was his wont. After pouring the old sot into his carriage, she would be waiting for Chase in the Cabots' library. They did not plan to read.

What to do from now till then? He took out his gold Howard pocket watch and checked the hour. He could slip down to a private gambling establishment on the seedier side of the city and play a few hands of cards. Perhaps if luck ran with him, he'd stay the night and let Agatha stew. She'd grown more possessive here of late than he preferred.

If only I could leave this accursed prison behind. Visions flashed through his mind of jagged pine-covered mountains, vast prairies undulating with buffalo stretching to the distant horizon, an endless sky so dazzling blue it made a man ache. The acrid taste of bile filled his mouth. He was trapped for as long as his mother lived. If one could call the way she was now "living."

He chose to remember her as she used to be when his father was alive, a tall, regal woman with thick golden hair who walked beside Vanishing Grass with pride. Life with the Cheyenne had been harsh, often dangerous, but for her it had been a liberation from the past, so much so she had taken the name Freedom Woman when she wed her Indian husband. She laughed often then and looked on her only child with warm smiling eyes filled with love. It was because of him that she had come back here. Better they had taken their chances on the reservation than endure the unspeakable obscenities inside the Remington mansion. The army might kill them, the Indian agents starve them, but either way it meant only death, and death, for a Cheyenne warrior, was nothing to be feared. But there were things in the white world even a warrior must fear. He washed away the ugly memories with a long swallow of whiskey punch.

Across the room Stephanie Summerfield tried not to stare at the uncommonly tall man standing alone. His height was not the only thing uncommon about him. His complexion was swarthy in contrast to the snowy whiteness of his shirt, and his unfashionably long straight hair brushed the collar of a jacket tailored to fit the magnificent expanse of his shoulders. But it was his face that held her so raptly. His glittering eyes, black as onyx, stared at some indistinct point in the distance, as if he were lost in a reverie. Thick dark lashes and heavy lids added to the disquieting intensity of his gaze, as did his sharply slashed eyebrows. In a room full of thin blue-blooded noses, his was larger, more boldly sculpted, yet it fit perfectly with the high prominent cheekbones and strong angular set of his jawline. One straight lock of hair fell across his forehead when he leaned over and set his glass on the table, then glided away with feral grace.

"Sinfully handsome, isn't he?" Addie Lake whispered from behind her fan. "Rumor has it, his father was a red Indian who carried off his mother. He couldn't speak a word of English when she brought him home. Then he ran off to the savages again when he was fourteen and had to be dragged back. No wonder poor Anthea Remington had to be placed in a sanitarium. Of course, he's not legitimate, but he is Jeremiah Remington's only grandson so that makes him incredibly rich. I suppose some could overlook his inferior blood, even his gambling and drinking, since he's a Remington—and such a gorgeous Remington at that." Addie laughed slyly as Stephanie's cheeks tinged pinkly. "Of course my mama would have the vapors if he ever looked my way. He has a terrible reputation with women. The Remingtons will have a difficult time getting a good family to allow their daughter to marry a half-savage."

"That half-savage, as you so quaintly call him, will graduate from Harvard next year. I seriously doubt if he's taken any scalps lately, not that I'd blame him, the way some people treat him," Stephanie blurted out. Then seeing the malicious light in Addie's eyes, she could have bitten her tongue.

"So, you do know Chase Remington! Lucretia said you did, but I just couldn't believe it."

Stephanie was saved from an awkward explanation when Rayburn Lawrence approached her and asked for another dance. She was ever so glad to leave the gossip mongering Addie behind, even if she did not find Ray the least bit appealing. He held her too closely when they danced and she disliked the treacly sweet smell of the pomade he used to subdue his frizzy carrot hair, but most of all she hated the way he talked down to her as if she were a child or an imbecile.

"I heard Chase's name mentioned. Does Miss Lake know him?"

"No, I do . . . or at least I did, many years ago when we were children. Are you his friend, Mr. Lawrence?"

"Now I've asked you to call me Ray, Stephanie," he scolded, then smiled, drawing her closer. "Yes, although I'm not exactly certain that Chase has any real friends. Not the sort, you know. He's a born loner. We were thrown together in Professor Thayer's philosophy class last term. I assisted him in writing a paper on Locke and Hume. Metaphysical stuff, you know," he added importantly. "Now don't bother that lovely little head worrying about what metaphysics is."

Stephanie stiffened at his patronizing tone and interrupted coolly, "Metaphysics is an inquiry into the nature of ultimate reality and the terms in which it can best be categorized. I've read John Locke and David Hume."

Damned Boston bluestocking, Ray thought with irritation. The last thing he wanted to do was to discuss philosophy with anyone, especially a girl he wanted desperately to impress. In fact, Chase had written the paper for him, but it served Ray's purpose better when told in reverse. Or at least he thought it did until now. "You're far too beautiful to be a bookworm, Stephanie. Oh, there I go again, putting my foot in my mouth," he said, noting her flush of embarrassment with satisfaction. "I didn't mean to be unkind." He gave her his most boyishly charming smile.

"That's quite all right," Stephanie said with a sigh. "Most of the girls at Miss Edgehill's Academy prefer piano lessons to philosophy, or painting silly little watercolors to studying art history. So, how did you and Mr. Remington meet?" she asked brightly, knowing it would annoy him to discuss Chase.

Gritting his teeth, Ray beamed at her as they swept

across the floor. "It was the past spring on the Common . . ."

Chase observed Ray dancing with Stephanie whatever her name was. That strange sense of familiarity washed over him again as they drew nearer and he could study her face close up. She was tall for a female, even among his people where women averaged five and a half feet. Her body was slender, not quite the full bloom of voluptuousness so in fashion, but she was young yet. There was an honest freshness, a vivacity to her that he found unusual among white women. He felt himself drawn to cut in on Ray and dance with her.

Absurd. Best if he stayed out of trouble for once and a girl like that one spelled nothing but trouble for the likes of him. Shrugging, he headed toward the library . . . and Agatha. He could sense the eyes of the women following him as he strolled from the ballroom, cat hungry young matrons on the prowl, silly little virgins tantalized with naughty thoughts, hostile and horrified respectable women who were appalled that a savage was allowed to contaminate their sacrosanct society. He despised them all.

Once there had been a white girl he had honestly liked. *Stevie.* The image of a freckled elfin face with a wide smile missing several teeth flashed into his mind. She couldn't have been more than eight. Hell, he was only twelve or so. Back when he was still naively trying to fit into white society. Before . . . *Don't think about it!*

He made certain no one was watching as he turned to the left heading down the hall instead of out the front foyer. The Cabot home, like so many of the Beacon Hill mansions, was an immense mausoleum filled with endless dark passageways and dank cavernous rooms. Chase was a little early but the silent library was preferable to the noisy chatter in the ballroom. Most of the time he was comfortable being alone. That was how he chose to live his life.

Selecting a cigar from old man Cabot's humidor, he lit it and stared out the window at the winter garden where ugly topiary huddled beneath a blanket of soot-stained snow. Could white men leave nothing in nature untouched?

* * *

Stephanie stood behind a large potted orange tree, praying
that she had escaped the notice of Rayburn Lawrence. Of
all her suitors, he was the most troublesome. Bumbling prep
school youths who stammered or brought her wilted nose-
gays she could handle, but Mr. Lawrence was older, a college man. Of course, so were a number of others. *But they
were not friends of Chase Remington*, her subconscious
rose to taunt. She tamped the thought down. Chase had not
even remembered her. She had felt his eyes on her several
times as she and Lawrence danced but he had not approached her.

The luster had decidedly worn off the evening. Her feet
were swollen from having clumsy young men trample them
on the dance floor and her head was beginning to ache from
the smell of overheated bodies and heavy pomade. Father
was doubtless closeted away in Mr. Cabot's private sitting
room discussing business with other rich Boston merchants.
She slipped quickly through the crowd and went in search
of him.

Her slippered feet made scarcely a sound on the Khor-
asan rugs as she wended her way down the hall. Strange,
all the rooms seemed dark. Had she taken a wrong turn?
The house was immense and she had not often visited here
in the evenings. Just as she started to turn and retrace her
steps, she heard whispered voices. Some instinct made her
freeze, flattening herself against the wall beneath the black
shadow cast by a huge ornately scrolled rococo cabinet. The
instant she heard Chase Remington's name she began to
tremble.

"He's in the library now. Expecting to have a tryst at
midnight. I've forged a note to the lady explaining that he'll
be detained until one."

"I expect the lady won't get 'er pleasurin', Gov'nor,
seein's 'ow Remington'll be dead before the clock strikes
twelve," a voice with a thick Cockney accent replied.
"Ain't nobody better with a dirk 'n me, Gov."

"Just be certain to make it look like a robbery. Leave
by the library window. His paramour will discover him

with his throat cut when she arrives. I wonder what tale she'll invent for sneaking into the Cabots' library at that hour?'' Then the tone suddenly shifted from nasty amusement to tight anger as the man with the cultivated Boston accent admonished, ''Don't botch the job—that damned savage is as hard to kill as a timber wolf!''

Where had she heard that voice before? Stephanie shivered with fright as the disembodied conversation concluded with an exchange of money and an assurance by the Cockney assassin that he would sail with the morning tide on the *Lady Jane*.

When a distinguished looking man dressed in expensive evening clothes walked past her hiding place, she was certain he could hear her heart pounding but his brisk stride never faltered. Then as he turned the corner the moonlight from a window struck him. Stephanie almost gasped aloud. She knew him! But surely she was mistaken. It must be a trick of the light.

She moved cautiously from her hiding place, praying the wharf rat with the dagger was not waiting to pounce on her and slit her throat. She had to find Chase and warn him! She recalled that there were two doors to the library. Since the assassin had not come this way, he must be planning to sneak in by the servants' entrance, which would give her time since that was a very circuitous route—if she could remember herself just where Mr. Cabot's library was!

Luck favored her. In a few moments she burst into the dark room, breathless and wide-eyed, frantically searching the moonlit interior for Chase. Before she could cry out his name a strong hand clamped over her mouth and she was slammed backward against a man's hard body. For an instant her blood froze with horror—was she too late?

Then a low smooth voice purred, ''If you plan any more mad, impetuous dashes, I'd recommend not lacing yourself so tightly.''

Her spine stiffened in outrage in spite of the difficulty catching her breath. He chuckled, then added, ''If you create a scene, I assure you that you'll be more embarrassed than I.'' What the hell was Ray's prim little heiress up to?

He eased his hand away from her mouth, but for some reason did not release his arm from around her tiny waist. The delicate scent of apple blossoms teased his nostrils as she struggled to twist around and face him.

"Chase, you're in danger! A man's been hired to kill you—he'll be here any—"

Her breathless whisper was cut short when Remington sensed the subtle air currents from another door opening across the room and once again muffled her mouth. "Quiet. I hear him."

His whisper was barely audible to Stephanie, but she froze in his arms as icy fingers of dread caressed her spine. They were both going to die! Chase was unarmed. Who knew what sort of an arsenal that awful sounding Britisher possessed! Chase set her behind him, then pulled something from inside his jacket. She caught a silvery gleam of metal as he melted silently into the shadows, moving toward the stealthy figure crouched somewhere in darkness.

Stephanie bit down hard on her fist to keep from making any sound which would alert the killer. She could not see him now, but she could hear him moving cautiously across the room. There was no sign of Chase. Had he vanished in a puff of smoke, leaving her to die alone?

Suddenly the dull *whump* of two bodies colliding broke the stillness. Curses and panting ensued for what seemed an eternity to the terrified girl, but could only have been a moment. Books came crashing from their shelves as the two men fought in the shadows. Then the struggling pair moved in front of the large bay window behind Mr. Cabot's desk. Dear God above, the assassin almost matched the half-breed's uncommon height!

The men rolled across the desk, locked in an embrace of death. Moonlight shimmered on their wicked looking blades as each strained to free his knife hand from the other's grip. A lamp shattered against the wall, knocked from the desk along with a flurry of papers. The combatants fell behind the desk. A loud grunt was followed by a gasp, then one man rose over the other, silhouetted against the snowy landscape outside the window. A blade arced like silver fire and plunged. The death rattle which followed was unmistakable.

Stephanie stood frozen in terror. Why had she not run for help while she had the opportunity? When she heard Chase call her name, she rushed across the room and flung herself into his arms, sobbing, "Oh, Chase, thank God it's you. I was afraid that awful man killed you!"

Chase held her tightly and stroked the silky skin of her bare back where her ball gown dipped low. "How the hell do you know my name, Miss Stephanie?" She raised her head and he could see tears glistening in the moonlight as they fell down her pale cheeks.

"You honestly don't remember me, do you, Mr. Remington," she replied stiffly, suddenly embarrassed to be blubbering like a schoolgirl while pressed indecently against the masculine hardness of his body. She tried to pull away but he did not release her. She swallowed for courage and met the glittering challenge in his eyes.

"No. I must confess I don't. Most mamas never let their virgin daughters within a mile of a mongrel bastard like me." He felt her flinch but she continued to meet his gaze.

A wobbly smile touched her mouth. "You always enjoyed shocking polite society. Even more, I think, you did it to infuriate your grandfather. Reverend Remington was certain we were both bound for hell when you were twelve and I was eight."

Recognition hit him like a punch. "Stevie? Is it really you?"

At the incredulous, almost wistful tone in his voice, her smile broadened. "Yes," she replied simply. Suddenly his embrace felt familiar and very dear but then he released her, taking her hand and ushering her away from the desk. She felt bereft of his body's warmth.

"I must get you out of here before—"

Just then the hall door opened and a husky feminine voice called, "Chase darling, I'm here. That old sot is asleep and—" Agatha Lodge let out a hiss of vexation upon seeing the slender figure of another woman just behind Chase's broad shoulder. Even in the shadows, she could tell the chit was young. "Am I interrupting something, darling?" she cooed wickedly, one slippered foot tapping angrily.

"You might say that, Aggie, love," Chase replied dryly, shielding Stephanie from the spiteful bitch's view. "You'd best go home to that 'old sot' before all hell breaks loose around here."

"All hell already has," she hissed, headed past Chase to confront the female bold enough to challenge her for his favors.

Chase took hold of her shoulders before she could reach her victim, backing her in the direction of the door. "You don't want to try my patience, Aggie," he said in a silky voice. "It brings out the redskin in me."

She pressed her voluptuous breasts against his chest and gave a theatrical sigh. "I'd love it if you got savage, Chase."

His fingers bit into her shoulders as he shoved her through the open door into the hallway. "No, you wouldn't, believe me, Aggie." With that he released her and slammed the door in her face.

Stephanie stood rooted to the floor during the exchange. Still reeling from a brush with death, she could scarcely believe her ears. Old Mortimer Lodge's beautiful wife was having an affair with Chase! " 'Aggie, love'?" she echoed in a huff.

"No time for indignation now, Stevie." Chase seized her wrist once more and pulled her stumbling behind him toward the servants' entrance to the room as "Aggie, love" pounded on the locked library door, shrieking curses Stephanie had only heard hackney drivers on Boston Common utter.

Carefully shielding the body lying behind the desk from her view, he held the narrow door open. "We have to get out of here before someone hears her and finds the body."

Stephanie picked up her skirts as they descended the narrow steps into the servants' quarters below. "Then . . . he's dead." She really had little doubt. "Do you always carry a knife on your person when you pay a social call?"

"It comes in handy from time to time." His voice was bitter. "I never know when I might want to scalp someone." When they reached the bottom of the stair, he led her down a long, narrow hallway, stopping to check behind the doors along the way until he located one leading back upstairs. In a few moments he pulled her into an empty sitting room on the main floor of the mansion. A gas light illuminated the elegantly appointed interior, which had apparently been recently vacated. The aroma of expensive cigars hung in the air.

Closing the door behind him, he motioned for her to have a seat on a balloon-backed easy chair, then walked briskly over to where a cut-glass decanter of amber liquid sat on a serving cart. Pouring two matching tumblers, he offered her one.

She shook her head. "Father forbids me to touch spirits."

A smile quirked his beautifully sculpted lips, then quickly faded as he shoved the glass into her hand. "No doubt he would also forbid you to attend knife fights. Take a sip. *Father* isn't here now and I don't want you fainting on me."

She drew herself up, reminding Chase of the plucky girl who had befriended him so long ago. "I never faint," she replied stubbornly.

"Drink it anyway," he commanded, tossing off his much larger portion and reaching for a refill. After taking another swallow, he leaned one arm on the marble mantel of the fireplace and studied her with troubled eyes. Now he could see why she had looked so familiar back in the ballroom. Her hair, bleached a paler straw color by the sun when she had been a tomboy, now had darkened to a rich deep bronze. The freckles were gone but the stubborn chin and clear golden eyes were the same. Her cheekbones were just beginning to take on the elegant hollows of definition and her lips were pink and full. She had grown into a beauty.

Feeling his intent examination as the silence between them thickened, Stephanie took a quick sip of the pungent liquor for courage, then burst into a fit of coughing. Chase set his glass on the mantel and knelt beside her chair, massaging her back with one elegant long-fingered hand while the other one held her arm. She had forgotten how dark his skin was next to her fairness. A frisson of sexual awareness danced along her nerves, tingling where he touched her.

"Take another sip, slowly, then tell me how you got mixed up in that little episode in the library." He guided the glass to her mouth and she obeyed. When the tip of her tongue darted out to cleanse the brandy from her lips he groaned silently. Damn the little minx, she was far more tempting than all the Aggies on earth!

Stephanie felt the second taste of liquor hit bottom and was oddly soothed by it. She cleared her throat and began. "After losing my way while I searched for Father, I overheard two voices in the darkened hallway. One man was paying the other to sneak into the library and kill you. As soon as they parted, I rushed there to warn you."

"I'm greatly in your debt. Most women would've swooned on the spot or run dithering for help that would have arrived too late to do me any good. You always were brave for a paleface kid, Stevie." He flashed her a devastating grin.

At the old teasing nickname, she smiled in return and the years fell away . . . almost. Then he had been a rangy boy poised on the brink of adolescence, she a scrawny tomboy, but now they were no longer children. She could feel her heart pound so wildly it must surely sound as loud as the base drum in the Salvation Army band that played on the Common.

Chase stared mesmerized at the tiny pulse fluttering rapidly in the hollow at the base of her delicate throat. Earlier, when Ray was dancing with her, he had thought her a skinny schoolgirl. Now, watching the soft swell of pale breasts above the azure silk of her gown, he reconsidered.

"I'm not a paleface kid anymore, Chase," she whispered, unknowingly echoing his thoughts.

Damn, this was Stevie Summerfield, a Boston heiress, an innocent. What the hell was he thinking! Removing his hands from her as if scorched, he stood up and paced quickly across the carpet. "I'd better return you to the party before you're missed."

Stephanie watched him move, restless as a caged wild animal. She was confused by his abrupt withdrawal. "Yes, I . . . I suppose I'd better find Father . . . but there is something else I didn't tell you, Chase." She hesitated, uncertain of how to broach the horrifying accusation—or even if she should. The light had been dim. Surely she had been mistaken.

"What is it?" he prompted.

"I . . . I believe I recognized the man who paid that sailor to kill you."

"It was my uncle Burke, wasn't it," he said tonelessly, without a hint of doubt in his voice.

☙ 2 ❧

Chase brushed past his uncle's officious secretary and strode into Burke Remington's private office. Knowing it useless to protest, the sputtering Gibbs closed the door after the wild Remington boy. Chase looked contemptuously at the distinguished blond-haired man seated behind the immense mahogany desk. Burke calmly sipped from a cup of sweetened Darjeeling tea. The only thing betraying any emotion in his patrician face was a tiny tic at his graying temple—that and the narrowing of his ice blue eyes.

Smiling coldly, Chase tossed a bundle of bills onto the desk, saying, "Quite a shame, wouldn't you agree, Burke, that one cannot ask to see references when hiring a cutthroat? That tar botched the job. It'll cost you more than a couple of hundred to see me dead."

Burke set his Haviland cup down in its saucer and rose, placing his well-manicured hands, palms down, on the desk. Leaning forward, he let the naked loathing he felt for this dark-skinned savage blaze from his eyes. "Are you prepared to prove that wild accusation?"

"No. I can't. Unfortunately your sailor won't get burial at sea . . . but he will get burial. I was forced to slit his throat before I could make him talk. You must really be getting desperate, Burke." He watched with satisfaction as the distinguished blond man's complexion turned waxy pale for a moment, but his big barrel-chested body remained poised over the desk. Even dressed in a custom-tailored wool suit and silk shirt, he exuded power . . . and menace.

"As usual, you display the same flair for the dramatic as your dear grandpapa . . . even if you are a trifle more bloodthirsty,'' he added in a pleased tone of voice, watching Chase's jaw muscle bunch in fury when he gritted his teeth. ''Oh, you do so hate being reminded of how much you're like old Jeremiah, don't you?''

''I've often been told I resemble my mother.'' The blow struck home as Chase knew it would. Burke hated the fact that Anthea's classically chiseled features had been passed along to a half-breed bastard.

''There is nothing of my sister in you.'' Burke bit off each word precisely.

''Half my blood is Remington, no matter how much I hate it.''

''*You* hate it!'' the older man roared, leaning farther over the desk as if ready to climb across and attack. ''You insolent half-breed trash, how do you think I feel having a mongrel like you claim the Remington name!''

Chase's lips thinned in disdain. ''I am the son of Vanishing Grass and Freedom Woman. I never wanted to claim the Remington name. It was your father who dragged me back here. I'd rather have gone to prison with my father's people than live in Boston.''

''Spare me your noble airs. You've been willing enough to spend the Remington millions carousing with your worthless college friends. Women, cards and whiskey. Red savages have quite a problem with whiskey, so I've been told. Can't hold their liquor worth a damn.'' Burke smiled nastily.

''It isn't just the money, is it, *Uncle* Burke? You don't care about my inheriting half the old man's estate as much as you care that I'm Anthea's son and you—''

''I'll see you in hell—right along with that filthy savage who raped my sister and put a bastard like you in her belly.''

''My father didn't rape my mother. She came willingly to him. She loved him.''

''You're pathetic—just as ignorant as one of those greasy illiterate savages if you believe that.'' Burke forced a pose of condescension.

''I believe my mother, and what gnaws at your rotten

guts is that you do, too. She never lied in her life.''

"Anthea doesn't know lies from truth. She's scarcely had a lucid moment in the past seven years."

"And we both know why, don't we, *Uncle* Burke?" There was a sinister undercurrent to the question.

The elder Remington stiffened. "I pray nightly for your death and I always have my prayers answered. After all, I am the Reverend Jeremiah's son," he added darkly.

"You'll have to pray harder, then. Your assassination failed. Maybe you ought to get off your knees and try killing me yourself next time . . . the Lord helps those who help themselves."

"I wouldn't contaminate my hands by touching you."

Chase shrugged. "Yes, after all, I wouldn't want you to get any of that greasy Indian filth on them. But on my honor as a 'filthy savage,' I promise you'll pray for your own death before I finish with you."

After Chase stalked from the room, Gibbs appeared at the door, Adam's apple bobbing nervously. "Are . . . are you quite all right, Mr. Remington?" he asked timidly as if half expecting to find his employer lying on his desk scalped.

Burke waved the little man out of the room impatiently. Shoving his teacup aside, he poured himself a stiff shot of expensive Scotch whiskey. He downed it neat, then stared out of the window, remembering the past . . . regretting it.

As the driver reined in the matched chestnuts at the front entry of the forbidding gray stone building, Chase jumped impatiently from the sleek black brougham. He hated the Remington family mansion worse than a prison, which for him and Anthea it was.

Unwillingly, his eyes swept across the massive walls to the crenellated tower at the end of the east wing where his mother was held, quite literally, in the silken restraints which kept her from harming herself when one of her "fits," as the doctors called them, overtook her. Most of the time she was quiet, engrossed in a solitary depression so bottomless little could draw her from it. Only when

Burke or the reverend came near her did she display violence, screaming like a demented thing, frenzied and clawing at herself as if trying to rip open her own veins and drain her life's blood from them.

Anthea wanted to die. And Chase understood her reasons all too well. Yet there were occasions, although fewer and fewer this past year, when she was lucid enough to ask for her son. Wonderingly she would drink in the sight of him, her pale trembling fingers contrasting sharply against the dark bronze of his face when she touched him. They would live in the past when Vanishing Grass was alive and she was Freedom Woman. How illusive that freedom had proven for her . . . and for her only child.

His troubling reverie was interrupted when he entered the house and a butler announced in sepulchral tones that the reverend wished to see him in his study. Chase walked down the opulent carpeted hallway. A typical New England day in winter made lighting the gas lamps a necessity in the cavernous house. Gleaming cherrywood wainscoting complemented by French burgundy wallpaper lined the corridor. He paused with one hand on the inlaid ivory door handle as childhood memories once again assailed him.

Every time he entered this room he remembered the terrified six-year-old Cheyenne boy trembling before the tall *veho* who claimed to be his grandfather. Chase would never have believed it if his mother had not assured him it was so. He could not speak a word of English then and did not want to learn either. The whites were his enemies. Had they not attacked his village and killed his father? The tall, cold-faced old man with piercing blue eyes had done nothing to dispel his fears that awful day.

That was nearly fifteen years ago, he reminded himself, turning the doorknob and peremptorily striding inside.

The Reverend Jeremiah York Remington still possessed the ramrod-straight posture and intense glare of an Old Testament prophet . . . or a Puritan fanatic. He was an ordained Congregational minister, pastor of the oldest and most prestigious church in the city, and he took his calling very seriously. As always he was dressed in an impeccably tailored blue wool suit without any adornment. His thick head of hair was snow-white now, immaculately barbered with heavy muttonchop sideburns. Sitting back in the leather upholstered armchair he steepled his big blunt fingers together and stared crossly at his grandson.

"Even three years at Harvard hasn't improved your manners."

"Why should college at twenty-one do what you couldn't when I was six, beating me bloody with a cane switch?"

" 'He that spareth his rod, hateth his son but he that loveth him, chastiseth him betimes.' Proverbs, thirteenth chapter, twenty-fourth verse," Jeremiah quoted in the rich deep voice that held his congregation spellbound when he preached.

A bitter smile twisted Chase's lips. "Then you must've loved the hell out of me, Old Man. You sure did an almighty lot of chastening."

"Do not profane the word of the Lord!" Jeremiah thundered. "As to the fires of hell, I don't doubt you'll be seeing them firsthand soon enough."

"I don't doubt you're right," Chase replied genially. "We 'primitives' love a good crackling fire, but you and I have been over this road before. And it always forks at the same turn. You wanted to see me for some particular reason?"

Jeremiah studied the boy—no, no longer a boy but a man grown now, arrogant and self-assured. "You're not the illiterate little savage Anthea brought to me fifteen years ago, Chase, even if you still act rashly now and again. You've reached your majority this year. In another you'll graduate from Harvard. Have you given even a moment's thought to what you'll do with your life? Considered your vocation?"

Amusement did dance in Chase's black eyes now. "Well," he drawled, "it certainly won't be a calling to the ministry."

Jeremiah snorted in disgust. "Must every discussion we have be occasion for levity? I assure you I am not amused.

Nor do I propose to continue funding your profligate immoral ways. 'The wages of sin is death,' Chase.''

" 'But the gift of God is eternal life.' Romans, sixth chapter, twenty-third verse,'' Chase replied beatifically. "See, you did beat a few lessons into me.''

"If only you would take them to heart.'' There was the faintest hint of regret in the old man's voice but Chase did not hear it.

"Maybe red savages don't have hearts—or souls to save. Did you and your missionary friends ever consider that, Old Man?''

Jeremiah winced inwardly at the appellation *Old Man*. Never once in all the years beneath his roof had his only grandchild addressed him as Grandfather, no matter how often he prayed to his God—or how often he beat the willful boy. He had been forced to accept Old Man, a term of respect among the savages, or so Chase had informed him. "You are only half-Indian—''

"I am Cheyenne,'' Chase said proudly.

"Cheyenne, whatever,'' Jeremiah replied, dismissing the distinction. "The fact is that you are heir to the Remington name and as your uncle has no issue, also to the family fortune.''

"Give it to charity. I don't want it. All I've stayed for is my mother. Once she's gone—''

"Anthea could live years yet,'' Jeremiah quickly interjected. "Her mind is afflicted, not her body.''

"And we both know the reason for her *affliction*, don't we?'' Chase felt a red haze envelop him.

"Silence!'' Jeremiah commanded. "We've had this discussion before, too. I did not summon you to rehash the past. It's time you grew up and accepted your responsibilities as a Remington. I know you won't pursue a career of public service such as Burke has, and we both agree you're highly unsuited for the ministry. But there is the family's business. It's been in the hands of hired managers since my brother Jasper passed on. You have a good head for figures. You could run Remington Enterprises.''

Chase shrugged, pacing gracefully across the luxurious

Turkish carpet which had come from one of the family warehouses. "I imagine it would be a divertissement," he said indifferently. All he was doing was marking time with the *veho*, waiting for the day when he could ride free once more. *Anthea could live years yet.* The old man's words mocked him.

Reverend Remington watched the enigmatic young man, struggling to leash his own frustration and fury. "You think you'll just ride off to live with those savages one day. Do you honestly believe they'll accept you back a second time?"

"You're the one who had me dragged off in chains and shipped here after I was taken prisoner at Washita. I never deserted my people."

"Little matter how you got here. You're white now. You sleep on clean linens and eat crepes for breakfast. You've received a classical education. The stink of an animal skin hut wouldn't hold the allure it did for a fourteen-year-old boy."

"You understand nothing about how the Cheyenne live." Even as he made the retort, Chase feared himself that the old man spoke the truth. Could he go back? Would his father's people accept him? And even if they did, could he now accept them?

"I don't need to understand them—I know how the Remingtons live. We accept the responsibilities the good Lord gave us. It's only a year to your graduation. You need to stop fornicating with whores and committing adultery with Delilahs such as Agatha Lodge."

Chase turned from the window with a faintly surprised expression fleetingly on his face. "So, you've had me followed. I expect your investigator had a good time . . . vicariously."

Ignoring the jibe, Jeremiah replied, "It's time you thought about taking a wife."

The statement hung suspended in midair as blazing blue eyes dueled with glittering black ones.

Chase finally broke the silence. "You're actually serious, aren't you?" *No wonder Burke tried to kill me. The old man really does intend to make me his heir.* "Have you a demure Christian virgin from a socially prominent family who is willing to martyr herself by marrying a man with tainted blood? For damn certain there can't be many candidates in Boston," he added with grim humor.

"In spite of your less than desirable paternal bloodlines, our good name has induced a number of prominent families to consider a marriage alliance."

Chase scoffed. "Our good name with a few million from your father's business ventures to sweeten the bargain."

"Coralee Vandeventer would make you an exemplary wife, as would Alice Ralston," Jeremiah said, ignoring Chase's jibe.

"What about Stephanie Summerfield?" some insane impulse made him ask. Instantly he regretted the rash question. *What the hell made me say that?*

The old man stroked his chin consideringly as he leaned back in his chair. "I seem to recall the child, Josiah's girl. Wasn't she that wild little hoyden who followed you around like a puppy dog?"

"She's grown since then," Chase said dryly, recalling his reaction to her soft curves and the scent of apple blossoms.

"Still a bit young, but if she's amended her childish ways, she might do. Might do quite well." He studied his grandson with renewed interest. "Have you met her socially?"

"You might call it that. But don't go asking her father about a dowry just yet. I haven't agreed to marry anyone. As you pointed out, I still have another term at Harvard."

"Which will be completed soon enough. Arranging a proper marriage alliance in our circles takes time, as you well know. And remember, a virtuous woman's price is far above rubies."

"Ah, but I believe the exact quote is 'Who can find a virtuous woman?'" Chase strolled to the door undismissed, a habit he knew infuriated the old man. "I'll let you search for me. Personally, I prefer the other kind of woman."

"We have not concluded this discussion," Jeremiah blustered, knowing it was useless trying to stop his arrogant grandson. He leaned back once again in his chair and began to scheme. He would have the boy married off as soon as he graduated. Once he'd taken a wife and had a child on the way, he'd be bound to remain in Boston, to assume his duty to the Remington name.

"Stephanie Summerfield, eh?" Jeremiah scratched his thatch of white hair, trying to recall some scandalous incident that took place between the girl and his grandson when they were children. Useless. Chase's entire life in Boston seemed to be composed of an uninterrupted series of scandals. Ah, well, they were little more than cubs then. Surely by now Josiah's daughter had learned to behave properly, even if Chase had not. He would have her investigated. If she proved acceptable, he would proceed. All the better that the boy was attracted to her.

The old man smiled to himself. Perhaps the Lord was at last answering his prayers.

"I have the most splendid new Portland Cutter and the snow's fresh as an October apple, Stephanie. You simply must say yes," Oliver Standish cajoled. His pale earnest face was lit with boyish excitement at the prospect of showing off his latest toy. As the only son of the Standish banking family, he was allowed all the toys his heart desired. Unfortunately the one he most devoutly wished for he had not yet obtained—Stephanie Summerfield.

"You've been cooped up here for ages. Cynthia told me you haven't been out since the Cabots' ball over a week ago," Oliver stated, as if such solitary confinement was beyond human comprehension.

She had spent the past week moping about the big lonely house. Her father worked long past the dinner hour every night, leaving her with far too much time to dwell on her incredible encounter with Chase Remington. At first she had hoped he would call on her. But then Cynthia had come gossiping two days after the ball, cattily delighted to relate how she had seen Chase with Sara Gidion, a famous British opera diva touring the eastern seaboard. The two of them were very cozy in an elegant private dining booth at Wellingtons.

He had made his preferences clear. Chase preferred older sophisticated beauties like Agatha Lodge or the glamorous Lady Sara. How he must have laughed at her girlish flustering. Other than surprising her by grabbing her in the darkened library, he had not made any physical overtures. In fact, after she had told him the shocking truth about his uncle, he had been politely solicitous as he escorted her back to the ballroom. He had not even attempted a kiss.

Not that I would have refused him.

"I say, Stephanie, are you quite the thing?" Oliver asked in affected British cant.

Stephanie placed her hands to her flaming cheeks. "Yes, yes, Oliver, I'm perfectly all right. And I shall be delighted to go sleighing with you this afternoon."

As soon as the Standish boy left, she regretted her capitulation. He was childish, spoiled and not very bright, but at least the ride would get her out of the oppressively silent house. If only her father had not forbidden her volunteer work at the charity hospital. She had so enjoyed feeling useful and needed for those brief months until Josiah Summerfield learned that she was tending Irish immigrants with cholera and flatly refused to allow her to engage in such a scandalous and dangerous activity.

What he truly wished was that she find some proper young man to wed and leave him in peace with his account books. Her mother had died when Stephanie was five and Josiah had never remarried. Indeed, the encumbrance of a daughter had been sufficient distraction for him to enlist the aid of his wife's spinster sister, Paulina. He had happily left child and household in her hands while Stephanie grew up.

Paulina proved to be a free spirit and a bit of a bluestocking who encouraged Stephanie's interest in literature, history and philosophy, even the suffragette movement. She had an unconventional childhood and if she missed a father's love, she could always rely on her aunt. Then when she was fifteen, her beloved confidant died suddenly of a heart ailment, leaving Stephanie once more alone, poised on the brink of womanhood with no one to guide her.

Josiah offered a sizable dowry and suitors began to flock about her. But the insecure girl always felt they were more entranced with her father's bankbook than with her. She knew Rayburn Lawrence was. At least Oliver was not interested in her money. If only he were not so boring! She doubted he had even read a book since leaving St. Vincent's Academy two years ago.

Hardly a Harvard man, she mused as the dark, sinfully beautiful image of Chase Remington rose in her mind's eye. Chase, with the magical white smile and the razor-sharp wit. Chase who had always been as much of a misfit and an outcast as she felt herself to be. "I'm being foolish. He's a libertine who would never have given me a second look if I hadn't come running to warn him about the plot to kill him," she scolded herself as she checked her appearance in the mirror one last time.

Haunted amber eyes stared back at her from a pale ivory face with a nose a trifle too long and a chin decidedly too bold for conventional beauty. And to make matters worse, her hair was neither blond nor brown but some strange almost metallic color, so coarse and heavy it defied all her maid's attempts to style it in the sleek poofing pompadour currently the fashion. No help for it, she was tall, thin, with a decidedly unpretty face . . . lord, perhaps even a bit hatchetlike because of that accursed chin. And she liked Aristotle. Poor Oliver with his double chin and sweetly vapid mind was probably the best she could do unless she wanted to settle for a fortune hunter like the Lawrence boy.

Just then her maid, Constance, entered the room bearing the new sable coat her father had given her for Christmas. The lustrous furs would have utterly delighted her if Josiah had not tartly informed her that if she did not like it she could take the matter up with his secretary's wife, who had been sent to select it. Slipping into the satin-lined wrap, she prepared to enjoy her afternoon sleigh ride with Oliver. Her father would not even notice she was gone.

*　*　*

"Don't you think we're going a bit too fast?" Stephanie asked Oliver, chewing her lip nervously as she watched the gleaming blades of the Portland Cutter slice through the crisp white snow at a constantly accelerating rate of speed.

"Nonsense, my dear. There's no way to overturn a cutter as heavy as this one," Standish replied, snapping the reins across the horses' rumps once more.

The Neponset River wound alongside the rolling hills as they raced by its frozen course. They had left the city behind hours ago, speeding southward over the trackless mantle of white. Now as the pale winter sun began to drop low on the horizon, Oliver urged his team homeward. Billowing gunmetal clouds began to mass ominously, ready to dump a fresh deluge of January snow on them. Her eyes scanned the riverbank ahead looking for a passable refuge if they could not outrun the impending storm.

The Remingtons' country place was only a mile or two away, but it was unlikely to be occupied in the dead of winter. *As if I'd want to appear a soggy, snow-covered beggar at Chase's doorstep*, she thought tartly. Yet remembering long-ago summers spent here brought a bittersweet pang to her heart.

Her childhood reverie was interrupted as she was flung sharply against the side of the seat when the sled sharply changed course. "What are you doing, Oliver?" she gasped, holding onto the seat awkwardly with mittened hands.

He was forced to lean closer to her to be heard over the noise of the rising wind. "I'm taking us down to the river. We'll make better time on the flat surface."

High above on a bluff, a lone figure sat on his ebony stallion, watching the expensive conveyance careen onto the frozen river. Muttering a curse, he kneed the horse into a canter. Didn't that fool driver realize last week's warm spell had partially thawed the big river? With the past few days of dropping temperatures and heavy snowfall most of it had refrozen, but it was sheer stupidity to put anything as heavy as a Portland Cutter on that ice.

The horseman swooped downhill at an angle to intercept

the sleigh. Snow flew up in stinging clouds beneath the stallion's churning hooves. As they neared the bank of the Neponset what he feared occurred. The sleigh tilted sharply to its side as one heavy runner sliced through the broken ice. Over the howl of the wind a sharp cracking sound heralded the breakup of the ice and freezing gray water bubbled up, sucking under the gleaming red and silver sledge. A woman's sharp scream echoed as she was thrown from her seat, tumbling into the icy grasp of death.

Ignoring the stupid driver who was struggling to whip his team into pulling his fancy toy away from the water, the horseman urged his big black to the water's edge. The woman was clawing frantically at a broken slab of ice which bobbed in the rising current. Her heavy fur coat, so excellent a protection from the storm a moment ago, now might well prove to be her shroud as its waterlogged weight dragged her under.

Stephanie felt her grip on the ice slipping as her whole body went from icy cold to a terrifying numbness in what seemed like only a heartbeat. The rushing gray water took her into its embrace. Suddenly a powerful vise seemed to squeeze the breath from her lungs. Stephanie was pulled from the water and flung soggily against the hard wall of another human body. The harsh force that had literally taken her breath away was a man's strong right arm. Before she could see her deliverer's face, he tossed her over his shoulder and dashed off the frozen river as the ice cracked and broke behind them.

When he reached the bank, her deliverer put her down in front of him, still holding onto her arms to steady her. "Chase," she gulped from frozen lips. Her mouth did not seem to work properly.

"Don't try to talk. You're half-frozen," he explained as he helped her to sit down on the snow-covered ground. Then he turned to the big black horse waiting patiently and unfastened a blanket from behind his saddle. He wrapped it around her shivering body.

Frantically she looked over her shoulder at the river for a trace of Oliver Standish and his sledge. One gleaming silver runner was lodged at a peculiar angle in the ice, all that remained visible of the conveyance. "Oliver! You must find my friend!" she gasped.

Chase could see a man's head bobbing in the water as he clung to one of the two thrashing horses which miraculously began to scramble back onto solid ground a dozen yards away. "As far as I'm concerned that idiot can drown for pulling such a reckless stunt," he yelled over the wind.

"But he's hurt," she cried, seeing the bright crimson stain spreading across Oliver's temple as he dropped from the horse onto the ground.

Snow had begun to fall in earnest now. "I have to get you to a hot fire and dry blankets immediately." Feeling her stiffen in his arms, he knew she would not allow him to leave her companion to freeze to death, no matter how richly deserved the fate.

Oliver was up on all fours now, his head injury bleeding freely. With a particularly vile oath, Chase reluctantly left Stephanie and went to assist her companion. Stripping off his gloves, he reached inside his greatcoat for a handkerchief, which he quickly tied around Oliver's head to staunch the bleeding sufficiently for him to be able to see.

"I'm going to boost you up on this horse as soon as I unhitch it from the other. You'll have to ride it bareback or else I'll be forced to leave you," he yelled as he began unfastening the heavy harness in a race with the growing numbness in his fingers.

Once the horses were free, Chase seated Standish on the gelding, then led it over to where Stephanie huddled on the bank. The blue blanket around her shoulders was already white and stiff with snow. He lifted her up onto his horse and swung up behind her. As the frozen trio headed up the hill toward the house, he was grateful it was only a few hundred yards beyond.

When they reached the mansion, the steward, Essex, took one look at his master's two frozen charges and set to work with typical New England practicality, stripping the ice-encrusted clothes from the man, discreetly leaving the young lady for his womanizing employer to deal with.

"See to his head injury. Once he thaws out it may start to bleed again," Chase instructed Essex before carrying a semiconscious Stephanie down the hall to his bedroom at the end of the hallway. Sheltered beneath a huge chestnut tree, it was the coolest place in the house in summer and, because it faced south, the warmest in winter.

"I'm so sleepy," she murmured thickly, her head lolling against his chest. She felt so safe held tightly in his arms. When he laid her on the big bed and moved away, she cried out, bereft of the solid comfort of his body. Her eyes roamed blearily around the room which was spacious and masculine. She was barely aware that he frantically tugged off her wet clothing, beginning with her boots.

"Did you shoot that deer?" she asked, staring at a magnificent rack of antlers hung above the fireplace.

"No. My people don't waste meat killing for trophies," he replied, cursing to himself as his fingers, numb from the cold, fumbled over the loops holding the heavy fur coat closed. *The first time in years I've been clumsy undressing a woman*, he thought wryly as he pulled her up against him so he could peel off the coat. As soon as her arms were freed from the coat, she threw them around his neck, hanging onto him with surprising strength.

"You're so warm," she breathed next to his ear.

"Well, you're not," he replied, slinging the ice-covered coat onto the carpet, then unpeeling her arms so he could lay her back and attack the myriad of tiny buttons down the front of her heavy twill suit. By the time he reached the frilly white lawn blouse beneath, he was not cold anymore. In fact, parts of his anatomy were most definitely heating up.

By the time Chase rolled her over on her stomach and began to unlace her corset stays, Stephanie was beginning to thaw as well. His hands touching her bare skin felt blissfully warm and incredibly deft. "Bet you've had a lot of practice doing this, haven't you?" she blurted out as he pulled the damp restricting garment from her waist. Lord above, here she was lying in a man's bed nearly stark naked while he touched her in unmentionable places and that was all she could say!

Ah, but could she feel! Her frozen arms started to tingle as he massaged them with powerful long fingers until the blood seemed to roar in her ears. When he moved down her legs and took one small foot in his big dark hands, she closed her eyes in bliss, giving in to the utter madness of the moment.

Chase watched her thick dark lashes flutter down, closing over those fathomless amber eyes. His own black ones were drawn to study her lithe young body as he worked over it. Her skin was alabaster pale as much from residual shock as from her fair coloring. But he could feel the pulse thrum steady under the silky skin behind her knee. His hand glided up over the curve of a long, slim thigh. She was slender but sweetly rounded, poised on the brink of womanhood. Against his will his eyes were drawn to the steady rise and fall of her chest as she started to drift off to sleep. Palest pink nipples puckered tightly in spite of the torrid warmth penetrating the room. Her breasts were small but perfectly formed, upthrust proudly without need of whalebone supports. The foolish corset was completely unnecessary. Her waist was tiny, her belly flat and sleek.

Before he allowed his hands to trespass down the path his errant eyes traveled, Chase reached for several of the blankets at the foot of the bed and tucked them securely around the dozing girl. *She is only a girl*, he reminded himself sternly. A beautiful fairylike creature, virginal, innocent and completely unsuited to a man like him. A white woman from a wealthy family who would demand marriage as the price of her purity.

And he was a half-caste who belonged two thousand miles away . . . or at least he hoped that he still did. Unless he rejoined the Cheyenne, he would not have any identity, for he could never be a Remington.

Stephanie opened her eyes and met Chase's troubled gaze as he looked down on her. In spite of the warm room, she began to shiver beneath the scratchy wool blanket.

"Your hands . . . they warmed me," she whispered, her voice hoarse and husky.

"You're still cold inside. Here, this should help you," he said, rising to step over to the bedside table where a crystal decanter of brandy sat. His legs were actually weak and his hands trembled as he poured the drink. He knelt beside her and raised her head so she could swallow.

"Why is it you're always forcing spirits on me, Mr. Remington?" she asked dreamily.

But she swallowed obediently as he held the glass. "Not for the usual reason, I fear."

"Too . . . too bad," she said through chattering teeth, not really aware of what she was saying. The hot silky warmth of the French cognac eased the chill a bit but she still shivered.

He smiled bleakly. "Yes, it is." *Leave now while you still can*, an inner voice of conscience screamed at him. "I'm going to fetch some hot soup from the kitchen—"

"N-no! P-please don't l-leave me, Chase." She sat up and her arms reached out to him. "I don't n-need soup— I need you."

The blankets dropped to her waist and those perfect little upthrust breasts gleamed like pearls. *Not half as much as I need you*. With an oath, he began stripping off his boots.

⧉ 3 ⧉

Chase slid beneath the sheets and pressed Stephanie's shivering body against his, then pulled the warm blankets over them. Inside the soft cocoon he could feel her heart pounding in cadence with his own. In his haste to get her out of the frozen clothes and warm her numb flesh, he had left her hair coiled tightly in a heavy chignon. Seeing the pins digging into her delicate scalp, he rolled up on one elbow, partially covering her body with his and began to work them loose, using his long fingers as a comb. "You have so much hair," he murmured hoarsely as the thick, lustrous waves spilled across the white pillowcases like bronze satin.

Her trembling began to abate. His trembling began to accelerate when her small hands reached around his shoulders. Stephanie levered herself more tightly against him and felt the buttons on his shirt press into the tender skin of her breasts, which had inexplicably begun to ache. The tautness of that ache quickly spread lower into her belly and throbbed in her most secret place when his rough wool trousers scraped against her lower body.

If only he had removed his clothes, some devilish inner voice whispered, as she clung to his big, hard male body. The idea of their flesh pressed together without any barrier of clothing should have horrified a proper Boston virgin. However, Stephanie Renee Summerfield had been raised by a free-thinking woman little concerned with the strictures of society. But Aunt Paulina had been a spinster, completely unaware of the powerful currents that could surge between a man and a woman.

Stephanie had overheard the tittering whispers of classmates at the academy but until her debut the past spring, she had virtually no contact with boys since childhood. And none of the young men courting her had interested her in the slightest—intellectually or physically.

No one but Chase.

And now fate seemed to have gifted her with him . . . alone . . . half-naked . . . in a bed. She could feel the pounding of his heart and sense the tension in his bunched muscles. He was holding himself back from her. Being honorable. Or, the shattering thought suddenly struck her— what if he did not find her desirable? She was just a green girl, too thin and too plain for his jaded taste.

Stephanie had to know. With the wisdom born of Eve, she ran her fingers down the swelling biceps in his arms, then glided her hands across his chest, reaching between them to unfasten the buttons of his shirt. He groaned and buried his face in her hair but did not stop her as she placed her fingers on the springy pelt of night-black hair on his chest. When she nuzzled her face against the hard slab of muscle, he shifted his weight suddenly, almost like a bucking horse. His hips ground down into hers and she could feel something hard prodding low against her belly through the placket of his trousers.

If Stephanie had felt any lingering doubts, she no longer did, even though in her innocence she possessed only the vaguest intuition about what men and women did in bed together. The sudden change in his anatomy and the harsh rasping of his breath certainly indicated that she was soon to find out. Instinctively she raised her face to his and pursed her lips for a kiss, murmuring softly, breathlessly, "I love you, Chase."

I love you, Chase.

He felt the virginal innocence of her lips, primly closed, pressing against his as the words registered. The fiery heat of a moment ago evaporated as surely as if he had been dropped beneath the ice in the Neponset River. He rolled from the bed flinging the covers back over her with an oath, still gasping for breath like a drowning man. The rigid erection in his pants was not as easily subdued as he stood towering over her with his shirt hanging open and his fists clenched at his sides.

When she let out a soft gasp of dismayed surprise and sat up, reaching out for him, he backed away, snarling angrily, "Cover yourself before you catch pneumonia."

Tears of mortification and misery welled up in her eyes as she coughed. Clutching the blankets, she pulled her knees up to her chest and laid her head on them, letting her unbound hair fan down her bare back as she sobbed. "I . . . I'm sorry, Chase. You m-must despise me."

He cursed again and dragged in a deep gulp of air trying desperately to bring his body under control. Looking down on her huddled there so small and forlorn with all that glorious bronze hair spilling across her milky shoulders made his groin ache with renewed viciousness.

"I don't despise you, Stephanie." He barked a harsh, self-deprecating laugh. "Hell, look at me. Do I look like I don't want you?" When she raised her head and timidly inspected his body, blushing at the protrusion against the soft wool of his trousers, he muttered, "You don't have the slightest idea what you do to me, do you?"

Her cheeks blazed fiery hot. "I thought . . . that is, I hoped you wanted to . . ."

"Oh, I wanted to all right."

Her eyes dared to meet his. "But then, why did you get angry and jump away?"

"Among my father's people it is a great shame to a man if he takes advantage of a maiden before they are properly wed. I may have broken most of the rules of Cheyenne honor, but this is one thing I will not do."

"So, it would seem you're more honorable than I am," she said, swallowing down her tears. "After all, white civilization teaches the same thing."

"There is seldom honor among the *veho* . . . but you . . . you're different. Pure and good and honest. My only happy memories of this place came from my time with you. I don't want that to change."

"You're remembering our childhood, but we're not children anymore. Things have to change.'' *Do you still care about me, Chase?*

He turned away from her and paced over to the window where a wilderness of white howled outside the frosted panes. ''You live in Boston, Stephanie. Things never change there. And we're stranded alone until this storm abates. We have to think of your reputation. God knows I've none of my own to worry about.''

''Oh yes, you do. You've worked hard building a reputation as a carousing libertine. Is it permissible in Cheyenne society to carry on with married women?'' Her jealousy was out of control and she knew it, but she also wanted to know why he lived as he did.

His smile was rueful. ''Well, it can get pretty expensive. A man has to make restitution if he dishonors another's wife—sometimes as much as his whole herd of ponies, his lodge, all his possessions. Unmarried men live under the same rules of chastity as unmarried women.''

''But here among the *veho*—is that what you call us— you've abandoned the rules.''

He shrugged. ''I had some encouragement,'' he replied bitterly. ''Hell, you should remember how it was even when I was a boy—'the dirty Indian.' When Jeremiah found us fishing in the creek, after your father's servants dragged you home, the old man caned me within an inch of my life.''

Stephanie remembered that day, the last time they had played together. It was etched forever in her memory, the heat of the afternoon and his tall, skinny, twelve-year-old's body. He had stripped down to his trousers, rolling up the legs so he could show her how the Cheyenne caught fish with their bare hands. It looked like such fun, she had wanted to try it, too. With her typical eight-year-old pluck and disregard for convention, she had taken off her shoes and socks and hiked up her skirt between her bare legs to wade in after him. She could still feel the fierce wriggling of that fat trout she'd caught. The sounds of their childish laughter echoed through the tall stand of alders as they tossed the slick, plump fish onto the bank, splashing each other with water in the process.

Now, she looked at his tense body, the broad shoulders hunched as he leaned his hands on the window sash, standing barefooted across the room, so long-legged and tall, refusing to face her. The harshly beautiful profile of his hawkish face gleamed like a copper mask of some fierce Aztec god. Her throat constricted remembering the lonely boy, always an outsider. "Was that what made you run away back to your father's people?"

He stiffened as the old shock and dread seized hold of him. "No. I endured lots of beatings before that one. Old Jeremiah tried his damnedest to whip the Indian out of me. Couldn't change the color of my skin no matter how much he prayed or used the hickory cane. The only reason I'm tolerated in society now is because of the size of the Remington bank account. Most of the good mamas of the city lock up their daughters when the dirty half-breed walks in."

"And you've taken pity on me because I don't have a mama to protect me."

The trace of impatient asperity in her voice caused him to turn around and face her. Unwillingly, he felt himself start to smile. "All this nobility is wearing on both of us. Why don't you bundle up in those blankets and I'll see about getting us some of that soup Essex made this morning?"

The mention of the manservant suddenly brought back visions of him stripping a bloody bandage from Oliver Standish's head. She bit her lip and asked, "Is Oliver all right?" Overcome by guilt, she added, "He was bleeding."

"Not nearly as much as he deserved. I saw the entire fool accident from the hill. He could've killed you."

Remembering the insane way Oliver was driving, she couldn't argue with that. "But he's going to live?" she persisted.

He grimaced as he tugged on his cold boots. "Yes, he'll live."

He started toward the door as she called after him. "You

will come back, won't you? I mean . . . not send that servant?''

Her uncertainty was matched by her tenacity. He had always admired that in the stubborn little tomboy. He smiled. ''I'll come back, Stevie.'' *And may the Powers protect us both.*

Essex had the Standish boy well in hand, liberally dosed with good brandy, bundled in blankets and sleeping soundly on a chaise placed in front of the hearth. It was twilight now and the storm raged on. Little help for it, they would be snowed in at least overnight, perhaps for several days.

Chase had come up to the deserted country place for a few days of peace away from the Remington clan. He had needed time to think about what he would do with the rest of his life. The day he had been captured at the massacre when Custer's soldiers stormed Black Kettle's camp on the Washita, the wounded young warrior had sworn a blood oath to return to the Cheyenne. Learning he was the half-breed heir of the powerful Remington dynasty, the Blue Coats had not killed him, although there had been one young officer who had tried his damnedest to convince Custer to disregard the orders to take him captive. Custer, ever eager to curry favor with the powers in Washington, had refused to listen to the second lieutenant. They had been forced to shackle the boy hand and foot in order to place him on the train headed back to Boston.

Over the years that followed, Chase continued his white education, marking time, gaining knowledge of their civilization, but always assuming that his destiny lay west with the Cheyenne. That was before Stevie came back into his life. He cursed to think it was the old man who had introduced the insidious idea of marriage. And even worse that he had instantly thought of her.

Deep in thought he stirred the steaming kettle of thick vegetables and venison, the latter a product of his hunting skills. There were times when he had to cleanse the stink of the city from his body, even if his soul was still tainted.

That need was what had caused him to desert the delectable Sara's bed and go hunting in the bitter New England winter. "What the hell will I do about her?" Chase muttered aloud as he dished up the fragrant food. He was not thinking of the diva but the innocent lying in his bed down the hall. Damn, it had been a near thing, climbing in bed with her that way. Only an idiot would have placed himself in such an impossible situation. *Maybe you intended to deflower her. Then you'd have to marry her.*

He almost dropped the bowl. Was that what he'd been about? Would marrying her be so awful? Bitterly he realized that it would. It would mean accepting the Remington name and living the rest of his life surrounded by men like Jeremiah . . . and Burke. No matter how brave and hardy Stevie was, she could not survive on the plains. Look how his mother had ended up—widowed and starving with a sick child for whom she had sold her soul and her sanity.

No, if he chose the girl, he would have to abandon his Cheyenne heritage. He rubbed his eyes as a headache thrummed behind them. "I have to think." But thinking under the same roof with Stephanie Summerfield was not all that easy. As he returned to the bedroom with their supper, he prayed the storm would clear by morning.

The day dawned gray and cold with snow still falling. The sounds of clanking pots from the kitchen awakened Stephanie. She blinked and sat up, alone in Chase's big bed. They had talked little as they shared the simple meal he brought. He had been taciturn, deeply preoccupied, answering her questions with monosyllables or turning them back on her. She had been exhausted from the ordeal and he quickly insisted she go to sleep.

Chase had brought back one of his servant's old nightshirts, explaining that he owned none. She had blushed at the sudden image of his bronzed body naked between the white sheets and accepted the soft cotton garment which was nearly a fit. Essex was a slight man and she was tall for a female. Stephanie gingerly threw off the covers and swung her legs across to the icy floor. Someone, probably

Chase, had kept the fire blazing all through the night while she slept, but now it had burned low.

Experimentally, she stretched and stood up. There were a few bruises but considering she had a near brush with death, nothing of note. Her feet were freezing. Picking up the old plaid robe Chase had left her—it did belong to him—she bundled up in it, belting the tie around her slender waist, then rolling up the sleeves that hung ridiculously long on her. A wardrobe stood across the room. Surely somewhere inside the massive piece she would find some house slippers or at least a pair of warm woolen socks, no matter how much too large. She opened one massive door, knelt down and began to rummage.

After spending an exceedingly uncomfortable night sleeping on a straight-backed Louis XVI sofa, Chase was in no mood for Standish's imperious demands or the affected English accent.

"I say, you know I'm grateful you happened along, old chap, but Miss Summerfield and I simply must get back to the city. I shall need medical attention," he averred, gingerly touching the bandage on his head. "Mamá will be beside herself thinking we've perished in the storm."

"You might just perish yet if you try to ride back to town through this snow. If it clears by noon, I'll see if I can get us through in the sledge. If not"—he shrugged—"you'll just have to let Mamá stew."

"But—but surely you can see how damaging this could be to a lady like Miss Summerfield. Think of her reputation if it ever got out that she spent days without a chaperone locked up in your house," Oliver said, trying another tack.

Chase raised one heavy black eyebrow. "Especially considering I'm in it."

"Well, I didn't mean . . . that is . . ." Oliver's florid complexion grew waxy as he looked up at the tall, powerful man whose austere swarthy face bore obvious testimony to his savage origins. "What I mean is that being here with only three men is most improper. Of course, I could do the honorable thing and marry her." He brightened suddenly at the inspiration. "Yes, of course I could!"

"Or I could."

The words dropped like stones between them and the younger man looked goggle-eyed at Chase, as if the idea were beyond preposterous. "But you don't even know her!" Oliver protested. "Stephanie and I have been courting for some time now and I have always intended to offer for her," he added righteously.

"I've known her since she was six years old," Chase replied calmly. "Say what you really mean, Ollie, old chap. That I'm unfit to touch a white woman." His voice was laced with an undertone of menace.

"Now see here," Standish replied, gulping for breath and backing away from Remington, who remained standing by the hearth. "I never said any such thing, but now that you bring it up, you do have a libertine's reputation."

Chase threw back his head and laughed. It was not a nice laugh.

"Don't you two *gentlemen* think as an interested party that I might have a vote," Stephanie said, padding into the middle of the tense confrontation. Both male heads swiveled toward her in surprise, but before either could speak she continued, "My reputation is my own concern and I shall not be coerced into a marriage meant only to silence the wagging tongues of silly gossips."

Flames shot from those dark golden eyes. Chase leaned against the basalt stones of the fireplace and crossed his arms over his chest, admiring her as she stood there with his robe dragging the ground around her feet, a pair of beat-up old house slippers many sizes too big for her sticking out beneath it. Despite being cinched tightly at her slender waist, it gaped open at the neckline. She clutched it closed with both hands as the rolled-up sleeves flopped around her elbows. A dim shaft of light from the hearth caught the bronze highlights in the silky hair that cascaded around her shoulders.

"Now, Stephanie," Oliver temporized, hesitantly drawing nearer her, "you must know that I have always held you in great esteem—as does Mamá."

"But she might not after this little episode," Chase interjected most unhelpfully.

Stephanie looked over at him. Smirking with typical male arrogance, one booted foot crossed over the other, he rested a broad shoulder against the mantel. "I ought to take you up on your gallant proposal and see just how long your bravado would last," she spat. He only made it to aggravate Oliver and to assuage that infernal pride of his, not because he really cared about her . . . or did he? She studied him, suddenly wary as he pushed off from the mantel and stalked toward her.

"I might just surprise you," he said softly, surprising the hell out of himself.

Essex chose that propitious moment to open the front door and stamp inside staggering under a load of firewood. "I believe the snow is stopping, sir," he said to Chase, who began removing the heavy pieces of wood from his arms and standing them on the hearth.

By early afternoon the storm was over and a weak winter sun glistened on the new-fallen snow. The trio rode back to the city in an old sledge pulled from the shed behind the house. It was not nearly so glamorous as Oliver's much lamented Portland Cutter, but it saw them anonymously home before anyone recognized Stephanie in the company of the notorious Chase Remington and looking for all the world as if she had spent the night in a lovers' tryst.

Anthea was having a good day . . . at least as good as they ever were for her, lost in her isolated world of internal torment. Her once glorious golden hair was now faded to a drab gray, hanging limply around her shoulders. She refused to allow her maid to do more than simply wash and brush it, nor would she wear the constricting dress of a white woman, but remained clad in a loose night rail and woolen robe both day and night. It mattered little, for she had not set foot outside her lonely tower room in seven years.

When Chase entered, she sat rocking slowly in the heavy oak rocking chair that belonged to her maternal grandfather,

Ellis Blackthorne Chase. Her only son was named for him. Chase knelt beside the chair and took her dry, veined hand in his. "Good morning, Mother," he said in the Cheyenne tongue. "Verity tells me you slept well last night, but now you must eat your breakfast." He studied the sagging hollows of her wrinkled cheeks and mouth, which were ravaged by scars from her nails, self-inflicted injuries. Sadly he realized that she was only thirty-nine years old. She looked seventy. When she did not respond, he stroked her hand, then just held it in silent communion, knowing she would acknowledge him in her own good time, if she chose to do so.

Finally, her pale eyes lifted and met his and she smiled. "Chase the Wind," she said softly in her husband's language, the only one she had spoken since the madness overtook her the fateful night he had run away.

He smiled in return at her use of the Cheyenne name he had been given as a boy. "Would you eat for me, Mother?" he asked.

She shook her head and he knew it would do no good to argue. Sometimes she fasted for days. When he returned after living for three years with the Cheyenne, he had been appalled at her mental and physical deterioration and guilt stricken because he had left her behind.

"I hear Vanishing Grass calls me sometimes," she said at last. "Soon I shall journey on the Hanging Road to the Sky to join him."

"I will miss you, Mother," he said simply.

She nodded. "But then you will be free." Before he could protest she added, "And so will I."

With a pang he accepted that. There was nothing more to say, no way to explain to her all the complications of his white life, least of all about his confusion over Stephanie.

His heart ached for the father he had so little time to know. When Vanishing Grass had been cut down by Blue Coat bullets, Chase was only a small boy, but the memory of a tall, handsome man with a wide smile remained with him. He knew his mother remembered far more, so he spoke to her as he always did when he visited, of his more recent time with her husband's people. He told and retold her of his great-aunt Red Bead and Vanishing Grass's brother, Stands Tall, the uncle who had been his mentor during the years when he proved his manhood and became a Cheyenne warrior. The stories seemed to comfort her even though they both knew that way of life was coming to a close with the passing of every year . . . and they were both prisoners thousands of miles away.

Finally, when he felt her drifting off to sleep, he stood up, gently placing her hand on the wide armrest of the rocker, then covering her with a blanket. These brief periods of lucidity when she recognized him were becoming more and more infrequent as her mind drifted deeper into its own tortuous labyrinths.

Would it have been different if I hadn't run away and left her? The question had tormented him ever since he was brought back here to find her locked away in the tower. The worthless *veho* doctors declared her raving mad. Burke wanted her moved to an isolated sanitarium run by a friend of his. Chase was grateful that the old man had refused to allow it. It was the first time Jeremiah had ever done something Chase had wanted.

Once she recognized her son, grown so splendidly tall and handsome, Anthea had joyfully cried and held him, speaking to him in Cheyenne. Chase knew then he could never leave her again, no matter what had happened in the past.

And now he had another woman to trouble him. *Stevie*. He had been summoned to Jeremiah's office the day after he returned from the country house. Thankfully, the old man had not learned about his overnight adventure with her, but he had learned that she was acceptable marriage material for the august Remington name. He announced that her father would countenance the match as well, reminding Chase none too gently that it was a major concession, considering his tainted Indian blood and wildly profligate ways.

Of course, neither of the old men had bothered to consult

either him or Stephanie. Such was the way of dynastic marriages between wealthy families. The custom was little different among his father's people, although if either bride or groom were unwilling, the Cheyenne never forced the issue. Jeremiah at least had the good sense to do likewise. He had laid his cards on the table and left the next move to his stubborn grandson.

And Chase had, for the first time in his life, done something Jeremiah wanted. He had called on Stephanie Summerfield. Even though he told himself it was madness, that he was Cheyenne, that he did not belong in the *veho* world and would not remain there, that he would only break her heart, he could not stay away. In the past week he had escorted her to a ball, taken her ice skating in the park, even dined with her sour old father, Josiah. She was Stevie, the beloved companion of his childhood, so refreshingly bright and without artifice in a world of vapid debutantes and jaded matrons who possessed the morals of alley cats.

He headed toward his room for a few hours of studying before class. His professors were growing restive with his absences and missed assignments. Time to apply himself sufficiently to pass the term. In fact he found many of the subjects fascinating, particularly military history and the natural sciences. Closing the door, he began to shrug off his jacket when a sultry feminine voice interrupted.

"Do get comfortable, Chase darling," Sabrina Remington purred in her slow Virginia drawl.

Chase turned, tossing his jacket across the bed, then folded his arms across his chest and scowled. "What the hell are you doing here, Sabrina? Burke will flay you alive if he catches you."

She raised her milky shoulders, scandalously revealed through the sheer ice blue silk of her peignoir, then shrugged dismissively. "Burke hardly notices me," she replied, tossing her thick mane of deep brown hair back, a preening gesture that accentuated her heavy breasts, the dark nipples indiscreetly peeping through the sheer fabric.

"Well, I'm not interested either. Find someone else's bed to sleep in."

"Oh, my, my," she cooed, placing one tiny beringed hand on her chest, stroking it consideringly. "That's right, you're practically engaged now, aren't you?" She glided over to him with a swish of her hips. "Some pallid little schoolgirl. I hear she's a veritable bluestocking. Must be something of a wallflower. Odd, I never fancied you to be smitten by the marriage bug."

He smiled nastily. "Observing how splendidly you and Burke rub on, I could be forgiven for entertaining doubts about the institution," he said dryly.

"Oh, marriage *is* splendid if a woman needs a rich husband. Burke leaves me to find my own divertissements in return for being seen with him at his important political functions."

His eyebrows rose sardonically. "A marriage made in heaven."

"And what about yours? Is she pretty, Chase?" She ran her fingertips up and down the taut biceps in his arm, then leaned toward him, pressing her breasts against him.

Chase uncrossed his arms and set her away from him, looking at her with disgust, not only for her but for himself. She'd stalked him like a hungry tigress from the day Burke brought his young bride home from Washington two years ago. Chase had taken her to bed just to cuckold Burke. But the satisfaction had not overridden the guilt. *I'm no better than the rest of the Remington clan.*

"It's over, Sabrina. I told you that six months ago." That announcement had provoked a screaming, vase smashing, clothes ripping tantrum. "Why the sudden renewal of interest in me after telling me I was a boring college boy too stupid to appreciate what the gods had gifted him with, hmm?"

"Perhaps I'm curious. After all, this Stephanie Summerfield must be—"

"Stephanie is none of your concern," he said through gritted teeth as she grazed by him, her heavy attar of roses perfume wafting around him in a seductive cloud.

"So testy. Does she know how to please you the way I did? I doubt it. A Boston virgin, hmm . . ."

"Stevie's a woman with morals, a concept beyond your comprehension."

She studied him speculatively, then let out a light trill of triumphant laughter. "Ah, just as I suspected. You haven't touched her, have you! But you've wanted to. A man like you can't be long without a woman. You're tense, Chase . . . hot, frustrated." Sabrina licked her lips as her eyes glowed with excitement. "I love it when you're frustrated. Remember when you tore my clothes off like a savage? Do it now, Chase, please," she cajoled, letting her peignoir robe slither from her shoulders and hang at her wrists in silken bondage while she once more rubbed against him like a restless Persian cat.

He almost weakened. Sabrina was right. The past week had been an ordeal. He was unused to self-denial and all he could think of was Stephanie, naked and entreating him while they were snowbound.

Sabrina's knowing fingers stroked his throbbing erection and she played her ace, whispering, "Do it to spite Burke."

All at once he felt sickened by her, by himself, by everything in this corrupt house, everything the Remington name symbolized. All desire fled as he pried her busy hands away and yanked open the door not caring if a servant or Burke himself saw her coming from his room in dishabille. "Get out and stay away, Sabrina. You have a lot more to lose than I do if your husband finds out what a slut you are."

He slammed the door in her face and locked it.

At long last after an interminable New England winter a hint of spring finally beckoned, providing Chase and Stephanie with their first opportunity for an afternoon outing, riding along the Charles River. The sun was glorious, lighting her bronze hair with brilliant richness. The deep golden shade of her riding habit perfectly complemented her eyes, which were fixed on him as they walked their horses sedately along the river road.

A faint breeze stirred his long, straight black hair. She tried to imagine him living with the Cheyenne, dressed as a savage warrior. There had never been privacy for them to discuss his past during the brief courtship. Now that they were not surrounded by people, she suddenly felt tongue-tied and afraid to ask.

As if reading her thoughts, he smiled, glancing back to where their groom rode a discreet distance behind them. "This is the first time I've been allowed to take you away from the crowd. I'm afraid my reputation isn't as sterling as Oliver Standish's."

"You're nothing like him, thank heavens. And sterling reputations are easily tarnished in the Neponset River."

He smiled grimly. "You were lucky to escape."

"Him . . . or you?"

He looked over at her and his smile warmed. "Still the same outspoken Stevie."

"Not quite the same. I've learned enough decorum to hold my tongue now and again . . . just not around you." Her cheeks flamed as she added, "I behaved quite shame-lessly the night you rescued me from the river. I was afraid you thought I was a . . . a hussy, that you wouldn't want to see me again." There, at least she had the courage to say that much.

Chase studied her lovely profile, noting the delicately heightened color in her cheeks as she swallowed and stared straight ahead. "Ah, Stevie, you aren't a hussy or anything close to it—and believe me, I should know," he added wryly.

Her head turned toward him. "You were the one who exercised good judgment while I . . ."

"You'll never know what that 'good judgment' cost me. Because of you I found I could behave honorably even in a *veho* world where there's damn little honor to be had."

"You don't like us, do you?"

"I like you just fine, Stevie." He was continually de-lighted with her artless blushes.

"I mean, white people in general. I remember your teaching me some Cheyenne words when we were children. The word *veho* means spider, not very flattering."

"It can be taken two ways, I suppose. Spiders are clever and industrious, but they spin webs that ensnare their victims until they're helpless. Then they destroy them.''

"Like the white man is doing to your father's people now?"

He nodded grimly. "A whole way of life is coming to an end on the plains. The buffalo are almost gone. The government is herding the tribes onto desolate reservations, land no one else wants. They're getting us out of the way for the railroad and the wagon trains headed west, like the one my mother was on."

"How is she, Chase?" He had never before spoken of Anthea, although Stephanie had heard dreadful rumors. She had always wondered what would make a lady such as Anthea Remington do such a reckless thing. The society gossips had quite a time of it when Anthea mysteriously vanished, then reappeared with an illegitimate Indian son. Stephanie watched the muscles in Chase's jaw clench and unclench as he battled for control of his emotions.

"There are days when my mother recognizes me."

"I'll understand if you can't talk about it." His pain wrenched her heart. "I lost my aunt, who was like a mother to me, but it was a clean parting."

"Her illness is the most insidious kind, taking her mind, leaving her body a shell."

"You must love her very much."

Chase nodded. "Yes, I do. She sacrificed everything for me. The Cheyenne live for their children."

"You speak of her as if she were Cheyenne, too," she said, puzzled. Anthea had been a captive, the dreaded "fate worse than death" for a white woman, an experience about which Stephanie would never dare inquire of Anthea's proud and lonely son.

"She is Cheyenne in her heart, her spirit," he said simply, unable to explain about Freedom Woman and Vanishing Grass and a time in the long-ago past. "The Remingtons have destroyed that spirit, destroyed her soul."

"I remember your grandfather from when we were children, sitting in the church pew while he thundered hellfire and brimstone on the congregation. It must have been hard for you to understand each other."

"Literally as well as figuratively. I couldn't speak a word of English when I was brought to him as a six-year-old. I learned English quickly enough."

"But never to understand him? He's a harsh man. I'll never forget that day he caught us fishing in the river." She shivered, remembering Jeremiah Remington's piercing blue eyes and harsh voice as he towered over them, dragging them dripping from their innocent childhood game.

"Neither will I." He smiled wryly, patting his buttocks. "I paid a dear price for enticing a young girl to take off her clothes."

Under his teasing grin she felt her face heat once more. "The punishment must have been singularly ineffective judging from how adroit you've become at undressing females over the years," she retorted.

"Miss Summerfield, you are a caution," Chase replied, throwing his head back and laughing heartily.

"I like you this way . . . laughing and happy."

"I suppose I am happy when I'm with you," he said consideringly, surprised to find it was true. "You're the only woman I know who I can talk with and not end up in bed with."

"That's where we began as I recall. I must really be a bluestocking if my conversation is more stimulating than . . . the other."

"I was speaking about your mind, Stevie, which I happen to enjoy purely aside from your body, which as you damn well ought to know I want in the worst way." He glanced back to where their groom had dismounted and was examining his horse's hoof. "Let's play hooky," he said softly. "Follow me."

He kicked his stallion into a gallop and Stephanie urged her own mount to follow at the breakneck speed. They raced off the road into a stand of evergreens down by the river. Chase brought his big black to a stop at the bank of the river with Stephanie close behind. The thick hemlocks completely hid them, encircling the gentle slope down to the bright rushing current below. They were completely alone.

He swung down from Thunderbolt and reached up to her. "Now, allow me to reassure you of your desirability, Miss Summerfield."

Stephanie's heart began to pound uncontrollably.

4

The fire in his eyes was smoldering as those dark, long-fingered hands encircled her waist. Her breath caught as she leaned toward him, placing her hands on his shoulders, allowing him to lift her from the sidesaddle as if she, tall, gawky Stephanie, weighed no more than thistledown. He did not play the gentleman and set her cleanly on the ground, but rather drew her body intimately against his, so that she slid slowly down the length of his tall, hard frame.

Stephanie could feel every muscle in spite of the layers of clothing separating them. When her feet finally touched the earth she continued to hold onto his shoulders. One of his hands slid from her waist to press against the small of her back while the other reached to her face, stroking her cheek and jaw with delicacy. The whole time their eyes locked, soft gold with hard obsidian.

"I recognized this stubborn little chin before anything else that night across the ballroom floor," he said in a husky mesmerizing voice, stroking her jawline, then splaying his fingers on her throat to feel the furious race of her pulse.

His eyes studied her mouth now, examining it with such intense deliberation that she could feel her lips tremble in response. "Are you going to kiss me, Chase?" she asked boldly.

The whiteness of his smile flashed, breaking the intensity of his heavy-lidded gaze for an instant. "Yes, I am. Do you want me to, Stevie?"

The pulse in her throat raced when his hand gently cupped her nape, cradling her head, drawing her closer,

closer. Her eyes fluttered downward as his mouth brushed hers, softly at first, velvety, warm and firm.

Stephanie dug her fingertips into the heavy wool of his jacket, feeling her whole body sing with his touch. His gentleness was at odds with the glowing black fire banked in those fathomless eyes, the tension radiating from his long body. She knew he was holding himself back, unwilling to frighten her, she who had seldom been kissed and herself never allowed more than the most perfunctory pecks, stolen by awkward boys who posed no threat.

Feeling a frisson of his frustration touch her, she instinctively pressed her body closer to his, moving up onto her toes, raising her mouth for more of the sweet enticement of his lips.

Chase could tell she was inexperienced, yet her instincts were passionate. She was eager to learn and unafraid. When she arched against him, he groaned and gave in, deepening the pressure of his lips, rimming the seam of her mouth with his tongue. She gasped in soft surprise and he glided inside, dancing a ballet with her tongue, teaching her how to answer. God, she was an apt pupil!

Emboldened by the shocking intimacy and the fact that it pleased her so, Stephanie returned the startling caress, exploring his mouth as he had done hers. Unconsciously her pelvis arched, answering his when he rocked his hips rhythmically. Then his hand glided down to the curve of her derriere, cupping one small cheek with strong fingers.

She came to him so artlessly, so eagerly, unlike any other woman he had ever possessed. His mouth grew restive, opening wider, savaging her soft pliant lips as he slanted his own across them, drinking in her proffered sweetness like a parched desert drinks up cool spring rain. His arms gathered her to him, wanting to absorb her pure yet heady essence.

Stephanie heard the low feral growl that rumbled deep in his chest as his kiss grew rough, his body more demanding. His hands trespassed over the curve of her hips and buttocks, then reached up to the soft swell of her breasts. She should be scandalized and appalled. A lady

would break free and slap his face. But she did neither.
Instead she reached up and ran her hands through his thick
glossy hair, tangling her fingers in the straight locks that
brushed the collar of his shirt. She had wanted to feel its
coarse texture and to touch the hot skin beneath from the
first moment she had seen him standing across the ballroom.

When he began unfastening the buttons down the front
of her heavy jacket and insinuated his hand inside, all coherent thought fled. The sheer lawn of her blouse felt more
like gauze as his fingers worked dexterously past frilly ruf-
fles to cup a breast, lifting it in one scorching palm. She
felt the nipple pucker tightly sending tingling shivers to her
belly and lower.

His lips finally broke away from their hot insistent kisses
and trailed a searing pathway across the hollow of her
cheek, over her jaw to the side of her neck. He exalted
when she threw back her head, allowing him access to her
pale vulnerable throat. The feel of her small perfect breast
pebbling in his hand nearly drove him mad with desire. He
would have sunk to the ground in mindless passion as randy
as a green fifteen-year-old boy if some primal instinct from
his days on the plains had not made him aware of a rider
approaching.

The groom! Chase heard his plaintive call, both aggra-
vated and timorous. Cursing, he pulled his hand from inside
her jacket and quickly began to refasten the buttons.

Stephanie felt him pull away abruptly and a faint cry of
protest bubbled up as she continued to hold onto his neck.
If she had let go, she knew she would have fallen to the
ground, blinded and breathless. Her eyes opened and fell
to where he was straightening her disheveled clothes with
such practiced ease. Taking a deep, shuddering breath, she
withdrew her arms from around his neck and stepped back,
brushing against the side of her horse. Burning heat stung
her cheeks and it no longer had to do with passion.

"This is the second time I've thrown myself at you quite
shamelessly. Now you must think I'm truly wanton."

"A truly wonderful wanton," he replied, his own voice

betraying none of the fierce angry frustration his body was feeling as the groom approached.

Only when Stephanie caught sight of the poor servant did she realize what had almost happened. What she would have *allowed* to happen!

"I'm that sorry, Miss Summerfield, but me horse come up lame," he said nervously as the tall half-breed's night-black eyes bored into him. In spite of Remington's expressionless face, the groom felt the tension and cleared his throat nervously, awaiting instructions. His employer's daughter looked flushed and guilty as if the breed had been taking liberties, but she only nodded to his remarks.

"We were just resting the horses until you caught up," Chase said, noting the way the surly youth was looking at Stephanie. *Damn, I'll ruin her reputation yet!*

The groom noticed that her hand continued to rest on Remington's arm. Whatever had been going on, old Josiah's prim bluestocking daughter had liked it well enough. No accounting for tastes, he thought sourly. Rich folks, who could figure them out? As the breed helped her remount, the groom waited an appropriate distance, curious about the soft murmurs of conversation exchanged between them, yet unable to hear.

"I apologize for my actions, Stevie. I didn't intend to let things go so far," he said as they turned their horses back toward the city.

She looked at him with defiance blazing in her eyes. "Well, I'm not sorry. I enjoyed it . . . immensely."

His breath caught, then erupted in a laugh. "You always say what you mean. Don't ever change, Stevie."

"I can't seem to help it," she replied ruefully.

"Good." He smiled at her.

"Then . . . you're truly not scandalized by my behavior. I'm not trying to trap you, Chase."

He studied her earnest expression as they rode in silence for a moment. "Maybe I'm trying to trap myself," he replied enigmatically as they approached the outskirts of Boston.

* * *

After her disturbing ride with Chase, Stephanie was too excited to eat her lonely supper that evening. As usual Josiah worked late. She slept restlessly that night, dreaming of the wicked pleasures of Chase Remington's mouth on hers, his hands on her breasts. Awakening at dawn with the covers tangled about her legs, she arose, knowing it was useless to try going back to sleep. Perhaps Chase would call today!

With that thought in mind, she performed her morning toilette quickly and headed downstairs, surprised to find Josiah at the dining room table. Normally her father did not eat breakfast but headed directly to his office.

"Good morning, Father," she said pleasantly, easing onto a chair as a servant held it for her, then poured a cup of steaming coffee. "I'm surprised to see you at home for breakfast."

Josiah Summerfield was a small man with perpetually stooped shoulders which came from a lifetime spent pouring over account books. His thinning tan hair was cut short by the personal barber who shaved him every morning in his office while he reviewed the day's calendar of appointments. He peered at his daughter from behind heavy bifocals that magnified colorless light eyes. His thin lips were turned down in a scowl that, like the shoulders, had been acquired by years of habit.

"We have a matter of some importance to discuss," he began in his usual preemptory manner, waiting for a maid to serve their omelets and tinned fruit compote, then leave the room.

Josiah seldom took the time to discuss anything with her. A flutter of apprehension washed over Stephanie as she thought of her most unseemly behavior with Chase Remington. When he resumed speaking she almost dropped the napkin she was spreading across her lap.

"Jeremiah Remington paid a call at my office yesterday. It seems he's looking for a wife for that hellion grandson of his and you are one of the candidates." He studied her face, which went from pale to rosy as he spoke. He supposed the chit was passably good-looking if a bit tall for a female, but she had inherited his late wife's delicate features and heavy shining hair. Of course Paulina had filled her head with a lot of nonsense but that was unavoidable and would probably not mean much if he took a hand in matters now.

"Oh, and what does Chase have to say about all this?"

"Chase, is it now? He's called on you less than half a dozen times and I suppose you've already given leave for him to call you Stephanie."

"Stevie," she corrected, then wished she could call back the word. "It's an old nickname from when we were children."

Josiah cleared his throat, dismissing any mention of her lonely childhood. "Be that as it may, I suppose you find the boy to your liking, even if he has . . . er, questionable parentage?" He raised one pale eyebrow and gazed myopically at her.

"Chase has every right to be proud of his Cheyenne father," she defended hotly.

Josiah allowed himself one thin laugh, as if he rationed them. "Even if that makes him—to put it crudely—a bastard? Lots of gels' mamas wouldn't let a man like him near their daughters. I pointed that out to old Jeremiah, don't think I didn't. Of course, he knew the boy'd already caught your scent. The Remington name is prestigious and as the heir, the boy will be worth a fortune one day. As will you, since you're my only child. Now my question to you, Missy, is will you marry him?"

Stephanie twisted her napkin until it was almost shredded in her lap while her father spoke his piece. "So you and Reverend Remington have decided to arrange our betrothal—without consulting Chase, I'm certain. I won't marry a man who won't speak up for himself. If Chase wants to marry me, he can ask me himself," she said, throwing the napkin onto her plate and rushing from the room.

Josiah called after her, then shook his head in vexation. Silly romantic dribble. Marriages in their class were made for sensible fiscal reasons, not on the whim of callow youths or flighty girls. It appeared she was smitten with the Remington boy, half-breed bastard that he was, not to mention his crazy mother. Well, if Stephanie threw up no vaporing objections to Chase Remington, the matter was settled as far as Josiah was concerned. He would tell Jeremiah that his grandson had better press his suit quickly so the serious business of a settlement could be worked out.

That afternoon a note arrived from Chase requesting the pleasure of Stephanie's company to attend the opera the following evening. By the time he called to pick her up, she had changed her gown three times, nearly driving her little Irish maid to distraction. She finally settled on the gold silk with cream lace trim, deciding it was the most sophisticated thing she owned and would make her look more mature. Fussing with one errant strand of hair which kept slipping from the heavy knot atop her head, Stephanie gave herself one final inspection in the mirror.

Do I look as frightened as I feel? What will happen? She gnawed her lips, afraid that he was only going to ask her to marry him because it was what his family wanted. No, Chase would not be swayed by the reverend. But he might propose because of some absurd notion about compromising her honor. It seemed they could not spend even a few moments alone without her ending up unclothed, letting him take appalling liberties. Was she so transparently in love with him? What if he pitied her?

Stop it! she scolded, then forced herself to go and face him. He stood at the bottom of the stairs, dressed in black evening clothes. The snowy whiteness of his silk shirt contrasted with his swarthy skin and night-black hair. The bloodred satin lining of his opera cape added an almost savage aura as he waited, so tall and handsome. She could not read anything in his face.

Lord above, she was stunning, his Stevie! Chase held his breath as she floated down the stairs, a glittering vision, spun of soft golden sunbeams. The faint scent of apple blossoms filled his nostrils as she approached. At once he could detect a wariness to her that had not been there before. She was always so impulsive, spontaneous and honest. .

Old Josiah's told her. He swore to himself, knowing how much tact the sour old merchant had probably used. About as much as Jeremiah had. He should have thrown the whole dynastic merger back in the old man's face just to spite him. But he could not do it.

I want her, he admitted to himself now that he was face-to-face with her again. Oh, he'd told Jeremiah that he would consider the marriage just to rattle Burke. But even then he'd known saying that was only a sham. He desired her as he had desired no other woman, even though he knew it meant his dreams of returning home would end irrevocably the day he wed her. *Am I crazy as Mother?* At that moment he honestly didn't know.

Chase reached for her hands, ensconced in elbow-length cream kid gloves. Taking both, he raised them to his lips for a chaste salute that somehow became something far more charged and erotic when he felt her pulse leap through the thin soft leather. "You're beautiful," he said simply, then asked, "Where is our chaperone?"

"Mrs. Wright is waiting for us in the study. Anthony was to ask you to wait there with her while he informed me of your arrival."

"He did, but I decided I'd rather watch you make a grand entrance. Every head in the opera hall will turn when I enter the box with you."

She blushed with pleasure and murmured, "I wish we could leave Mrs. Wright behind."

"What would people say?" he asked with mock indignation, always caught off balance by her combination of pristine innocence and free-spirited lack of concern for convention.

"What indeed?" she echoed.

"Do you like Salieri?"

"No," she replied honestly. "Do you?"

"No. He's a boring composer but the opera was an excuse to ask you out for a late dinner."

"I have an idea. Father won't return until around midnight. He spends every Thursday evening at his club and it never varies. If I know Mrs. Wright, she's already been tippling his sherry . . .''

He raised one dark eyebrow speculatively, unable to stop the grin spreading across his lips. "What do you have in mind, vixen?"

"An earlier dinner without Signor Salieri's pompous arias—unless you must hear the divine Sara sing?" she couldn't resist adding.

Unbelievably, Chase felt himself blush beneath his swarthy skin. "Sara and I parted ways some weeks ago." *After I found you again.* "How did a sheltered miss like you hear about such a thing?"

"Society misses gossip worse than fishwives," she said dismissively, unwilling to let him know how much the rumor had pained her when first she heard it. "Now let me introduce you to Mrs. Wright. We'll take a few moments for sherry. I guarantee you by the time our carriage reaches the opera, she'll be snoring fit to frighten the horses!"

They entered the study and Stephanie very properly introduced Mrs. Wright to Chase. The chaperone was delighted to join them in a bit more sherry.

The older woman was a distant cousin of Josiah's father, paid to fulfill the duty of chaperoning his headstrong daughter. While Stephanie hated having no real family to rely on for social occasions, Mrs. Wright's fondness for sherry could be useful. The day of her disastrous sledge ride with Oliver Standish, the chaperone had been left behind at the last moment due to an "indisposition." Josiah had not been present to say her nay, so Stephanie had done what Paulina would have let her do—left without benefit of a chaperone. She prayed her plan to "indispose" the old harridan tonight worked.

When it was time to leave, Chase offered an arm to each lady and they walked through the open walnut door and out into the cool spring evening. Once they were securely ensconced inside the coach, the fumes of sherry on the plump old woman's breath were almost as noticeable as had been her stiff reaction to Chase.

She's worried I might scalp her, he thought in grim

amusement, then ignored her as she stared out the carriage window at the gaslit streets, making no pretense at being anything other than a paid employee. He was desperate to speak with Stephanie alone, but all they could do was make polite small talk en route.

As predicted, Mrs. Wright was soon snoring noisily. Slipping the driver a large banknote, Chase instructed the man to take them to the Remington mansion so they could pick up his phaeton. The coachman was to drive Mrs. Wright home, wait outside the incapacitated matron's house until she awakened, then escort her to her door with the assurance that Miss Summerfield and Mr. Remington had enjoyed the opera and hoped she had, too. The befuddled woman might wonder about how she had sat through *Cyrus und Astyages* without remembering any of it, but she would be too embarrassed to dare question anything or breathe a word to anyone.

Once they were alone in his spider phaeton, Chase slowed the horses to a leisurely walk and turned to her. All the earlier conspiratorial amusement had fled. "It's time to discuss serious matters, isn't it, Stevie?"

"You make it sound funereal," she said, striving for a light tone as her heart seized with dread.

"I take it your father told you about the esteemed reverend's proposition."

As he spoke he guided the matched team effortlessly around the corner of a narrow street. Stephanie did not know where he was taking her and did not care. She studied his hands on the reins, encased in immaculate pearl-gray gloves, those long-fingered dark hands so devastatingly skillful, so masterfully gentle. "Yes, Chase, he's spoken to me. I told him I would not be party to a dynastic arrangement made by two old men."

She waited a beat but he said nothing, forcing her to look up and meet his eyes. They glowed like live coals in the moonlight yet revealed nothing. Swallowing for courage, she continued. "I told you before, I won't trap you, Chase. I don't want it that way between us. If you want to marry me, you'll have to ask me yourself . . . and mean it."

A sad smile touched his face as he reached up and brushed the side of her cheek with one hand. "I never thought I'd marry a white woman . . . until you came along."

Her heart raced as the implication sunk in, but there was more. He seemed almost reluctant to admit that he would consider courting her. "You always planned to return to your father's people and marry a Cheyenne woman."

His eyes took on a faraway depth as he stared out into the darkness. "Ever since the old man had me brought back in chains I've dreamed of nothing but escaping the Remingtons."

"They brought you back in chains?" Her voice was appalled. "Why did you stay?"

"Because of my mother."

Of course. Now she was beginning to understand a great many things about the brooding and rebellious Chase Remington. "Your mother needed you."

"She speaks nothing but Cheyenne . . . when she speaks at all. I should never have left her alone in that house, never have run away."

"You were only fourteen, Chase," she replied gently.

His expression hardened. "I made a deal with the old man. I'd behave, learn to dress like a *veho*, eat with the right fork, even go back to school if he'd keep his son from having her committed to an asylum."

"What will happen when—" She stopped short. "Oh, I'm sorry, Chase. I had no right—"

"Yes, Stevie, you have every right. When she's dead, I'd always planned to leave forever and never look back." *After I killed Burke.*

"And now . . ." If there was hope in her heart that he loved her enough to stay, there was also fear, which she voiced. "She held you here all these years, unintentionally, but against your will. I won't take her place, Chase. Not that way."

He smiled sadly. "Always so forthright. More so than I've been, rehashing the past. I think it's time to put it behind me. I've never been certain if I could go back—if the Cheyenne would even have me after all the *veho* have done to them. I may not be socially acceptable in many Boston homes, but I have learned to survive here. If you married me, you'd be shunned in some quarters, too, Stevie.''

''Do you think I'd care?''

''No, not now . . .''

''Not ever, Chase.'' She held her breath, waiting for him to say the rest, to tell her he loved her, ask her to marry him.

''You're so young, so idealistic and untouched by life's ugliness. There are things so evil you could never begin to imagine them. The Remington money's been my passport to respectability but the Remington name is a sham. To borrow a phrase from the old man, 'a whited sepulcher.' I'll always despise it.''

She could see in his face the naked pain of a little boy trying to be brave in the face of the Reverend Jeremiah Remington's blistering denunciations. ''I understand why you hate the Remingtons.''

His eyes flashed with a sudden savage fire. ''No, you could not possibly,'' he replied in a clipped, cold voice, at odds with the momentary lapse he had revealed to her.

Stephanie placed one small hand on his arm, feeling the terrible icy fury he was masking. ''I can imagine a great many things. I was there when your grandfather caught us in the water, remember? And I was there when your uncle paid a man to kill you for your inheritance.'' She shivered.

He placed his hand over hers. ''And you'd still marry into the Remington family, knowing all that?''

''No, not the Remington family. Prestigious names and money don't mean anything to me. I would marry you if . . .''

He felt her hand tremble. She had been honest about her feelings. He owed her the same—if only he knew clearly what his feelings were! ''Stevie . . .'' he began uncertainly, ''I've never felt this way about any other woman. I admire you, I desire you, I want to be with you and I'm happy when we're together . . .''

"But your heart's still out west . . . with the Cheyenne," she said softly as tears gathered, stinging her eyes, trapped beneath thick sable lashes. She refused to let them fall. *I won't cry and humiliate myself any further in front of him.*

The phaeton neared the restaurant which had a discreet, private back door for wealthy men entering to keep assignations. Knowing he had bungled the whole thing badly, Chase reined in the horses as the doorman approached. With a silent oath, he tossed Harry a generous tip as the old man took the lead horse's bridle, saying, "Evening, Mr. Remington."

Even though she had never been to the exclusive restaurant, Stephanie understood the significance of the back door entry—and the fact that Chase was a regular customer used to bringing women here who could not afford to be seen in public with him—women like Agatha Lodge. She was a foolish young virgin who was behaving just as scandalously with a man she really did not know or understand at all. A man whose heart belonged to no one . . . if he even had a heart.

"They have private dining rooms upstairs where we can talk," he said softly, reaching for her hand.

"Perhaps it would be better if you just took me home, Chase," she said stiffly, pulling her hand away from his. "I seem to have lost my appetite." She stared straight ahead into the darkness.

Chase felt the tension in her body. She sat ramrod straight on the softly upholstered seat as if it were a bed of nails. She was desperately fighting back tears and he could not blame her. She had let down every barrier and told him she would marry him if he asked her. A bold and forward thing for a properly raised Boston bluestocking to do, especially one scarcely out of the schoolroom. Caught up with his own private demons, he had humiliated her without ever intending it. If he asked her now she would probably tell him to go to hell!

Better to let her regain her dignity and indulge in a good private cry. Tomorrow he would send flowers with a carefully composed note. Perhaps once he sorted out his thoughts, he could put in writing what he had not said in person.

Anthea Remington walked out of her tower cell for the first time in seven years. She had to learn if what Dr. Walters said was true. The old physician had come for her monthly checkup that afternoon. As he had examined her, she had listened to his conversation with the nurse.

Like everyone else, they spoke as if she could not understand them. Since she only spoke Cheyenne, when she spoke at all, it was a reasonable assumption. But sometimes she understood. Today when she heard the words *savage* and Chase's name, she had willed herself to listen. They discussed the railroad and how that New York millionaire Jay Cooke was going to build it westward through the hunting grounds of the Sioux and Cheyenne. The Northern Pacific would destroy the last of those "filthy red savages" who had driven her out of her mind and saddled her with the shame of Chase, an "illegitimate half-breed."

Anthea had seethed at the lie but said nothing, for she had grown cunning in the ways of madness. Let them say what they would as long as the doctor did not sedate her or have her tied to her bed again.

When the house grew quiet she had slipped past her dozing maid, Verity, and wended her way through her childhood home, a soulless cold mansion in which she had always felt a stranger. She had no way to judge the time, only that it was late. She prayed they were both asleep by now, especially *him*. Anthea was not certain if she could hold onto this thin thread of sanity if she came face-to-face with him.

Her destination was the library where all the issues of the newspaper were kept until her father finished reading them on Saturday night when they were thrown out. She must read for herself if the railroad was coming to destroy her people—Chase's people.

He must help them. *He must leave me*, she thought. Could she bear it? To be alone in this house without her son's protection? *I am Freedom Woman*, she reminded her-

self with a single-minded intensity which left no room for
fear or doubts.

Then she heard *his* voice and the old terror seized her.
Her heart hammered and a sour brackish taste filled her
mouth. The room spun crazily and she knew she was going
to scream and scream . . . but no, she would not. *I am Freedom Woman, Mother of Chase the Wind*, she repeated like
a mantra. Her nails dug into her palms until they drew
blood in spite of being carefully pared short by the maid.
She stood in the hallway for a moment as another voice
rumbled deeply.

She forced each leaden footstep nearer, flattening herself
against the wall outside the slightly ajar door, shivering in
the darkness like a wild creature.

"Chase's marriage is all arranged whether you like it or
not. I've settled everything with old Josiah."

"What makes you so certain he'll go through with it?"
Burke asked. "You know how defiant the damned savage
is."

Jeremiah chortled, self-satisfied. "Oh, he'll marry her all
right. He's been squiring her about for several weeks—first
eligible female he's kept company with since he was out
of knee britches."

"And into breechclouts," Burke interjected with sar-
casm.

"None of that matters anymore. He's in Boston to stay
now. I'd always feared when Anthea died that he'd up and
run off to those benighted savages again. I know she's the
only reason he's remained here for the past four years. But
once he's tied to the Summerfield heiress by marriage, there
will be children. Then he'll have to face up to his responsibilities as the Remington heir."

"I never thought I'd live to see the day you'd bestow
everything on Anthea's bastard. Good God, Father, he's a
damned red-skinned savage!"

"Since you and that Virginia belle you married haven't
seen fit to provide me with any white grandchildren, I have
no choice in the matter! Besides, I will hardly be leaving
you destitute."

"God damn you, you pious old hypocrite—you'll be sorry for this!"

" 'Thou shalt not take the name of the Lord thy God in vain!' 'Honor thy father!' You will not blaspheme in this house ever again, nor rail at me!" Jeremiah boomed out. Burke slammed the heavy oak door on his way out, storming down the hallway, oblivious of the figure huddled on the floor in the darkness.

🥀 5 🥀

For several hours Anthea simply remained in a fetal position curled up in the deep shadows of an ornately carved kast. *He* had left the house. Yet her terror would not let go of her. Finally, she became aware of her surroundings once more. And she remembered what she had just overheard.

Chase was being forced to marry a society girl handpicked by her father. Her son would be chained to this terrible house and the curse of the Remingtons for the rest of his life. All because of her. She had brought him here to save his life when he was a child. Would that act now cost him his soul?

"I cannot allow him to do this thing because of me. He must be free to leave this place and never return."

Slowly, like a woman twice her age, she unfolded her arms and legs, feeling the pinpricks of restored circulation as she walked very stealthily into the library. First she must write a letter to Chase. That would be the most difficult part. After that, the rest would be so simple . . . and welcome. . . .

Chase and Stephanie rode in stiff uncomfortable silence. Mercifully the distance from the restaurant to her home was a short one. When he escorted her to the door, she would have quickly fled inside had he not detained her at the top of the porch steps.

Stephanie felt his hand on her arm and tried to pull free. She was desperate to reach the privacy of her room and release the torrent of tears held in check for so long. But his grip was as firm as his voice.

"I never thought you were a coward, Stevie." She stiffened in outrage and tried again to break away. "Look at me," he commanded, cradling her jaw in his other hand. The jewel-bright glitter in her eyes tore at his heart and he cursed himself for seven kinds of a fool. "I do love you and I do want to marry you," he said simply.

"Not as much as you want to leave Boston and rejoin your father's people, Chase. You don't want the onus of the Remington name. Marrying me would tie you to it more tightly than caring for your mother ever has." She waited a beat, some tiny part of her hoping he would deny it.

But he did not.

Instead he muttered a frustrated oath and swept her into his arms, kissing her fiercely, possessively. She started to resist, then surrendered, letting him savage her mouth with the blistering passion she had come to crave so hungrily. *Good-bye, Chase.*

Chase felt her melt against him, returning his passion with an unpracticed ardor that was a far more potent aphrodisiac than all the skillful wiles of women like Aggie or Sabrina. When he was near her he could not think . . . but he could feel. Ah, could he feel!

Their embrace was sheltered by heavy wooden rose trellises casting black and white shadows on the lovers as the moon peeked in and out of cloud banks. Both of them spoke more eloquently with their eager young bodies than they could with words. Finally Chase's team grew restive and pawed at the cobblestones, snorting impatiently. The sudden noise from the street echoed up and down the silent residential neighborhood, bringing them out of their magic world of sensation. A chill spring wind swirled around them as they broke apart.

"I love you, Stephanie," he repeated again.

"Good-bye, Chase," she repeated aloud, slipping from his grasp like a wraith, vanishing into the darkness beyond the massive front door.

When Chase finally neared the Remington mansion, it was well past three A.M. He had driven around aimlessly, stopping in several of the less respectable haunts he frequented, drinking more than he should have. But he could not seem to get drunk. After the waterfront tavern closed its doors, he realized how feckless it was to attempt drowning his pain in liquor and turned the phaeton toward home.

Home. Had he ever had one since his father had been killed and his mother had been forced to bring him to this hellish place? Rounding the corner, he saw lights burning in all the windows of the big ugly stone monolith. It looked like a sinister black jack-o'-lantern squatting in pale moonlight.

A sudden premonition of dread tightened in his guts as he whipped the team into a fast trot and reined in on the front drive in back of Dr. Walters's battered old brown buggy. An ashen-faced butler held the door open for him. "What's happened, Amos?" he asked the elderly black servant.

"I'm so sorry, Mr. Chase."

He knew. Bounding up the stairs, he raced toward the tower room where the doctor was conversing in hushed tones with Jeremiah as Anthea's maid, Verity, sobbed, quietly comforted by one of the cook's helpers. Several other servants, all in their robes and slippers, stood about, whispering behind their hands, their eyes round with shock.

"What happened?" Chase asked the doctor without preamble.

Walters turned from the haggard Jeremiah to his enigma of a grandson. The physician's myopic brown eyes would not meet Chase's fierce black ones. "Your mother has passed on, Mr. Remington. It really is for the best. She's not been coherent for some time. That's why—"

"She was healthy enough yesterday," he snapped. "What happened to her?"

Both the doctor and Jeremiah stood frozen like statues for an instant. The reverend recovered himself first. "There's been an accident. The Almighty has seen fit to take her."

Chase knew, yet he could not bear for it to be true. "Just how did your *veho* god *see fit* to do it?" he asked harshly.

Jeremiah bristled at the irreverent question but the doctor

replied hastily, "Somehow in the night she slipped from her room while the servants were sleeping—"

"It's my fault, Mr. Chase," Verity blurted out, interrupting Walters. "I should've heard her."

"Nonsense," Walters admonished, then turned back to Chase, not unkindly. "Miss Remington has been in a mostly vegetative state for months. There has been no need for restraints for at least two years. No one expected her to awaken and wander out of the safety of her room in the middle of the night. She was, of course, quite disoriented in the dark. I'm sure that's how she fell from the widow's walk. How she ever found her way up the stairs in the dark is a mystery in itself."

"The widow's walk?" Chase echoed in amazement, picturing the narrow deck around the third floor dormer in the west wing. "That's clear across the house. Why the hell would she go there . . . ?" His voice faded as the reason came clear. The widow's walk's heavy wrought-iron railing was waist high and quite sturdy. "She jumped, didn't she." It was not really a question.

"Certainly not!" Jeremiah replied, his tone oddly strained. "She would never imperil her immortal soul by committing suicide, no matter how far gone her mind."

The old physician looked far less convinced of the issue but wisely kept any comment to himself, adding only, "When she fell the noise of her body breaking a dried branch on the oak out front raised one of the servants. Otherwise no one might have found her until morning."

"Where have you taken her?" Chase asked in a toneless voice.

"In here, sir," Verity said, wringing her thin, work-reddened hands, leading him into Anthea's tower room. "She didn't suffer, sir. At least there's that blessing. The doctor said her neck broke in the fall."

Anthea lay in her bed, with her hands folded across her waist. She looked for all the world as if she were asleep, if not for the slightly odd tilt of her neck. The rotten oak limb must have broken her fall.

When he heard the old man and the doctor step into her

room, he turned with the look of a cornered animal glittering in his black eyes, wounded and dangerous. "Get out! Leave me in peace with her!"

Jeremiah started to protest, but in a surprising reversal of roles, the quiet little physician took the big man's arm and guided him out, shaking his head. The reverend did not protest as Walters closed the door behind them.

Chase knelt beside the bed on the step stool she used to climb into it. How small and frail she seemed lying on the plush coverlet. He touched a wisp of grayed yellow hair, tucking it against her ear gently. "At least you can go to my father whole, not disfigured," he murmured. The Cheyenne believed that a person who was maimed in death went forever afterward carrying that physical stigma. She had plaited her hair in the Cheyenne fashion and dressed in a loose red silk robe which Chase had bought her last Christmas. It was the nearest thing she had to Cheyenne finery. Jeremiah had burned her doeskin wedding dress as soon as they arrived here.

"You look at peace." He stroked the pale dryness of her cheek, which for the first time in years seemed unlined and free of the fear and shame that had tormented her as long as she lived under the Remington roof.

His throat ached as he began chanting low and slow at first, the words coming back to him gradually from the past. It was a Cheyenne death song to send her on her journey up the Hanging Road to the Sky. As he chanted, he withdrew the knife he always carried from inside his jacket and made several diagonal slashes on his palms. The red of his blood dripped onto the red of her robe, blending with his tears.

When Chase had finished he stood up, dazed and disoriented, and began to walk to the closed door, but as he reached for the cold brass knob, a woman's voice, choking on a sob, stopped him. He turned quickly, startled to find Verity still in the room. Her eyes were round as she stared at his bloody hands. "What savages you must think we are," he said in a neutral voice, not willing to explain himself further.

Hesitating only slightly, the old woman approached him, offering the envelope she had clutched in her hand. Tears streamed down her wrinkled cheeks. Swallowing them back, Verity whispered, ''She's at peace now. Like you said, with yer pa.'' She thrust the envelope at him. ''When . . . when I woke up hearin' the commotion downstairs, this was beside my pillow.''

Chase took it gingerly in one bloody hand. His name was written on it in delicate spidery letters. Odd, he had no way of recognizing his mother's handwriting. He had never seen it before but he knew that it was hers. ''Thank you, Verity,'' he said quietly, then opened the door and walked out of the room.

One bloody handprint stained the polished brass knob black.

Alone in his room, Chase sat staring at the unopened envelope as he wrapped strips of white linen around his hands. Both Walters and the old man had been horrified at his self-mutilation. ''Savages, chanting to heathen gods. 'Thou shalt have no other god before me,' saith the Lord!'' Jeremiah had thundered. Nervously the doctor offered to tend Chase's injuries but he had brushed them both away with no more concern than he would have given a swarm of gnats.

When he completed the hand wrapping, he took a swallow from the whiskey bottle on his desk, then opened the letter and read:

My dearest son,

When you read this I will have gone to join your father. Had I been of a stronger mental constitution I would have done so years ago that you might have returned to our people. Please forgive me.

I know you are being forced into an alliance with a woman the reverend has chosen. He boasted how it would tie you to the Remingtons irrevocably even after I was gone. This evil place would destroy you as it did me if you bound yourself to this woman. I give you your freedom.

Our people need your guidance. I have heard that the rails are coming onto the sacred ground. The buffalo will scatter and the Long Knives will try to herd the Cheyenne onto reservations. You have learned the *veho* ways, my son. Use what you know to help our people.

But before you go home, my son, I beg you to promise me one thing: Do not kill Burke. The Remington arm has a long reach. *Veho* law would take your life for his. That would not help our people. I implore you to heed my final request.

Remember me not as you see me now but as I was once in a happier time.

I love you.

Your mother, Freedom Woman

Stephanie took the heavy velum envelope from the butler with thanks, then closed the door to her room, where she had sequestered herself all morning. She recognized Chase's bold scrawl addressed to her. After leaving him last night she had cried until dawn. Now, holding the missive in her hands, she felt a premonition of disaster. Best to sit down before she read it, an inner voice cautioned. She walked over to the windowseat where she had watched the sunrise. Suddenly gray rain clouds obscured its weak light, an omen of the sort of day it would be.

Stephanie sat on a fat steel blue cushion and carefully opened the letter as her heart thumped fast and hard against her chest. Her eyes were puffy and burned from her tears. She blinked, struggling to hold the paper steady as she read.

My dearest Stevie,

You knew me better than I knew myself. How does a young lady grow so wise at only seventeen? Please believe me when I say again that I do love you as I shall love no other woman. But you were right about my allegiance to my father's people, which would always have stood between us if I had remained in the world of the white man and we had married.

The Cheyenne were my mother's people, too, for in her heart she was more Cheyenne than white, and I am her son. Anthea, Freedom Woman, my beloved mother, is dead. Last night she made the ultimate sacrifice to free me from the Remingtons. Her final request was that I return to the Cheyenne to try and help them during the tribulations which lie ahead. I cannot in conscience do otherwise.

You have grown into an extraordinary woman who will make some very fortunate man a splendid wife. I regret deeply that I cannot be that man.

Be happy, Stevie.

Chase

Tears seeped unchecked from her eyes, rolling slowly down her cheeks and dropping onto the paper. With deliberation she took the letter and crumpled it in her hands. The heavy velum formed a small tight ball, crushed like her heart.

He had chosen. And his choice was as she had always known it would be . . . those savages over her. He said he loved her and perhaps he did, but not enough. Never enough. Never in her life had Stephanie Renee Summerfield been worthy of enough love. Only Aunt Paulina had truly cared for her and even she had deserted her niece in a premature death.

"I have no one," she whispered in the empty room. The sound of her desolate words echoed in the gathering silence. Now she realized, after her night of stern resolutions and high-minded anger, that she still had held the faint hope that against the face of all reason, he would come back to her. Perhaps if Anthea had not killed herself—for that is what he must have meant by "ultimate sacrifice"—he would have.

But she knew, too, that keeping him that way would have been a hollow victory. The lure of the West, that land of endless sky about which he had spoken so passionately, would always hold him in thrall. And so would his father's people, the strange, savage Cheyenne who Anthea Remington had adopted as her own. What would make a white woman abandon every tenet upon which she had been raised?

A man like Chase.

But Chase was gone forever. Stephanie laid her head on her bent knees and huddled in the windowseat as a spring storm blew in, gray and angry, pelting the glass with splinters of sleet. She felt as if the icy shards were penetrating her heart as well.

Spring finally arrived to stay. Daffodils and hyacinths bloomed and the skies cleared. The whispers over Anthea Remington's tragic death—which everyone knew was by her own hand, poor demented thing—were quickly eclipsed by the far more titillating rumors surrounding her scandalous bastard son. The half-breed heir to the Remington millions had simply up and vanished without a trace. Among all Boston's upper crust, he had left behind only a string of angry cast-off lovers—and Stephanie Summerfield.

The gossips had instantly seized on Remington's squiring about that most unlikely young miss. Agatha Lodge sniffed that Stephanie was thin and drab, not to mention a boring bluestocking. Whatever had he seen in her? To further fuel the fire, the servants' grapevine circulated the story that a marriage alliance had been agreed upon by the Reverend Remington and old Josiah Summerfield. Then the prospective groom had fled, no doubt gone back to join those hideous red animals who were raping and pillaging across the plains. He was, after all, tainted with their inferior blood and nothing better could be expected of him, regardless of a Harvard education.

But Josiah Summerfield's daughter was from pure-blooded Boston Brahmin lineage. Much better was expected of her, even if her late aunt had raised her a bit unconventionally. Had the unscrupulous libertine taken advantage of the girl? Perhaps that was why she'd agreed to marry a man like Chase Remington.

For the first few weeks after Chase left, Stephanie remained barricaded in her room, awash in the self-pity only the very young are capable of feeling, utterly unaware of the fustian of gossip sweeping Beacon Hill. Then gradually her natural resilience and the stubborn courage that had always been uniquely hers asserted itself. She must get on with her life and forget Chase Remington. Surely by now thousands of miles away, he had forgotten her. Stephanie made her valiant resolution and emerged from her cocoon, ready to dazzle even the spiteful Agatha Lodge.

Ever immersed in his account books, the dour old Josiah took no notice of such trifling matters as gossip, even if anyone would have dared to broach such a subject to the sharp-tongued, sour-faced old merchant. When he was notified by the Reverend Remington that his errant grandson would not be fulfilling the marriage contract, Josiah had been annoyed still to be saddled with a daughter of marriageable age. Just as quickly he left her to her own devices and returned to work. He was confident that another suitor of good family would come along shortly, considering the huge dowry he was willing to bestow to settle the matter.

Only when Stephanie accepted her first social invitation to a cotillion given for Addie Lake by her doting parents, did she realize that her association with Chase had done more than break her heart. Her finishing school roommate Addie greeted her with a coo of delight when Stephanie walked into the big ballroom on her father's arm.

"Ooh, Stephanie, you've come out of seclusion at last! I was positively delighted when you accepted the invitation. What a luscious gown."

Josiah snorted in disgust. "Dress ought to look good on her. Cost me enough." Then seeing August Lake talking to several bankers by the punch bowl, he quickly excused himself from the frivolous female company and headed off to talk business, the real reason he had come.

"Most girls could never wear that color successfully, Stephanie," Addie added, eyeing the pale shade of green which would have made her sallow complexion look utterly jaundiced.

Embarrassed by her father's brisk dismissal, Stephanie smoothed the delicate embroidered sprigs of leaves on her skirt. "I'm pleased you like the gown, Addie. Your own is quite lovely, as is the party. Thank you for inviting us."

"Why, you poor dear, of course I wouldn't have dreamed of excluding you, no matter what those vile-tongued old harridans say. I never listen to gossip," she added with a self-righteous lift of her plump double chin.

Stephanie paled. "Gossip?"

"Why about you and that wicked Chase Remington, silly. Oh dear, don't tell me you didn't know?" She placed four chubby fingers on her powdered cheek in mock regret. "But of course you didn't. You've been hiding away like a virtual hermit since he jilted you."

Stephanie stiffened her spine and her eyes darkened with indignation. "Mr. Remington and I were never engaged, so he could not have jilted me. I merely went on a few social outings in his company."

"Whatever you say, my dear," Addie said in a sweetly patronizing tone. Then her eyes took on an avid glow as she asked, "Did you keep company with him because of your old childhood friendship? You never did explain how you knew him at the Cabots' ball last winter."

Stephanie had never really liked Addie, even though they had been thrust together by necessity in school. The girl always had been catty and backbiting in spite of the loving indulgence of both parents. "No, I never did explain since there's really nothing more to it than a brief acquaintance when I was a little girl."

Before Addie could launch into another line of questioning, Tom Bennington and George Gordon sauntered over and asked the ladies to dance. Prior to approaching the young women, the two young gentlemen had tossed a coin to determine their prospective partners. Tom lost and bowed over Addie's hand while the winner George swept Stephanie into the strains of the waltz.

She was used to the succession of self-important and shallow sons of the city's elite fawning over her and expected the evening to be like many others had been since her debut. But as she traded partners through mazurkas, schottisches, polkas and waltzes, she detected a subtle difference. Instead of the compliments and braggadocio, there were odd assessing looks and stilted conversations about the weather. A few of the bolder ones had held her too tightly or issued invitations to stroll in the Lake's English garden out back. One man possessed the audacity to ask her to slip out for a carriage ride! She indignantly declined every one.

What sort of gossip had Addie been hinting at? Even if Chase had broken an engagement—which he had not— why would anyone blame her? After all, she was the aggrieved party! Surely no one had learned about that disastrous night spent with Chase in the snowstorm. Would Oliver Standish have been cad enough to disclose it after all this time?

When the late supper was announced, Stephanie had no appetite and wanted only to leave, but as usual, Josiah was closeted away with his cronies, discussing stocks and bonds. She went in search of him with no success. En route back to the ballroom she heard Addie's thin titter amid the giggles of several other debutantes. When they mentioned her name, she froze.

"What do you suppose it feels like? Ooh, I wish I could ask Stephanie."

"I dare you!"

"Just imagine, doing *that* with a half-wild red Indian."

"Half-wild, my aunt Fanny's bloomers—Chase Remington is a Harvard man, after all. And so wickedly handsome he would be hard to resist."

"I heard poor Stephanie was hiding because she was in a family way, but after seeing her tonight, I suppose that's not true."

"Maybe not but if she kept company with that awful half-breed, she must've let him bed her. He never bothers with any woman who won't."

"She must've been a disappointment. After all, he *did* leave town!"

Gales of laughter followed the last sally. Stephanie felt nauseated. Balling her hands into fists she prepared to wade into the midst of the vicious little cabal of "ladies" who were supposedly her friends and tell them precisely what she thought of them.

Suddenly a musical tenor voice with just the hint of a Southern drawl said, "I don't believe a word of it. No one with any sensibility—not to mention a grain of common sense—would."

Stephanie gasped and turned to face a handsome stranger in the blue and gold of a cavalry officer's dress uniform. He was tall and very slender with wavy light brown hair and warm brown eyes that were sympathetic without a trace of pity. "Please accept my apologies for startling you. I didn't intend to cause you further undeserved discomfort."

Stephanie warmed to his smile, which seemed honest and kind. "Your apology is duly noted, Lieutenant—?"

"Phillips. Hugh Phillips, but since I'm only a second lieutenant, technically I should be addressed as a mere mister, Miss Summerfield."

"Have we met before? Surely I'd remember so chivalrous a gentleman," she added, returning his smile.

"No, but I inquired about the identity of the beautiful woman whirling across the dance floor when I came into the room. Would you do me the honor of allowing me to escort you to supper?"

She nodded in assent, taking the arm he gallantly offered, and they began to stroll toward the groaning buffet tables in the Lakes' immense dining room.

"I was late for the ball, I'm afraid. A hazard of duty when one is a soldier."

"Are you stationed here in Boston then?"

"No, I was only sent here from Washington to deliver dispatches to Colonel Breckenridge. My permanent assignment will be with the Seventh Cavalry, in Elizabethtown, Kentucky. My family is from Baltimore but I have a married aunt living here in Boston. Marybelle Kenyon. I'll be staying with her for a while. You see, I have a month's leave coming. I'd be honored if you would consent to spend a brief bit of it in my company, Miss Summerfield.''

Hugh Phillips was balm for her wounded soul. She quietly relished the look of amazed jealousy on the other debutantes' faces when she passed the buffet table in the company of the dashing young officer. Their plates heaping, they found a quiet bench in an alcove where they could dine privately.

After a few moments more of polite conversation, Stephanie laid down her fork and looked at Hugh. ''How do you know the gossip about me is not true?''

''I could not be more certain. You are a lady. Just watching the way you conducted yourself on the dance floor convinced me. There is an air of innocence, of honor about you that is inviolable. If your father saw fit to agree to a betrothal with the Remington heir, it would have been an honorable marriage. The man was a bounder to leave you— not to mention an utter fool.''

''Most people in Boston would not agree with your assessment . . . of me, at least,'' she replied darkly.

''Most people in Boston are stuffed shirts with nothing better to do than polish their own tarnished halos by attempting to tear them off the real angels.''

Stephanie felt a small burble of laughter well up at his earnest assertion. ''I'm not guilty of having an affair with Chase Remington, but that scarcely makes me an angel.''

''When you smile, you are. I have a feeling you haven't done nearly enough smiling in your young life and I propose to remedy that. Will you take tea with Aunt Marybelle and me tomorrow afternoon?''

Stephanie smiled again. ''Yes, I believe I'd enjoy that.''

In the weeks that followed, Hugh Phillips became Stephanie's constant escort. They attended ice-cream socials and dances, went on picnics, and horseback rides. His aunt Marybelle was a kindly older matron with the same innate Southern gentility as Hugh. Although Marybelle was nothing like Aunt Paulina, Stephanie grew fond of the lady. And of her nephew. He was charming but never slavish like Oliver Standish. He was warm, but never forward like Rayburn Lawrence. Hugh made her feel safe, something she had never felt with Chase.

Hugh talked a great deal about his lifelong love of the army and high hopes for serving his country. He came from a fine old Baltimore family who lived in genteel poverty after the war. Winning an appointment to West Point had been the dream of a lifetime. He had graduated third in his class back in 1868, then was sent immediately to join Lieutenant Colonel George Armstrong Custer on his summer campaign against the Plains Indians.

If he adored the army, he idolized his commander, General Custer. Hugh explained to her the general's rank was only breveted to the great man for heroic exploits during the war, but his star was definitely on the rise. And Hugh Phillips's star would ascend right with it and the Seventh Cavalry.

"You should have seen the general at Washita," Hugh said with his eyes aglow as they sat around his aunt's dinner table one evening. "He split his command into four forces and they rode into old Black Kettle's camp at dawn, cutting off every hope of escape for the savages."

"Now, Hugh," Marybelle admonished gently, setting aside the Waterford wine goblet she had been sipping from. "You mustn't frighten us womenfolk with such blood-thirsty tales of red Indians."

"What do you think of the Cheyenne, Hugh?" Stephanie knew Chase had been captured during that raid, nothing more. He had not wished to speak of it. Understanding his pain and resentment at being dragged back to Boston in chains, she had not pried. But now she wondered if Hugh had seen Chase as a seventeen-year-old prisoner. If so, he gave no indication of it. She dared not reopen old wounds by asking. She would not want Hugh to think her crazy—or still in love with Chase—if she mentioned what Chase had told her of his people. But was what he had described true? Or were the Cheyenne really the savages everyone thought?

Hugh considered her question thoughtfully, as he did every one Stephanie posed to him, a trait he knew pleased her. "They are primitive, of course, but not without their own code of honor. They make dangerous adversaries on the battlefield. Beyond that, I've had no personal dealings with them. The best thing would be for the army to contain the Cheyenne and their Arapaho and Sioux allies far away from miners and settlers.''

''But they held the lands in the West for centuries. Have we the right to just take it from them?''

Before Hugh could answer, her father interjected, ''Don't be a ninny, girl. What can an ignorant savage do with fertile soil or gold? He doesn't farm and he doesn't mine. White civilization—good old American enterprise—has the God-given right to use that land. And with the army's help, we'll do it.'' He gave her a quelling look that might have indicated he was angry with her defense of Chase Remington's people . . . or more likely meant that he simply found her romantic altruism bad for business. She had subsided and the topic of conversation changed.

''I'm to report to the general in Kentucky next week,'' he announced the following week as they rode through the park, the Summerfield groom following at a discreet distance.

Stephanie could sense the regret in his voice. ''After all you've told me about the general's exploits, I'd think you would be thrilled to finally rejoin him.''

''It will mean leaving you behind. As much as I want to return to active duty, I don't relish being without that smile.'' He reached over and touched her cheek gently, bringing forth the desired effect.

When they dismounted by the fountain and let the groom cool their horses, Hugh took her hand in his and said earnestly, ''Soon we'll be leaving Kentucky. Bound for the High Plains. Stephanie, the West is incredible. Vast, wild, magnificent!'' He made a sweeping gesture with his arm, then stopped himself self-consciously. ''You must think me an incurable romantic . . . or a fool.''

''Never a fool, Hugh. As to being incurably romantic, I don't think that's such an awful thing.''

He squeezed her hand gently. ''I'd hoped in the past month that you'd come to regard me fondly, Stephanie. I know that I'm not a rich man but my lineage is good and your father has approved of me. I would like to pay you court, with your permission.''

The hesitancy tugged at her heart. Hugh was the polar opposite of Chase, who took whatever he wanted without an instant's hesitation. Blazes! Why did she keep making comparisons between them? Chase was gone and Hugh was here. Chase had deserted her for his savage red brethren. Hugh was steadfast and decent and, she was certain, quite desperately in love with her. But was she in love with him? Or was her heart so bruised and battered that she could never truly love again?

Grow up, young lady. Stephanie could still hear aunt Paulina's sensible admonition. *It's a dreadful thing not to become a woman when one ceases to be a girl.* She must possess the courage to live again.

''I would like that very much,'' she replied to Hugh.

Over the next several months, they exchanged letters regularly. He wrote of the boring routine of camp life in backwater Kentucky. When they were given a special assignment in the Dakota Territory, he painted a vivid picture of the vast herds of buffalo blackening the great plains and even described the imperious yet jovial charm of the Russian Grand Duke Alexis, whom Custer had the honor of squiring on a hunt.

His letters were utterly wonderful. Stephanie read them and pictured in her mind's eye the vastness of a cloudless bowl of blue, the Endless Sky the Cheyenne called it. Plains filled with huge shaggy bison, snow-capped mountains and icy clear rivers, all beneath a brilliant beaming sun. The images were her solace through the bleakness of another Boston winter.

When Hugh received leave the following spring, he rushed straight to Boston and asked her to marry him.

Stephanie accepted.

They were wed in a grand Episcopal Church in Baltimore, for Hugh's family was High Church and asked that the ceremony be held in the cathedral. Oddly during the elaborate nuptial mass, Stephanie caught herself fleetingly wondering what the Reverend Jeremiah Remington, stern

Congregationalist that he was, would have thought of it. Any memories of his grandson, she forced from her mind, vowing to be a good wife to the handsome man who beamed down at her with a look of complete adoration on his pale handsome face.

✧ *6* ✧

Bighorn Mountains, 1872

Chase stared down at the teeming village below, stretched in a horseshoe configuration with the opening facing east, as was the custom of the People. Every camp he had visited looked the same from a distance, young men practicing with their bows, girls hauling buckets of water, women scraping buffalo hides while old men smoked and prayed and small children laughed and played with toys. Perhaps this time he would find them. Hopefully, he guided his big stallion down the ridge toward the village.

The Elk Society sentries scrutinized him suspiciously but let him ride past. *They know I'm a breed,* he thought to himself. Dressed in old buckskins and a pair of worn moccasins he had bought from an Arapaho trader, he rode without a saddle in the manner of all horse Indians. Outside of a locket from his mother and Thunderbolt, he had kept little from his old life in Boston, only a small amount of money, which was almost gone now. He had been searching for nearly a year. What if they were all dead?

But no. In every camp he had visited they remembered Stands Tall and Red Bead, brother and aunt to Vanishing Grass whose half-blooded son had been taken prisoner by the White Eyes. From all accounts, his family had returned to the mountains from where their Northern Cheyenne relatives had first come south. Tracking down the survivors of the Washita Massacre had not been easy, for Black Kettle's band had scattered to various camps ranging from the Nations to the Yellowstone country.

And so he had gone from one camp to another, not certain of the welcome his white blood would bring. The People's hearts had been hardened against all *veho* since Sand Creek and Washita. The White Father had broken the Medicine Lodge Treaty and sent his Blue Coats to attack peaceful hunters and burn more villages filled with women and children. Quickly he had learned he must disavow all traces of the white world. He could not look completely Cheyenne, but he could at least abandon hard-soled boots, hats and haircuts. Most camps received him warily but hospitably, offering food and shelter, telling him what they knew of his uncle and great-aunt to aid in his search.

The task was not a simple one for the hunting grounds of the Plains Tribes stretched fifteen hundred miles from the Canadian border to the Staked Plains of Texas. His search was further complicated because the main bodies of Northern and Southern Cheyenne left their large summer encampments every fall, scattering into small bands.

Sooner or later he would find his remaining family. *Then what?* The question had nagged him when he slept alone beneath the vast canopy of stars. He felt a kinship with the land but could he reestablish his ties with the People?

Thunderbolt picked his way through the loose rocks to the edge of the camp. By this time two small boys had discovered the visitor and watched with wide, glistening black eyes as he dismounted. The women ignored him, continuing their chores, but a group of young warriors whose weapons bore the markings of Crazy Dogs, the most militant of the warrior societies, approached him.

A big barrel-chested warrior with Sun Dance scars proudly displayed on his chest blocked Chase's path. "What do you want here, White Eyes?" he sneered.

"I search for my father's brother and their mother's sister who have rejoined the Northern Cheyenne," Chase replied fluently in their tongue. "My uncle is Stands Tall, son of Iron Kite and brother of Vanishing Grass who was my father. I am called Chase the Wind."

The suspicious look on several of their faces began to dissipate but their leader's expression only hardened more.

"Stands Tall spoke of your capture. You have lived

among the White Eyes many seasons. Why do you return now?"

"That is for me to explain to my uncle," Chase answered levelly as a sudden wave of excitement caused his pulse to leap. "Is he with this band?"

"He is here," a second Crazy Dog replied, stepping past his more hostile companion. "I will take you to him."

When the first man reached menacingly for the knife at his waist, another placed a restraining hand on his arm, saying, "It is for the council to decide, Pony Whipper. Let him pass."

Chase's steady gaze never left Pony Whipper's face. He stood poised on the balls of his feet, his hands hanging loosely at his sides, waiting to see what the other man would do. Only when Pony Whipper muttered an angry curse and stalked away did Chase nod to his guide to lead the way. He walked past the rest of the Crazy Dogs, feeling their animosity. *They want nothing to do with whites, even half-whites.* After seeing what the coming of the railroads with their influx of settlers had done in the south, he understood their hatred.

He followed the young warrior through the village, looking neither to the left nor right, letting the People study him in open curiosity. There would be time to learn their names later—if the council allowed him to stay. Soon they stood in front of one of the largest lodges in the village, at least seventeen skins. When he saw the bent shoulders of a thin old woman straighten up from the quilling she was doing on a ceremonial shirt, his heart leaped in his chest. Red Bead was still alive! Her wizened face was seamed like ancient parchment and her toothless gums gave it a hollow appearance but her small black eyes were clear and shrewd, still shining with keen intelligence as she nodded in recognition.

Just then the lodge flap opened and a tall figure emerged. Age had not diminished Stands Tall, who at fifty-two was still as lean, straight and vigorous as ever. Silvery hairs gleamed in his heavy black braids and the creases around his eyes and mouth had grown deeper. When he smiled at Chase the years fell away.

"You are just as I remember you," Chase said simply as the older man opened his arms to his dead brother's only child and Chase embraced him.

"And you are a man grown now," Stands Tall replied, holding his tall muscular nephew's arms.

"What of the others—Song Bird and Red Water?" Chase asked, glancing to the lodge door.

"My wife and my younger son are dead."

"I know Little Sun perished in the Washita Massacre," Chase said sadly, remembering Stands Tall's elder son, a fearless warrior. "But I saw Song Bird escape with Red Water."

"Only to fall prey to another of the white man's killing ways. The spotted throat destroyed them two winters ago."

Although his uncle's face remained impassive, Chase could feel the older man's pain. "I am sorry I was not here to mourn with you."

"Always our aunt said you would return to us. I confess I doubted Red Bead. My heart is glad that I was wrong."

"There was a reason for Chase the Wind's sojourn with the spider people but it is over now. Freedom Woman has joined her husband," Red Bead replied in a voice that rasped softly with age.

Chase embraced the old woman. "I stayed with her until the end. She is at last truly free."

"And so are you. I will have Kit Fox prepare food while you and Stands Tall talk. You will have much to say to each other, I think," the old woman said judiciously as she scrabbled off with surprising swiftness.

Chase followed Stands Tall into the lodge where a small fire flickered gently against the approaching chill of dusk. His uncle motioned for him to take a seat as he himself did so, then began to prepare a pipe. After the ritual of pointing the stem to the sky, the earth and the four winds, he inhaled a draught of fragrant smoke, then handed it to Chase.

They smoked in silence for several moments. He knew

Stands Tall would speak when it was time and it would be rude for him to break the silence first.

Finally, the older man set the pipe aside and studied his nephew's face. "I can see your father in you . . . and your mother. When the soldiers took you away, back to their cities, to your white family, I thought you lost forever."

"I could not leave my mother again. Her brother was going to have her locked away in an evil place. While I was with the Cheyenne, her mind was destroyed. She would speak only in the tongue of the People and only about the old days when my father was alive."

Stands Tall nodded. "Sometimes when life in one time is too much to bear, the spirit returns to a better one."

"She killed herself to free me," Chase said bleakly.

"And so you followed her wishes and came in search of us. Now that you have found us, what is it that your heart tells you to do?"

Chase looked up suddenly from where he had been studying the flames, surprised at the blunt question. "I have come to live with the Cheyenne."

Stands Tall smiled. "That does not answer what I have asked you. Does your heart wish to be Cheyenne . . . or does part of it yet remain with the whites?"

Not a day had passed during the last year of wandering when Chase had not thought of the life he left behind, the woman he left behind. *Stevie*. How could he explain her to Stands Tall when he did not understand his own feelings?

"My heart never belonged with the white man . . ." he began uncertainly. "They looked at me and saw an Indian, a savage in a silk shirt. No matter how diligently I studied in their schools, I was still considered ignorant. All those years when I lived in the house of my mother's father, I dreamed of the endless sky, of riding across the plains, of hunting the buffalo and becoming a warrior once again . . . of belonging."

He felt uncomfortable under Stands Tall's scrutiny, as if his uncle waited for him to say more. Finally, he did. "There was a woman, a white woman whom my mother's father wished me to marry."

"And did you wish this also?"

"She was not like the others. I . . . cared for her, but I could not have made her happy. I could not be white," he said bitterly.

"And now you have come to see if you can be Cheyenne. You will not succeed if you feel only a debt of honor for your mother's sacrifice."

That touched a nerve. Had he only left Stevie because it was Freedom Woman's dying wish? "No. My mother's madness had been touched by the Powers. She knew the marriage would have been doomed, *I* would have been doomed, if I had not left. I've seen many things during my search for you. I've seen what the coming of the railroads has done in the south, slaughtering the buffalo, scattering other game, bringing settlers and miners in swarms . . . and the army to protect them and drive our people into the hot dry lands where they must live on a dole of putrid government rations."

"What you say is true. One reason I decided to rejoin my grandfather's people here in the North was to escape that fate."

"The rails are coming here, too. Already the rich spider people back east make plans to build through the north up all the way into the Yellowstone country. And the one called Long Hair, Custer, will bring his horse soldiers next summer to scout the course of this railroad."

Stands Tall pondered his nephew's news gravely. "I feared we could never escape."

There was a dangerous glint in Chase's eyes as he said, "I cannot seem to escape Custer. Will your council allow me to join the band?"

"They will allow it. There are still a few among us who remember your valor at Washita. We could never have led those women and children to safety if you and the other young warriors had not held the Blue Coats at bay, fighting like wolves."

"All of my friends were killed by the Long Knives. Only I was spared, because I was a powerful white man's grandson," Chase said bitterly, remembering that awful day.

"They dragged you away bleeding and unconscious, chained like an animal. There was no dishonor in that for you. As a youth your hatred of the whites burned hot as a flame. Since then you have lived among them, learned their ways, even considered taking one to wife. We have fled before the Blue Coats for many seasons. What you have just told me means that soon there will be no place left to run. We and our Lakota cousins will be forced to fight. Can you kill the whites as easily now as you did at Washita?"

An image of Burke Remington flashed across Chase's mind, then blurred with that of the long-haired cavalry officer with the insane pale eyes, Custer, and his young lieutenant who took special delight in dispatching Chase's helpless wounded brothers. "Yes, I can kill them," he replied with cold certainty.

Stands Tall nodded. "I will speak for you and tell of Washita for all to hear in the council. Then you will have your opportunity to live the Cheyenne way."

"That is all I ask," Chase replied simply, praying that it would work, that he could at last belong.

Bodies lay sprawled grotesquely, some burned beyond recognition in the fires. Others had crawled clear of the lodges only to be hacked to pieces by rifle butts and hunting knives. An old woman lay cradling a parfleche filled with pemmican. Two small boys had fallen together, their skulls crushed, still clutching small bows in their hands, children's toys. A young woman stared sightlessly up at the brilliant azure of the sky with a bullet hole in her forehead. Her tunic was rucked above her thighs, which were parted obscenely and smeared with the seed from repeated rapes.

Chase stared down at the desolate remains of the small Lakota camp. In the months since he had come to live with his father's people, he had found a measure of peace, but the encroaching whites robbed him and the beleaguered Plains Indians of that peace, of their very lives with every vicious atrocity such as this one. How would it all end? Looking around at the obscenity, he feared the answer.

The trill of an icy stream mocked the horror-struck silence of the Cheyenne warriors around him as they made their way into the remains of what had once been a thriving camp. Blackened lodge poles, with their buffalo hide coverings burned away, stood like skeletons amid the cold ashes. Pottery lay smashed, the contents scattered by the restless winds, meat rotted in the warm sun and insects feasted on the remains. Blood pooled around the unburned corpses drawing flies which droned ominously on the still air. The metallic stench had grown all too familiar. Closing his eyes he saw that other village on the banks of the Washita, far to the south. When Custer's Blue Coats had finished, it looked much the same. Massacre, rape and mutilation. *And they dare to call themselves the civilized ones!*

"White men who gouge the sacred earth for the yellow metal have done this. I say we turn our hunt to human game!" Pony Whipper cried, his face contorted with rage.

"The murderers might have been soldiers," Chase said quietly. Random army patrols had been trespassing on their hunting grounds since spring.

"Do you fear the Long Knives?" Pony Whipper challenged, leaning across his horse's withers.

Several of the other warriors sucked in their breaths at the insult while Strikes Back and Plenty Horses, also Crazy Dogs, waited to see what Chase would do.

Chase stared intently at Pony Whipper, fighting the urge to knock him from his horse and kill him with his bare hands. Knowing that would be a violation of tribal rules, he leashed his fury. "You speak like a foolish boy if you think a handful of warriors should attack a company of Blue Coats. We are armed with bows. Only two of us have guns." He gestured toward Elk Bull's ancient muzzleloader with his own Sharps breechloader, the best he had been able to obtain in barter for his gold Howard watch. "These guns speak only once, but Long Hair's soldiers are armed with Henry repeaters, and the miners are even better armed with Winchesters." His voice was laced with scorn, daring Pony Whipper to make the first move.

"We will do nothing until we see to the dead. Their spirits cannot rest this way," Elk Bull said forcefully, eyeing the two antagonists. He was an older warrior, chief of the village and the leader of this hunting party. The responsibility for keeping peace between the young hotheads fell to him.

Strikes Back and Plenty Horses murmured angrily while Pony Whipper glared at Chase, then spat in the dust with contempt, but made no reply. No one challenged Elk Bull. Several of the other warriors cast glances at Chase the Wind as everyone dismounted but no one said anything to the half-blooded son of Vanishing Grass. No one had to—Chase knew how they felt. In spite of his father and uncle's prowess as warriors, his white blood and the years he had spent in the East had left him tainted in the eyes of many, especially other young men eager to prove their worth in battle against the white invaders who perpetrated obscenities such as this.

Chase could not blame them for their distrust. All the years in eastern schools had imbued him with a lot of emotional and intellectual confusion that was not easy to slough off. Life with his father's people was primitive and at times harsh. He had grown soft and debauched during his college years. Since coming to Stands Tall's band last fall, he had not yet proven himself worthy.

Grimly they all applied themselves to the task of carrying bodies from the village to a series of small caves across the stream. All that could be done now was to seal the cave opening with rocks against the predators of nature. The predators of white society had already done their work so well there was no way to properly cleanse and dress the dead in their best finery as was customary. Everything they owned had been destroyed with them—or stolen by the white scavengers.

As he worked, Chase concluded that these marauders had likely been gold seekers, the riffraff who lived on the periphery of white society, cutthroat drifters in search of quick riches. The would-be miners must have stumbled upon this small camp and decided to help themselves to food, furs and females. Not that soldiers had ever been adverse to ruthlessly attacking a camp of Indians, killing women, children and old men along with the warriors. He'd seen that firsthand at Washita. But officers like Custer only killed for glory, to advance their military careers. Petty thievery seldom interested them.

Could Elk Bull keep Pony Whipper and the other Crazy Dogs from rushing off after revenge? It would simplify Chase's life if they did it and ran afoul of a well-armed patrol. Pony Whipper had taken a personal dislike to him from the first day they'd met. When the council agreed to let Chase join the band, Pony Whipper had been furious. Then to further complicate matters, Plenty Horses's sister, Kit Fox, had taken a fancy to Chase, after spurning Pony Whipper's offer of marriage. Sooner or later he would have to deal with his enemy, but he could not simply kill him as he would have done back in Boston, for tribal law forbade one Cheyenne to take the life of another. The punishment for it was banishment.

The irony of the reversal did not escape Chase.

When they had done all they could for the dead Lakota, the small party of Cheyenne hunters began the trek back to camp. It was near dusk when they came upon the drunken white man who literally stumbled out of a stand of lodgepole pine and into Elk Bull's horse, which shied, dancing backward in spite of its heavy load, for the pony carried a dressed deer the warrior had shot that morning.

Staggering back in goggle-eyed fear, the man turned to run, bellowing at the top of his lungs, "Injuns! Christ Almighty, Injuns!"

He got no farther than the edge of the trees before Pony Whipper had nocked an arrow and taken aim but Elk Bull's stern words prevented him from firing. "Do not kill him! Take him prisoner."

Before the older man had finished speaking, Chase kneed Thunderbolt into a gallop and cut off the terrified man when he emerged from the copse of pines mounted on a shaggy mustang. Pony Whipper came from the opposite side but was too late. Chase had already knocked his captive from his horse and begun tying him securely.

When the white man started to cry out as Chase yanked

him to his feet, Pony Whipper knocked him unconscious
with his war club. "He'll slow us down deadweight like
this," Chase ground out as he struggled hefting the burly
man across the saddle of the mustang and tying him securely.

They quickly rejoined the others and rode away in the
opposite direction from which the man had come, hoping
the rest of the *veho* had not heard the outcry. After about
an hour, when there was no sign of pursuit, the hunting
party halted.

Elk Bull walked over to Chase who was dragging the
captive from his mount. "Has he regained consciousness
yet? I would have you question him about what happened
in the Lakota camp."

"If Pony Whipper did not cleave his skull," Chase replied darkly as he hauled the moaning man into a sitting
position. His pale eyes glazed with fear as he looked around
at the armed warriors' hostile faces. Then he moaned a
muffled curse as his bladder gave way, soaking his filthy
wool britches.

"You have excellent cause for fear, white man," Chase
said in English.

The man squinted up at the menacing figure who towered
over him while kneeling on one knee. "You speak American?" he croaked in amazement, studying Chase's black
eyes and gleaming braid adorned with eagle feathers.

Chase smiled grimly. *American.* As if his people were
the immigrants! "Yes, I speak your language and you had
best heed me. Tell us why you have trespassed onto our
land."

The prisoner again stared at Chase, noting for the first
time his elegantly chiseled features. "Yew a breed?" he
blurted out, then paled at the flash of fury in those ebony
eyes. "I—I didn't mean nothin' by it, honest," he choked
out. "Me 'n' my friends, we was just pannin' fer a little
gold, that's all."

"You didn't by any chance run across a small camp of
Sioux yesterday, did you?" Chase asked.

"Ain't seen no Injuns till I run onta yew, I swear it!" he averred.

Chase was almost certain the man was one of the marauders but could not be positive unless they found the others with their stolen booty. He walked over to the man's horse and began rummaging through the saddlebags. With an oath of disgust, he pulled out a Lakota breastplate made of elk rib bones held together with elaborate beadwork. Unrolling the ceremonial piece, he threw it into the dust where the captive sat cringing. "I suppose you brought this along from the Red Cloud Agency when you came prospecting."

"N-no. That is . . ." He wet his lips, looking from Chase to Elk Bull's impassive face, then back to Chase. "Listen, yer part white. You can't let them—"

"You will die as our friends the Lakota did, only without honor," Pony Whipper said with relish as he knelt beside the captive. He and the others had watched the interrogation in silence up to this point.

"Wait," Chase said in Cheyenne. "We need to ask him how many men were with him. If the army might—"

"No! You only wish to save another White Eyes' miserable life!" Pony Whipper snarled as his blade slashed across the captive's wrists, cutting the bonds but also scoring his hands in the process. He would enjoy toying with the miserable coward before he slowly cut him to ribbons.

Chase, too, freed his knife and pointed the wickedly gleaming blade at Pony Whipper's chest. "What is between us can be settled later. I can make him tell us who the others are who did this and where they have gone."

"Chase the Wind speaks sensibly," Elk Bull said, nodding to the half-blood.

"Now," Chase said, turning his attention back to the captive. "You can do this easy . . . or hard . . ." He pressed the tip of his knife into the fat gut of the killer.

"I . . . I was only with 'em. I didn't start it. It warn't my idea," he begged. "It was that damn bluebelly, a shavetail who just made first lieutenant. He caught up to us two days ago. Said he had to 'escort us' out of here. Then we run

across these two young Injun gals. Nothin' would do but
that damned fool had to find the camp. Said he was here
to kill Injuns first, not baby-sit miners. Damn if it warn't
all his fault!''

''Damn you, indeed,'' Chase said softly, knowing the
prospector had joined in the looting and rape, even if he
had no stomach for the actual fighting. ''How did you come
to get separated from this band of soldiers?''

Before the miner could answer, a shot rang out, then
another. The soldiers rode into the clearing at a hard gallop,
a whole column of them firing at the running Cheyenne.
With a quick grunt, Pony Whipper slit the prisoner's throat,
then ran for his horse along with the others who were scattering beneath the withering fire.

A young lieutenant with his saber raised shouted orders
at his troopers who raced in pursuit of their illusive quarry
as the light faded quickly into dusk. Chase felt a jolt of
recognition. Could it be? The officer's hard features and
cold dark eyes came into his sights as he drew a bead on
the man. Just as he squeezed off a shot with his Sharps the
lieutenant seemed to sense him and wheeled his mount
around. Chase's shot grazed his cheek with a shallow
bloody furrow.

Yelling wildly, the officer charged directly toward the
man who had marked him, intent on cleaving him in two.
Without time to reload, Chase reversed his hold on his
Sharps, to use it as a club against the horseman's saber.
Suddenly, he was struck from the rear. A blinding explo-
sion of colored lights went off in his head. Then everything
faded to black as he fell unconscious to the ground.

''I got one of them sons o' bitches, Lieutenant!'' a grizzled corporal exalted.

''Tie him up and we'll take him back to camp with us,''
his superior said. Fingering the wound on his right cheek,
he yelled, ''Where the hell's the damn surgeon!''

༄ 7 ༄

The rhythmic rocking of the railway car lulled Stephanie into pensive reverie as she stared unseeing out the window. So much had happened in the past two years since she left her father's home to build a new life with her husband. How naive and dependent she had been that night in Baltimore when she became Hugh's wife. The fumbling painful coupling of consummation had ended that naiveté. Two years as an army wife had taught her a self-reliant resourcefulness beyond anything even the intrepid Paulina could have imagined.

Her spinster aunt would indeed be proud of how her charge had adapted, but perhaps she would also be wistfully sad that Stephanie fared little better in love than had she. *Am I doomed all my life to be an outsider looking for someone who will understand me?*

Stephanie blinked back tears of regret for the kind of love she had never experienced. Perhaps her childhood fears were valid and she was truly unworthy of love. In spite of her best efforts to love her father and her husband, she had not been able to surmount the barriers around their hearts. With Josiah it had been his business, with Hugh it was the army.

She closed her eyes and laid her head back, remembering those first few months of marriage. Not even at the onset had it been idyllic by any stretch of her imagination. In spite of her dissatisfaction in the bedroom, Stephanie had believed Hugh loved her, and she felt crushing guilt for making silent invidious comparisons between the way she felt when he touched her and when Chase Remington had. She had continually reminded herself that Chase had deserted her and she had chosen to wed Hugh.

Her husband had been polite and considerate of her ladylike sensibilities during their long journey from Baltimore to Kentucky, letting her prepare for bed and douse
the lights before he entered their private railroad car, a luxury paid for with her dowry. When they arrived at his post
in Elizabethtown, he had spent profligately again, securing
her quarters in the town's best hotel, which only majors
and colonels could afford. In fact she soon learned that
most junior grade officers, even first lieutenants, did not
marry because their salaries were too meager to support
wives. Stephanie was forced to live with the wives of rank-
ing officers. She found them to be much like the ladies of
Boston, insular, boring, and single-mindedly obsessed with
the military protocol afforded the wives on officers' row.
As the wife of a lowly second lieutenant, she was on the
bottom rung of the social ladder and would have been content to spend her days with the hotel manager's sprightly
young bride, but Hugh had been adamant that she must
mingle only within their proper social circle.

"Hattie Wilcox is an Irish immigrant, for heaven's sake,
Stephanie," Hugh had remonstrated. "Being from Boston,
surely you know what that means. Next thing I know you'll
be having luncheon with the company laundresses!"

"But Hattie's bright and friendly," she protested.

"She's still your social inferior," he reminded her
sternly. "You must associate only with my superiors'
wives."

"Captain Alexander's wife is insufferably pompous, telling everyone who'll listen how her great-aunt someone or
other married into the Astor family. And Mrs. Reynolds,
Hugh, she wouldn't even speak to a mere lieutenant's wife
until Mrs. Custer told her my father owned Summerfield
Mills."

"I don't plan to be a mere lieutenant—second or first—
for long, my dear. But in the meanwhile, don't dismiss the
importance of having enough money to impress the likes
of Major Reynolds's wife," he added darkly.

"I don't care about money, Hugh," she said, pressing

one hand tentatively on his sleeve, needing reassurance, not chastisement.

He turned to stare down at her through eyes that had lost their earlier warm brown color. Now they looked pale and cold as frozen earth. "That's easy for you to say, Stephanie. You have always enjoyed the comforts of wealth. The Maryland Phillipses have not been so fortunate for a number of generations—in spite of the blueness of their blood."

Stephanie was taken aback at his bitterness. "I'm sorry, Hugh. I didn't mean to sound flippant. I shall try to befriend the other officers' ladies. Mrs. Custer seems quite sweet . . . even if all she can speak of is her beloved 'Autie.' "

At once Hugh recovered and warmth again suffused his face as he took her in his arms. "The general's lady is devoted to the army life. That's what it takes, Stephanie. I know you will not fail me."

The "army life" had not proven to be an easy one. After a brief stay in Elizabethtown chasing Klansmen and moonshiners across Kentucky, Hugh became bored and restless. His discontent was greatly exacerbated by the departure on extended leave of his hero, the general, who was off to glittering New York City with his wife. Hugh at once requested a transfer west where the Indian wars afforded him greater hope for promotion.

The West. The sky might be endless, but oh how desolate the alkaline plains. Stephanie learned to face the vicissitudes of being an officer's lady, no easy task on the rough frontier outposts. Hugh's first duty station was a far cry from Kentucky and the genteel rusticity of the Elton Hotel. Situated on the rolling buffalo grass–covered plains of eastern Colorado, Fort Lyon was nothing more than a collation of bleak adobe buildings with heavy shutters over the doors and windows to keep out the stinging, choking misery of sandstorms, wind and rain. Unfortunately, they did not keep out rodents, spiders or other loathsome creatures.

The second morning when Stephanie went to the kitchen stove to oversee breakfast preparation, a large rattlesnake slithered down the vent pipe, its tail making a sinister click. Dropping the granite coffeepot, she shrieked as her striker

O'Shaughnessy calmly cut off its head with a cleaver. The trooper explained that snakes often came in that way, seeking warmth from the stove on cool Colorado nights.

Stephanie had been determined to adjust to post life. Although Hugh was preoccupied with the search for hostiles, and often gone on patrol, he saw that she was provided what comforts an army post could afford. Enlisted men often worked as strikers for extra pay, doing all the cleaning, cooking and heavy work for the officers' wives. Hugh hired a brawny Irishman for their household. O'Shaughnessy was a jewel for whom no task was too arduous. At Hugh's insistence, they also took on a laundress, a Chinese girl from the nearby mining camp, who worked for such a meager wage that Stephanie felt guilty. Hugh assured her it was all any Chinese expected and she should not cause trouble with the other ladies by increasing the pay scale of "menials."

She acquiesced. But when he returned after several weeks on patrol to find her fishing clothes out of the boiling laundry kettle he was livid. "What the hell do you think you're doing?" he hissed, seizing the pole she was using and throwing it and a clean bedsheet into the dust while Soo Lin cowered against the wall.

Stephanie held onto her dignity in front of the servant, allowing him to take her inside their small adobe quarters on the line, on officers' row. Fighting back tears of weary frustration she shoved a heavy strand of hair from her sweaty forehead. This was not how she envisioned his homecoming at all!

Hugh studied her mended old gingham dress, liberally stained with soapy water. "No wife of mine will demean herself in front of the other ladies by doing laundry! Why do you think I hired that damned Chink! You look like a slattern on suds row."

Shocked by his language and accusations, Stephanie's temper ignited. "I had to do something! The storm yesterday blew Lin's washing across the camp. What wasn't shredded to bits by the sand was gray with filth. She had to have help. Lord knows, with you gone for weeks at a time, I need something to do."

"Perhaps you'd prefer returning to your father's mansion in Boston," he suggested coldly. "Lord knows, on a lieutenant's pay I can't provide you with the sort of life to which you're accustomed."

She watched him turn his back stiffly and stare out the window at the undulating gold of fall grass billowing in the relentless wind. Swallowing the lump in her throat, she fought down panic. Back to that cold lonely house with Josiah who was gone even more than Hugh. *At least my husband loves me.* Somehow the thought rang hollow in her heart. She pushed aside the feeling and touched his shoulder. "No, Hugh. I don't want to leave you. I—I shall try harder to do as you wish."

He gave her that same boyish smile he had the first night they'd met when he defended her honor so vehemently. She flew into his arms with a sob.

In the months that followed, the rigors of military life did not lessen. They were "ranked out" of their quarters when a superior officer arrived at the post and chose their home, forcing them to move to a less desirable location on the line. Hugh seethed with resentment, but Stephanie took it in stride, learning military protocol, enduring outposts in Texas and Kansas. Finally they ended up at Fort Fetterman on the sagebrush-covered High Plains of Wyoming.

Hugh's restiveness grew. Minor skirmishes with hostile Indians did not bring his dearly desired promotion. He had barely made first lieutenant after five years in the army, a fact he increasingly bemoaned especially the night he received word he had been passed over for a captaincy.

"I graduated from the Point in '68, Stephanie. Five years, five miserable years—do you realize during the war men rose from second lieutenant to full colonel in half that time?" Hugh sat at the kitchen table clutching a glass of whiskey in his hand. The bottle in front of him was well on to half-empty.

Stephanie had come home from nursing one of Mrs. Turner's sons through a bad case of croup. She was cold, hungry and exhausted from the ride across the river where the rancher's home was located. "You'll get the promotion,

Hugh,'' she temporized, ''just not as quickly as you'd hoped. This is peacetime.''

''Peace, ha!'' he snorted, draining his glass. ''I was promised there'd be a damned Indian war out here. If only those fools in Washington would stop vacillating and turn Sheridan loose, by God, I'd make captain in a trice!'' With that pronouncement, he looked at his wife, who stood by the kitchen stove, warming her hands.

He scooted his chair back, irritated with the way she held her distance when he drank, letting him rave as if he were a child on a tantrum. In fact, it seemed to Hugh that his cool Boston lady held herself aloofly superior to him altogether too often here lately. ''I've been neglecting my little wife, haven't I?'' he said, nuzzling her neck as he pulled the heavy pins from her hair with clumsy, drunken fingers.

Stephanie felt the sting on her scalp as he tore loose her chignon. ''I feel a bit weary tonight, Hugh,'' she murmured softly, hating the sour smell of whiskey on his breath.

He laughed mirthlessly. ''Weary now, is it? You always have some excuse. How do you ever expect to have those babies you want if you're always 'too weary' to do your wifely duty?''

Guilt overwhelmed her. From the first she had disliked what they did in bed, the perfunctory swift and silent way he took her, only to roll over after to snore softly while she stared off into the darkness and thought of Chase. Was that why God had not seen fit to bless her with a quickening? Was barrenness her punishment for the secret adultery in her heart?

She turned in his arms and let him pick her up to carry her to the bedroom.

When the word arrived on the army grapevine that the ''boy general,'' Custer, had been commissioned by Sheridan to gather the scattered forces of the Seventh Cavalry and head for Dakota Territory, Hugh at once petitioned to join his old idol. He was jubilant when the transfer came through. Stephanie once again packed up what they could effectively transport and sold off the carefully acquired excess in household furnishings—for the fourth time in less than two years.

Because Fort Abraham Lincoln had been an infantry post before the arrival of the Seventh, it had no stables for the horses. When barracks were converted to that end, the shortage of housing on the upper end of the scale resulted in no remaining facilities adequate for the officers' ladies. Libbie Custer and several other wives in the Custer entourage, dubbed the "royal family" by those on the outside, decided to return East for the duration of the summer campaigns across Western Dakota Territory into Montana. Stephanie and a number of the other wives elected to remain in nearby Bismarck, the railhead from which the Northern Pacific's crews surveyed westward.

Now that Hugh had been reunited with his blond commander, Stephanie hoped his brooding silences and heavy drinking would abate, but they did not. She hated being cooped up in another hotel room in the rough frontier railhead after growing accustomed to the freedom of riding her own horse at their previous posts. The long separations from her husband she had grown used to. Indeed, at times she felt a small guilty relief when he was sent on an assignment, freeing her from his moods and demands. But then the hollow emptiness of her lonely existence haunted her.

Hugh was expected to return to Bismarck within the week, according to the last brief letter he had sent to her. She was tired of spending her days at endless teas, piano recitals and dinner parties, but there was no alternative in Bismarck. Even if there had been, she knew what an ugly scene Hugh would create if he found her helping her striker in the kitchen or volunteering to nurse sick soldiers at an infirmary.

Mrs. Harris, the captain's wife, drove her home from a luncheon late one afternoon. As the small rig made slow headway through the muddy streets, Thelma Harris said, "I'm certain you'll be relieved to see your husband safely returned from the wilderness. One never knows what might happen with those bloodthirsty savages on the rampage."

She shuddered and her gelatinously plump cheeks shook rather like a bulldog's jowls.

"Have you had much experience with the Indians? I must confess we've been posted West for nearly two years and I've yet to see any savages, only a few rather pitiful creatures who lived around the small posts where Hugh was stationed. He never even allowed me near his Arikira scouts."

"I should hope not," Thelma exclaimed. "They're all dirty and disgusting, even the tame ones. It will be a blessing when the army has them all secured on reservations in the Indian Territory down south. Then decent people can civilize this heathen land."

A sad smile tinged Stephanie's lips. "That's my father's opinion, too."

"Well certainly, it's yours as well," Thelma said with a hint of a question in her voice.

"I'm not so sure we have the right to take all the good land away from people who were here for hundreds of years before us."

"Humph, you'd not say such a foolish thing if you'd ever seen white captives brought back from the hands of those sadistic miscreants. I for one would take my own life before I'd allow a filthy savage to touch me!"

Looking at Thelma Harris's fat, doughy white face, Stephanie experienced a twinge of doubt that any self-respecting savage, except for a cannibal, would want her, but forbore making such a shocking remark. *I wonder if Chase has ever taken any white captives?* The thought ambushed her, as thoughts about him always did, no matter how she tried to suppress them. Feeling suddenly uncomfortable with the self-righteous Mrs. Harris, Stephanie said, "My hotel is only a block away and I need to stop in the mercantile for some thread. Please, just let me off in front of it. I can walk the short distance from there."

After thanking Thelma for the ride and bidding her farewell, Stephanie made her purchase in the store, then strolled toward the hotel. At the next intersection she spied a narrow back street that seemed a shortcut. On impulse, she started down it, passing a rather seedy looking saloon. *Well, it is broad daylight,* she assured herself, crossing the street to avoid the swinging doors. That was when she saw the horse tied in the alley.

There was no way she could mistake the big chestnut with the white star on his forehead. The powerful thoroughbred was Hugh's. The thought that he had come back from his western assignment early and sought solace in a bottle instead of her arms hurt, but she had admitted for some time that their marriage would never be the idyllic one of her girlhood dreams. Then another thought occurred to her. What if someone had stolen Hugh's horse? He could be lying in some gulch outside town or even in that very back alley, grievously injured or dead while some outlaw sat in the saloon drinking up his pay!

What could she do? If she called the corporal of the guard and Hugh was in the saloon, he would be humiliated and vent his spleen on her, especially if he was drunk. *But what if he is hurt?* Her conscience would not allow her to walk away. Clutching her reticule tightly to her chest, she crossed the street, hoping to peer into a side window of the drinking establishment and see if he was indeed at the bar.

Stephanie was not certain whether she wanted him to be there or not, but when she edged closer to the grimy window and gazed inside, her blood froze. Everything seemed to go black for an instant, then a harsh buzzing filled her ears. She watched Hugh bend a yellow-haired harlot over his arm, kissing her open-mouthed with passion. His hand kneaded one of her big white breasts, which he had pulled free of the scanty confines of her garish purple satin gown while two other laughing whores cheered him on.

Surely he must be so drunk he did not know what he was doing! But as Stephanie stood rooted to the rough wood planking outside, Hugh picked up the voluptuous blonde and walked straight as an arrow to the stairs at the rear of the room and climbed them with effortless ease. He knew which room was hers, too, kicking open the rickety wooden door and disappearing inside without hesitation.

By the time he returned to the hotel the next afternoon,

Stephanie had considered her response carefully. Although his uniform was dusty from the trail, he was freshly bathed and shaven. No traces of cheap perfume or rouge betrayed his sins. She studied him with cool, remote eyes as he walked into the sitting room of their suite, a suite paid for with her dowry money. How handsome he looked standing there, hat in hand, smiling at her.

When she remained behind the drum table unsmiling, he asked, "What the devil's wrong, Stephanie? Aren't you glad to see me after three weeks in the wilderness?"

"Not nearly as much as that yellow-haired whore at the Birdcage Saloon was," she replied calmly.

Hugh blanched, then his complexion mottled and his jaw clenched as he ground out, "What the hell are you talking about? What does a lady like you know about whores?"

"Only what I see with my own two eyes, Hugh."

"You spied on me!" he accused incredulously.

"Not on purpose. I was taking a shortcut on my way home from Major Ferguson's yesterday afternoon when I recognized your horse. I thought someone had stolen it . . ." Her ironic smile crumpled. "How could you go to a place like that—to a woman like that?"

Hugh shrugged and walked across the room to the decanter of whiskey and poured himself a drink. "A man has needs that a woman like you wouldn't understand."

"Make me understand," she said, masking the pain that clawed at her.

He snorted in disgust and tossed off the drink. "I most certainly am not going to discuss such a vulgar topic with my own wife."

"A vulgar topic or your vulgar behavior? In spite of our differences, your unhappiness over the promotion, everything else, I believed you loved me, Hugh."

He studied her with cold dark eyes, his gaze raking from her flushed face down to her plain brown skirt. "You're not going to let this drop, are you?" he asked with an air of disgust. Polishing off the drink, he sat the glass down on the cabinet with a sharp rap and turned back to her. "Love is an illusion for children and fools. It has nothing to do with what men do with their whores—or what they do with their wives.''

He watched her flinch as if he'd struck her and felt a vicious stab of satisfaction. ''Believe me, you have a far better arrangement with me than Letty does.''

''Why did you marry me, Hugh, if you don't love me?'' some self-punishing instinct forced her to ask.

''Why, to advance my career, of course. Your family name is not only prominent, your father is a very wealthy man. How many junior officers can afford the luxuries we have? Can entertain their superiors?''

If she thought the pain was terrible before, the queer hollowness that struck her now was perhaps worse. ''You only wanted my money—like some—some cicisbeo!''

''Don't be so prigishly self-righteous, Stephanie. It was a fair exchange. The protection of my name at a rather vulnerable time in your life. After your little fling with that half-breed bastard Remington, you were a social pariah in Boston. Everyone believed you'd given yourself to him. The question did occur to me as well. I must confess I was relieved to find you a virgin on our wedding night. It would have been intolerable raising an Indian's brat, not that you seem to be in any danger of ever being able to conceive a child.''

Humiliation washed over her in waves. He had lied to her, deceived her, used her. ''I had wanted your child desperately. I don't now,'' she said flatly. ''All that earnest protestation about my innocence the night we met—it was all an act. You thought I . . .'' She turned away realizing that if Chase had wanted to take her she would have willingly given herself to him. In her heart she was guilty. When she had married Hugh, her virginity had merely been an accident. *I'm as much a whore as Letty.*

Hugh assessed the various expressions flickering across her face. *She never could hide her emotions*, he thought with satisfaction. ''You actually fancied yourself in love with that mongrel, didn't you?'' he asked, almost pityingly. ''And you believed I was in love with you.''

''I've been disabused of both notions,'' she replied, grip-

ping the edge of the table but refusing to crumple before
his hard stare. "Where do we go from here, Hugh?"

"Oh, I believe we can reach an accommodation, my
dear. You've proven a charming hostess, a lovely ornament,
an uncomplaining army wife, once you learned what was
expected of you. Now that I'm up north where the real
Indian campaigns will be getting underway, I expect the
promotions will start to come. In a few years, when I make
major, even colonel, we can return East and live with all
the amenities."

"And I'm simply to turn a blind eye when you go to
other women like that . . . creature, Letty!"

He shook his head as if annoyed with a child having a
tantrum. "Other wives do it, I assure you, especially in the
army where long separations are part of the rigors of cam-
paigning."

"And what if I'm not like the 'other wives'?"

His eyes riveted on hers as he asked, "Do you really
want to return to Josiah's big empty house and live in disgrace for the rest of your life?"

Hugh watched her crumple at last, taking a seat on the
chair next to the table. "I thought not," he said smoothly,
turning back to pour another drink.

"Hugh, there is one thing I would ask of you."

At her surprisingly level voice, he turned back to her,
one eyebrow cocked questioningly.

"Will you at least be discreet? I don't fancy being the
subject of post gossip."

He nodded coolly as he rose and walked into the bedroom to change into a fresh uniform.

The next day Stephanie received a wire informing her of
her father's sudden death. Since Hugh was scheduled to
lead another expedition of railroad surveyors into the wilderness, there was no question of his requesting leave, thus
jeopardizing his chances for promotion. Mrs. Phillips would
attend her father's funeral alone.

It was a relief to take the cars east to Boston without
Hugh. She had time to think, to take measure of her mar-

riage and decide what she might do to salvage it . . . if she wanted to salvage it.

Once more returning to the present, she rubbed her fingers over her burning eyelids and looked out the railcar window. *When I'm in Boston, perhaps everything will seem clearer.*

She doubted it.

• ''All right, you murdering red son of a bitch, time to wake up,'' a voice yelled as the slap of ice cold water drenched Chase head to foot. The sergeant stood with the empty wooden bucket in his hand and a nasty smirk on his wide, ugly face. Sun and wind had etched lines and creases on his pockmarked skin. His blunt features were contorted in a scowl as he watched the prisoner revive.

'' 'Bout time you come around. The lieutenant wants to see you 'n' he ain't exactly happy, since you marked up his purty face.'' The sergeant gave an ugly laugh.

Chase moved his head gingerly as blinding flashes of bright pain ricocheted through his skull. His hands were tied behind him, so excruciatingly tight that the circulation had been cut off. He was lying on his side in the dirt near a smoldering campfire. At least a couple of dozen Blue Coats went about their duties. Several of the men near the fire watched him warily. They were green recruits who had probably seen few live red Indians before the butchery in that Lakota camp. His eyes quickly swept past them to where a rope corral held their horses at the edge of a neat row of small canvas tents. He did not see Thunderbolt. Perhaps the horse had escaped. He could not hope to do so unless he could free his hands and reach that remuda.

His swift inventory was interrupted when the sergeant's big meaty fist seized his braid, trying to yank him to his feet. ''Come on, you got a date with the lieutenant.''

Chase bit his lip to keep from uttering a sound as the pain in his head hammered in sharp staccato bursts when the sergeant's grip on his hair tightened. His feet were free. He could have kicked the burly noncom to the dirt, but that would only have earned him a swift and doubtless brutal reprisal. He stood up slowly, shaking his head carefully once he was released. His vision was still slightly blurred. *Must have hit me from behind with the butt of a carbine.* Docilely, he allowed the noncom to prod him toward a slightly larger tent in the center of the camp.

The tall brown-haired lieutenant whom he had grazed was sitting at a small campaign table with maps spread out in front of him. Two civilians clad in heavy denims and grimy flannel shirts glared hostilely at Chase as the sergeant shoved him in front of the table. They were arguing with the officer.

"Now, Lieutenant, we got as much right to be here as them railroaders. They's gold in these here hills and the army can't keep honest miners from finding it," a fat, red-faced man with long stringy gray hair said.

His companion, a small thin fellow, glared at Chase with open loathing. "He's one of the ones who killed Charlie, ain't he! I say string the bastard up!"

As he reached the table and the officer turned to face him, Chase felt the jolt of recognition. He tamped down his blazing anger behind an impassive facade. This was the son of a bitch from Washita, the young lieutenant who had taken such brutal delight in taunting and tormenting the chained half-breed boy whose life the soldiers were forced to spare. The narrow bloody furrow on the lieutenant's face had been sewn, but the stitches were large and sloppy. *It'll leave a bitch of a scar*, he thought in silent satisfaction. His expression gave nothing away as he stared into the furious dark eyes of the officer.

The lieutenant ignored both of the irate miners and fixed his attention on his prisoner. "So, you're awake at last," he said, standing up to stare across the table. Unconsciously one hand came up to touch his cheek. Seeing the savage's eyes take note, he angrily jerked his hand away and walked around to inspect the captive.

Chase held his breath but the bluebelly did not recognize him. He had been a seventeen-year-old boy then. Had he changed so much—or did all breeds look alike to men such as he? Both men were the same height, well above six feet.

Hard brown eyes clashed with glittering black ones for a moment. Chase's face remained expressionless, waiting to see what the officer would do.

"I am Lieutenant Hugh Phillips, United States Army, assigned to protect railroad surveyors and escort any other whites here illegally off treaty land. You're in a lot of trouble. I could have you shot . . . or turn you over to the tender mercies of these miners. Ever see a man hang, Indian? I've heard your kind have a superstition about it—something to the effect that it traps the soul inside the corpse."

His tone was light, conversational as he strolled around Chase, taunting his prisoner, who stood rigidly erect, staring straight ahead, giving no sign that he understood a word of English.

Phillips studied the Indian's profile for a moment. "You have the look of a breed about you. Some dirty squaw spread her legs for a white man, huh?" he drawled.

Chase willed himself to remain absolutely immobile, giving no indication that he understood the threats or the insults as Phillips stood behind his back. His eyes glanced down across the maps and papers on the table. The daily march of the troops was neatly marked in tiny x's across the page. They would cross the Belle Fourche River in three days time.

"You really don't understand a word I'm saying . . . or, I wonder, do you?" He stepped up close beside his captive. "Filthy mongrel savage, you made a mistake marking me this way . . . a very big mistake indeed. I'll pay you back tenfold . . . before I let you die."

His last words were a low purr whispered in Chase's ear so that no one else could hear them.

⚭ 8 ⚭

"Have your men take him over to that tree," Phillips said to the sergeant, pointing to a tall fir surrounded by a thick copse of chokecherry.

As two troopers seized Chase's arms and dragged him away, he studied the lieutenant impassively. There was a cold, feral cruelty behind those eyes, a kind with which he was most familiar. *Burke.* He blocked from his mind any thought of what they would do with him, letting them take him without protest as if he were docile, already beaten. He scanned the camp as they walked through it. Half a dozen Henry rifles were stacked neatly beside a felled log about fifty feet from the rope corral where the horses were penned. Then he heard a familiar nicker and looked through the milling herd of sturdy cavalry mounts. Thunderbolt stood tied securely behind the other horses, his nostrils flared, scenting Chase's presence.

"Lieutenant's got plans for you, redskin," one of the troopers said in a sly voice.

"You should've kilt thet purty boy clean, not marked his face. Thet made it real personal," his companion said with a chuckle. As they approached the tree, he slipped a knife from its sheath and slashed the tight leather holding the prisoner's wrists. Shoving Chase toward the tree he instructed his friend, "Tie his hands around the trunk while I keep him covered."

Suddenly, the distant sound of music and the low vibration of hoofbeats filled the air, along with the furious baying of hounds. Both troopers paused as the sound of martial music grew louder, followed by yells of recognition.

"Damn if it ain't the general hisself, announcing his arrival with *Garry Owen*, just like always," one man said with a grin. "Got them damned dogs with 'em, too."

Custer. Chase stiffened but gave no other sign he understood as the camp erupted in a chaos of welcome. Custer's column rode in with the long-haired "boy general" far ahead of his men as was his usual wont, surrounded by the pack of hunting hounds he always took on campaign with him. The man was tall and gangling, with a thin face and receding chin that was disguised with a heavy mustache and goatee. George Armstrong Custer's eyes were his most unforgettable feature. Icy blue and penetrating, they glowed with the gleeful delight of a schoolboy . . . or a madman.

Phillips and his sergeant snapped smartly to attention as the buckskin-clad lieutenant colonel dismounted. The arrival of the troopers created a billowing cloud of dust. Dogs darted in and out between the horses. Men laughed and shouted. Every eye in the camp was on the two officers conferring across the clearing.

With both of his captors momentarily distracted, Chase knew this was his only chance. He whirled and seized the rifle behind him by the barrel, shoving the stock with all his strength into its owner's solar plexus, knocking the breath from him, then swung the weapon like a club, smashing it into the head of the trooper in front of him, who crumpled while his companion doubled up, choking and gasping.

Not pausing to look back, Chase raced toward the corral, stopping to scoop up another of the new Henrys as he darted into the throng of horses. He heard the shout of alarm go up from several men but only one stood in his path, a young unarmed private frozen with fright. Chase clubbed him with one of the rifles as he ducked beneath the ropes of the makeshift corral, whistling for Thunderbolt.

The big black pulled free of his restraints and cleared a path to his master. Chase swung up on his back and broke through the cluster of horses as shots began shearing the air close to him. As he zigzagged his mount through the clumps of sumac, he heard Phillips curse and yell, "Don't shoot that horse—it's worth a fortune!"

Custer barked furious orders at several of his troopers who were still mounted and they spurred their horses after the escaping prisoner, but their tired mounts were no match for the rested and infinitely faster black thoroughbred. Chase quickly outdistanced them after a few shots skimmed harmlessly over his head. Within half an hour he was in the clear, unhurt but for a dull headache, two good repeating rifles the richer for his brush with the Blue Coats.

Custer and Phillips owe me a lot more than these rifles, he thought with grim humor as he rode into Elk Bull's camp late that night.

When he neared the fire, Pony Whipper's eyes narrowed, concealing his surprise at seeing the half-blood still alive. He looked to where their sentry stood watch on a hill at the opening of the ravine, then back to Chase. "Did you bring the Long Knives back with you?"

Chase ignored the nasty taunt and approached Elk Bull offering the older warrior the two new rifles he had pilfered. "A 'gift' from the Blue Coats. As I escaped I stole these. Long Hair has many more."

Elk Bull examined one of the weapons after handing the other to Stalking Owl. "This is a fine weapon. We have heard Long Hair's pony soldiers have brought many fine guns, even the big earth gougers, with them."

"They also bring men who plan the route for their wooden rails," Chase replied. "The railroad is more dangerous than cannons."

"The iron horse comes through the hunting grounds of the Lakota and Cheyenne?"

"While I was a prisoner I saw some maps. Day after tomorrow they will ride through a narrow pass leading to the rocky hills river, the one the whites call Belle Fourche. If Long Hair's soldiers do not remain with the lieutenant who captured me, it would be easy to ambush them and take many more of these fine guns."

Elk Bull studied Chase in the flickering firelight. "We would need more warriors. I will send a rider to our village."

"Here is what I think we should do," Chase said after

a warrior had been dispatched with word about the iron horse surveyors trespassing onto their lands. He began to sketch a map in the dust with a broken twig.

"You would let this half-blood lead us? How do we know he will not take us all into a trap where the Long Hair's soldiers can shoot us down like dogs?" Pony Whipper asked angrily.

Elk Bull raised his eyes to Pony Whipper and replied simply, "Because Stands Tall has vouched for his nephew. And with my own eyes, I saw Chase the Wind struck down as he aided our retreat."

Shamed and furious, Pony Whipper subsided with a harsh glare at Chase. Feeling the Crazy Dog's burning eyes piercing his back, Chase continued to sketch out a plan for an ambush. As he did so, an idea took root in his mind. He decided to discuss it with Stands Tall when his uncle arrived.

The raid on Lieutenant Phillips's company was a great success. The soldiers were taken completely by surprise as they rode through the narrow neck of the ravine. The warriors split into two groups, one attacking frontally to draw fire and attention while the rest made a lightning foray from the rear, seizing several horses laden with guns and ammunition. Then the whole war party vanished back into the hills with their booty.

Several days later, Chase stood before the council of chiefs. "The key to holding the whites at bay is modern rifles and enough ammunition to enable our warriors to practice," Chase explained. He felt the dampness on his palms as all eyes in the august assembly studied him. Stands Tall had arranged for him to speak before the great council composed of chiefs from most of the Northern Cheyenne bands, now gathered together for the summer hunt in the Tongue River country. Among them were Little Wolf and Morning Star, who was known as Dull Knife among the Lakota, two of the greatest of Cheyenne leaders. Would they trust a man whose blood was half-white, who had lived half his life with the enemy? He forced the doubts from his mind and concentrated on explaining his plans.

"You all know I have lived in one of the White Eyes' great cities far to the east, by the great waters of the Atlantic. I learned their ways but I am Cheyenne, the son of Vanishing Grass, the son of Freedom Woman. It was my mother who sent me back to the People. She bid me use what I have learned from our enemies to aid you in preserving our land, our heritage, our lives."

"I believe your heart speaks truly," Lame White Man, a Cheyenne from the South who had joined the Northern bands, replied with grave courtesy. "But how can you help the Cheyenne? Lean Bear, a great chief, journeyed all the way to the great waters in the east that you speak of, to this Washington. He brought back a piece of paper signed by the White Father, Lincoln himself. He was carrying it the day the pony soldiers shot him down and trampled him. They did not want to read the message of peace."

Unable to conceal his bitterness, Chase replied, "I would go among the white men as one of them not to beg for peace, but to read their newspapers bragging of when they will attack us, listen to their soldiers' drunken talk about battle plans, watch their merchants load up wagons and mules with guns and gold to buy guns. I would bring this information back to my people—just as I brought word of the soldiers crossing the rocky hills river. They mean to destroy us, but we will learn where their weapons are and we will raid swiftly, using their own weapons against them, then return to the safety of the hills."

"My brother's son has spoken from his heart. He speaks wisdom. What do you say to this?" Stands Tall asked the others as Chase sat down for them to deliberate.

Even as he spoke, Chase had known that any victories against the whites would not be enough to save the Cheyenne. The red man could never hope to turn back the tide of whites pouring across the High Plains in search of gold and farm lands. *But we can make them pay for destroying us . . . pay dearly.*

That was all that he could ask. Freedom Woman's dying hopes that he could save the Cheyenne were as doomed as she herself had been. At least now he understood his mission in life. For a fleeting moment a small heart-shaped face with soft gold eyes and a stubborn chin, surrounded by a mass of bronze hair, flashed through his mind.

Stevie. Scarcely a night went by that he did not dream of her. Cursing silently, he suppressed the painful image and focused on the discussion among the tribal leaders.

"You are young and unproven in battle before this raid, yet what you say has merit," one chief said. With the hint of a smile, he added, "We would be fools to let pass the opportunity to use the White Eyes' ways against the White Eyes."

Stout Lance, father of Pony Whipper, stood up angrily. "This half-blood belongs to no warrior society. He bears no marks of honor from the sacred Medicine Lodge. By his own admission he has spent half his life with the enemy. How can we trust such a one?"

"My nephew has fought for our people not only at rocky hills river but at the distant Washita."

As the debate raged on around him, Chase sat silently, waiting to see what they would decide. Such deliberations often went on for hours, each warrior having the right to speak his piece in front of the assembly. He understood their doubts. He was an outsider, a man caught between two worlds trying desperately to belong to the only one in which he saw honor—even if it was doomed to destruction . . . perhaps especially because it, like him, was fated for death.

Finally when a lull in the speeches came, he stood up again, having made up his mind that it was time to do what he and his uncle had spoken of on numerous occasions. "You are right to question my youth, my inexperience, my white blood. I am too old to join a warrior society, but I will undergo the ultimate test—the sacred Sun Dance that all may know I am a true son of the People."

Sweat drenched his entire body . . . or perhaps it was blood, he could not tell. *Focus on the sky, not the pain. Search for the vision. It will come.* Stands Tall's words echoed in his mind as he felt the agonizing pull of the rawhide tongs tied through his pectoral muscles. He danced slowly around the circle, all the while straining steadily at the tongs which were attached by a long rope to the tall lodge pole set up in the flat open plain where their summer camp had been made.

Chase was one of half a dozen warriors pledged to this dance. None of the men looked at the others, each intent on his own inner struggle and purification, the intense concentration that would bring a vision to guide his destiny and bring him peace. Two men had already fallen, their flesh tearing free from the bindings. An elder male member of each man's family, who had also undergone the Sun Dance, carried them away to have their wounds tended.

Stands Tall waited patiently as Chase the Wind endured. It was a sign of great bravery to last long at the ordeal, but Chase was not thinking of courage or honor or even his beloved uncle. He summoned every fiber of his being to the vision quest, forcing aside the engulfing terror that his white blood—cursed Remington blood—would deny him a vision.

Images floated behind his eyes of faraway places, long-ago times, of his father Vanishing Grass teaching him to shoot a bow, of his mother Freedom Woman singing to him as she prepared an evening meal. Black terrible images came, too, of Jeremiah and Burke, of his mother screaming and tearing at herself in madness. But more frequently than any of those, the one face which haunted his fevered brain was Stevie's.

Stevie. As a skinny freckle-faced girl with wispy sun-bleached hair following him in worshipful adoration when they were children, and as a beautiful woman, her eyes radiant with love, her heavy bronze hair spilling around that unforgettable face as she looked up at him from the feather mattress in his bedroom at the country house.

He could smell the apple blossom scent of her through the blood and the dust, feel the soft creaminess of her flesh over the merciless scorch of the sun, hear the lilting ripple of her laughter instead of the steady thrum of the drums.

She is your destiny.

No! She was a white woman, forever lost to him, thousands of miles away. He had forsworn his love for her. Chase shook his head, tugging at the bindings. An agonizing shock wave of pain shot across his chest, causing him to break stride with the steady beat of the drums. Just as he started to stumble, the vision came, stark as a flash of lightning.

Wolves! One iron gray, sleek and fat, faced another that was pure white. The white wolf's fur blazed like sunlight on new snow, dazzling in its brilliance. An aura of power surrounded it as it fixed cold eyes on its foe, stalking the gray wolf, which snarled with feral viciousness. The combatants circled, circled. Then both leaped at once, crashing into each other with incredible impact.

They tore at one another's heavy pelts, slashing and ripping until both were covered with blood. Suddenly a woman's scream shattered the sound of their labored breathing. Stevie's face, pale and distraught with terror, was imposed above this fight to the death, both over it and yet a part of it, more than an observer. Then the white wolf lunged one final time and brought the gray down, breaking his neck and tearing open his throat. The scene blurred into another in which the white wolf bounded slowly away while the woman followed him, crying his name, *Chase . . . Chase . . . Chase.*

"Chase the Wind, it is over." Stands Tall's voice broke into his trance.

Chase could still hear the echo of Stevie's voice calling him as his uncle spoke. He blinked his eyes, dazed, and opened them to see the deserted circle. Stands Tall's face was wreathed with pride as he spoke.

"You were the last to fall. And your eyes have seen a vision. I can tell, but we will not speak of it now," he said as he took Chase's arm and helped him stand.

"You will be a great warrior, a leader of our people."

After Red Bead had tended his wounds, placing a healing poultice of red dock root over the bloody lacerations on his chest, he drifted into a troubled sleep.

After several days of feverish delirium, Chase awakened. He found himself surprisingly refreshed and rested, prepared to assume the role he had described in front of the council. Yet in spite of his certainty that he could move among the whites, spying on them and using the information to aid his people, he still felt Stephanie Summerfield's presence.

"I shall be called the White Wolf," Chase said to Stands Tall.

"This was your vision. It is good. Do you wish to speak of it now?"

After a moment's hesitation he replied, "Yes." The older man nodded and Chase described the vision with the two wolves but he did not mention Stevie's mysterious and troubling presence. He did speculate about what the gray wolf might symbolize—Burke Remington, a man he hated above all other enemies. When he had finished he looked at Stands Tall.

Although his uncle's expression revealed little, he was thoughtful. "There is a mystery here. Often the Powers do not give a man understanding all at once. Perhaps you are destined to destroy this man . . . or he you."

"In the vision, it was the white wolf who vanquished the gray."

Stands Tall nodded gravely. "Perhaps, but hatred seeps into the soul and destroys all who nurture it. Be careful, my son, if ever again you meet this man."

"I will, Uncle. Believe me, I will."

Chase began to implement his plan to infiltrate the white world as soon as the debilitating effects of his ordeal were over. Drifting into a frontier outpost dressed in greasy buckskins with his hair hanging loose around his shoulders, he spent the last of his money to buy enough cheap white man's clothing, tack and trinkets to enable him to pose as a half-breed drifter who traded with various tribes in the Yellowstone country. He did not ride Thunderbolt when he went among the whites, for such a splendid animal would cause suspicions and draw trouble. His plan was to remain invisible, a contemptuous outcast living on the periphery of white society, a man no one paid any heed to, a man others spoke freely in front of, a man who listened, observed, read and analyzed.

His plan worked. By early 1874 army contractors and overland stage companies had placed a thousand-dollar reward on the head of a raider known from the Platte to the Arkansas as the White Wolf, but no one could catch him. Nor did anyone understand how he knew which stage-coaches, supply trains or army details carried guns or gold.

In the spring of the year, Lieutenant Colonel George Armstrong Custer received his marching orders to invade the sacred Black Hills, searching for the gold so many miners had sworn lay waiting in chunks in the rivers and streams. The Northern Cheyenne and their Sioux and Arapaho allies girded themselves for the war everyone knew was coming.

A few men on both sides still hoped for peace. William B. Allison from the office of Indian affairs wanted to negotiate an amicable cession of mineral rights to the hills and Red Cloud of the Sioux came to listen, but their cause was hopeless against the overwhelming forces of public opinion across the nation. The common sentiment was that it would be easier to raise a turkey from a snake egg than to raise a papoose to be a good citizen. There was rich agricultural land and a fortune in minerals just waiting to be taken by the God-fearing pioneers and miners who looked to the army for protection.

And the army, under Phil Sheridan, was eager to oblige. The general handpicked his favorite young officer, Custer, to open what would become known as the "Thieves Road" into the Black Hills. The final showdown grew increasingly inevitable as the days of 1874 spun on.

But for Stephanie Summerfield Phillips a "showdown" had already been lost. Josiah was dead. Stephanie had never really known her father, certainly never felt the kinship of love that an only child should feel for a sole parent. Her grief was not because of his death, but rather for his life, a life of isolation and indifference, even impatience dealing with a frightened child who had turned to him at her mother's death. Josiah had not responded. During her lifetime Paulina had. Paulina she could mourn. For Josiah, Stephanie felt only profound regret.

Coupled to that regret now was a stunning sense of shock. Before the will had been read, Stephanie knew the vast extent of her father's worth, millions in mercantile houses, banking and shipping industries. What she had never guessed, even imagined, was that Josiah would leave it all to Hugh.

Not a cent to his only child.

Shortly after her marriage, the will had apparently been rewritten, naming Hugh as heir. If she produced no male offspring by the union, Josiah's fortune would revert upon her own and Hugh's death to his brother, Frazier. Stephanie had always detested her husband's cold patrician family, most especially Frazier Phillips, the elder son who, like Josiah, was a merchant. Unlike her father, however, Frazier had already produced three sons.

I never mattered in the slightest to my own father. When he had seen her at all, it had been only as the potential means of guaranteeing male heirs to run his empire. She, Stephanie Summerfield, meant nothing . . . nothing at all.

How pleased Hugh would be. Of course it would probably motivate him to return to her bed in hopes of impregnating her. She shuddered in revulsion, thinking of the stale smell of whiskey and cheap perfume from his whores. Tears clogged her throat as she paced across the sitting room floor. A thin shaft of early spring sunlight filtered in the window. Boston in April was every bit as bleak and chilly as she remembered it.

Drawing her cashmere shawl more tightly across her shoulders, she took a seat on the Voltaire chair. Every man who had been important to her had betrayed her—her father, her husband . . . Chase. In spite of this most recent sting of rejection from Josiah, she knew in her heart of hearts that Chase Remington's desertion would always cause her the most pain. Not a night since he left Boston and she moved on with her life had she failed to dream of him. Perhaps she did share the blame with Hugh for the failure of their marriage. *Did I marry Hugh so that he would take me west . . . to Chase?* She flinched at the harsh unvarnished truth, admitting to herself that unconsciously she had done just that. "Whether I was aware of it or not doesn't matter. I must go back to Hugh for there's nowhere else to turn," she murmured to herself bitterly.

Not that she had not considered all manner of desperate alternatives, from bargaining with him for a modest settlement from the Summerfield estate in return for a divorce to simply leaving him and applying somewhere for a position as a governess in order to support herself. But her own common sense had quickly prevailed. Hugh would never countenance the scandal of a divorce any sooner than he would give up the hope of bestowing the Summerfield wealth on his own heirs. And no one would ever hire a governess who had left her husband. Indeed, no one would hire such a person to scrub pots, for that matter! She would have to return to Hugh.

Perhaps she might yet conceive. A child might fill the void in her heart, someone small and trusting, someone who might love her just a tiny bit in return. . . . Upon that slender hope, Stephanie resolved to make the long arduous journey to Bismarck as soon as the snows allowed passage by cars from Chicago into Dakota Territory.

Hugh lounged against the crude clapboard shack that passed for a railway station in Bismarck, waiting impatiently for the afternoon train carrying his wife. Stephanie was rejoining him, considerably chastened, he imagined with a cool smirk. He had been stunned and utterly delighted when the documents from old Josiah Summerfield's attorneys had arrived. How bereft his poor little wife must have been to learn that her husband, not she, was heir to the family fortune. How relieved he had been!

After their hostile parting a month earlier, he had feared that she might decide to ensconce herself in Josiah's Boston mansion and prosecute a divorce, using her newfound wealth to finance such long, drawn-out and expensive pro-

ceedings. He would have been utterly ruined both socially
and financially if she had done it, and he had little doubt
that she would have. Stephanie had always been headstrong
and heedless of social censure in spite of her deep-seated
insecurities.

Hugh smiled to himself, remembering their first meeting.
He had handled her well then, playing on her shock and
hurt at being snubbed—not that she did not deserve it. On
their wedding night he had frankly been amazed that she
proved a virgin. But he had planned to wed her, maiden-
head or no.

The Phillips family had been long on noble lineage and
short on cash for several generations. All his life he had
burned to succeed where the other men in his family had
failed. Fools, all of them, giving themselves to losing
causes, joining the Confederacy and wasting what precious
little remained of their resources. But he knew his best path,
the one chosen by destiny for him, lay with the Union
Army. He was born to be a soldier, had dreamed of nothing
else since he was a boy, filled with tales of illustrious Phillips ancestors who had distinguished themselves in the Rev-
olutionary War, the War of 1812 and the Mexican War.

To succeed in the army, however, required more than
courage, dedication and fierce ambition. Climbing the ladder of rank was as much a social as a military process and
the former required money. That was why he married Stephanie. He heard the faint echo of a whistle. *My beloved
will be here soon.* He chuckled sardonically.

Best if he handled her with tact at this point. She might
still prove troublesome and cause him some embarrassment.
Gossip on any officers' row was worse than that in the
highest social circles of Boston or Baltimore. To date Stephanie had gained a reputation as something of an angel of
mercy, tending sick soldiers in the infirmary and even civilians in Bismarck since he had been forced to leave her
here while construction of Fort Lincoln was completed.

She had such strong maternal instincts, he thought with
a smile. Best if he got her breeding. Babies would occupy
her leisure time when he didn't require her services as host-

ess. Also, he reminded himself grimly, providing a direct heir would keep the Summerfield fortune from passing to Frazier's sniveling brats.

"Yes, my dear, I do believe we shall begin a new phase in our relationship," he murmured, stroking his chin as he watched the train rumble and hiss to a stop in front of the station.

Stephanie climbed down from the car, tired and sooty, looking as wilted by defeat as she felt. But she had washed her face and freshened her heavy hair into a sleek chignon beneath a fashionable bonnet at the last stop. Even if propriety demanded she wear black for months yet, she must still look the part of an officer's lady. Hugh approached, smiling broadly at her. There was more than a hint of self-satisfaction in his expression.

"My dear, I've missed you," he said, pressing a chaste kiss to her cheek and taking her arm proprietarily. "I assume the journey was not too arduous."

When he looked down at her, she gasped softly in surprise, reaching up to touch the wide white scar across his cheek. "You've been hurt." *Probably in a bar brawl or cut by one of your whores.*

His expression darkened and the naked fury in his eyes turned his face from the boyish handsomeness of a moment earlier to a cold, frightening mask. "A half-breed renegade shot me while we were out on campaign, but I will effect retribution," he replied stiffly.

"I'm sorry, Hugh," she said, feeling guilty for her earlier uncharitable thoughts.

He stroked the scar unconsciously as they walked to the elegant George IV phaeton he had purchased upon receiving word of the inheritance. With a flourish, he lifted her into it. "For you, my dear. A present to celebrate your safe return. I know how you love to go visiting the other officers' wives. This gives you the means to do it in style."

"It's . . . it's quite beautiful, Hugh." *Purchased with my money,* she thought sadly, reminding herself that it was no longer hers but his now. "Do you think it will be practical in the mud at Fort Lincoln?"

Hugh shrugged as he slapped the reins and the phaeton took off. "It will serve well enough now here in Bismarck. After that we'll have it stored until we return to a larger post—when I'm promoted." He paused, waiting for her reaction, then went on. "Oh, my last letter didn't have time to reach you, did it? We aren't going to Lincoln. I've applied for a transfer to Wyoming Territory on the Union Pacific rail line, to Fort Fred Steele."

"But the general and Mrs. Custer are here," Stephanie said, bewildered by the sudden turnabout.

Hugh had not written to her at all regarding the change. It pleased him to throw her off balance. "I believe it in the best interest of my career to part company with Autie. He's incurred the disfavor of President Grant over some scandals in Washington. Even Sheridan hasn't been able to rescue him. Anyway," he added dismissively, "I have a special reason for requesting this posting to Steele. That's where the action is, where a man can earn his captain's bars. You've heard the rumors about the Indian raids to the south, on payroll details, stagecoaches carrying gold, even munitions trains—"

"That renegade called White Wolf—a Sioux, isn't he? Or at least so the Eastern papers say." She nodded, feeling for some inexplicable reason a sense of disquietude steal over her.

"He could be Sioux, no one's certain, any more than they can figure out how an ignorant savage always seems to pick targets that are not only vulnerable but carrying weapons or money. The reward on him's just been raised to five thousand dollars."

"And you plan to be the one to capture him," she said in understanding.

"No, I plan to flush him out and kill him and his whole cutthroat band."

When they reached the hotel he turned the team over to a stable boy waiting at the porch, then assisted her down. "I expect it'll take you a while to unpack, once the striker brings your trunks from the depot. Let's plan on a late supper, here in our suite."

The husky intimacy of his voice took her by surprise. "Hugh . . ." She moistened her lips nervously as they smiled greetings at another first lieutenant's wife and passed through the small lobby headed upstairs.

Once they were inside the parlor, he closed the door and drew her into his arms. She came woodenly, pressing her hands against the stiff wool and cold brass buttons of his uniform jacket.

"So chilly, Stephanie. I'd hoped so long an absence might warm your blood a bit."

"You haven't complained of a cold bed for some time, Hugh. You've always found some woman more than willing to warm it."

"Ah, but those women aren't my wife. They can't provide me with children. You do want children, don't you, my dear?"

A suffocating panic squeezed the breath from her. "Yes, I do, but you don't. You want heirs for the Summerfield estate, Hugh."

He did not deny it.

"What do you want, eh, wife? Did you ever stop to think it was your coldness that drove me from your bed? All you've ever done was lie rigid as a stick, enduring your duty."

The accusation stung for she did hate his touch and had indeed forced herself to endure rather than welcome it. "A lady isn't supposed to know how to . . . how to . . ." She stumbled over the words in a misery of shame and guilt. *With Chase you responded—you knew what to do!*

Hugh tilted her chin up so her gaze met his. "I propose we turn over a new leaf tonight, Stephanie. A child would occupy your days while I'm off on campaign, which, you'll be relieved to know, will be most of the time once we reach our new post. But until then . . ." He let his words linger like a threat as he began unfastening the buttons on her blouse.

⚜ 9 ⚜

Fort Fred Steele, Wyoming Territory

The silence was eerie. Stephanie stood on the porch of the post commissary watching as women, shivering in the chill autumn air, held babies while older children clung to their ragged, filthy skirts. Many of the little ones were practically naked and all were round eyed with fright as the soldiers prodded them with gun butts against the stockade wall, segregating the pitiful handful of men, the majority of whom were old, the rest too badly injured to give further fight.

Most of the troopers focused their attention on the men, gathering them into a sullen group that they forced into the small, windowless log cabin that served as a guardhouse. The women and children were herded inside one of the corrals used to hold livestock before it was slaughtered for the enlisted men's mess. It had rained the preceding night and the ground was ankle deep with sticky, foul smelling yellow mud. Huge black eyes stared out from weathered faces, erased of all expression except for infinite weariness . . . and perhaps resignation. They were beaten.

"The children don't cry," Stephanie murmured to herself, watching in horror.

"They are taught not to from infancy on, for even the tiniest noise could alert an enemy." The respondent was a small thin woman clad in a plain gray dress and unadorned bonnet. She studied the prisoners with compassionate eyes that were a shade darker than her faded cotton clothes.

"I've never seen any Indians this close before, only the scouts on the posts where we've been stationed and a few tame ones who trade in the towns. These people look different.''

"They are from Red Cloud's Oglala Sioux, a small group who did not wish to live on the reservation lands to the south. They attempted to flee and join the Hunkpapa who roam from the Bighorn Mountains into the Powder River basin.''

"Sitting Bull's people?" Stephanie asked, having listened to Hugh rave about the thousands of Sioux and their allies who still refused to accept government handouts on the reservation and insisted on the old free-roaming way of life, following the buffalo.

"Yes, Sitting Bull's people . . . but these have not succeeded in escaping oppression.''

Stephanie looked startled at such unpopular sentiments so bluntly spoken in a soft melodic voice. Gold eyes collided with gray and held as the two women took each other's measure. Although Stephanie had only been at Steele a few days, she was certain this shabbily dressed woman with the ageless face was not an officer's wife. "I've never heard anyone say the Indians were oppressed before . . . although I can scarcely disagree, especially seeing women and children herded like cattle into that filthy pigsty of a corral.''

"Thee is new to the post," her companion said merrily as an approving smile bowed her thin lips, making her small pinched face seem almost pretty for a moment. "Everyone here knows the Quaker troublemaker, Hannah Wiette." She nodded gravely to Stephanie, offering a reddened, work-worn hand.

Stephanie took it, surprised at the callused strength in the small thin fingers. "I'm Stephanie Phillips and I am happy to make your acquaintance. On an army post, troublemakers, especially female troublemakers, are a rare find, indeed," she added, returning the smile.

Both women chuckled, sensing in the exchange that each had just made a friend.

"If you're a Quaker, then you're not married to a soldier, are you?''

"No. I am here with our missionary society, although even among my own, I do tend to disturb tranquillity. Rather than tend their souls with preaching, I am more inclined to fix on their bodies. Thee can see the poor people are cold and hungry and all too often prey to our diseases. I am a nurse. I assist Dr. Farmer, the post physician, when he asks me. Most of the time I tend sick Indians in the small hospital I've been allowed to set up." She pointed to a long, low rectangular building newly constructed of rough-cut logs. "It is not much to look at, but we try to keep it clean and comfortable for our patients—the ones who Colonel Boyer allows us to house there," she added tartly, then studied Stephanie with a shrewdness at odds with her seeming ethereal frailness. "Would thee be willing to assist us?"

"I've had some experience tending the sick on other posts. I would like very much to help at your hospital," Stephanie replied, knowing an angry confrontation with Hugh was inevitable. "You said 'we.' Who else volunteers?" she asked, praying at least one or two of the higher-ranking officers' wives were involved.

"There is Sarah Verly and Faith Ballium . . ."

Hannah named a series of women, only two of whom were married to soldiers, one a second lieutenant and the other a sergeant. No, Hugh most certainly would not approve. Stephanie looked over at the pitifully clad Sioux women in the muddy corral and heard the racking cough of a small boy who huddled protectively beside his injured mother. *That could have been Chase when Anthea Remington was captured.* "When may I start, Hannah?"

"I absolutely forbid you to go near those filthy savages ever again," Hugh said, white lipped with fury when he returned from patrol the following week. He had come storming into the small infirmary and seized her by the wrist in a bone-crushing grip as she sat bathing a fevered boy's face with cool compresses.

She had left the building rather than create a scene and alarm the already frightened patients. Once they were alone behind the building, she broke free, struggling to gather her thoughts as she massaged her aching wrist. It would be discolored with bruises by morning.

Think, think, how can you make him understand? She had spent the past week so enmeshed in her work at the hospital she had pushed the thought of Hugh's return from her mind. "These people are human beings, Hugh—in spite of what the army thinks. They require food and shelter and medical care the same as white people. They've been rounded up like cattle, many of their young men killed, the rest imprisoned, the women and children confined quite literally in a pigsty, forced to sleep out in the open in foot-deep mud! They need better food—and blankets."

"I've already heard from Captain Shaffer about your going around to all the officers' wives begging for these savages, collecting cast-off clothes and blankets as if you were some pathetic Salvation Army worker!"

"I'm only trying to—"

"You're only trying to humiliate me further than you have already—if that's possible."

"Hugh, they're dying—of fevers, malnutrition—things we can cure, if only we care! Think of the children, Hugh!"

He gritted his teeth and grinned mirthlessly at her. "Sheridan said it best—nits make lice."

"I can't believe you'd make war on babies in their mother's arms," she said, ashen faced. But she could believe it, looking at him now, really seeing him.

"You will do as I say—do you understand me!" he shouted. Then glancing quickly around, he lowered his voice, struggling to appear calm and reasonable in spite of his desire to choke the defiant romantic nonsense out of her. "We've had this discussion before, Stephanie. I've explained to you how damaging to my career these kinds of associations can be. Coddling savages in the company of that female riffraff is unconscionable. I cannot permit it."

"What will you do, Hugh, confine me to quarters? Court-martial me?" she snapped, goaded beyond endurance.

In pure reflex he lashed out, backhanding her across the cheek. The red haze of fury her temerity had occasioned quickly passed as it always did. He seldom left visible marks on women. This was the first time he had struck his wife. He cursed her for provoking him into it, yet felt oddly relieved to have let out some of the frustration he had always felt toward her. Calmly now, he said, "That was most unwise, dear wife. Such unladylike insolence is quite foreign to you."

When he reached out to stroke her injured cheek, he was annoyed that she did not flinch. Beneath the red mark of his hand, her complexion was waxy pale as she studied his elegantly sculpted face with wide, stunned eyes. She did not back down but stood her ground, refusing to move, even when he leaned forward intimidatingly.

"We have never known each other at all, have we, Hugh?" she said. "I fear I've always been stubborn—'willful' I believe Josiah called it. You call it unladylike, but then, gentlemen don't strike ladies, do they?"

"I am an officer and a gentleman by act of Congress, my dear, which means you must be no lady at all," he replied genially. "But you are my wife, so we shall just have to make do."

"You can't lock me up every minute of the day, Hugh. I must have some meaning to my life—something more useful to do than pour tea and arrange masked balls for the regiment. I've done everything you've asked of me for the past two years, but I can't spend the rest of my life with nothing worthwhile to show for it."

"Advancing your husband's career isn't worthwhile any longer but nursing savages is?" he sneered. "Defy me in this, Stephanie, and I shall make you pay far more dearly than you could ever imagine."

There was a chilling edge to his voice that sent a frisson of fear down her spine. His eyes were soullessly flat, almost yellow-brown as they bored into her, willing her to acquiesce. Dear God, would he murder her in her sleep? He already had her money. He didn't need her now. She had to get away from him, to gather her thoughts and plan what to do next. Shaken, she replied, "I had best return to our quarters and put some cold compresses on my face. We wouldn't want any scandal now, would we?'' She noted with great satisfaction that her husband flinched ever so slightly.

The following morning, while Hugh was at roll call, an answer to Stephanie's dilemma materialized in the person of Emma Boyer, the post commandant's wife. Plump and flighty on the surface, she was a shrewd and manipulative campaigner who knew every whisper of gossip on the post.

Praying the cold water soaking last night and a liberal morning application of rice powder hid the discoloration on her face, Stephanie smoothed her skirts and opened the door to admit her unexpected guest.

''Abigail Shaffer and I were planning an impromptu trip to Rawlins for some shopping, a bit of holiday while the gentlemen take their troops into the ghastly Powder River country after hostiles. Since Lieutenant Phillips has been assigned to accompany Colonel Boyer and Captain Shaffer, I thought I would ask if you'd like to join us.''

''That is very gracious of you, Mrs. Boyer. I'll have to discuss it with my husband, of course.''

''Of course,'' Emma parroted with a nod that sent her pudgy cheeks to jiggling. ''The men should be on patrol for several weeks. That will allow us plenty of time to enjoy the amenities in Rawlins. Even if it is only a small town, they have several respectable hotels and adequate mercantiles.''

Fully expecting Lieutenant Phillips to comply with her invitation to Stephanie, Emma bid her good day after refusing the offer of a cup of coffee, saying she had to go home and supervise packing. Stephanie felt her curious blue eyes study the discoloration beneath the rice powder but offered no explanation or excuse. If it tarnished Hugh's reputation, she did not care.

As Stephanie, and the colonel's lady expected, Hugh was delighted to have her included in the exclusive little excursion to Rawlins. ''Do have some more stylish gowns made while you're there—even though they must be black for your period of mourning. Mrs. Shaffer's giving a dinner party next month and the Boyers always have an autumn ball.''

She did not argue even though the thought of endless fittings appealed little more than spending the evening in his company. Her trunks were already overflowing with more clothes than she could ever wear out here on a frontier army post. At least the trip would allow her a few weeks of peace away from Hugh. But what after that? The question haunted her as she packed. The marriage was in shambles, perhaps beyond all hope of repair, but she had been raised under a stern Congregationalist code which allowed no sundering of solemn vows. She had sworn to love, honor and obey Hugh Phillips before God, for the rest of their lives. The thought of the bleak years ahead chilled her to the very marrow of her bones.

If only he could gain his captaincy, perhaps things might be better . . . but no, for then he would only burn to be a major. Ultimately, nothing short of general would ever satisfy Hugh Phillips. A general staff appointment to Washington was his life's dream. And he would achieve it climbing over Indian bodies. This mission into the Powder River country was to pursue the raider they called White Wolf, some mysterious leader who had become Hugh's obsession in the past year. She prayed he would capture the renegade. Not only would it garner him that next promotion, but it might also restore a measure of peace to the plains.

''That still won't change the ugly situation between us,'' she murmured to herself as she sat at her dressing table massaging her aching temples that evening. They would leave at first light in the morning. Hugh was not home yet. Probably he was out drinking with Captain Shaffer again. Such had become a common pastime. Although she hated the reeking smell of whiskey and his abusive moods, he usually passed out quickly after an evening of over-indulgence and did not touch her.

The front door slammed. Hugh was home. Stephanie looked in the mirror, seeing the pale, hollow-eyed face staring at her. She fought back tears as she heard him shamble with a drunken gait toward the bedroom. Stumbling against the door frame he glared at her back, watching her expression in the mirror in front of her. "You have good reason to look afraid. I told you to stay away from those damned meddling Quakers and the savages!"

"Little Otter was asking for me. I had to see if his fever had broken and to take the last of the blankets and clothes we gathered."

He lurched across the floor and seized a fistful of her heavy hair, which she had just finished brushing. Tears spilled as the stinging pressure of his hold tightened. She did not utter a sound, only stared at his reflection in the mirror.

"Little Otter needed you, eh? You and those damned redskins! What is it about them—you prefer dark meat, is that it?"

"Hugh, Little Otter is only seven years old!" She sat rigidly, furious at his crude remarks.

"Too bad that Remington bastard jilted you. Maybe you wouldn't have been so cold in his bed!" he blurted out, then reddened even deeper beneath his already drink-stained complexion. He released his hold on her hair as if it had scorched him and staggered back a step, staring at her as she continued to sit with her back to him, spine straight, but her eyes were downcast now, no longer meeting his reflection.

"So, it's true, isn't it," he said softly.

She turned around and faced him, her hands clutching the seat of the chair tightly. "Whatever I once felt for Chase Remington has nothing to do with us now, Hugh. You're right. He jilted me three years ago. And I made myself a promise that I'd begin a new life. I've tried my best to be a good wife to you, but you never intended to be a good husband. You used me, Hugh—you wanted my money and my family name so you preyed on my naiveté and vulnerable position after Chase left to get me to marry you. You pretended to be someone you weren't, but you knew who I was all along. You just never wanted me to be me."

He stared at her, slack jawed at her truthful accusations, hating her for all of it, too befuddled by liquor to refute her logic and furious that he had revealed his jealousy to her. He cursed roundly, then turned and stumbled against the bed, falling on his back, spread-eagle atop the covers.

Stephanie sat and watched him fall asleep, snoring loudly. Then she slipped into the parlor with a quilt and made her bed on the settee. Hours passed before she finally drifted into an exhausted slumber.

The ride into Rawlins took several hours because Mrs. Boyer insisted on stopping to rest midway, saying the jouncing ambulance in which they rode was giving her a migraine. Stephanie took the time to enjoy the pungent scent of sagebrush and saltweed bushes and watch the breeze rippling miles of gramma grass. Rawlins was typical of newly constructed rail towns across the West: raw, boisterous and tentative, situated amid jagged escarpments of sedimentary rock on one side and the level stretch of the High Plains on the other. The North Platte flowed serenely past it, with cottonwoods and willows growing profusely along the banks, breaking the starkness of the landscape.

Stephanie spent the evening with Emma Boyer and Abigail Shaffer. After a hearty meal in the dining room of the Rawlins House Hotel, she excused herself, pleading a headache, which was not far from the truth. After the latest ugly scene with Hugh, she felt drained. The idea of a room—and a bed—to herself—was greatly appealing.

The next several days the women spent poring over pattern books and selecting fabrics in Mrs. Carmichael's modiste shop. By the end of the third day of fittings and endless gossip, Stephanie was ready to scream with boredom.

"And I said to the colonel, my dear, I said, you simply must do something about these quarters. Why, how could I be expected to give a regimental ball—"

"Pardon me, Mrs. Boyer, I do hate to interrupt," Stephanie said as she entered the stuffy dressing room where Emma was holding forth to Grace Carmichael as the intrepid Irishwoman adjusted a bustle. The scent of Emma's heavy perfume blended with the stench of moldy lumber and old sweat, assaulting her nostrils. "I'm going to take a walk around town while you and Mrs. Shaffer finish up here."

"Do you think it safe to do that unescorted?" Mrs. Boyer asked doubtfully.

"I'll only walk a few blocks. I'll be fine."

Before the older woman could raise any further objections, Stephanie was gone, eager to begin exploring the raucous railhead.

There was a sense of raw vitality and freedom in the West that she had grown to love, especially whenever she was able to escape the rigid social protocol of an army post and spend time in a neighboring settlement. Best of all, she loved her occasional rides across the incredible open expanse of the plains, to feel the wind and the sun beating on her, to smell the tang of sagebrush and listen to nothing but the echoing majesty of silence, broken only by the shrill cry of the hawk.

Perhaps she would see about renting a horse for a short ride, if she could slip away from the troopers the colonel had assigned as escorts for the officers' ladies. Stephanie observed the bustling activities all around her. In front of a barbershop, two indolent looking cowboys in shabby denims and sweat-stained collarless cotton shirts argued amicably over who would go first for a badly needed shave and haircut. Across the street a heavy freight wagon rumbled past her, its driver cursing and popping a whip over the team of straining mules. A female of the sort ladies never mentioned leaned on the upstairs railing of a shabby saloon, calling out a crude invitation to passersby. Prosperous looking merchants in dark wool suits rubbed elbows with hard looking gunmen while a cluster of "pumpkin rollers," as the homesteaders in their stained muddy coveralls were called, ogled a display of iron tools in the window of France's General Merchandise.

As she strolled into the dim dusty interior of the livery, she could see through the broad barn to the open double doors at the opposite end where a large corral was situated. A team of horses was being unhitched from a freight wagon by the boys employed at the stables while the driver talked with a trooper from Fort Steele. Stephanie slowed her step, disappointed that one of her chaperones was there to stop her impromptu ride. She slipped quietly next to one of the stalls in the gloomy interior where a delicate little sorrel filly let out a wicker of welcome.

Patting the horse's nose she blinked her eyes, letting them adjust to the poor light. Then she heard the low conversation between two men who were standing partially hidden just behind the corral post.

"This here looks like a real heavy wagon. Could carry a pretty considerable of a load, I 'spect," a drawling voice said.

"Yep, this here wagon was plumb loaded down with bullion from the mines outside Helena. They come 'n' put it on th' train. After that White Wolf feller got ahold of the supply wagons last week, I reckon they's figgerin' they wuz lucky to git it to th' railhead safe 'n' sound," the grizzled old man volunteered, spitting a wad of tobacco into the dust at his feet.

"Heard 'bout the reward for the White Wolf. Wouldn't mind collectin' some of it."

"Five thousand—say who wouldn't, Asa," the old man said with a cackle, "but them soldier boys figger they can catch that renegade theyselves. Course with you bein' a quarter Osage, mebbe you could scout for 'em 'n' get a cut of some kind."

The trooper ambled over, joining in the conversation at this point, as did the wagon driver and one of the stable boys, but Stephanie's mind did not register their casual speculations about where Colonel Boyer's forces had been deployed. She stood frozen, straining to catch a glimpse of the Osage breed who was leaning with his back against the corral post, now silent while the others talked.

In spite of his drawl and uneducated speech patterns, his voice sounded exactly like Chase's! Deep, low and slightly gravelly. All she could see was one shoulder clad in a dirty homespun shirt. The brim of a greasy flat-crowned hat with a rattlesnake band shaded his face, which was further obscured by straight black hair falling to his shoulderblades.

I'm imagining things, she scolded herself. What on earth would Chase be doing here in Rawlins, dressed shabbily like a tramp, talking like an illiterate drifter? Ever since she had come west, Stephanie had entertained fleeting thoughts of encountering him again one day, especially when Hugh was posted to Wyoming Territory, but she had always suppressed them. Not only was such a notion disloyal to her husband and certainly most unlikely since Chase intended to live as a Cheyenne, but even more devastating was the very idea of what such a meeting would do to her. Seeing him again after he had broken her heart, when she was irrevocably bound to another, would destroy her.

Still, some self-punishing, desperately hungry part of her ached to hear that familiar voice, to see those fathomless glittering eyes, that blinding white smile. Biting her lip, she inched across the stable to the opposite side of the wide center aisle where she could see more of the Osage, cursing herself for a fool with every step.

He was tall and lean like Chase. She could see one long leg bent at the knee, the heel of his boot resting against the corral post. He was several inches taller than any of the other men, even leaning back, slouched down. Suddenly he shifted his weight away from the post and straightened, his face in clear profile to her. The man's complexion was coppery dark like a mixed-blood Indian, yet his features were classically sculpted, the nose straight and prominent, the eyebrow a heavy black slash, the jaw clean and strong, the lips . . . the lips that had kissed her!

Chase! It could not be. She had longed for him so deeply over the lonely years that she must have convinced herself that the handsome stranger was her love. *My love, yes, admit it. He will always be my love, my only love.*

A low prickle danced down the back of his neck. Chase sensed someone watching him from inside the stables. He casually turned his head toward the open door, his hand nonchalantly resting on the old Navy Colt on his hip. The shadows were too deep to see clearly, but it was a woman's figure. There was something eerily familiar about her. He turned his back on the group of men and took a step toward her. A flash of bronze hair caught the sunlight as she turned in a flurry of skirts and vanished like a wraith in the gloom.

She was tall and slender just like Stevie. He shook his head. No sense making a fool of himself over some unknown white female who was probably already having heart palpitations because a breed had looked at her. He knew the rules, even harsher out here than they had been back east where the Remington name had allowed him a little more freedom—white ladies could look at him with secret lascivious thoughts but he dare make no public overtures in return without risking a killing—his or somebody else's. Here on the High Plains in the middle of an Indian war, those consequences were apt to be even more swift than usual. He could not afford to draw attention to himself by getting into a fight.

Too long without a woman, he thought with a curse. That was what made him think the bronze-haired female looked like Stevie. Shaking his head to clear away painful memories, he turned and ambled off toward the corral gate, leaving the group of men behind. He'd learned all he needed to know from garrulous old Hyram Wimbley and the dumb young trooper. Gaston de Boef would tell him the rest tonight. The wily little Frenchman sold information to anyone with the price of a bottle but he had been as good a friend as Chase had ever encountered in the white world. The best thing he could do after their meeting was to relieve the itch that had been growing inside him with a few hours of recreation at the Rocky Road. Hell, Rocky would be glad to see her old customer Asa Grant, the Osage quarter breed. If Rocky Rhoades' voluptuous whores couldn't take his mind off Stevie, he might as well turn himself in to the army and let them hang him!

Stephanie stopped in the alley half a block from the livery, leaning against the wall, her arms wrapped protectively around her waist. *Chase!* It was Chase. Once he turned and started to walk toward her there could be no mistaking that long-legged pantherish stride, the way his broad shoulders rolled gracefully as he moved. And his face! No matter that he wore a scruffy beard and his hair fell in shaggy strings past his shoulders, she would know him anywhere.

But he had changed in more ways than the obvious. The greasy, cheap Western clothing and lethal looking arsenal of weapons were not as dramatic a difference as the expression on his face. He looked hard and dirty and dangerous. There was a flatness in the cold black eyes which had once glowed with passion and laughter. What had happened to make him change this way? Why did those men call him Asa and think he was Osage? He looked like a drifter, a mercenary gunman who would kill without blinking an eye. She had fled, terrified of the stranger who was Chase.

Then the thought struck her like a lightning bolt. What if he had never found his Cheyenne family—or worse yet, what if they had all been herded onto reservations to die like those poor Sioux she had been nursing at the fort? What despair he would be feeling, already cut off forever from the Remingtons, and now his father's people lost to him as well.

Her heart ached, wanting to run to him and embrace him, to offer her love, her comfort. Yet she could do nothing of the sort. She was married. If he knew she was Hugh Phillips's wife, a man who had spent years hunting down and killing Indians, Chase would despise her . . . and she could not blame him.

Tears swam in her eyes, blurring her vision. She wiped them away impatiently. "What am I to do? Can I simply let him ride away again?" The answer of her conscience squeezed her heart in pain.

But she could not let go of the old dream so easily. Her mind churned, thinking of the way he had talked back there, like an illiterate.

Why?

She pulled a handkerchief from her pocket and repaired her tear-streaked face, then stepped back into the street with a new resolve. She would make discreet inquiries where this Asa the Osage stayed, then attempt to learn what he was doing in Rawlins. Whether she would have the courage to confront him face to face, she was not yet certain.

That nagging prickle had returned for the past fifteen
minutes or so. Chase rubbed the back of his neck and
cursed as he walked down a dark section of the street where
stores and warehouses were closed for the night. The meeting with Gaston was always in the back room of the Rail's
End Saloon, just up the street. Chase doubted the man
would have any information of sufficient interest for him
to risk another raid this soon in the area. It was time for
the fall hunt anyway. He should make ready for the long
journey to the village in the trackless Bighorn country. No
Blue Coats would ever find them there . . . he prayed.

Damn, his concentration was off. Someone *was* following him. Could de Boef have gotten drunk and let slip who
Asa Grant really was? He glided around the corner of the
deserted apothecary shop and began to run on silent moc-
casined feet, circling the little clapboard building, emerging
on the other side. A shadow moved, then halted by a pair
of rain barrels directly in front of him. Chase slipped the
knife from its sheath on his hip and stepped into the street,
seizing the slim figure around the neck and pulling it
roughly against him.

Stephanie felt the impact of her body slamming into a
man's chest but when she tried to scream, a hand clamped
over her mouth stifling her cry, and a sharp blade pressed
against her throat.

"Don't make a sound."

Even before he spoke, she had recognized the feel of
Chase's body, his scent. Sweaty buckskin clothes could not
disguise it from her, even after all these years.

He could tell even before he grabbed her that it was the

bronze-haired woman. Then as she struggled ineffectually in his arms the scent of apple blossoms teased his nostrils. "Stevie," he hissed, sheathing his knife and turning her in his arms, unwilling to let her go. "What the hell are you doing here?" He waited as she coughed, trying to catch her breath.

Her mind simply shut down. After over three years she was in Chase's arms again. What could she say? She looked up into his face but the moonlight was behind him, shadowing his expression. All she could see were hard planes and angles through the grizzled beard. And those cold black eyes, glittering like the windows of hell.

"I—I thought it was you this afternoon but I couldn't be sure . . ."

"So you waited and followed me in the middle of the night, through the worst part of a wide-open rail head? What the hell is going on, Stevie?"

She stiffened at his harsh angry accusations. "I could ask you the same thing—Asa the Osage!" She stiffened and tried to draw back from his tight painful grasp. "You're filthy as a wharf tar and you were talking to those men as if you'd never seen the inside of a schoolroom, much less attended Harvard."

, He gave a scoffing curse. "In case it's escaped your notice, out here no one flaunts their academic credentials. How did you get from Boston to Wyoming Territory, Stevie?" He could feel her trembling now as she struggled to dredge up some kind of answer.

"I'm married, Chase. I came with my husband."

The misery in her voice was genuine. The thought of her being touched by some other man had always haunted him, even more now if she was unhappy in the marriage. He gentled his hold. "I always assumed you'd marry a proper Bostonian blueblood and live in a mansion on Beacon Hill."

"Really? When you ran off, I doubted you'd given much thought to me at all," she blurted out, unable to stop the retort that revealed her pain.

"You know why I had to go," he replied, stung anew with guilt.

"Your letter said you were going to rejoin your father's people, not become a gunman. Why, Chase?"

"No, you don't. You're not answering my questions with other questions. What is your husband doing out here? Who is he?" When she would not meet his eyes and began to tremble even more, he knew she was hiding something.

Just then a pair of half-drunken cowboys came ambling down the street, headed for the Rail's End. He pulled her back into the darkness between the two buildings, forcing her to hide behind the rain barrels until the men had passed. "Be quiet if you value your reputation," he whispered. "I doubt the respectable folks in town would understand your being caught in a back alley with a breed in the middle of the night. Neither would most husbands."

When the men were out of earshot, he stood up and helped her to her feet. "What do we do now, Stevie?" he mused aloud, almost as much to himself as to her. "Why won't you tell me about your husband? Won't he notice that you're missing?"

"He's not in town right now." The minute she said it, she bit her lip in vexation.

"Oh? Why would he leave you alone in Rawlins? I know you don't live here. I've been in and out of here a dozen times the past year. Where is he?"

Then it hit him like a fist. The column of bluebellies that had ridden out last week chasing the White Wolf. He'd heard talk some officers' wives had come to town for a shopping spree. With an oath he swept her up in his arms and strode down the street. When she started to cry out in protest, he reminded her, "Remember what I said. You'll be in almost as much trouble as me if someone hears you."

"I'll be in trouble if I'm found in your arms, too," she replied breathlessly.

"Well, then," Chase growled, "shut up and maybe no one will see us."

"Where are you taking me?" She felt a frisson of fear

in the pit of her stomach. This dangerous stranger was no longer the Chase she had known.

He did not answer her, only muttered another curse and slipped around the corner toward the back door of a big sprawling two-story building. It looked seedy and rundown to Stephanie, but that described most of the town. Despite the late hour, lights glowed in all the windows and piano music carried faintly from somewhere inside. Chase tapped on the back door with his foot and it quickly creaked open a scant few inches, spilling a narrow beam of light directly in his face.

"Howdy, Asa. What ya got there? Lordee! Bringin' yo' own meat to da' bar-bee-que?" a fierce looking black man the size of a bison asked, grinning as he swung wide the door.

Stephanie blinked at the sudden light as Chase carried her inside. The walls were lit by ornate brass lamps that cast flickering shadows on the garish purple-flocked wallpaper. A stained red carpet ran the length of the hall that ended in a large open room from which the piano music and bawdy laughter echoed. "What sort of a place have you brought me to?" she whispered, aghast, for she knew exactly where they must be.

Ignoring her he asked the woolly-haired giant, "Do you have a private room free? I need to discuss something with the lady."

Looking dubiously at Stephanie, he shrugged and nodded. "Miz Rocky be fit ta chew a railroad tie 'n' spit toothpicks she see this 'un," he muttered, leading them to the third door.

Before he could open it, a woman of Amazonian proportions emerged from another room down the hall. She was almost as wide as she was tall, which made her wide indeed. Her girth was accentuated by the garish puce satin gown that swished with every purposeful stride as she made her way straight toward Chase. A mound of cleavage bulged up from the front of the low-cut bodice like two giant loaves of rising bread, doughy and pale. Her face was equally pale but well camouflaged with rouge and gritty looking powder which was caked in the creases lining her skin. Bits of red lip paint flecked at the corners of her mouth when she smiled at Chase.

"Asa, baby, it's been too long! The gals and I missed you somethin' fierce." Her puffy little putty-colored eyes shifted from the tall man to the woman he was carrying. She narrowed them and studied Stephanie assessingly. "You bringin' me a new whore, darlin'? I already got plenty—'n' none of 'em are that skinny."

She cackled and slapped one mammoth arm around his broad shoulders, leaning close to give him a kiss. Stephanie nearly gagged at the odor of heavy perfume, reeking breath and stale perspiration.

"Rocky, sweetie, this here's Stevie . . . uh, an old acquaintance I just run across. Seems like she was followin' me 'n' I aim to find out why," he added ominously.

Rocky peered at the girl again. "Now, darlin', I know you're one great lookin' stud, but even you don't go gettin' females trailin' after yer scent down back streets at midnight. If she's trouble, my boys can get rid of her for you— or I could always put her to work here, once I fatten her tits and ass up a mite."

"Thanks. I appreciate the offer, but I'll handle her myself," Chase replied, chuckling when he felt Stephanie stiffen in outrage. "You see, the little lady's married to one of them bluebellies from Fort Steele."

Rocky grunted. "Asa, I don't need to hear that shit! Them soldier boys is nothin' but trouble."

"Can you let us talk in private for a few minutes?" He indicated the door the black man had opened.

"Wal, I reckon," Rocky replied grudgingly, eyeing Stephanie with mistrust. "Once yer through with her, get 'er out, and you come back 'n' talk to a lonesome ole woman, you hear?" She winked flirtatiously.

"I promise, Rocky darlin'." Giving a cheeky grin, he returned the madam's wink, then stepped inside the door and set Stephanie down, still holding tightly to her wrist.

Rolling his eyes as if imploring heaven for deliverance, the black man closed the door on the couple and shambled down the hall, muttering to himself. Chase crossed his arms over his chest, staring at Stephanie. However, before he could open his mouth, she launched into him furiously. "You have red lip rouge smeared all over your cheek, 'Asa, baby.' Why is it all men find cheap women so fascinating?" she asked scathingly.

"I'd say it's something a lady is never supposed to ask about . . . but then we both know you aren't a lady," he replied, remembering her forthright and unconventional behavior back in staid old Boston.

The gleam of faint amusement in his eyes made something inside of her snap. Before she could even think, her hand flashed up and connected stingingly with his cheek. "And you're a gentleman—consorting with prostitutes? In Boston at least you were discriminating enough to choose society matrons for your dalliances."

His eyes narrowed as he stared down into her flushed, furious face. What in hell had set her off—jealousy? He scoffed at himself and said, "Funny, but after sampling both society 'ladies' and prostitutes, I decided the prostitutes are a hell of a lot more honest . . . and less costly."

She stared at the red imprint of her hand on his cheek. She had struck him so hard her fingers stung. He was furious, but she refused to show fear. She raised her chin in its old pugnacious set and glared defiantly at him.

His flash of surprised anger ebbed as he regarded the slender enigma of Stevie. *If she were Cheyenne she would make a real warrior woman.* Absurd! Where had such an idiotic thought come from. She was pampered and delicate and . . . white. He forced himself to be calm. "Now," he continued patiently as if nothing had just transpired, "let's go over everything again, starting with who your husband is and why you were sneaking after me down a back alley at midnight."

Her mouth felt cotton dry and her heart hammered in her chest. But as he leaned arrogantly against the door and stared at her with that harsh piratical expression, his voice so cold and reasonable, she felt another blaze of righteous anger building. All the fury mounting over all the years of her life focused on Chase Remington. Josiah's neglect and disinheritance and Hugh's deception and infidelities had been painful, yet hurt nothing like Chase's desertion. Most of all she was furious with him, for he above all men possessed the power to wound her to her very soul. Hugh frequented places like this and it shamed her but in her secret heart she had grown to prefer that he spend his lust on whores rather than on her. However, it was intolerable that this man was no different than her husband. Whores knew Chase here and no doubt in dozens of other places like it from Omaha to Denver. And this infidelity from a man upon whom she had no legal claim hurt so much worse than her own husband's. Damn him! Damn him for making her love him still!

"How dare you," she ground out in a low voice, advancing toward him with fists balled up, quivering with rage. "How dare you drag me into this—this sinkhole and stand glaring at me as if I were the one who's guilty of something! I didn't leave you—you left me! What did you expect? That I'd wither, an old spinster pining away for you? I have a right to a life!" *I have a right to love!*

Chase stood calmly as she glared up at him, raising a fist to pummel his chest while the other hand came toward that same stinging cheek again. He seized her wrists and held them tight, pulling her against him as she kicked and struggled to break free.

"Stevie—"

"Don't call me that! Don't ever again call me that! You're just like all other men—lying, deceiving users. You aren't even using your own name! What sort of a masquerade are you playing, I wonder, convincing that freighter and those troopers you're just an Osage bounty hunter looking for a reward on that renegade White Wolf?" She sensed the subtle tensing in his body. An expression of amazed alarm flashed in his eyes before they returned to stony shuttered blankness. And she knew! "Dear God, you're him! You're that awful raider—spying, posing as a tame Indian, gathering information so you can lead a pack of bloodthirsty savages to rob and kill!"

His face had looked hard before. Now it blazed with fury. "Bloodthirsty savages! You married a damned blue-belly and you call us bloodthirsty? We're fighting for our lives," he snarled in a low, deadly voice.

"Hugh Phillips isn't a thief stealing soldiers' pay or a murderer scalping innocent victims!" she shot back in blind fury. Whatever his shortcomings, he was her husband and being a soldier did not reduce him to the level of a renegade such as Chase had become.

Chase felt poleaxed. "Phillips—you married that glory seeking sadist?" he asked incredulously.

"What if I did!" she shot back defensively. How dare he accuse her!

"I'd have expected Josiah Summerfield's daughter wouldn't have settled for less than a full colonel. Phillips is a mere lieutenant."

She wanted to strike that sneering expression of disgust from his face with her fists, to hurt him the way he had hurt her. "A mere lieutenant! After the way you destroyed my reputation in Boston, I was a pariah! Hugh Phillips was my best prospect," she said bitterly. Suddenly the adrenaline surge of blind anger was spent. She felt weary, exhausted to the bone and utterly heartsick for the death of all her dreams.

Chase studied her as the words registered. He hadn't considered what his abrupt departure might do to the reputation of a young heiress keeping company with a libertine like him. Knowing Boston gossips, it was even possible word of the marriage agreement between Jeremiah and Josiah Summerfield had gotten out. Perhaps she did have good reason to hate him, he thought bleakly as he felt the tension draining out of her slender body. Her face was pale with large dark smudges beneath her eyes. The look of fragility was at odds with the spitting furious hatred of a moment earlier. Had she come after him to learn who his contacts were, to turn them and him in to the army? He found it difficult to believe. But after three years as an army wife—trapped in what seemed to be far from a love match—

perhaps she desired revenge against him. And maybe she even deserved it.

His troubling ruminations were interrupted by a sharp rap on the door. "Asa darlin', Strop just heard several of them officer boys ride into town. Seems like them men tangled with some Sioux northeast a ways. If that gal's husband misses her, I don't want him comin' lookin' for her here."

Chase yanked open the door with an oath. "Where did the officers go, did he hear?"

"Straight to the hotel, most of 'em."

Would Phillips come searching for his wife after he found her absent from her room? He swore again, looking at the pale slender woman who stood ramrod stiff, glaring defiantly at him. "What the hell am I going to do with you, Stevie?"

"I'm not yours to do anything with, Chase. Let me go," she said quietly.

"I don't think so," some gut level instinct made him reply as he reached out and seized her wrist.

"Don't you dare grab me again! I'm not a sack of flour you can just sling over your shoulder and walk away with."

He ignored her squirming protests and said to Rocky, "If they come here, you never saw me or the lady."

"You got that right, baby." She stepped back as he strode through the door, dragging Stephanie with him.

Then he paused and turned back to the madam with a grin. "I owe you one, Rocky."

"I'll collect, Asa. I always do," she replied, returning the smile as she watched him vanish out the back door into the inky night.

Stephanie became alarmed when the darkness enveloped them. He dragged her behind him, his long legs moving in ground-eating strides. When they reached the corral behind the livery stables, she grew really alarmed. Fighting to catch her breath, she tugged against his iron-tight grip. "What are you planning, Chase?"

He could hear the fear in her voice. Irrationally it angered him. "Be quiet if you don't want old Willis to pepper us with buckshot for horse thievery."

He walked stealthily around the corral to a small lean-to where all sorts of tack was stored. Rummaging through his saddlebags, which he had stashed there earlier in the evening, he pulled out some rawhide strips and a none-too-clean handkerchief, then began binding her wrists tightly together.

"You can't—you wouldn't—"

"I can and I am," he said curtly.

Before she could protest further he stuffed the cloth in her open mouth, then secured the binding on her wrists to an iron wall hook in the lean-to, hoisting her up so high that her feet barely touched the ground. She tried to spit out the gag, then to rub it out of her mouth against her arm, but nothing availed as she twisted and struggled ineffectually. Leaving her to thrash and make muffled cries, he quickly slung his saddle up on one shoulder and called softly in Cheyenne for his big dun gelding. The horse came to the corral gate obediently and he let it out, then quickly saddled up, grateful he had been prepared to ride out after meeting the Frenchman. De Boef would just have to wait till another time.

He led the horse the few yards to the lean-to. Reaching over, he lifted her off the hook, and threw her across his saddle. Then he mounted and walked the horse down the deserted back street.

Slung so awkwardly across the saddle, Stephanie could not even get her breath, much less scream. The horse picked up speed as they reached the outskirts of town, bouncing her against the unyielding hardness of leather and Chase's thighs. It was oddly intimate. Her breasts pressed against his leg and her hair, worked loose from its pins, flowed like a heavy cloud around his boot. She tried to kick with her feet but he stopped her struggle with a sharp swat to her derriere.

"Lie still or you'll fall and break that beautiful little neck," he whispered, but she continued to squirm until he cleared the last of the small shanties scattered at the edge of town.

Then he kneed the dun into a ground-eating canter,

which so winded her that she ceased struggling, afraid she would suffocate. After what seemed an eternity of the pounding punishment, he reined in and slipped gracefully from the horse, then eased her down. Her legs buckled beneath her and everything started to go black as she coughed and choked through the gag. Her head throbbed from being upside down so long.

Chase removed the gag and cut the bindings from her wrists, then swept her up in his arms and carried her to the edge of a small stream. After placing her on the ground, he walked back to his horse, took a tin cup from his saddlebags and filled it with cool water from his canteen. "Here, drink," he ordered.

Stephanie wanted to hurl the cup in his face but her mouth was parched from the gag, her throat literally closed off. She held it up in her numb hands and drank greedily. Finally stopping after she had drained the cup, she wiped her hand across her chin awkwardly, then watched him drink directly from the canteen. The strong bronzed column of his throat moved with each swallow.

Limned in moonlight, his profile was even more beautifully sculpted than in her erotic fantasies. In Boston she had been a green virginal girl. Now she was a woman who knew a man's touch. *God help me! I never wanted Hugh but I want you!* When he, too, finished drinking, he refilled the canteen at the stream, then walked over to his horse, seeming to ignore her. "What are you going to do with me?" she asked in growing alarm when he shrugged off his tattered shirt and moccasins, then began to unbutton the fly of the greasy denims.

"Not what you think," he answered with a wicked leer. "I hate the stink of white men's clothing. I'm going to bathe in the stream and change. Nobody will be after us this soon."

Stephanie sat appalled as he continued removing his pants. The muscles of his arms and shoulders flexed with each movement, gleaming hard and satiny in the soft light. She could see the dark thatch of hair on his chest and remembered its texture. Mesmerized, she still knew every nuance of his body, the male scent of him, the heat and the hardness when he had crushed her to him and kissed her. She squeezed her eyes closed, shamed to the core of her soul by her base physical cravings. Her eyes flew open when he kicked away his pants and turned toward the stream, completely naked. She watched his long-legged stride, taking in the breadth of his shoulders, his small tight buttocks and lean sinewy thighs. What was wrong with her, ogling her naked abductor! She had just been given the opportunity to escape while the arrogant savage was in the water.

Stealthily, she stood up, then began edging slowly to the dun gelding. She grabbed the reins and swung up onto the horse, kicking him into a gallop. A shrill whistle split the air before she had ridden a dozen yards. The dun skidded to a halt, then turned toward Chase, his ears held forward, waiting obediently. No amount of cajolery would budge him. In that instant, she remembered how he had trained Thunderbolt the same way back in Boston. The big black had always come to him. No one could ever steal him.

"I'm not by nature a careless man, Stevie," Chase said as he casually wrapped himself in a soft buckskin breech-clout and pulled on fringed buckskin leggings. After slipping the beaded moccasins on again, he strolled casually toward her.

"What if I'd reached for your gun instead of your horse?" she asked.

He shrugged enigmatically. "Then I imagine we'd both have found out if you could pull the trigger."

"You don't think I could."

He studied her face in the shadowy light. "I'm not sure. Once I thought I knew you but that was before you married Phillips."

"Why do you hate Hugh so much?"

"You accused the White Wolf of being a killer and I am, but I don't attack women and children. My warriors don't rape thirteen-year-old girls and club old men's brains out either."

"You're saying Hugh does that?" She felt faint and

dizzy, remembering those helpless captives being herded into corrals by Hugh's men—young girls and old people, treated as if they were livestock being sent to the slaughterhouse. Was it possible?

"Believe what you want," he replied when she sat mute, staring down at him. He turned his back on her and walked over to the edge of the stream, stuffed his white man's gear in his saddlebags, then returned to fasten them behind the saddle.

Stephanie sat astride the horse with her legs indecently exposed. If Chase was aware of the bare flesh, he gave no indication of it until she tried to pull down her rucked up skirts to cover herself. Then he reached out one hand and closed it over the curve of her calf.

"Don't," he said softly as his dark fingers glided over her pale smooth skin.

She held her breath, her mouth once more gone suddenly as dry as it had been when he removed the gag. Moistening her lips she asked, "Why did you kidnap me, Chase? The whole army will be scouring the territory searching for me."

"It was that or kill you," he replied tersely as he swung up behind her on the dun and kicked him into an easy lope.

"You think I'd tell them you're the White Wolf?"

"Probably. After all, you're a soldier's wife and I'm a bloodthirsty savage with a price on my head."

"How did this happen, Chase? When you left Boston you said you wanted to find your father's people. Couldn't you locate them . . . or were they all dead?"

"No. I found my uncle and great-aunt among the Northern Cheyenne, although it took nearly a year."

"Then why aren't you with them? Why not live away from white civilization, just be Cheyenne?"

"You mean, why become a raider? Have you lived out here the past three years and seen nothing? The Cheyenne can't live as they did when I was a boy. The buffalo are vanishing, most other game is scarce—wantonly slaughtered in a deliberate policy to starve us and the other plains nations, to drive us all onto reservations where we can live on the White Father's dole . . . and our spirits can die slowly.

"Red Cloud of the Oglala and Morning Star of the Northern Cheyenne tried to make peace—to keep to the great hunting preserve supposedly given to the tribes in the Fort Laramie treaty of 1868, to trade with the government agencies. Then last summer Custer came riding right into the heart of the sacred Black Hills, looking for gold. Do you know what they call the glorious trail he blazed on our land—the Thieves Road."

She could feel the bitterness emanate from him as he sat behind her and they rocked with the steady cadence of the horse's gait. "So you chose to fight back—even though you must know it's hopeless. All you're doing is giving men like Custer and my husband the excuse to kill you."

"They don't need excuses, Stevie. I'd rather die quick and clean as a warrior than slowly as a beggar."

"That's why you masquerade as a tame Indian to learn where best to strike. What are you doing with all the gold you've stolen? Buying more guns?"

"Sometimes. We can't fight Henrys and Winchesters with bows and lances. We also use the money to buy food, blankets and medicine when I can't steal them directly. White men's diseases kill my people even faster than bullets or starvation."

"I know," she said softly. "I nursed the prisoners at Fort Steele. A remarkable Quaker woman named Hannah Wiette recruited me to work in her hospital." His harsh mocking laughter surprised her.

"You always were tough and resourceful, even though you are a rich man's daughter." He paused, scrutinizing the black dress she wore as a thought suddenly occurred to him.

"Is Josiah dead?"

"He died several months ago," she replied.

"I'm sorry," he said, feeling awkward, knowing there had been no love between father and daughter.

"Don't be." Her voice was cold now. She would never reveal to him that she had been disinherited by Josiah.

Shifting the subject back to her nursing skills, at which he had scoffed, she asked, ''Don't you think I'm capable of nursing sick Indians?''

''I don't doubt you're capable of a great many things, Stevie.''

''Now who's playing the bigot? You obviously think the worst of me simply because I'm white, don't you, Chase?''

''I think you and all those do-gooder Quakers and others like them simply don't understand. You can't make red men into white. We can't live caged. Even if you keep our bodies alive, our spirits will die that way.''

She had no answer.

They rode in silence until the first faint streaks of dawn reached across the eastern horizon, shafts of breathtaking pink and golden light. Chase veered from the direction they had been traveling for the past several hours, heading for an outcropping of shale surrounded by a scraggly copse of alders. Reining in behind the shelter of the trees, he slid from the horse and lifted her down, then began to unsaddle the gelding.

''A buck riding with a white woman would get himself shot, if we happened on anyone. So, we'll rest by day and travel by night,'' he said tersely. His back was turned as he slung the heavy saddle onto a boulder beside the dun. ''You can wash up in the stream over there if you want. I have some food here for us to eat.''

She saw the small clear creek gurgling just beyond the rocks. ''Do you know every water hole in the territory?''

He shrugged as he knelt with his back still to her, fishing something from the leather pouch. ''This territory and several others. The Cheyenne once ranged from the Canadian border all the way onto the Staked Plains of Texas following the buffalo.''

Stephanie glanced at the earth which was strewn with small hunks of loose shale interspersed with several solid rounded rocks, any one of which might bash out a man's brains. Perhaps she could just stun him and make good her escape before he could signal the horse.

As if reading her mind he said, "I wouldn't try anything foolish, Stevie."

When he heard her stomp off to the water's edge, he let out a sigh. What insanity had he committed? She was right, the army would hound him relentlessly if they ever found out he had taken her. Of course, he was certain Rocky Rhoades would not incriminate herself by revealing it, but there was always the possibility someone else might add up her mysterious disappearance and Asa Grant's sudden absence and put the two together.

He cursed his rotten luck, then considered the options. Leaving her to reveal his identity would mean giving up his disguise as the bounty-hunting Osage and that he could not do. It was an edge his band had that no other Cheyenne or their allies possessed. He provided essential survival tools and valuable information to use against their enemies. The only alternative to bringing her with him was to kill her . . . and that was really not an option, for he knew he could never harm Stevie Summerfield.

You still want her. He tried to deny the nagging voice in his head but could not. What the hell would he do with a spoiled, beautiful rich girl when he reached their camp?

As if echoing his thoughts, Stephanie walked back from the stream and stopped beside him. Using every ounce of the courage she had worked up, she asked, "You still haven't said what you plan to do with me, Chase." He stood up and faced her. Her face paled as she stepped back, wide gold eyes riveted to the scars on his bare chest. He had not been marked that way when he undressed the day they were snowbound. "What . . . what happened to you—did the soldiers do this?"

Chase smiled grimly as she stared, horror-struck. "I imagine this seems a barbaric disfigurement to you," he said, striking his chest with one fist, "but among my people these scars are a badge of honor."

Over the years spent at half a dozen frontier posts, Stephanie had overheard talk about the savage self-mutilation rituals performed by the Indians. "The . . . the Sun Dance. You underwent the Sun Dance?" she asked incredulously.

His eyes narrowed dangerously on her as a sudden surge of anger coursed through him. "Difficult to believe, isn't it? That a Harvard man would participate in something so primitive and offensive to civilized sensibilities," he sneered.

She swallowed her gorge as images of his flesh ripping free of crude rawhide bindings flashed before her eyes. "I didn't mean to sound superior," she said defensively.

"Yes you did. Everything I am has always offended white people. Even when I dressed in silk shirts and Oxford tailored suits I was still nothing more than a stinking dirty redskin to the good people of Boston."

"Not to me, Chase," she replied defiantly. Still afraid of the half-naked scarred stranger who had once been her love but unable to stop her yearning to touch him, Stephanie reached out tentatively and grazed the raised welts of scar tissue on his chest.

At once his hand came up and seized hers, pressing the palm flat against the swift thudding of his heartbeat. "I feel anything but civilized right now, Stevie," he said raggedly as they stood motionless, facing each other.

✧ *11* ✧

He could feel the pulse in her wrist racing as wildly as his
heart. This was insane. She was another man's wife—a
bluebelly's wife. She was forbidden to him. *But she was
Stevie.* He forced himself to remember how he lived now,
the path he had chosen. She could never survive with the
Cheyenne—even if she wanted to. Would she want to share
his lodge, bear his children? The sudden thought shook him
to the core and he angrily shoved her hand away as if it
bore a rattler's sting. "Use the chokecherry bushes over
there to relieve yourself. After living out west this long I
assume you know to watch for rattlers."

Stephanie glared at him. Then, red faced, she headed for
the shelter of the bushes, too desperately in need for pride
to rule. As she struggled with her skirt and petticoats, she
heard the unmistakable sound of him making water a few
yards away, on the opposite side of the shrubbery. Memories of their childhood suddenly flashed into her mind and
she cringed, recalling the forthrightly curious little girl who
had asked him how he could pee so much faster than she
could when they were romping in the woods behind his
grandfather's country place. When he was too embarrassed
to explain, she had spied on him the next time but could
see nothing from her position behind him. He simply stood
with his drawers still up . . . doing it. She had thought it
mysterious and frustrating because girls couldn't perform
such a basic act of nature with that ease and she told him
so! Afterward he had teased her, knowing she had followed
him. Still red faced, Stephanie wondered if he was recalling
the same incident right now.

As she straightened her clothing, she muttered to herself,

"I can't cower in the bushes until he comes looking for me." Steeling her courage, she walked back to the stream where Chase waited.

"I've laid out the food. Not lobster bisque, I'm afraid, but you'll eat if you're wise," he said, gesturing to the parfleche packed with pemmican and a dozen hardtack biscuits all carefully placed on a clean piece of cloth. Then he stalked to where he'd thrown the saddle and began to unroll some blankets.

Still trembling, she sank down in front of the meager cold food, humiliated by her forwardness and his rejection. What had possessed her to touch him like that? Placing her hand on his scars seemed even more intimate than the moments they had spent in his bed together so long ago. Her stomach growled and cramped, reminding her that she had skipped dinner last evening and spent the night bouncing madly on horseback. Gingerly she reached out for a biscuit, eyeing the strange grayish looking substance he called pemmican with uncertainty. The biscuit was hard and salty, difficult to get down without something to moisten it. She broke off a piece of the soft greasy stuff and placed it on the bread. It had the tang of chokecherries and other wild fruits, combined with the almost buttery flavor of well-refined white lard. All in all, not too unpalatable.

Chase watched her eat, surprised that she would not find camp food too repulsive to taste. But Stevie had always been a game one, even as a kid, he mused as he spread his bedroll on a bit of moss growing in the shade beside the stream. Then he rejoined her, grabbing a couple of hunks of hardtack and making a sandwich with the pemmican as she had. "White man's biscuits and red man's suet and fruit. Half-breed food. Fitting, don't you think?" he asked, taking a bite.

"Why do you blame me for what's happened to your life, Chase? I didn't leave you—you left me. I never cared a fig about your mixed blood."

"That was back in Boston . . . before you saw me as I am. And I am Cheyenne, one of those savage inferior people who require enlightenment and inspire pity."

Her cheeks flushed as she remembered just those very feelings the first time she had seen red men and women after coming west.

"You'd have made a good Quaker yourself," he said scornfully, taking in her guilty expression. He finished off the last of his food and washed it down with a draught from the canteen, then offered it to her, as if daring her to wipe off the rim before she drank.

"Damn you," she muttered, taking it and gulping down several fulsome swallows.

He tsked mockingly. "Well, perhaps you wouldn't have made a good Quaker after all."

"I could never exercise enough Christian charity to be like Hannah. She would forgive you for abducting her."

He laughed darkly. "What makes you think a bloodthirsty savage like me would have taken some homely old Quaker woman captive? I might have scalped her and left her in that alley."

Stephanie studied his expression—what there was of it to read. Did he make some sort of ghoulish jest or had he changed so utterly from the man she had loved back in Boston that he could actually do such a thing? She shivered in spite of the warm morning air, then noticed the bedroll he had spread in the shade by the stream.

Chase followed her eyes. "I don't know about you, but I need some shut-eye after riding all night."

He gestured to the pallet, which looked suspiciously narrow to her. "Where do you propose to sleep?" she asked with feigned innocence.

"I'll use one of my saddle blankets as a hammock," he replied dryly. Then his tone became firm. "We sleep together."

"No!"

"Yes. After all, you might bash my brains in with a rock . . . or try for my gun this time." When she refused to move, he walked over to her and reached down for her hand as if she were a recalcitrant child. She snatched it away. "Are you afraid of me, Stevie?" he taunted softly.

She shot up and glared harder. "No."

"Liar," he said softly, taking her arm forcefully and compelling her to step over to the pallet. "Now lie down and go to sleep. You have my word of honor that I won't ravish you. Oh, but I forgot, you don't believe bloodthirsty savages possess any honor, do you?"

Stephanie had never been so physically aware of her husband as she was of the man standing in front of her right now. At first, Hugh had never even bared his chest in her presence, but come to her in the dark, clad in a nightshirt. In the past years as he began to drink more, he had stripped in front of her but she had never looked at his body, had never wanted to see it or feel it. But perversely, she still longed to touch Chase whenever he came near her, to sink her fingers in the springy black hair on his chest, to feel those alien and frightening scars. She could smell his scent, horse, leather and male sweat all blended together. It should have offended her sensibilities but it did not. Maybe Chase was right. She was no lady at all.

She seemed to look right past him ignoring his taunt. Well, he supposed she really did believe he might rape her. He knelt on the pallet and pulled her down beside him. "Lie down. I don't want you sliding off the horse in the dark tonight because you're too exhausted to stay awake." When she was this close, he could smell that faint apple blossom essence and it sent most unwelcome sensations racing through his body. The journey to their camp would take at least three more days. Three days of lying beside her. Chase gritted his teeth and suppressed the ache in his groin as he willed her to obey him.

Perspiration glistened on her face, which was flushed from the growing heat. She was miserable. "I'd advise opening the collar on that prim little gown. Wouldn't want you getting heat stroke," he added, unable to resist the jibe even though the idea of her baring that creamy throat was torture.

Stephanie was hot. Her mourning dress was black, trimmed with a high scratchy collar of deep violet lace, which seemed to be slowly strangling her as the sun arched higher in the sky.

"I won't unfasten anything. I have no intention of making it easy for you," Stephanie replied crossly.

He gave her a nasty smile. "That's only fair since I have no intention of making it hard for you."

She blushed down to the roots of her hair, too shocked to make a retort. Mustering her resolve, she retreated behind a wall of cold stoicism, staring at him with disdain.

But the prim facade of calm was quickly broken when he produced that heinous length of rawhide that he had used to bind her wrists. "What are you doing?" she croaked as he seized one of her hands. He tied the rawhide around her wrist, then slipped the other end around his own, leaving barely a foot of play between them.

"Just making sure you don't do any exploring while I'm trying to rest. Oh, I might mention, Cheyenne warriors are very light sleepers. If you make any move at all, I'll know. Now lie down," he commanded, as he stretched out on the pallet, yanking her right arm so she plopped on her side next to him.

Stephanie lay rigid as a board, trying desperately not to touch his body with her own, an almost impossible feat on the narrow confines of the blanket. She could feel his body heat radiating across the scant inches separating them. Sweat pooled between her breasts and soaked the tight waist of her dress. Her legs felt as if they were bundled in wool and fur instead of thin lawn petticoats and a polished cotton skirt. She stared straight up into the branches of the aspen, waving lazily in the faintest of breezes, green-gold against the brilliant azure dome of sky . . . and itched to unbutton her collar as he had suggested.

Gradually she became aware of a reciprocal tension in him. It was simply a matter of sixth sense, or feminine intuition at first. Then, from the corner of her eye, she could see his profile. His head rested with his right arm behind it as he, too, stared stonily heavenward. A secret smile tugged at her heart. Perhaps there still was a tiny bit of the old Chase left in this violent stranger. As children they had always been amazingly in tune with each other's thoughts and feelings. She had still felt some of that old familiar kinship when he courted her four years earlier.

Before she could stop herself or analyze what mad impulse made her do it, she began unfastening the buttons at her neck, quickly moving all the way to where her camisole covered the swell of her breasts. The whalebone of her corset, which had saved her belly from a pummeling when he had thrown her across the horse, now felt horribly constricting, not to mention hot. Suddenly a horrible thought occurred to her—how long would she have to keep it on before being allowed the privacy to rest in a night rail?

Chase felt his stomach clench when her left hand moved up her throat and began to open the front of her dress. By the time she stopped, he was rock hard, his staff straining against the confines of his breechclout, throbbing. He gritted his teeth, suppressing a groan, then casually bent his left leg at the knee, raising it to shield the telltale bulge of his erection. His own barb came back to mock him: *I have no intention of making it hard for you.* So much for intentions.

It would be so easy to roll on top of her and bury his face between the pale mounds of her breasts, to tear off her clothes and drive himself deep inside her. Damn her for taunting him. Didn't she know she was playing with fire? But if he took her even once, would he ever be able to let her go?

No, dammit, I can't do it! I'll take her to Red Bead and let my aunt have charge of her. She can spend the winter observing how my people live, share our privations. Let her see we are not animals. Then I'll send her back to Phillips.

The idea of that butchering bastard ever touching her ate at his gut. From what she said—and did not say—he gathered that the marriage was miserable. After being captured by savages, Chase knew the bluebelly wouldn't want back a soiled wife, one sullied by Cheyenne "bucks." Perhaps it would be best if she returned to Boston. After all, she was a rich woman now that Josiah was dead. He looked over at her again. Exhaustion had finally closed her eyes. Her breasts rose and fell evenly in sleep. Hell, he'd think about what to do with her next spring. All he had to do now was keep his hands off her and get them both back to the fall hunting camp in one piece.

They awakened near dusk, ate a bit more, washed up in the stream and rode through the night, repeating the cold camp the following morning. By late that afternoon, Chase had awakened and gone down to the small water hole to wash up, leaving Stephanie still sleeping. Tomorrow they would reach his band. He must ride in dressed as befitted a Cheyenne warrior, free from the taint of white civilization. He took jewelry from its wrappings, then began to work his freshly washed hair into a braid, which he tied with a leather thong and adorned with several hard-won eagle feathers.

Stephanie heard him splashing in the pool as she came out of the deep slumber of exhaustion. Every bone in her body cried in protest as she sat up. The whalebone staves of her corset must have permanently fused rib cage to spine by now, she thought in misery, longing desperately to peel off every stitch and dive into the cool depths of the pool. Of course that was impossible. Chase was there.

Chase. She watched him emerge from the screen of cord grass and sit down beside his saddlebags, looking refreshed and cool as he began to plait his hair and decorate it with feathers. Then he donned several copper bracelets and placed a pair of large silver loops in his ears. So that explained those tiny holes in his earlobes! Watching this pagan adornment ritual, she would have thought him a full-blooded red savage if not for the thick black hair on his chest and the bristling beard he had to shave off every night. He turned to her as if sensing her eyes on him.

"You can go down to the stream and wash up while I'm gone. I heard prairie chickens over the ridge. We're far enough into Cheyenne and Lakota hunting grounds now. It'll be safe enough to chance a fire for a hot supper tonight."

Stephanie stood up, stiff and shaky from the days and nights spent sleeping on the ground and riding across the wide harsh plains. Now they were headed into rough, mountainous country. Dear God, where was he taking her?

She considered the transformation in him since they had parted in Boston so long ago. Then he looked the epitome of a wealthy young Brahmin. Now he stood before her, half-naked and scarred, adorned with gaudy jewelry, his long hair in a braid. All he needed to complete the picture of one of George Catlin's splendid savages was to don an elaborately beaded bone breastplate.

Chase knew what she was thinking. He smiled thinly. "A warrior doesn't ride in with a captive unless he dresses the part. Go perform your own toilette . . . unless you want to look like the dirty hag Cheyenne women believe white females to be."

With that parting sally, he leaped agilely onto the unsaddled horse, rifle in hand, and rode up the hill. Tears of angry frustration filled her eyes. *Damn him!* Dirty hag was she! Looking down at her dust-covered, wrinkled black dress, Stephanie knew she must look as bad as she felt. He had left a small bar of plain soap and a clean length of cloth out, even a heavy comb made of some sort of animal bone.

Grimly, she picked up the items and stomped down to the pool. Peeling off her dress and petticoats was wonderful, but unlacing the corset and taking her first deep breath in three days was pure bliss. She seized the soap and jumped into the pool, which was deep and colder than she would have imagined. After paddling about for a few moments, Stephanie realized Chase might return soon. She could not let him find her mother naked in the water. That would be tempting fate too much.

Do you want to tempt him? that inner voice asked, scouring her conscience. Sternly she reminded herself that she was a married woman. There could be nothing between her and Chase Remington—or White Wolf the renegade. Even if she had not wed Hugh, she could never give herself to the man Chase had become. *But what if he takes you anyway?*

The thought both tantalized and tormented her. *Dear God, what is happening to me?* She hugged herself, shivering in the cold water. What would he do when they arrived at his village? She would be his slave, utterly at his mercy. He could force her . . . if he had to. Back in Boston she had been the one to throw herself shamelessly at him. But then she was not wed to another man. Like it or not, she was now Hugh Phillips's wife. She must never again succumb to her old weakness for Chase Remington. The fear of sleeping beside him, of having him touch her squeezed her heart painfully. With a shuddering breath of resolution, she sudsed from head to toe, then rinsed and waded quickly to shore.

As she dried off, she eyed her corset and dirty clothes with distaste. There was no help for donning the ugly black dress again. She took the damp towel and wiped as much of the dust from the gown as she could, then smoothed it out on a big boulder to dry in the afternoon sun while she put on her undergarments. The whalebone corset lay on the ground like a menacing skeleton ready to pounce. She kicked it into some elderberry bushes and slipped on her petticoats and camisole, then the slightly damp dress, leaving the top several buttons open. "If he can parade about half-naked, I can damn well be dragged captive across the Rocky Mountains without a corset!" she muttered to herself, then set to work untangling her hair.

Just as she finished combing the waist-length masses and started to plait them, several shots rang out. She thought it was Chase bringing down the prairie chickens, but when she heard yelling in English, she leaped up and began to run in the direction of the ruckus. White men! Rescue, before the unthinkable had happened. *Before you gave in to him!*

"Help me! I'm Stephanie Phillips—I've been kidnapped," she cried out, running through the thickets of kinnikinnick toward the firing. She reached the trail across the opposite side of the ridge and burst into the clearing. Chase was afoot, his big dun some distance away in the buffalo grass. In front of him stood an old gaudily painted medicine wagon with a sign blazoned across the top proclaiming: SAVAGE CANNIBAL CHILDREN!!! One rider was already a distant speck on the southern horizon, out of Chase's rifle range. A second man in a frock coat came tearing up the road toward her, whipping a big piebald into a hard gallop.

"Please, take me with you. I'm a cavalry officer's wife. I've been kidnapped," she yelled, but he would have ridden her down if she had not thrown herself clear at the last second. As she rolled off the rocky road, the horse's hooves thundered by, just inches away. When the rider passed her Chase fired, but it was too late. The escapee had vanished into a dense stand of blue stem grass. A fat man wearing a garish stovepipe hat clutched a rifle to his chest, slumped across the open wagon box on the driver's seat. He was dead. Stephanie fought the nausea rising sourly in her throat as she stood up and took in the carnage. "You attacked a harmless medicine show and tried to kill all these men just because they're white!"

Chase strode toward her, fury blazing across his face like a molten brand, cursing in a mixture of English and Cheyenne. At least one of the men who escaped had heard her yelling and might report to the authorities that she had been abducted by Indians. Luckily she had only given her name, not his or his tribe. There was a slim chance he could catch one of the men but he had no hope of overtaking both of them.

"You damn little fool! He could've trampled you to death," he snarled, grabbing her wrist and yanking her to him, then inspecting her for injuries. "Are you hurt?" He touched her cheek where a scrape from the flying gravel had drawn blood. "I'll have to clean that. Cuts fester quickly in this heat."

"Why, Chase . . . why?" she asked. How could he be so tender now and have committed such a brutal savage act only moments ago?

"I didn't attack them because they were white," he said wearily, seeing the fright and disillusionment in her eyes. "I was only trying to parlay with them to free the children but their leader there"—he gestured to the corpulent corpse—"decided it would be better to kill me. He pulled out that rifle from behind the seat. Guess he thought he could stuff me for a display in their little freak show." He pointed to the bright orange calligraphy on the bottom of

the wagon proclaiming the world's greatest display of tax-
idermy.

"Freak show?" she echoed, looking again at the banner
drooping across the side of the wagon—which had curtains
drawn behind a set of bars.

Just then a frail whimper sounded from inside. "Come
see what your civilized white men have done," he said
tightly, turning his back on her and walking over to the
wagon. He pulled back the curtain revealing two small Indian children, huddled together in one corner of the
cramped, filthy cage. The smaller one, a girl, was sobbing
while a slightly older boy tried to console her in some
strange dialect.

Savage cannibal children indeed! They were terrified Indians barely six or seven years of age. "My God, the poor
things—get them out of there, Chase," Stephanie said, approaching the wagon slowly to avoid frightening them.
"Hello. We mean you no harm. We're going to set you
free," she said softly. Two huge pairs of round black eyes
stared at her in awe, but they made no reply. She turned to
Chase who had climbed up onto the wagon box and was
searching the corpse. For an instant she was horrified, certain that he planned to scalp the man, but he was instead
searching his pockets. He pulled a key ring from one, then
let the dead man fall from the opposite side of the wagon.

Ignoring the dull thud of two hundred pounds of dead
meat hitting the ground, Chase jumped down and began
trying each key on the rusty old lock as Stephanie watched,
all the while talking soothingly to the children.

"They don't seem to understand English. Speak to them
in Cheyenne, Chase," she said.

"It would only frighten them more. They're Crow,
sworn enemies of my people. Their village was wiped out
by smallpox and their mother was one of the few survivors.
She took them to Camp Baker looking for help. Her husband had been an army scout before he died. The soldiers
offered to let her whore for them. She died after one of
them beat her to death. Then the captain sold the children

to these dandy fellows.'' He finally tried the right key and the lock clicked open.

''How did you learn all this?''

''The fellow who hightailed it out of here using you for cover was real loquacious while his partner was sneaking out his rifle to kill me.''

''If they're Crow and your people are their enemies, why risk your life to help them?'' Chase was becoming more of an enigma to her every moment.

''We don't make war on children,'' he replied impatiently. ''Any little ones captured in raids—red or white— are adopted into our tribe.'' He opened the cage and extended his hand to the boy hovering protectively over the girl. ''The fat man said you spoke some English. We set you free. Will you come with us?''

''No more cage?'' the boy asked suspiciously.

''No more.''

''You Cheyenne?''

''Yes, but you heard what I told the white woman. My people will offer you a home, food, a warm lodge.''

The boy digested this for a moment, studying Chase intently. Then apparently deciding he trusted his rescuer, he nodded and murmured something to the girl, who was staring at Stephanie in awe. He turned back to Chase and replied, ''I, Smooth Stone. My sister, Tiny Dancer.''

''I am called White Wolf,'' Chase replied with a smile as the boy climbed out of the wagon followed by his sister.

''Who is she?'' Smooth Stone asked after his sister whispered the question in his ear.

''My name is Stephanie,'' she replied to the children, smiling and kneeling down in front of them.

''Are you White Wolf's woman?'' the boy asked.

Stephanie bit her lip, uncertain of how to reply, not wanting to frighten the children by saying she was a prisoner. Nor did she want to deceive them by saying she was his wife. ''Once our families pledged us to wed, long ago,'' she equivocated. Their pitifully thin little bodies were filthy and their hair matted with some noisome snake oil, probably mixed up by the wagon owner. ''Are you hungry?''

she asked. "We have food at our camp." She opened her
arms to Tiny Dancer, who stood shyly beside her brother,
a graceful little wraith clad in a garish yellow breechclout
covered with cheap feathers dyed red and blue. Both children had been outfitted like performers in some tawdry
Wild West circus, with bones tied in their hair and hanging
around their necks.

Tiny Dancer hesitated for a moment, then went into Stephanie's arms. "Smell good," she whispered with a slight
lisp caused by her missing front baby teeth.

"Come, little warrior," Chase said to Smooth Stone.
"We will let your sister and Stephanie ride my horse back
to our camp. We will walk." He whistled for the dun, then
helped Stephanie to mount and handed up the little girl into
her arms.

Smooth Stone followed his savior proudly, while keeping
an eye on the white female carrying his sister. "You live
Cheyenne, but you are part white," the boy said, looking
at Chase's hairy chest. He had spent enough time among
white men to recognize the difference between the races.

"My mother came from far beyond the Father of Waters
to wed my father," Chase replied. "I have chosen as she
did, to live with his people."

"What of your woman? Did she choose same?" Smooth
Stone asked, watching the way Tiny Dancer clung to Stephanie who talked softly to the girl, stroking her head as
she carried her.

Chase found himself in the same dilemma as Stephanie.
How should he answer? The boy was uncommonly shrewd,
seasoned by bitter experience far beyond his years. There
was no way to deceive Smooth Stone. "She is my captive.
I am taking her to my band where she will learn that red
men have honor . . . just as some whites do."

"Huh! I do not believe white man has honor. Soldiers
lie to my father. Share my mother. Sell us to bad men who
put us in cage. Others look, spit on us, laugh."

Stephanie listened to the boy as they walked back to their
camp and her heart broke. That supposedly civilized human
beings could behave so callously appalled her. Yet after

listening to the other officers' wives discuss the "Indian problem" and witnessing the army resettlement policies, she knew few whites really believed the Indians were human beings, even the children. *Nits make lice.*

After they reached camp, Chase left Stephanie in charge of bathing the children who eagerly shucked the chafing and garish costumes they had been forced to wear by their captors. Shrieking in delight they scampered into the pool, laughing and splashing.

"How could anyone call those beautiful children cannibals! And subject them to such an ordeal," she said furiously, feeling more than a bit of guilt for the cruelty of her race toward those considered inferior.

"It's not unusual. Everyone likes a freak show—the Elizabethans thought it a merry jest indeed to trip and kick dwarves and lame children. It isn't unknown among some tribes of Indians. I'm glad those fools got lost and wandered off the trail. At least two little ones have been saved. They'll find a good home with my people."

But will I, Chase? She did not voice the question aloud. Instead, she asked, "When I've finished cleaning them up, what shall I dress them in? Do you have any more clothes in your pack?" she asked, thinking she could cut something down, perhaps shirts.

"They can go naked," he replied casually.

"Naked! Most certainly not—why that's . . . that's . . ."

"Barbaric?" he supplied to her sputtering. "Children that young most often don't wear clothes in warm weather. They wouldn't want to be rigged out in layers of hot restricting cloth," he said, his eyes sweeping over her wrinkled black cotton dress.

"I'm going after supper. Stoke up that fire while I'm gone." He turned and strode away, then looked back at her for a brief moment and said, "At least you ditched the corset," his eyes lingering suggestively on the curve of her breasts. Then he was gone, leaving her standing by the campfire, staring mutely after him.

How did he know? Her hand came up involuntarily and brushed her breast and she gasped for both nipples were rigidly hard, the points stabbing shockingly against the thin cotton bodice of her dress. She crimsoned in mortification at the tingling ache he had caused with only one scorching look.

What is happening to me?

12

Chase was gone over an hour. It took him only half that time to locate the birds. He shot enough for them to feast well that evening, but he stayed away from camp, circling his gelding around the area instead of returning. He dreaded the thought of facing Stephanie. God, every time he looked at her his body throbbed and the facade of scorn became more impossible to maintain. He wanted her. How he wanted her! When he had seen the impudent outline of her nipples protruding through the ugly black cloth, he had wanted to take her right there on the ground. If not for the children, he might well have lost control and done it. Lord knew, she felt the same way he did—or at least her body did, if not her mind. He could imagine the soft supple grace of that slender body now freed of the hard confinement of corset stays and lacing. No, thinking of that would only bring disaster!

After stopping at the medicine wagon to unhitch the two mangy nags and put hackamores on them, he turned his gelding back to camp, leading the other horses. They were old and ill treated, but would serve to carry the children. Stephanie could not be expected to ride bareback even if he could have trusted her not to attempt another foolish escape.

Only one more night of riding with her body pressed so closely to his. He gritted his teeth against the thought as he neared the camp. The children had looked hungry. They would enjoy the fresh meat. He, on the other hand, would just have to curb his hunger for the bronze-haired *veho* until he could turn her over to his aunt for safekeeping. Beyond that he refused to consider.

As he approached the pool, dusk was thickening and the tang of woodsmoke from the fire filled the air. The musical sound of children's laughter blended with the richer timber of Stephanie's husky chuckles. He reined in the dun and looked down on the scene below.

Stephanie knelt at the pool's edge with a length of white cotton in her hands as two small brown naked bodies cavorted around her. The three of them played some sort of game. Tiny Dancer skipped near and Stephanie grabbed her in a fierce hug, enveloping the little girl in the cloth, drying her wet glistening body as the child giggled and shrieked. Then Stephanie released the girl when Smooth Stones skipped close enough and seized him with the towel, repeating the process.

When both children were dry, she gathered them in her arms and spoke softly with them. They squatted obediently beside her on the towel which she laid out. Then she produced a comb and began to work on unsnarling their hair. He could see she had a natural way with children, obviously loved them. Why had she and Phillips never had any of their own? The question seemed to ask itself. Thinking about her bearing a child to the sadistic bluebelly made him angry.

He kicked the dun into a trot and the nags followed as he rode down the ridge into camp. Sliding from his horse's back, he tossed the hens to the earth in front of the fire. Stephanie walked across the open ground from the pool with the children gamboling around her. When she approached the fire, she glanced down at the blood-spattered game, then met his steady gaze.

"I see you were successful," she said neutrally, still unnerved by how savage he looked. Even before he spoke she knew what he was going to say.

"Prepare these birds and roast them." He pulled the knife from his belt and tossed it into the earth, then began to secure the horses. The blade sank into the moist ground at her feet with a solid thunk.

"Aren't you afraid I'll use that on you?" she asked, eyeing the wicked looking knife.

· "In front of the children? For shame, Stevie," he replied caustically after he completed his task and the horses began to graze.

"I've never plucked a chicken in my life, much less cooked wild game over a campfire. I haven't the first idea of how to go about cooking quail."

Chase was not surprised but Smooth Stone and Tiny Dancer were. "What kind of woman cannot cook what hunter provides?" Smooth Stone asked in amazement.

"In Boston my father had servants to do the cooking. Out west Hugh hired a striker to cook and clean for me," Stephanie said, staring defiantly at Chase, knowing the answer would anger him. She wanted to hit back in any way she could. He was punishing her for marrying his enemy, as if marriage to Hugh was not already punishment enough!

"Since I neglected to abduct a striker, you're on your own," Chase drawled, mockingly.

"If I pick up that knife it will most certainly not be to use on creatures already dead."

Tiny Dancer took in the exchange between her rescuer and the beautiful white woman with apprehension. She was too bold, speaking this way to a warrior. He would surely whip her! "I watch women cook. I do it," she said, shyly stepping in front of Stephanie.

Chase looked contemptuously at Stephanie, then turned his gaze on the little girl and smiled. "It is a kind thing you offer and I am grateful. When you grow up you will make some warrior a fine wife. But my captive is a woman grown and she must learn for herself. Go play with your brother while I teach her what must be done."

"It be as White Wolf say. Come," Smooth Stone said with dignity. He took his sister's hand and pulled her away, leaving the two adults confronting one another.

Chase knelt and reached for a bird with one hand, retrieving his knife with the other. "I'll clean one. You watch. Then you can do the rest."

"And you can go to hell," Stephanie replied through gritted teeth. "As you've pointed out several times, I'm your captive—not your squaw."

"Would you like to change roles, Stevie?" he asked softly, looking up at her with smoldering black eyes, daring her.

Her hands clenched into fists at her sides. She stared down at him with impotent fury. "Is this the way all Indian women are treated? Brought up from girlhood to wait on men? Tiny Dancer was afraid for me. Already she expects to jump any time a male speaks, to do whatever he asks."

"We have a cooperative society. Everyone has their assigned task to perform for the good of the group as a whole. Cooking and caring for children are women's work, not all that different in white society—except for the idle rich who have everything done for them."

"Now who's being superior and a hypocrite to boot, Mr. Chase Remington of the idly rich Boston Remingtons? Anyway, at least we idle rich abolished slavery. Servants are paid. *Captives* aren't," she snapped back.

Chase stood up, hiding his anger. She had scored a direct hit with her barb about the idly rich Remingtons. Damn her. His eyes narrowed on her, raking her from head to toe and back. "We might be able to arrange some sort of payment, Stevie . . . that *is* what you want, isn't it?"

The sexual innuendo hung between them as their eyes and wills clashed. "I am not one of Rocky's girls. The only thing I want from you is my freedom!"

"Is it, Stevie?" he asked in patent disbelief.

"I've told you not to call me Stevie."

"And I'm telling you, you'll learn to clean those birds or you'll go without food tonight. I suggest you make up your mind quickly. The children are growing hungry while you have a tantrum."

Stephanie felt a sudden inexplicable urge to burst into tears. She was hot and tired and hungry herself, frightened of this savage stranger, saddened beyond measure by the way things had turned out between them. Swallowing the hard knot of misery in her throat, she knelt and picked up one of the dead birds. "Show me how to clean this," she said tonelessly.

* * *

They rode through the night, Smooth Stone and Tiny Dancer each mounted on one of the old team horses, which they controlled with the ease of those born to ride. Stephanie remained mounted in front of Chase. They stopped to rest for a few hours when they lost the moon. Stephanie's only sense of direction was maintained by the setting and rising of the sun. Otherwise she was utterly lost even as the moon reappeared to illuminate the stark outlines of jagged mountain peaks looming ever nearer. They had crossed untold miles of flat open buffalo grass for the past two days. The third night the topography began to change dramatically. As they drew near the mountains, the plains gave way to hills, gullies and ravines, rocky, rugged land dotted with increasingly taller stands of lodgepole pine.

"Your village—is close, White Wolf?" Smooth Stone asked excitedly as the eastern sky began to lighten with a faint pearl-gray glow.

"It is close, yes," Chase answered with a smile. He reined in and the children did likewise beside a small sluggishly flowing creek. He dismounted saying, "I must make final preparations to greet my people."

Smooth Stone and Tiny Dancer slid effortlessly from their horses and sat down to watch with avid interest. Chase assisted Stephanie down, then brought out a razor and shaving gear from his saddlebags. He knelt with the mirror beside the creek to perform the daily ritual which he intensely disliked. "An unfortunate reminder of my white blood."

"Apparently the only one," Stephanie muttered.

"White men have much hair," Smooth Stone said. "Is good you cut it off face."

Stephanie had heard that Indians considered the facial and body hair of white men to be ugly. Chase had a dark bristly growth of beard every morning and a thick pelt of hair on his chest, all reminders that he was half-white. *He must hate that*, she thought. *But you love the feel of it*, an inner voice mocked. She turned angrily away from the enticing sight of the razor gliding along his face and stared at the horizon while he continued his toilette.

When he had finished shaving, he put away the razor and

took out the rest of his warrior's regalia—more jewelry and a breastplate. He was aware of Stephanie's apprehensive gaze as he made the final preparations for his homecoming. Smooth Stone and Tiny Dancer understood that a warrior returning to his people after a successful raid always dressed in his finery, but for Stephanie it was merely another indication of how deeply he had sunk into savagery. He finished dressing and motioned for the children to mount up, then swung into the saddle and swept her up in front of him.

"I'm surprised you don't ride bareback," she said breathlessly.

"If there were some place to stow the damn saddle, I would," he replied, kneeing the dun into a trot. As he flexed one bare arm around her waist, the heavy copper bands on his wrist and biceps gleamed in the dawn's light.

Chase pressed her back against his chest and felt her spine stiffen when the hard bones of the breastplate touched her. "Nervous about meeting the family?" he whispered lightly in her ear.

"I'm not 'meeting the family.' I'm being dragged in as a captive—a slave for you to parade in front of your friends."

He shrugged indifferently, hiding the hurt her stinging words brought. "Have it your way."

"If I had my way, I'd be asleep safely in Rawlins."

They rode in silence while the children chattered between themselves excitedly in a mixture of English and their native tongue. Just as the sun tipped over the horizon in a great golden ball, they crested a steep ridge and looked down into a wide flat bowl, a shallow valley through which ran a narrow stream of water. Between thirty and forty buffalo skin lodges were arranged in an orderly semicircle facing the rising sun, as was the Cheyenne custom.

Chase watched as Stephanie leaned forward, peering down at the activities around the awakening camp. "The rider moving from east to south around the camp is the crier," he explained. "He informs everyone in the village of the day's activities, who is raising a hunting party, who gives a feast this night, any news of interest or restrictions decided upon by the elders. Right now I imagine he's telling them of our imminent arrival.''

She turned her head back to him quizzically. ''How would he know?''

''Sentries,'' he replied, pointing to horsemen whom she had not seen on the perimeters of the valley's ridge.

Stephanie observed women gathering in clusters, laughing and gossiping as they listened to the crier. Some started cookfires while others already had heavy kettles boiling and were dishing up bowls of some sort of meat and vegetables. A group of preadolescent boys drove a small herd of horses into the center of the village while a dozen or so young girls carried in bundles of firewood. Old men clustered at the openings of some lodges, watching the sunrise and serenely puffing on their pipes while younger ones stood stretching and yawning, preparing to greet the day. Everywhere small children ran giggling and shrieking, as utterly naked and unashamed as were Smooth Stone and Tiny Dancer. As they drew closer to the village, an excited buzz began. All eyes were on the White Wolf, who led two little children and brought a captive female back with him. Young boys and girls ran ahead to greet their hero as a number of mongrel dogs yipped excitedly at their heels. Women turned from their chores to smile and men raised their arms in salutes of welcome.

They were an uncommonly tall and handsome race. Stephanie remembered hearing someone at Fort Steele refer to the Cheyenne as ''the beautiful people.'' Certainly they were nothing like the beaten starving wretches she had seen herded into the compounds of army posts with their heads bowed, ragged and stoic, awaiting their fate. These people were proud and free, their fragile way of life as nomadic hunters still intact, thanks no doubt to the half-breed renegade who stole and killed for them.

The men had long-boned muscular bodies and possessed strong features although none had quite the chiseled perfection of Chase's arresting face. Most were clothed only in breechclouts, a few with leggings, and all were adorned

with jewelry and feathered ornaments similar to those
Chase wore. The women were striking rather than conven-
tionally pretty, with large liquid black eyes. Their hair, like
that of the men, was braided but frequently coiled into
heavy rolls at the sides or back of their heads. They were
a great deal more modest in their dress than the men,
clothed in long tunics and high laced boots, all made of
soft tanned animal hides.

Everyone stared at her. Stephanie could sense a blend of
curiosity and hatred emanating from those who crowded
around the horses as Chase rode to a large lodge in the
center of the village. An older man with gray-streaked hair
and hawkish regal features stood waiting patiently with an
unreadable expression on his face. Chase's uncle. She remembered his name, Stands Tall, which fit him well. His
fathomless obsidian eyes studied her without revealing any
emotion but when they shifted to the children, a smile lit
his face.

Chase slid from the dun directly in front of him and the
two greeted each other by clasping arms. As they spoke in
Cheyenne, Stephanie could sense that they discussed her
and grew uneasy. The exchange seemed troubling to Stands
Tall. Other children crowded around Smooth Stone and
Tiny Dancer chattering in their tongue. The Crow children
could not understand them but it was apparent they were
friendly.

Chase had known his uncle would not be any happier
over his captive than he was, but at least Stands Tall understood the necessity of his actions. And his uncle also
intuited that there was something between him and the
bronze-haired woman. He looked up at her, sitting proudly
on the dun gelding.

"She shows no fear. Her heart is strong," he said.

Chase turned to Stephanie and lifted her down from the
horse. "This is my uncle, Stands Tall, a great peace chief
among our people, and this," he said as a wizened old
woman emerged from the lodge, "is my great-aunt, Red
Bead. They both understand English."

Stephanie turned her attention to the crone whose small

wiry body still moved with ageless grace. She bowed gravely to Chase, then returned Stephanie's perusal with shrewd black eyes. "Come," she commanded as she turned and disappeared again into the lodge, expecting her new charge to obey.

"Go with her and do as she says," Chase instructed.

"What about the children—"

"I'll see they're well cared for," he replied, then spoke in Cheyenne to the village children clustered curiously about the two old horses.

They stepped back, quieting as he summoned a plump, moon-faced woman who came forward and reached up for Tiny Dancer, opening her arms in a motherly embrace. The little girl responded instinctively and Smooth Stone bounded to the ground, eagerly awaiting his hero's instructions.

"This is Crow Woman. She is of your former people, captured in a raid as a child and adopted. She still speaks your language and will teach you ours. Go with her."

"You be big brother, White Wolf?" Smooth Stone asked wistfully.

Chase knelt by the boy and said, "I will teach you the way of a warrior and you will grow up to be fearless and strong." Satisfied with the pledge, Smooth Stone took Crow Woman's free hand. She walked off with him, carrying Tiny Dancer on her other arm.

There was nothing for Stephanie to do but follow Red Bead into the lodge. Blinking to accustom herself to the soft light filtering in from the rolled up bottom edge of the lodge skin, she observed a surprisingly spacious living area with a small fire pit in the center. Various tools and implements of war hung from the lodge poles. Pallets made of thick soft pelts lay against the outer perimeters and between them what looked like backrests made of willow poles and buckskin acted as dividers and storage units. Everything was neat and orderly.

"Sit," Red Bead commanded, her tone of voice neutral, as she squatted agilely on one pallet, gesturing for Stephanie to take her place at the opposite end of it.

"Chase said you speak English," Stephanie began with an uncertain smile.

"I speak English. You are from the faraway place where he was held prisoner?"

Her eyes squinted sharply, fixed on Stephanie, who nodded. "Yes, we knew each other when we were children . . . then again just before he returned to you." She volunteered no more, waiting to see what the old woman would do.

"The White Wolf has done a foolish thing, I think, following his heart. You will bring trouble for him . . . but the Powers will decide."

"The Powers? You mean the tribal elders?"

"No. If the White Wolf has captured you, you are his to keep. No man will stop his doing with you as he wishes. The Powers are spirits. You call God. Only White Eyes do not believe we share your God. Perhaps we do not," she added enigmatically.

Stephanie detected censure in the words and felt constrained to say, "I did not wish to be brought here. Chase kidnapped me from a white man's town."

"Chase the Wind no longer uses his boy's name. Now he is the White Wolf," Red Bead replied, ignoring Stephanie's remarks. "You eat, then I take you to the river to bathe and put on clean clothes."

Red Bead all but turned up her bony nose at the dirty wrinkled black cotton dress, by now so dusty it had paled almost gray. Stephanie was sure it smelled worse than a horse blanket! Her face reddened in mortification as Red Bead rose and scuttled outside, quickly returning with a bowl of bubbling stew.

Under the old woman's watchful eye, Stephanie took the bowl and a small knife, which she had observed was the Indian's major eating utensil. Gingerly she stabbed at a chunk of meat swimming in the brown broth, praying it was edible. Although somewhat flat, lacking salt, the flavor was sweet and the meat tender. She grew bolder and tried some of the unidentifiable vegetables which were also quite palatable.

"It's good," she offered politely to Red Bead.

"Yes. Fresh bear meat. Killed yesterday," the old woman responded.

Bear! For a moment the sweet taste started to roil on the back of her tongue, but Stephanie quickly quashed the impulse which might have offended her hostess. It *had* tasted good. A bear was wild game just like a buffalo or a deer and she had grown used to both, as fresh domestic meat on army posts was seldom available. When it was, it was either strong grass-fed beef or the world's oldest roosters, fit only for the soup pot.

She smiled at Red Bead and continued eating. Finally, when all that remained was the broth, she puzzled for a moment since she did not have a spoon. Red Bead answered the unasked question, saying, "Drink." She made a motion for her to upend the bowl. Stephanie did so, wiping her mouth on the back of her hand, which was far cleaner than the sleeve of her dress.

Red Bead nodded her approval and took the bowl. "Now you bathe," she said peremptorily. She rose, gathered up some items from one of the storage containers behind her, then walked outside, once more expecting Stephanie to follow her without question. When they emerged from the lodge, Stephanie glanced nervously around. Chase and his uncle were nowhere in sight, nor were any of the young warriors. A few old men sat smoking and working on ceremonial paraphernalia and a group of women knelt on the ground, sewing buffalo hides together.

"They make a lodge for Magpie this day. She is to marry Swift Antelope as soon as it is complete," Red Bead said as they passed the working women. Several of the younger ones glanced curiously at her, but quickly looked down, too shy to meet her tentative smile. An older woman with a stony impassive face stared at her boldly, almost as if challenging her.

"That one is Granite Arm, mother of Kit Fox, who expects to be the White Wolf's wife."

Stephanie's heart squeezed painfully. Of course Chase would marry a Cheyenne woman. The only surprising thing was that he had not already done so, she reminded herself.

"She has no reason to be jealous of me. I am his prisoner, not a rival. I am already married to another."

Red Bead said nothing in reply, only continued walking toward the winding stream that dissected the flat open ground. A stand of alder trees sheltered the rushing water from the early-morning sun's heat, affording seclusion for her bath.

Thank heavens I can bathe in privacy, she thought, but then she heard soft giggling and splashing as they rounded a copse of kinnikinnick bushes. A dozen or more Cheyenne women, several of them with young children, cavorted in the water, which surprisingly ran shoulder deep in places. Little boys and girls swam gracefully as young otters, as did several of the women. Two women sat on the bank, nursing infants. All were completely naked and totally unashamed of their bodies.

Heat rushed to Stephanie's cheeks as everyone's eyes turned to her, standing there fully clothed, filthy and bedraggled. How dearly she longed for a bath! Yet she desperately did not want to strip and have all these curious women see her naked body. No one had ever seen her naked in daylight, not even Hugh.

But Chase had. Memories of him stripping every stitch from her soaked, frozen body and rubbing her numb arms and legs came rushing back to her. *Don't think about it!* Red Bead interrupted her trance.

"Take off all your clothes and bathe," she instructed. When Stephanie still did not move, she said, as if talking to a dim-witted child, "Here is soap. Clean the stink of sweat from your skin. I will bring clean clothing."

"I—I've never undressed in front of anyone before," Stephanie confessed, clutching the small bar of soap, which was stamped as army issue, no doubt a product of another of the White Wolf's raids.

Red Bead gave an inelegant snort, indicating what she thought of white women's sensibilities. "No men invade the bathing place now. They know it is time for the women. You are safe undressing."

The old woman did not move but stood waiting until

Stephanie began to unbutton the front of her dress. If she had been white, no doubt she'd have tapped her slipper with impatience. Realizing there was no way out except compliance, and that procrastinating was only making her audience more curious, Stephanie set to peeling off her dress and undergarments as swiftly as she could.

The younger women stared in open fascination at her ivory skin, pale pink nipples and the light brown hair at the junction of her thighs. Several of them began to giggle and chatter among themselves. Stephanie fought the urge to shield herself against the invasion but Red Bead explained, "They were only curious to see if the color of your hair below matched that above."

One of the young mothers suckling her baby, pointed to Stephanie's breasts and asked something in Cheyenne. Stephanie turned to Red Bead who replied, "She asks if such pale nipples work the same way our dark ones do."

Having never nursed an infant, Stephanie did not know what to reply and quickly decided it best not to attempt any explanation. Instead, clutching the soap, she walked into the water as deep as she could go and began to paddle around. *Thank you, Aunt Paulina, for seeing to it I learned the unladylike sport of swimming!* she thought as she moved through the water. It felt different swimming without anything on, free and faintly erotic. What was wrong with her! Only a few hours spent with the savages and she was starting to think like one. This was all Chase Remington's fault, damn him. Why had he not left her in Rawlins? Why had she committed the insane folly of following him down a dark alley?

There was no use even thinking about it. All she could do was make the best of an impossible situation and pray Chase would set her free soon. To do what—return to Hugh? How would she explain her absence? Being a captive of Indians forever tainted a woman, placing her beyond the pale of civilized society. At best she would be pitied, at worst castigated for not killing herself. Chase had made no attempt to force her to submit to him . . . yet. But even if he didn't rape her, no one would believe it.

Stephanie forced the disquieting thoughts aside and lathered up her hair after scrubbing days of trail dust from her body. Then she plunged into the water and swam until she was completely rinsed clean. After completing her bath, she looked toward the shore, uncertain of what to do next. She had no towel, but neither did the other women who seemed content to sit on the rocks sunning themselves dry while they combed and replaited their hair.

Dare she join them? For the most part they had seemed friendly enough, if embarrassingly curious. There was nothing else to do until Red Bead returned with the promised clothing. She had hoped to salvage her undergarments and wash them but the old woman had taken every stitch with her when she left. Working her courage up, Stephanie began to walk through the shallows up to the rocky bank where she took a seat and started to wring the water from her sopping hair, then detangle it with her fingers. If only she had remembered the comb Chase had given her.

Then one of the young women shyly held out her hand offering a comb. "Your hair is good," she said in halting English. "Like the sun is caught in it. Magic."

Stephanie smiled and accepted the comb. "Thank you."

"I think it is ugly, like pale river mud," another woman said spitefully, also in surprisingly good English. Several of her companions gave her reproving looks but she ignored them and stormed away angrily.

"Do not listen to She Bear. Her man was killed by Long Knives. She has much bitterness," the handsome young girl who offered the comb said.

"You are kind and you speak my language well."

"I am Kit Fox." Her dusky cheeks darkened with a blush as she added, "The White Wolf taught me."

"Oh," Stephanie exclaimed, surprised. This was the girl Red Bead spoke of, who expected to marry Chase. No wonder she'd learned English! "I . . . I am Stephanie."

Huge dark eyes studied her face for a moment. "The others say you are his captive, wife of a Long Knife."

Stephanie swallowed, uncertain of what to say. "My

husband is a soldier, yes. And Cha— I mean, the White
Wolf did take me prisoner.''

"You knew him in a long-ago time." It was not a question.

"How did you know that?" Stephanie asked.

A look of wistful sadness came over Kit Fox's face. "He
did not say so . . . but I know he loved a white woman
before he returned to us.''

And this white woman was you. The words hung unspoken between them. Had Chase ever really loved her? Over
the years, Stephanie had agonized about the question, but
it was far past the time for regrets now. "I am wed to
another now. I do not wish to be your rival, Kit Fox.''

The girl looked into her eyes for a moment, then, as if
satisfied, nodded. "If you are not my rival, then will you
be my friend?''

"I would like that very much. I have need of a friend,
Kit Fox," Stephanie replied with a strained smile.

13

"The half-blood brings death among us! The white woman belongs to a Long Knife. The soldiers will come searching for her," Pony Whipper said, gesturing angrily to where Stephanie stood, pale and trembling. Red Bead had just brought her up from the river after having her don a Cheyenne tunic and moccasins. The group of women with her looked on in silence at the confrontation between the White Wolf and Pony Whipper.

Chase stared with impassive calm at the seething troublemaker. This was not the first time they had tangled but bringing Stephanie here had certainly given his old foe good ammunition in his campaign to unseat the half-blood from his position of leadership among the young warriors. As soon as Pony Whipper rode into camp and learned that Stands Tall's nephew took a Blue Coat's wife captive, he had searched out Chase, spoiling for a fight.

"The soldiers will never find us in the vastness of the mountains at our winter stronghold. Already we have begun the journey away from the other bands' great summer camp. No one in the white town even knows that I took her."

"Why did you bring her here?" Elk Bull asked, not unreasonably.

This was the question he had been dreading. "She knew me as Chase Remington in the East. When she saw me in Rawlins she figured out that I was the White Wolf."

"If she would betray you, why did you not kill her?" Pony Whipper snarled.

"I do not know for certain that she would betray me. She was my friend when I was a child, and I do not repay kindness with death. But I also could not take chances," Chase replied.

Pony Whipper spat on the ground and looked at Stephanie, then back to Chase. "Her white blood calls to you! You desire her—and you would endanger all of us to have her!"

"I would never do anything to place my people in danger. It is time to move into the mountains where we will be safe for the winter. Then I will decide what to do with the white woman." Against his will, Chase's eyes strayed to Stephanie and she returned his troubled gaze. In spite of the buckskin tunic Red Bead had given her, there was no way she could be mistaken for anything but a white captive with her shimmering bronze hair, golden eyes and pale skin.

"If you do not desire her, sell her to me then. I will give three fine ponies for the shining hair," Pony Whipper said with glittering triumph.

He knows I can't do it, the bastard. "No, Pony Whipper. I would not sell you a dog. She is my captive and I choose to keep her," Chase said arrogantly.

Stands Tall, who was a tribal elder, stepped between them as the two men bristled, ready to erupt in violence. "There will be no fighting over women or anything else," he said sternly.

"You protect him because he is your brother's son," Pony Whipper accused.

"My uncle knows I have no need of protection, but unlike you, I honor our laws. A Cheyenne cannot shed Cheyenne blood."

"You are no Cheyenne. Your have lived among the White Eyes for too long. Your blood is tainted!"

Involuntarily Chase's hand went to the knife on his hip but he did not draw it. The half-breed stigma had never left him. Even here with his father's people, the people of his heart, he knew there were others who agreed with Pony Whipper. But he would not shed Cheyenne blood.

"The White Wolf has brought us food when we were hungry, medicines to cure the spider people's diseases, guns to fight them. He has proven he is one of us, a leader of worth,'' Elk Bull said.

Since the older man, too, was a member of the Crazy Dog Society and a tribal elder, Pony Whipper was forced to subside. He stepped back from Chase with an angry oath and stalked away.

"He will not let this rest," Stands Tall said to Chase. "I am sorry I told the council that the woman belongs to a Blue Coat."

"You had no choice but to answer their questions," Chase replied.

"Will you keep her with you?"

Chase knew there was more to the question than what was immediately obvious. "I cannot return her."

"Then she will betray you?"

Chase sighed. "I honestly do not know."

"And you cannot kill her." It was not a question.

"No, I cannot kill her," Chase echoed softly, looking over to where Stephanie stood, so slender and delicate among the strong and sturdy Cheyenne women.

She watched the terse exchange among the men and knew it concerned her. What would Chase do with her? What did she want him to do? Her apprehension mounted as he walked over to her.

"What did that man say?" she asked. "I know you were arguing over me."

"Bringing you here endangers my people. He was right about that, even if he is an old enemy."

"You could take me back to Rawlins," she ventured.

"Or I could do what Pony Whipper suggested . . . kill you."

She stepped back, her heart pounding in her chest as if he had struck her a blow. She refused to give in to fear. "You always did enjoy shocking people, Chase, even back in Boston."

"We aren't in Boston anymore, Stevie," he replied bleakly, as his eyes swept over the soft doeskin tunic she wore. "Not exactly conventional attire for an officer's lady."

"Kit Fox gave it to me. Your people are very generous," she replied, noting his slight flush at the mention of the lovely young Cheyenne's name.

"For bloodthirsty savages, we do have our redeeming qualities," he replied in a combination of black humor and bitterness.

"You'll never let me live down those words, will you, Chase?"

He hardened his heart against the whisper-soft entreaty in her voice. She was another man's wife, a white woman. He had chosen a different path. He could not succumb, so he must not forgive. "Go back to Red Bead." He turned on his heel and stalked away, leaving her standing alone.

With a troubled expression on his face Stands Tall observed the exchange from across the camp. His beloved nephew was drawn to the white woman. He had confessed that he knew her since they were children and that their families had considered a marriage between them just before Freedom Woman's death. Did he still love her, even though she had now been given to another? He pondered the question of what was to be done . . . and saw no answers.

"There will be a feast this night to celebrate the return of the White Wolf," Red Bead told Stephanie as they made their way back to the village after an afternoon spent digging roots with cumbersome wooden instruments. The other women wielded the tools with ease and skill. Stephanie had done a minimum of gardening at a few of the posts where they remained long enough for crops to grow, but she was an abysmal failure at the task assigned her. Instead, Red Bead sent her to pick wild berries along the riverbank, in clear sight of the other women toiling across the flat open ground of the valley. The sun was high and Stephanie felt hot, sweaty and tired, altogether out of sorts by the time the old woman signaled it was time to stop.

A feast to honor the White Wolf indeed!

"Will I be expected to attend?" she asked Red Bead, still uncertain of her place among these people.

"You are my nephew's captive: You will serve him."

During the day, Stephanie had observed the women and young girls preparing food for the men and boys and waiting upon them. Then they and the small children ate afterward. She had thought the custom demeaning. And now he expected her to act the part of an obedient lackey? She bit back a sharp retort to Red Bead. It would do no good to antagonize the old woman, who had been kind enough in her own peculiar way.

Stephanie was a stranger, a captive at the mercy of savage people who could kill her with as little thought as they'd give to swatting a mosquito, she reminded herself. The best thing would be to swallow her pride and do as she was bidden. Perhaps if they feasted, they would drink, too, and fall into a stupor. Then she might steal a horse and make good her escape, although finding her way back to civilization would not be easy. Yet anything was preferable to remaining a prisoner. Anything was preferable to remaining so close to Chase.

Kit Fox, carrying a heavy basket overflowing with thick whitish roots, approached Stephanie.

"Would you join us at the river? The day has been hot and Swan Flower, Green Grass and I go to bathe again before we prepare for the feast."

Stephanie looked to Red Bead and her old guardian nodded. The laughing, chattering young women quickly took the roots and berries to the village, then headed for the grove of alder trees at the river once more. The quartet stripped and dived into the cooling water. This time Stephanie did so less self-consciously than she had that morning when the hostile older women had been present. The young women laughed and played for a short time but Green Grass and Swan Flower had family duties back in camp. After they departed, Stephanie and Kit Fox decided to stay a bit longer.

"I would practice my English," the Cheyenne girl said with a smile.

"You want to please the White Wolf, don't you?" Stephanie asked, deciding on candor with her newfound friend.

Kit Fox's expression was uncertain as they made their way to the shallows and began to dry off. "Yes. I wish to please him so that he will offer my brother a bride price. But I do not think he will . . ." She hesitated.

"And you think it's because of me?" Stephanie shook her head. "No, Kit Fox. He left me over three years ago. He chose this life—he chose *your* people. I am married to another man now. There can be nothing between us."

"You cannot undo what already has been done," Kit Fox said simply. "Do your laws not allow a wife to leave a husband if she does not love him?"

Stephanie considered the question. Kit Fox had obviously learned enough about white society to comprehend the concept of divorce. "It is possible," she said hesitantly, "but very, very difficult, especially for a woman to obtain a divorce." She shook herself mentally for even saying such a thing aloud, much less discussing it. "I can never divorce Hugh for Chase. It would be . . . immoral— wrong."

"Yet it is right to live a lie? White men have strange ideas," Kit Fox said, shaking her head in perplexity. "Our people do not often separate once a man and woman have joined their lives together, but if the husband or the wife no longer wishes to be married, it is right to part. No one thinks less of a woman who has done this thing. All she need do is set her man's possessions outside their lodge and he must go away."

"It's a great deal more complicated in my world. Women have few rights," she said softly, recalling the painful betrayal of her father who had given her inheritance to Hugh as if she were less than nothing.

"I am sad for you, then . . . if you still wish to return to such a life."

Kit Fox sees too much, Stephanie thought to herself, but there seemed to be no adequate response. She changed the subject, asking, "Do you think the Crow children we brought with us will be happy with the woman who took them?"

Kit Fox replied, "Yes, I know Crow Woman will love

them as if they were her own. And because she speaks their tongue, she will quickly teach them ours. You grew to care for them?"

Stephanie nodded, biting her lip. "Yes, very much. Do you think I might be permitted to visit with them from time to time?"

Her companion considered this. "Perhaps you could ask Red Bead. She and her husband were never blessed with children. She might understand your longing."

Stephanie smiled. "You are wise, my friend." She reached out her hand and clasped Kit Fox's and they stood smiling, holding onto each other for a moment.

Then the two women finished dressing in silence. Divining that Stephanie needed some time alone to think, Kit Fox said, "I promised my mother I would gather some chickada to make a sleeping potion for Grandfather. I will see you this night at the feast."

After she had departed, Stephanie sat and stared at her reflection on the smooth surface of the water. What might it be like to be master of one's own destiny? To have the freedom to begin all over again? Undo past mistakes? *Hugh was a mistake.* "No! I married him in church, of my own free will. I cannot abandon my vows even if he has his." If ever she were to have children of her own, they must be Hugh's. The thought offered no consolation for she had already concluded that she did not want a child of his.

You would want Chase's baby, wouldn't you?

"No! I cannot," she cried in the silence. Stephanie massaged her aching temples with her fingertips as the ironic thought came to her—Chase had given no indication that he would ever touch her, much less marry her even if she *were* free! Kit Fox had unwittingly placed troubling thoughts in her mind. Best if she supported her young friend in her pursuit of the White Wolf. He had always intended to wed a Cheyenne woman and Kit Fox would make a perfect wife for him.

Her painful thoughts were interrupted by the sound of angry voices—a man and woman arguing. The woman was Kit Fox and the man was the big hostile warrior who had confronted Chase earlier. A sudden muffled scream followed by the sounds of a struggle brought Stephanie running through the trees to help her friend.

Kit Fox glared at Pony Whipper. She had clearly spurned his advances, yet he refused to accept the rejection. When he reached out and seized the front of her tunic, tearing it, she was incredulous and furious. As she slammed against him, her left hand brushed the war club hanging at his belt. She yanked it free, angry enough to cleave his skull with it but at such close quarters she could not maneuver. He wrenched it from her grip and tossed it away, then continued ripping her tunic. When she tried to scream, he covered her mouth with one large hand. He was going to rape her!

Pony Whipper had her friend pinned beneath him. Her tunic was ripped down the front, baring her breasts. He held her with his powerful thighs while clamping one hand over her mouth. His other hand had pulled up her tunic and now was unfastening his breechclout! She must stop him at once before irreparable damage was done to Kit Fox!

She started to run at him, intent on pummeling him with her bare hands, anything just to get him to stop, but then she saw the club lying on the ground and scooped it up. Just as she raised it to strike, he sensed her presence and turned. His flushed face contorted and he gave a snarl of rage but before he could raise a hand to stave off the blow, Stephanie swung and the club struck his temple. He crumpled to the ground, knocked partially clear of the struggling girl, out cold.

Choking back a sob, Kit Fox wriggled free of the big man, then pulled down her skirt and covered her breasts with the ripped pieces of doeskin. "He has no more shame than a weasel," she spat, looking at his bare genitals, obscenely revealed when he tore loose his breechclout. "You have saved my honor. I owe you my life," she said gravely to Stephanie as the white woman helped her to her feet.

"Come, let's get you some help. Then send the chief to deal with him. I hope the punishment for such a crime will be swift and terrible."

"No!" Kit Fox cried, surprising Stephanie. "You must tell no one."

"But—I don't understand. Is such an act not punished by your leaders?"

"Yes, of course. We never kill our own people, but he could be banished—if my brother Plenty Horses asked for it. But Plenty Horses would never do that. He is Pony Whipper's friend and he has been pressing me to accept Pony Whipper's offer of marriage. They are both members of the Crazy Dog Society and they hate the White Wolf. My brother does not wish me to wed him.

"Among our people, when a crime has been committed, the chiefs prefer to arrange for a payment to make up for the injury rather than to banish the offender. My brother would ask that Pony Whipper atone for dishonoring me by offering marriage. I would be forced to accept."

"They planned this together to make you marry against your will! But that's terrible."

"You see why we cannot tell anyone about the shameful thing Pony Whipper has done," Kit Fox said as the man groaned and rolled over.

Both women stepped back but he did not attempt to arise, only reached one hand to his head and massaged the lump forming on it. "If he had not turned and dodged the full force of my blow, I might have killed him. Dear God, the other Crazy Dogs would have demanded my death, wouldn't they?"

Kit Fox nodded. "As a captive, you do not have the same rights as a Cheyenne. We could hardly banish you," she added with impish amusement. Then she sobered. "Come, you have made a deadly enemy. Pony Whipper dare not speak of his dishonor, but he may try to harm you for spoiling his plan. I will protect you. I will speak with my brother. Plenty Horses has much to answer for. I think he will be ashamed for this day's work."

The two women left the dazed man sitting on the ground and quickly returned to camp. Kit Fox slipped into her lodge before anyone saw her torn clothes. Stephanie returned to Red Bead, deeply disturbed by the dangerous situation in which she had now become embroiled. *As if I were not already in* enough *trouble.*

Chase spent the afternoon in discussions with the chiefs and leaders of the warrior societies, planning the move for the winter into the high isolated region of the Bighorn Mountains to the north. There they would be safe, far from the Long Knives, the railroad and all the deadly dangers of white civilization. But soon they would be hemmed in. The Union Pacific was already established in the south and the new Northern Pacific would run to the north. The High Plains tribes were slowly being squeezed by a pincer of rails. How long could they hold out, fighting the hit-and-run sort of war he had taught them?

Deeply preoccupied, Chase walked back to his lodge only to find Stephanie waiting outside it. What was he to do with her? He must take her with him to their secret hideaway. Yet that bastard Phillips would love nothing more than to ride into the stronghold and massacre every man, woman and child. Once she had journeyed there, could he ever risk freeing her? *Isn't that what you want? To keep her forever?* He repressed the disturbing thought, concentrating on how to treat with her for the moment. She looked lovely with her hair falling like molten silk over her shoulders. The Cheyenne clothes fit her tall slender body perfectly. He could almost make himself believe that it would work out if he took her, but he knew he was deceiving himself. She had pledged herself to his sworn enemy and if there was one thing of which Chase was certain, it was that Stephanie Summerfield would never break her vows.

Stay clear of her. He smiled coolly as he approached her. "I see you're ready for the feast."

"Red Bead said I was to wait for you." Her tone indicated how much the idea appealed to her.

"Come," was all he replied, turning sharply.

He expected her to heel like some damned camp dog! Fleetingly she wished for the war club to bash in the thick skull of another Cheyenne male, but common sense prevailed. Best to play along. Perhaps there might be a chance for escape later. She followed him to the open clearing surrounded by the semicircle of lodges.

The area was already filled with people of all ages, laughing and talking excitedly. Many greeted Chase in obvious friendliness and admiration but here and there she noted several hostile young warriors watching him with narrowed eyes and angrily furrowed brows. Were they all members of the Crazy Dog Society Kit Fox had mentioned? Stephanie could not discern enough about tribal insignias and nuances of dress to be certain.

As he approached the front row of the circle of men seated around the large fire, he turned to her. ''Go to Red Bead and she will direct your tasks.''

''Of course, my lord. I am your obedient servant,'' she said dulcetly.

''And property,'' he replied with indifferent arrogance calculated to enrage.

She swallowed a retort and walked furiously over to Red Bead. Chase sat down beside Stands Tall who smiled thinly. ''I do not think she enjoys being your captive.''

''Whatever gave you that idea?'' Chase replied dryly.

''Only watch she does not scald you with a bowl of stew,'' the older man retorted with a chuckle.

Chase grunted, not at all sure of what Stevie Summerfield might do. When she approached him with a bowl of steamed trout, he was wary, but she sat it beside the basket of fresh gooseberries and hackberries. He knew some of the food would repel her, the roasted intestines of buffalo calf, stuffed with fresh meat and nuts, and the marrow bones that were broken open so the rich black marrow could be sucked out and eaten raw by the men. By the time she brought him a chunk of buffalo stomach filled with a gelatinous mass of congealed blood, Chase expected her to be pale and queasy looking, but she surprised him. Anger had always made Stevie even stronger. And he knew that playing slave was infuriating her.

He nodded to her with respect after all the food had been set out and the men were eating. Many warriors fed choice tidbits to their favorite sweethearts, wives or children.

Chase indicated that Stephanie should at last take a seat on the ground behind him and his uncle, then passed her some fruit and a chunk of roasted buffalo hump.

Tiny Dancer and Smooth Stone scampered around the fire, following the other children, begging for treats as was the custom. He motioned them to come sit with him, then offered them the fresh fruits and a spoon made of buffalo bone so they could dig into the various bowls of stew and other delicacies.

"This stew is my favorite," Tiny Dancer exclaimed after they had sampled many things under the indulgent eyes of Chase and Stands Tall.

"Yes, it is mine, too," her brother agreed, taking the spoon from her and scooping up a chunk of meat.

"You must try, Stephanie," Smooth Stone said, offering her a generous spoonful.

She had sat back, watching their eager excitement with pleasure. Smiling she said, "Very well."

"I would not advise that," Chase cautioned in a low voice as she took the spoon.

"Am I not entitled to the really good food because I'm a mere white captive?"

He shrugged. "Suit yourself."

She took a sip. It was faintly sweet, unlike any other game she had ever eaten, with a peculiar mushy consistency and a distinctive strong aftertaste. She chewed and swallowed manfully, not wanting to hurt the children's feelings. "It is . . . different. I've never tasted buffalo prepared quite that way before."

Tiny Dancer giggled as Smooth Stone said, "Not buffalo. Puppy."

She hoped she had misunderstood him. "You—you mean calf—buffalo calf, don't you?" she asked hopefully, feeling the bile rise dangerously in her throat.

He shook his head and both children laughed at the foolishness of this white lady. "No, puppy—young dog. Sweet, tender. You want more?"

"No! That is, no, no thank you," she said more calmly. Sheer force of will kept her stomach from rebelling further and humiliating her. *I will not give him the satisfaction*, she thought, glaring at Chase's back as he sat chewing on one of those noisome marrow bones.

"What is wrong, Stephanie?" Tiny Dancer asked in perplexity.

"My people do not eat dogs . . . er, puppies. They are domesticated animals, raised as helpers for people."

"So are cows, chickens. You eat them, no?" Smooth Stone's logic seemed irrefutable to him. "Give milk, eggs, help you, but you eat meat." He shrugged.

"It's not the same," Stephanie replied weakly. The children returned to their stew with zest, and the white woman fell silent remembering a scene she had seen that afternoon on her way to the river with Kit Fox and the others—a plump toddler outside one of the lodges, napping in the warm sun, nestled in a pile of sleeping puppies. Stephanie murmured softly, unaware that she was speaking aloud, "Chubby little babies don't cuddle with chickens or cows."

Chase heard the comment and the mouthful of food he was swallowing seemed to lodge in his throat. God, she sounded so forlorn so . . . lost. He looked at Tiny Dancer and Smooth Stone, but apparently they had not heard the remark. He wished to God that he hadn't.

Wanting to shake her gloom, Stephanie asked Tiny Dancer, "Are you happy with Crow Woman?"

"She is kind. She teach us to be Cheyenne. We learn to speak, to play stick ball, swim, do chores with other children."

Stephanie hated having to make the supplication. She knew she would only hurt the children if she made it in their presence and Chase refused to allow it. So she waited until Smooth Stone and Tiny Dancer ran off with several of their young friends to play. "Would you let me visit with them from time to time . . . as long as I'm here?"

He stared straight ahead in silence for a moment, hearing the entreaty in her voice. She loved the children, longed for little ones of her own. He thought of the beautiful babies they could have had together and the pain engulfed him. Cursing inwardly, he pushed the impossible thought aside and turned to her. It was almost his undoing. Her eyes were luminous in the firelight. Her skin gave off a soft golden glow for she had spent many hours in the sun during the past days of travel. The shimmering curtain of bronze hair glowed like molten metal, surrounding her face like a radiant nimbus. She was so utterly lovely he almost reached out to touch her, just to assure himself that she was real, that she was his.

But she was not his. She belonged to Hugh Phillips, he reminded himself angrily. "You may visit them, but don't interfere between them and Crow Woman. She is their mother now and will care for them long after you've left us. Come, it's time we retired," he said abruptly.

Stephanie was taken aback. She had hoped the revelers would drink to excess and pass out as she had always heard the tame Indians around the posts did. But there had been no sign of alcohol all evening. The men shared a mild beverage made of some sort of fermented roots, but it did not seem to affect them any more than would watered down beer.

"Aren't you going to join in the dancing?" she asked, observing some of the men and women moving gracefully about the fire, the males segregated from the females decorously. Perhaps they might dance until they dropped with exhaustion!

"I don't think so. Tomorrow I have to be up before first light and I need my sleep." Let her make of that what she would, he thought with grim amusement as her eyes widened and she moistened her lips nervously. "Let's go." He turned and strode swiftly toward their lodge.

He expected her to follow again . . . like some damned puppy—to the slaughter! She would not sleep beside him ever again, she vowed fiercely. Out on the plains he had teased and taunted her, playing his cruel sexual games until they had encountered the children and he was forced to act with more decorum. But now he could take her to the privacy of his lodge. She knew Stands Tall and Red Bead would allow him to do whatever he wished with his captive and never interfere. There was nothing to stop him from forcing himself on her . . . if he still desired her as he had back in Boston—and he'd given many indications that he did desire her even though he despised her and himself for it.

We're so alike, Chase. I despise myself for it, yet I long to have you touch me as you once did. She choked back tears. How bitter that admission. But she could never give in to her long repressed feelings. She would refuse him. Surely his sense of decency, some small vestige of the civilized man he had once been, would prevent him from dishonoring them both. Resolutely she followed him back to the lodge.

When they reached the opening, he stopped. "Red Bead will show you where you're to sleep." Noting with satisfaction the startled expression on her face, he said, "What's the matter, Stevie? Disappointed?"

"You are contemptible," she said, stung with humiliation. "Nothing could give me greater relief than to be free of your . . . snoring!"

He reached up and touched her cheek very fleetingly. As he dropped his hand he whispered, "Liar," then vanished into the darkness.

Stephanie watched him enter another large skin hut a couple dozen yards away, leaving her standing alone without so much as a backward glance. Red Bead's voice broke into her stunned trance, bidding her to enter. She bent over and slipped inside where the coals of a small low fire glowed faintly, casting everything in dim orange light.

"That is your sleeping place," Red Bead said, pointing to one of the pallets of soft furs.

There were only two pallets remaining in the big lodge where that morning there had been three. She had assumed one was for Red Bead, one for Stands Tall and one for Chase. She had also assumed she would be forced to share Chase's. "Where has Chase—er, where have White Wolf and Stands Tall gone tonight?" she asked, hating herself as the old woman's shrewd eyes studied her knowingly.

"They sleep in another lodge," was all she replied.

Red faced and burning with humiliation, Stephanie sank

onto the surprising softness of the pelts which were clean and fragrant from the freshly cut pine boughs laid beneath heavy buffalo robes, forming a mattress of sorts. The fox and marten furs were piled on top, making up a most comfortable bed. But Stephanie was far too upset to sleep in spite of physical and mental exhaustion. Her mind churned with hurt, anger and frustration well leavened with fear. What would she really have done if Chase had tried to make love to her?

✍ *14* ✍

It was the time of the plum moon when they began their journey to the north, into the vast impregnable reaches of the high mountains white men called the Big Horns, after the fierce wild sheep inhabiting them. Every winter since Stands Tall had rejoined his Northern kinsmen, he had led his small band to an isolated valley hidden in a box canyon, a place that even he had discovered only by accident. Laden down with the meat they had dried and the fruits, vegetables and other foodstuffs they had gathered and preserved, the small band of Cheyenne would once more set their faces toward the mountains and the winter.

After a restless night's sleep, Stephanie awakened that morning to the sounds of the village crier yelling out his announcements. Although she could not understand what he said, she knew something important was going on the moment she stepped outdoors. The tranquil morning routine they had observed from the ridge yesterday had changed. None of the old men sat smoking and no women stood about gossiping, nor did the children skip about or play stick ball.

An air of excitement moved through the village. Young mothers gathered their children, giving them instructions, which the little ones scampered to obey. Some women packed up cooking utensils while a few others prepared a hasty morning meal for the rest of the camp. Lodges were being taken down one at a time by groups of women working together with the precision skills of a military drill team.

The camp was breaking up today! Stephanie hadn't understood they would head into the mountains to that isolated hidden valley Chase had spoken of so soon! She should have chanced an escape last night even though the men had not gotten drunk as she had hoped. Now they would drag her to a place no white had ever seen. She would spend the rest of her life living like a slave!

She stood for a moment, looking around, forcing herself to calm down. Panic would serve nothing. It was a long way to those mountains and en route with all the horses kept close to camp she might actually find it easier to plan an escape in the confusion. Yet the way the Cheyenne handled moving seemed quite orderly as she observed the youths herding groups of their family's horses, then separating out those selected to carry the travois loaded with household goods. The men carefully packed their ceremonial pipes and war tools.

Stephanie had believed all menial chores were done by Indian women. Seeing a warrior gathering his war weapons into a leather bag, she decided the best thing was to engage Red Bead in casual conversation so that she could gain her trust, and perhaps make the old woman just a bit less vigilant. Walking over to her, she asked, ''Why doesn't that man let his wife pack for him?'' The woman and two adolescent daughters stood waiting patiently as he loaded his gear onto a travois.

''Women do not touch sacred things or war weapons. Brings bad medicine to a man if his pipe or shield—anything he uses to ensure luck in battle—is contaminated.''

''I thought as much. When the oaf goes into battle, what does he do with his 'contaminated' privy part, I wonder.'' Stephanie sniffed disdainfully to herself after the old woman turned away, busy bundling up her assortment of bone spoons and dishes. But then the soft ripple of laughter between a man and woman caught her attention. There was a husky warmth in his voice as he talked with a pretty girl who was obviously his very pregnant bride. He lifted the heavy buffalo hide roll of lodge skins onto a travois for her.

Stephanie turned away, feeling oddly like an intruder on such domestic intimacy. If only her life with Hugh could have been touched with just a tiny bit of that affection. But it never had been, never would be. She needed something to do. "Can I help you?" she asked Red Bead.

Soon she was busily occupied assisting the surprisingly strong old woman position and tie the heavy parfleches of foodstuffs onto a travois. The load had to be distributed carefully so it would ride smoothly, not pull to one side. Within an hour she and Red Bead had all her worldly goods packed up. Several younger women had come to help take down the big lodge, Kit Fox among them. When they knelt to bind the lodge poles together with rawhide strips, Stephanie asked her friend, "What happened after you returned yesterday? I did not see you at the feast last night."

"Plenty Horses was very angry. He would not let me attend the celebration which honored the White Wolf. My mother wishes me to wed Stands Tall's nephew. He will be a great leader one day. She and Plenty Horses argued," the girl said sadly.

"I imagine Granite Arm was angry, too, after what her son and Pony Whipper planned to do to you," Stephanie said in consolation. "Is there nothing you can do to expose Pony Whipper's evil?"

"Not unless I also shame Plenty Horses. This I cannot do." They finished strapping the lodge poles to a travois, then the younger woman said, "I must go now and help some of the other old women with their heavy chores."

"Is it always the custom among your people to help the old and infirm?" The army said the savages left their elderly out to starve, but all she had seen here gave the lie to that. Kit Fox looked puzzled. "Of course. With the passing of the seasons in men and women's lives comes wisdom. We honor them and their wisdom. Do your people not do the same?"

Stephanie nodded thoughtfully, knowing that life in civilization was not always as caring as it appeared to be with this small band of Indians.

And so the journey began. The village became a long orderly cavalcade of people and horses. Mounted warriors

led the way with several dozen riding point to safeguard
the women and children who followed with the laden travois. Some of the older people, who could not easily walk,
rode the travois, perched among cook pots, buffalo robes
and other household goods, as did the little girls. The boys
rode horses and the older ones were responsible for herding
the extra stock not in use. Dogs yipped and darted among
the people who walked at a slow steady pace, their faces
set to the mountains.

Chase and Stands Tall returned on the following day. As
soon as they drew in sight of the people, the younger man's
eyes swept the long column searching for Stephanie. Her
bright hair stood out like a beacon, glowing in the waning
afternoon sunlight.

"Any white who happened upon us would know she is a
captive," Stands Tall said, echoing his nephew's thoughts.

"I will see that she disguises her hair. I had not counted
on running across a party of miners. They are directly to
our south and could become nosy."

"Have you decided what is to be done with her yet?"

The troubling question had haunted Chase's dreams ever
since he had taken her prisoner. He'd hoped being away
from her while they scouted the trail to the mountains
would enable him to think more rationally about the situation, but it had not. He dreamed of her nightly. Sighing,
he shook his head.

"Perhaps she could become one of us as your mother
did."

Stands Tall's tone of voice communicated the doubt both
he and Chase shared. "She married that butcher Phillips,
and spent the past three years living as a soldier's wife. She
will never come to me as Freedom Woman did to Vanishing Grass."

"Never is a long, long time," Stands Tall said softly,
surprising himself almost as much as he did his nephew.

Stephanie watched Chase ride in on Thunderbolt, sliding
from the magnificent stallion's back with the effortless ease
of the High Plains horse Indians. He was practically naked,
clad only in breechclout and moccasins. If the proper ladies

of Boston had swooned when he appeared dressed in immaculate white shirts and custom-tailored wool suits, imagine how they'd react if he walked into one of their drawing rooms now!

He made his way to her after conferring briefly with Elk Bull. She refused to give him the satisfaction of waiting obediently like his horse until he deigned to speak to her. Instead she walked over to where several of the young women were unloading cook pots and other utensils and began helping with the task.

"You look too white," he said peremptorily, as he approached her.

Stephanie turned to him and sputtered, "And just what am I supposed to look like—a Celestial or an African?"

"You will use some walnut stain to darken your skin."

"Dye my skin!" she exclaimed aghast. He smiled sardonically. "What's the matter? Does the Boston matron shrink at the thought of dark skin?"

Her face reddened as she remembered loving the contrast between her paleness and his coppery darkness when they were in Boston. "I can't be what I'm not," she replied stubbornly.

"I'm not trying to remake you into a Cheyenne woman—as if I could. I only want to keep you from attracting any unwanted attention. If any white hunters or miners stumble on us, I'd hate to have to kill them just to silence them."

She looked at his implacable expression. "You'd actually do it, wouldn't you?"

"Go to Red Bead and have her disguise you. She'll know what to do," was all he replied before stalking off.

Stephanie seethed, resuming her tasks. If she made a loud clatter with the iron cook pots, no one commented on it. "I'm getting so sunburned I'll soon be dark enough to pass as an Indian anyway," she muttered to herself as she worked. She did not see Chase again until after the evening meal when she and several of the young women were on their way back from bathing in the river.

Stepping out from behind a copse of aspen, he barred

her way. The other women quickly left them, knowing there was trouble between the White Wolf and his captive. Even her friend Kit Fox lowered her eyes in resignation and walked away. Stephanie looked up at him, waiting to see what he would do. He held a small vial in one hand. With the other he reached out and took hold of her wrist, heading back toward the river.

"I have already bathed," she said as anger and panic took hold of her in equal measure.

"But you have not done as I told you."

"No, I have not," she dared him, trying to yank her arm from the steely grip.

He refused to relinquish it. When she continued to balk, he slipped the small vial into his waistband and quickly picked her up, tossing her over his shoulder before she could do more than let out an outraged gasp. Approaching the riverbank, he slung her down and released her. They stood facing each other, eyes glowing in the dim light of evening. Slowly he withdrew the vial and uncorked it. A pungent not unpleasant smell assailed her nostrils. She wrinkled her nose as he offered it to her.

"Smear it on your face, neck, arms and hands."

"It stinks." She refused to take it.

"It's only walnut oil. As soon as the stain dries you can bathe away the odor."

"No whites will see me here. There's no reason for this."

He looked at the damp skin of her throat where a small pulse raced. She had left the tunic unlaced at the neckline. A small smile curled about his mouth as he fingered the lacings. "Well, at least you've finally taken my advice about loosening up."

She backed warily away. "I'll scream, Chase."

He smiled broadly now but it was not a nice smile. "Go ahead. Do you think any of my people will interfere between me and my captive?" He poured a bit of the dark oil into his palm and then slid it along the pale column of her neck, pulling her to him. She could feel the calluses on his hand, the slickness of the oil, the warmth of his breath as he drew her closer. His fingers dropped lower across her collarbone and she gasped, looking down to see the dark stain spread across her light skin. By now he had clasped her wrist in his other hand along with the small vial, all the while continuing the soft massaging motion along her shoulder, sliding the loosened tunic dangerously low. When he grazed the swell of her breast, she reached up and clasped his hand with her free one.

"Please . . . don't do this," she whispered hoarsely.

"I don't know. The thought of massaging all that lovely white skin does hold a certain allure," he murmured, noticing she did not pull away, only pressed her hand against his to stop him from reaching inside her tunic to caress her breast. He ached to do just that. Suddenly she seized the vial from him and slid from his grasp, standing still, her breasts rising and falling swiftly, her lips slightly parted, breathless. He could see the dark imprint of his touch across her throat, a stark contrast to the pallor of her face.

"I . . . I'll use the stain. Just leave me."

Silently as a wraith, he turned and did so. Stephanie watched him go, still feeling the tingling ache where he had touched her . . . and where he had not. With a ragged breath, she began to rub the pungent oil over her face and arms as the sun slipped beyond the western horizon and night fell.

When she returned to the camp, Red Bead looked up at her darkened skin and grunted in approval, then scuttled through the packs to give her a length of soft blue cloth, no doubt trade goods obtained from a raid. "Cover your hair with it when we travel," she said, dishing up a bowl filled with fresh berries and handing it to Stephanie. She used a small knife to cut off a hunk of the roasting venison haunch still spitted on the campfire and began to chew, then offered the blade to Stephanie to do likewise.

The meat smelled wonderful although she was still not used to the lack of salt. Her stomach gave a small growl. She used the knife to help herself.

Then Red Bead said, "It was a good thing you did yesterday. Granite Arm told me how you saved her daughter."

She paused but before Stephanie could make a reply she said, "Kit Fox wishes to wed the White Wolf."

"I know. She told me." Stephanie refused to venture more, wondering if Red Bead believed she was jealous.

"You are not like other whites I have known," the old woman said, then turned her attention to the food, staring silently into the flames as she ate.

They broke camp at dawn, continuing the trek north. Stephanie muttered to herself but wrapped the blue cloth about her head after plaiting her hair. She was ambivalent about running across any white travelers, devoutly wishing for rescue yet not wanting to bring harm to these people, many of whom had been most kind to her. Nor did she wish to see Chase carry out his threat and kill any witnesses in order to keep her.

Chase rode point through the day. She watched him on the ridge riding his magnificent stallion, Thunderbolt. The only time he rode the stallion was when he was with the band. What a splendid barbarian he was, riding bareback with long muscular legs gripping the sleek horse's sides and the wind whipping his long feathered braid. The sun gleamed on his sweat-slicked skin, delineating the muscles of his shoulders, arms and chest. He did not wear a breastplate today so the scars of his Sun Dance showed through the thick pelt of dark hair on his chest.

"You look at him with longing in your heart," Red Bead said, startling Stephanie. The old woman had approached silently, catching the white woman unawares.

A denial sprang to her lips but she looked into Red Bead's shrewd sympathetic eyes and nodded instead. "Once long ago, we were in love. But he left me and I wed another. There is nothing that can change that."

Red Bead merely shrugged. "We do not always know what the Powers have in store."

Before Stephanie could reply to the enigmatic remark, Chase came streaking down the hill toward them, reining in next to Stands Tall and Elk Bull who rode at the head of the column of Cheyenne. They conferred briefly, then he approached the travois of Red Bead where Stephanie walked. Sliding from Thunderbolt's back he said, "Cover your hair completely," reaching out to pull the cloth shawl into a drooping hood that fell across her forehead, obscuring her face.

"Why? What is—" Before she could pull it back and look up at him, he reached out and seized her hand in an iron grip.

"Do as I say! A group of white men are just over that rise—miners looking to strike it rich in the Black Hills."

An expression of tortured ambivalence betrayed her before she could school her features to neutrality. Chase saw it and cursed. "Don't be a fool, Stevie. We outnumber them. I would have to kill them to protect my people."

"I won't reveal myself," she replied in a choked voice, knowing he would keep his word. She walked beside Red Bead under his watchful eye as he paced the restless stallion beside them.

She saw the miners when they crested the hill just as Chase had said, a rough looking company of about a dozen men. The leader was a gaunt looking fellow with a turkey feather in the greasy felt hat that shaded a face to which life had not been kind. Watery pale eyes narrowed as he studied the band of Indians whose path had cross sected his, noting that they were not painted for war and had all their women and children with them.

"Howdy! Any of you speak American?" he asked, spitting a wad of tobacco on the ground and patting the repeating rifle he held in his hands. His men were well armed. He did not realize that the Cheyene warriors were equally so. Chase had instructed that most of the men hide their Henrys and Winchesters in the baggage-laden travois and carry only their bows and lances.

"I speak, yes," Stands Tall said in far more broken English than Stephanie had ever heard him use before. "We peaceful—good Indians."

So Chase came by his duplicity naturally, Stephanie thought with grim humor as she listened to the exchange. One of the men caught sight of a travois piled with beaver pelts and offered to buy them for a paltry sum, which Stands Tall refused. They haggled as the leaders around Elk Bull became increasingly restive. Then a rumble of horses' hooves sounded and more voices in English echoed across the open plain. From behind the next rise a column of cavalry out of Fort Fetterman came riding smartly toward them. Stephanie recognized the insignia and had even met the young captain who was leading the column. Every nerve in her body screamed at her to rip the covering off her hair and run to Gus Ansil.

Chase was not certain what she would do. Yesterday they had sighted the miners but only an hour ago had he run across the column of cavalry apparently sent to head off the men who were illegally bound for the gold strikes in the Black Hills to the east. There was nothing they could do but pray the soldiers would let them pass peacefully. Stands Tall was now assuring the captain that they were headed north to receive rations at Fort Stanbaugh and settle peacefully for the winter there.

The issue of rounding up all Indians on the northern plains had not yet been settled by Washington, although many commanders in the field frequently attacked villages under the pretext of hostile provocation by the Indians, charges unfounded more often than not. During the fall of 1875 matters were particularly delicate since the government was negotiating with various tribal leaders, chiefly the Sioux, in an attempt to get them to cede mineral rights to the sacred hills. Chase knew neither his Lakota allies nor the Cheyenne would ever give away their hunting grounds, but until the dust of endless talks settled, he prayed these troops would stand down during this encounter.

The warriors might be able to successfully engage both groups of whites in a fight, but in a pitched battle it would be an appalling disaster if they were encumbered with women, children and old people.

The Stephanie of old would never knowingly endanger children or old people, even to save herself. But that was the woman he remembered from another life, he reminded himself. He could not trust her now. If anything happened to cause a fight, he would be completely to blame. As the arrogant looking captain sought to end the haggling between Stands Tall and the miners, Chase reached down from Thunderbolt's back and swept Stephanie into his arms. She started to cry out but before she could do more than gasp, his mouth came down hard on hers. Stands Tall and several of the other Cheyenne leaders, who he had talked to before they encountered the enemy, all began to laugh.

"What's that buck doin'?" one miner asked.

"Him just married. Now breechclout all time fall down. Then he fall on squaw," Stands Tall replied in the guttural dialect he had affected. Now even some of the other miners and soldiers joined in the laughter.

Chase heard the captain make some lewd remark as he carried Stephanie to the back of their caravan. With one hand he held the scarf tightly around her head while he pressed her against him with the other. His superbly trained horse responded to knee commands, stopping near the end of the long line of horsedrawn travois. He knew that Stands Tall had convinced the soldiers of the reason for his dramatic gesture. Now all he had to do was make Stephanie behave like an enamored bride. The thought gave him a sudden pang. *If only she could be my bride!* Her lips were startled and soft beneath his, tasting warm and sweet as he savaged them. Her body stiffened in surprise as she kicked and flailed, trying to push him away, but he was far too strong. He deepened the kiss, taking advantage of her breathlessness by plunging his tongue inside her mouth and losing himself in the soulful hunger that had so long tormented him.

From among the cluster of women, Kit Fox watched the White Wolf carry her friend toward a big travois piled high with pelts for the cold winter camp in the mountains. He tossed her onto the pile of furs and covered her with his body as she thrashed, then grew suddenly quiescent. His whole body moved over her in a dance as ancient as time. In spite of the roughness of the initial encounter, Stephanie responded. Hesitant and inhibited as it was, the subtle relaxing, then retensing of her body gave her away. Her hands fell loose, no longer pushing against his body's invasion, and her legs ceased their thrashing. Instead her fingers curled against his shoulders and one leg instinctively raised and rubbed against his thigh. As Kit Fox watched, the movements spoke volumes to her.

They are destined to be lovers, even against their wills. Her heart ached, yet she faced the truth. Her friend did not love her white husband. The White Wolf had taken no other woman to his blankets since coming to live among the People. This was the reason. *Good-bye, White Wolf, Chase the Wind. I will grieve a while . . . then I will live once more.*

Stephanie felt the heat and hardness of his body as he slammed it into hers, driving the air from her lungs when he flung her onto the travois and followed her down into the soft furs. At least, that's why she told herself she did not cry out or fight him further. She would not respond to the harsh caresses he bestowed upon her as he forced her to lie silently beneath him, hidden from the soldiers. She *would* not. She tried lying limply beneath him at first, letting him play out the charade for the soldiers and miners. Their coarse, ugly laughter still faintly echoed but Stephanie could no longer hear it. The world receded until all her universe encompassed was the man holding her in his arms, pressing her into the soft furs. His every movement was a brazen caress, from the hot intimate invasion of his tongue in her mouth to the way his hips rocked suggestively against hers.

Her senses blazed to life, remembering how it had been between them every time they had touched before. With a small moan her hands reached up to his shoulders and her body opened to his, weeping with a want she could not comprehend, had never been able to comprehend from that first day in the snowbound country house in Massachusetts.

Then before she could utterly disgrace herself, she heard a loud command for the troops to move out, followed by the thundering vibrations of their horses' hooves. Disgruntled, the miners followed. Chase suddenly rolled off her and sprang from the travois. She lay breathless and stunned, staring at him as he stood towering over her. His breath came in gasps as if he'd run a great distance and his fists clenched and unclenched at his sides. The expression on his face was angry and at the same time agonized, as if he were in great pain.

Or had she imagined it? "It was not necessary to shame me. I would not have betrayed these people," she whispered hoarsely.

He just stared down at her for a moment. "I'm sorry. I could not risk my people's lives," he said in a low intense voice, still out of breath. He willed his rebellious body to obey him but just looking at her made it ache. The scarf covering her hair had pulled away now, revealing its bronzed splendor. Huge golden eyes glistened with tears in her small dark face. Thank heaven he had forced her to use the walnut oil. *That was not all you forced her to do*, his conscience tormented.

"You will never trust me," she said simply, too emotionally and physically wrung out to conceal her pain.

"I cannot even trust myself, Stevie," he replied. Then he spun on his heel and leaped on Thunderbolt's back, galloping away, leaving the caravan far behind.

Stephanie felt as if everyone around her were staring, but the Cheyenne were too polite for such a thing. They had surely seen the way she fell in with Chase's ruse—only what had begun as a ruse had swiftly turned into something else. Desire—but not love. Never would she dare to call it love. Red faced beneath the stain darkening her skin, she climbed from the travois with trembling legs. That was when she met Kit Fox's eyes. And looked away quickly.

"There's a civilian feller here to see you, sir," the corporal said to Lieutenant Phillips, who sat in the small cramped office of the adjutant at Fort Steele. "I tole him you was real busy. He looked sort of down at the heels, a drifter . . . but he . . ." The corporal shuffled nervously, unwilling to meet his superior's eyes. "He said he seen a white woman with an Injun who attacked his medicine show wagon and killed his partner. Said she might be an officer's wife."

"Send him in," Hugh replied tightly, dismissing the noncom. Everyone at the post knew his wife had been missing for over a week now, mysteriously vanished without a trace from the Rawlins Hotel where she and the other officers' wives were staying. Gossips who knew the Phillipses were having marital troubles whispered she had run away with another man. All he needed to make matters worse was for her to have been captured by savages!

A tall gauntly built man wearing a moth-eaten frock coat and shabby boots shuffled into the office. A sour smell of cheap whiskey and body odor filled the stuffy little room. He needed a shave and his eyes and face were ravaged by prairie winds and drink, probably more of the latter.

"I understand you had an encounter with savages, Mr. . . ." Hugh waited for the man's name, not offering him a seat. *A cheap huckster by the looks of him. He couldn't possibly know anything about Stephanie.* Still the doubt niggled.

"Wallaby. Seth Wallaby, Lieutenant . . . Phillips, ain't that yer name?" the narrow faced man said.

There was a crafty gleam in the bloodshot eyes that unnerved Hugh. "I'm Lieutenant Phillips, yes." He waited for the man to speak his piece, volunteering nothing.

"Last week, Friday, it was, er, I think," he said, scratching his thinning greasy hair, trying to retrieve the event from whiskey blurred memory. "Me 'n' my pards, Laben 'n' Marty, we run on this buck. Had him a fancy Yellow Boy Winchester. We run a circus wagon 'n' sell a little tonic on the side."

"What did the savage do, Mr. Wallaby?" Hugh's patience was wearing decidedly thin.

"Tried to buffalo us into giving him these here two Injun brats we had workin' in the show. When I said no, he up 'n' shot Laben 'n' tried to do fer me 'n' Marty. Winged Marty. We split in opposite directions. Never did find him."

Hugh could wager how diligently Wallaby had searched for his injured comrade. "And this white woman?" he said, affecting a bored tone.

"All a sudden just after the fireworks started a woman come running out of the bushes—yellin' she was a cavalry officer's wife—Stephanie Phillips. Course, I was bein' shot at by a buck with a repeater, Laben was stretched out dead 'n' Marty wounded. I couldn't get near her to save her, but I thought the army might want to know." He shuffled his feet a bit more, one well-worn muddy boot, then the other. "I, er, I heerd they might be a reward for the lady."

"Until you heard that you stayed buried in a bottle in some Rawlins saloon, though," Hugh sneered. "What did she look like, this 'lady' you couldn't rescue?"

He scratched his head. "Kindy tall fer a female with lots of long brown hair—light 'n' shiny like metal er somethin'. Oh, 'n' she wore a black dress, like she was in mournin'." He studied Phillips nervously with crafty eyes.

Hugh felt poleaxed. How the hell had the damnable woman run into a savage? "Was the buck alone or with a war party?"

"I only saw him but there was a powerful lot of shootin' goin' on. Musta been a whole bunch of 'em. I was lucky to get away. Like I said, Marty 'n' Laben, they didn't make it."

"How far from town did this take place?"

Wallaby shrugged. "We got lost comin' from Cheyenne. Musta overshot the turn off to Rawlins. I ain't sure."

"And I imagine you aren't sure what tribe the buck was, either."

"Cudda been Sioux, mebbee Arap, or even Cheyenne, I reckon. But whatever he was, he was big, 'n' tall 'n' pure mean."

Hugh pulled a five-dollar banknote from his pocket and shoved it across the desk. "I better not hear anything about this matter or you'll answer to me, Wallaby," he said, indicating the man was dismissed.

Wallaby looked into those deadly cold dark eyes and shuddered. He needed a drink. Clutching the banknote he backed out of the room, nodding his assent.

But the gossip spread all too quickly once the first whispers about the snake oil man's visit were out. Wallaby had spoken to several people in town, once he sobered up enough to learn there was a Lieutenant Phillips at the nearby fort whose wife was missing. A drummer stopped off at the post from Rawlins, discussing with several troopers whether or not the female whom Wallaby had seen was the officer's missing lady. The corporal, eavesdropping at the door during Hugh's interview with Wallaby, quickly substantiated the fact.

By the following morning, Hugh Phillips was the object of sidelong glances and pitying looks from the officers' wives, awkward attempts at condolences, even false wishes for a blessed reunion with Stephanie from their husbands, and outright sniggering and foul jokes behind his back from the enlisted men, who detested the martinet lieutenant. If he had been eager to win military distinction before, now he became obsessed with finding Stephanie and the mysterious savage who had abducted her. He drove his men to the brink of exhaustion and past it, taking out one patrol after another, riding from first light to full dark. But weeks of scouring the foothills of southern Wyoming, from the Medicine Bows to the banks of the Sweetwater, yielded not a trace of any Indian war party or a white captive.

They did run across a pitiful bunch of Arapaho so decimated by smallpox that Hugh ordered their execution instead of taking any prisoners, then had the village fired to prevent contagion. Each time he returned to Fort Steele to face the other officers and men, his plight grew more unendurable. Soon winter would envelop the High Plains and surrounding mountains in a lethargic coat of deep white snow. When the winds howled across Wyoming, only fools ventured out.

Hugh knew the Indians were already splitting up into small bands to go to ground until spring. The odds of locating his wife were growing more remote with the passing of each day. He considered resigning his commission and going east to live in luxury on old Josiah's money, but money had only been a means to an end for him. Hugh wanted the recognition, the glory of being a general, of moving among the highest echelons of power in Washington, of showing his supercilious Southern family that his choice in attending West Point had been the correct one. Still, he despised the dust and the silence, the crude tobacco spitting troopers and opinionated settlers—he despised everything about the West. Most of all he hated the savages for threatening his plans and humiliating him by stealing his wife.

But he loved the killing.

Nothing would stop him until he had found Stephanie and her abductor and that damned renegade raider White Wolf. He would see to it they all died. Then he could return East, bathed in glory, a tragic hero. Meanwhile, he relentlessly patrolled in ever widening circles, searching tirelessly. Every opportunity he found, he attacked the Indians he located, searching their villages for a trace of Stephanie, bringing in the captives to be herded onto reservations. His energetic efforts came to the attention of General George Crook, head of the Department of the Platte. Lieutenant Phillips was commended . . . but not promoted.

Hugh's idol Custer also languished in rank, chomping at the bit during the summer and fall of 1875, albeit he ''languished'' with the rank of lieutenant colonel. On the far northern plains at Fort Lincoln, Custer had seen no outbreaks of hostility by the savages. South at Fort Steele, Hugh had at least consoled himself with the activity afforded by the White Wolf's raids. When he was not pursuing the renegade or searching for Stephanie, Hugh went into Rawlins and drowned his frustrations with cheap whiskey and cheaper women.

❧ 15 ❧

The days grew colder now that they were living in the Bighorns. The valley Chase and Stands Tall had brought them to was isolated, impossible for any army patrol to locate—if the army was even searching for her, Stephanie thought bleakly. She wondered from time to time what Hugh had thought when she vanished. Was he relieved to have her gone? Frustrated by her imagined defiance? She was certain how acutely Hugh would feel the embarrassment of having his wife desert him.

But her thoughts were seldom on her husband. They centered on Chase. He was gone now, as he was so often, off on some sort of spying mission this time. He had ridden with a saddle and worn white men's clothes, his hair unbraided and a beard bristling on his jawline. No one knew when he would return or where he had gone. At least, no one told her and she did not ask.

His avoidance of her caused both relief and heartache. She knew they could never act on the desire that had drawn them to each other over the years and the miles, but just seeing him walk across the camp or leap gracefully onto Thunderbolt's back gave her pleasure. Watching him covertly became a habit. Just knowing he was nearby gave her comfort. When he left her alone in this strange isolated place among his people, she had at first been frightened, but as the weeks wore on, she began to grow used to her new routine.

Every morning she awakened to the voice of the crier, rose and went out to watch the golden glory of sunrise in the mountains. The Bighorns were wild and magnificent and the hidden valley in which they lived was deep and fertile with clear running streams. There was even a remarkable natural hot spring that bubbled up into a series of pools. Everyone could bathe no matter how cold the weather. Wild fruit trees and bushes grew in abundance and small game was easily snared. All in all, it was an idyllically beautiful place, the sort she had fantasized about when a youthful Chase first described the West to an impressionable eight-year-old girl.

This morning she arose and donned a tunic and leggings, then pulled on a pair of the soft doeskin moccasins that were so comfortable. When she stepped outside she picked up a bucket and walked to the stream that flowed a few dozen yards from their lodge to draw fresh water as Red Bead smiled approvingly. Her second morning in camp she had used the clean water left sitting from the night before. The old woman had upbraided her for washing in "dead water." Each morning the women all drew fresh water for the day.

She made her way across the awakening camp, smiling greetings at those who had become friendly to her, bypassing others who still looked upon her as an outsider whose Blue Coat husband might yet bring them to grief. The village seemed to be split into three factions. Many were members of the Crazy Dog Society. They and their families resented Chase, mistrusting his white blood and thus, his captive. Others were grateful for the White Wolf's prowess as a warrior who could outwit the White Eyes and provide his people with weapons and supplies. They were willing to accept Stephanie. The third group simply waited to see how the strife would end, withholding judgment and their friendship from the white woman.

After splashing her face and hands in the icy waters of the river, Stephanie dried off, then completed her simple toilette by combing her hair and replaiting it into one fat long braid which hung below her waist. She lowered the bucket and filled it from the cold swift current. When she rose and headed back to Red Bead's lodge, she saw Kit Fox some distance downstream, but before she could call to her friend, a young warrior approached, smiling a shy greeting at the lovely Cheyenne. The morning air was chilly and he wore a heavy buffalo robe draped across his shoulders like a blanket. He opened it in invitation and Kit Fox stepped inside. The sounds of soft laughter echoed faintly as they stood, sheltered thus, talking in plain view of the camp. Such was the way a man courted a maid among these people. Kit Fox seemed well pleased by the comely man, whose name was Blue Eagle.

Stephanie felt a sudden pang of loneliness as she watched the young couple, then reminded herself that it was good Kit Fox had found someone who made her happy. When Chase had created that scene throwing Stephanie on the travois in front of the soldiers, she knew Kit Fox was aware of what still lay between them and had been hurt by it, abandoning her hopes of wedding the White Wolf. The white woman would not have blamed the Cheyenne if she had withdrawn her friendship, but Kit Fox remained her staunchest ally.

Now she has found someone who returns her affection. Be happy for her, Stephanie chided herself. Chase would not wed her friend. But Chase could never wed her either. Even if the insurmountable barrier of race did not separate them, Hugh would always stand between them. *What will become of me?* Forcing herself to abandon the melancholy thought, she walked briskly back to Red Bead's lodge to begin the day's chores. Today she would learn how to clean and tan the heavy buffalo hides which provided shelter, bedding and blankets.

Red Bead took the bucket of "living" water and dipped a bone ladle into it, drinking deeply, then wiped her mouth with the back of her hand and said, "Smooth Stone has gone with some of the older boys hunting rabbits. Tiny Dancer will spend the day with us while Crow Woman goes with the other women in search of the last of the grapes. Soon the frosts will kill them."

Stephanie's heart filled with joy for she loved nothing as much as watching over the winsome little girl. "I've seen some of the other girls with dolls. Could you teach me how to make one for her?"

Red Bead nodded. "If you wish. We will gather sticks and cattails for it this afternoon. Your heart is good for children."

"I always wanted children . . . but . . ."

"Sometimes the Powers withhold the gift of children. I, too, was barren." She studied Stephanie a moment as the young woman cleared away the simple breakfast. "I knew it was my lack, for my husband had children with his second wife. Perhaps your man, not you, was the one at fault."

Stephanie colored with embarrassment at the matter-of-fact way Cheyenne women discussed such intimate matters. The first time her monthly flow had begun, Red Bead had explained to her about their custom of sequestering menstruating women in a "moon hut" for the duration of her cycle. The blood taboos of their society seemed primitive but she had been even more distressed by the open discussion of bodily functions. Yet in spite of their candor in regard to speaking about sex, Cheyenne women were every bit as chaste as the most moral of white society. Courting couples did no more than innocently share a robe the way she had seen Kit Fox and Blue Eagle do. There were no whores and no marital infidelities among these people.

She floundered for a reply to Red Bead's speculations about Hugh. "I . . . I don't know if my husband had other children." Lord knows, learning of his repeated infidelities, he could have left a string of bastards from Baltimore to Bismarck. "We have only been married for three years." She could not explain their estrangement or the humiliating reasons Hugh had quit her bed. It might well give Red Bead ideas about matchmaking between her and Chase.

"Three years is plenty time to make a baby," the old woman said with a grunt. "Come, we work now."

They stepped outside the lodge into the cold. A stiff wind had arisen with the hint of a few frosty flakes of snow in it. Stephanie did not look forward to working outdoors all morning. When they collected Tiny Dancer, the little girl seemed impervious to the icy wind, dressed warmly now in a long-sleeved deerskin tunic and high leggings. She skipped alongside Stephanie, chattering happily in a hybrid of English and Cheyenne. The latter she endeavored to teach Stephanie.

As they approached the place where three large hides had been staked out on the ground, she observed the women rigging a windbreak around the area. They drove lodge poles into the earth at regular intervals and stretched lodge rolls across the spaces between them. Inside the shelter several small fires burned, affording warmth in which the women could kneel on the cold ground to scrape and cure the raw skins. Red Bead handed her an adz made of bone and illustrated how to use it. Stephanie set to work, letting the hard repetitious task cleanse her mind of troubling thoughts about Chase Remington.

Chase sat in the small shabby tent on the outside of the old frontier trading settlement of Fort Laramie, now the largest army post in southern Wyoming Territory. The waitress in the crude restaurant, an Arapaho woman, poured him a second cup of coffee as he scanned the newspapers in front of him. The information was several months old and not encouraging. Zachariah Chandler, former senator from Michigan and lifelong friend of George Armstrong Custer, had been appointed secretary of the interior. An avid expansionist, Chandler shared the views of Sheridan and Custer with regard to Indian removal. The Interior Department had been the last frail bastion against the onslaught of white settlers into the territories of Dakota, Montana and Wyoming.

The net is tightening with the passage of each season, he thought grimly. The Union Pacific Railroad ran seventy miles below the fort, effectively sealing off the Arkansas River hunting grounds to the south. Even though the stock market panic in 1873 had temporarily halted Jay Cooke's plans for construction of the Northern Pacific through Montana, Chase knew it was only a matter of a few years before it, too, would encroach. When he first began raiding as the White Wolf, he had resigned himself to dying as a warrior, but he had hoped to preserve for a short while longer the freedom of his people, even though he knew their way of life was doomed.

But that was before Stephanie had come back into his life. He wanted to live for her, with her, to have children and build a life with her. But where? How? He could not turn his back on the Cheyenne and she could not live as his mother had. Even if she could, Stephanie was bound by her vows to the Blue Coat Phillips, the very man who had brought him to Fort Laramie. The man he planned to kill. And once he had done so, he knew she would never forgive him.

When Chase had left the stronghold, his original purpose was to scout out a likely target for his raiders. The army would not expect them to strike during the winter. However, the more he drifted, the more tales he heard of the intrepid Indian killer, Lieutenant Hugh Phillips. Chase's plans changed. Now, he stalked the two-legged predator who had slaughtered so many of his people.

He had spent the past month traveling from one small army outpost to another, always a few days behind the damned butcher, who had become a worse scourge on the plains than Custer, Crooke and Mackenzie combined. In his pursuit of the White Wolf, Phillips systematically hunted down, searched out and destroyed every Cheyenne, Arapaho and Sioux village he could find. Chase had to face the fact that abducting the man's wife had added to his fanatical zeal. Before Phillips had been politic and cautious, attacking only when there was some slim pretext of Indian provocation to justify the wanton slaughter, but now he charged in, saber drawn, to give no quarter as Chivington and Custer had done at Sand Creek and Washita. He was a mad dog and Chase meant to stop him. He knew it was something that needed to be done, a matter of simple justice, regardless of the old enmity he felt for Phillips, regardless of the woman. Yet he still felt guilty prosecuting a personal vendetta. This was a weight on his conscience he would have to bear the rest of his brief life, a life alone, apart from all others.

What will I do about Stevie? Once her husband was dead,

Chase could send her home to Boston. Since old Josiah, too, was dead, she would be a wealthy widow with good prospects for remarriage, this time to a man of better character than Hugh Phillips. The idea of Stephanie with another husband did not sit well but he pushed the thought aside. Right now his task was to deal with Phillips.

The lieutenant was having dinner with the post commander after another "successful mission." He had ridden in yesterday, herding with him the pitiful remnants of an Arapaho band. Chase had learned the lieutenant favored a bit of entertainment on the seamier side, frequenting brothels and saloons in the towns and outposts along his way. For some utterly perverse reason known only to the twisted workings of Phillips's sick mind, lately he preferred to use Indian or mixed blooded women and he used them hard. Like most army outposts in the region, Fort Laramie boasted several such establishments. Setting aside the newspaper, Chase tossed some coins on the table to pay for his meal, then left the tent. It was getting dark. Phillips would be on the prowl shortly. So would he. Within half an hour he had located the lieutenant in a big old two-story clapboard structure called the Burning Bush Saloon and Palace of Pulchritude.

Since Indians were not allowed as customers, he sneaked into the place through a back window on the second floor by climbing a rotted old trellis that had supported rose vines in the establishment's better days. Once inside the dim hallway, he wrinkled his nose at the smell of cheap whiskey and stale sweat. The air was heavy with the musk of sex, couplings done roughly and repeatedly by the occupants of the long rows of tawdry rooms. He had no idea which one belonged to Phillips's partner, but knowing the man's predilections, he figured he'd soon hear enough to give away the location. Grunts and moans sounded through the thin warped doors as he moved soundlessly down the hall. At the fourth door he heard a pitiful thin cry of a woman, pleading in the Lakota tongue and Phillips's muttered oaths as he struck her repeatedly. The ugly sounds brought no one from downstairs to intercede.

Chase tried the door, which was unlocked. Easing his knife from its sheath, he slipped noiselessly inside. In the pale green light cast by a cheap chartreuse shade on an oversized lamp, he looked at the hellish scene. Phillips had his back to the door, kneeling on a bed behind a slender dark-skinned girl with long black hair. She was naked, tied to the heavy iron bedpost facedown, on her knees, writhing in pain as her tormentor pinched and slapped her buttocks. His belt, lying beside him on the bed, had already left an angry crisscross of welts on her soft flesh.

"You like it—say it, dammit, you red-skinned bitch— say you want it," he rasped out, pulling the turgid member from his open fly and ramming it into her anus. She screamed loudly, trying to escape from him.

Hugh was so intent on his lust he did not hear Chase approach the bed, but the shadow cast by the lamp alerted him to an intruder. He whirled around, pulling away from the whimpering girl and seizing his belt. In one swift movement he snapped it hard in Chase's face. Chase partially blocked the wicked blow with his forearm and reached for the belt with his free hand, trying to yank it out of Phillips's grasp. Refusing to release his end of the doubled up heavy leather, the lieutenant dodged the deadly arc of his foe's knife as he instinctively reached for his pistol only to find it was not there. The weapon lay beside his hat, tossed carelessly on the room's one rickety chair. He leaped from the bed, giving up the tug of war to escape his attacker's knife.

"You breed bastard! You won't escape this time," he snarled, recognizing the man who had scarred his cheek.

"I don't think you'll be in any shape to stop me—or to abuse any more helpless women," Chase replied, advancing with his knife.

Phillips lunged for the chair but Chase kicked it over before Hugh could reach the pistol. With a feral growl, the officer swung a looping right that landed high on the left side of Remington's head and grabbed his knife arm. They went down, crashing across the floor, struggling desperately for control of the blade. Used to the rough sport of wrestling among the Cheyenne, Chase quickly pinned Phillips's legs on the floor, then began to force the knife nearer and nearer his throat. The half-breed could feel the lieutenant's arm giving way and became a bit too confident.

Suddenly Phillips released his grip and jerked his upper body so the blade plunged into the rough wooden floor, missing his throat by a scant inch. Using Chase's momentum against him, he broke the hold pinning his legs and at the same time struck Chase's hand as it gripped the knife, trying to free it. The blade went flying across the floor, out of either man's reach.

Hugh caught sight of his gun which had fallen beneath the overturned chair. He rolled away from Remington and seized it, pointing it at his foe's chest. "Now, you breed bastard, I'm going to work my way up from your knees to your cock, then your gut. By the time I'm out of bullets, you'll be begging for me to kill you." As he spoke, he lowered the gun slightly and aimed.

Neither man had paid any attention to the girl on the bed as she untied the ropes that bound her wrists, using her teeth. She huddled in the center of the bed for a moment watching the desperate fight. Then she inched her way to the edge of the bed and reached down to pick up the knife which Chase had lost. An instant before Hugh fired, she plunged the blade into his back. Hugh felt the knife sink in, too high to be fatal, deflected by his shoulder blade. His shot went wild, hitting Remington high to the right on his chest. With a gasp of agony he jerked around, almost losing purchase on the gun.

As Hugh turned, Chase lunged forward and pulled the blade free. The lieutenant whirled back but could not get off another shot before the knife bit into his belly. Chase would have pulled it up and gutted his hated enemy, but suddenly the door burst open. A burly guard from downstairs raised an ancient Walker Colt and fired at the intruder. As Chase rolled away, he could feel the scalding pain where Hugh's bullet had ripped through muscle and sinew, but he was up on his feet even as the guard fired a second shot and missed again.

Hugh lay deathly still as Chase dove through the window onto the porch roof. He slid to its edge, then dropped to the ground while the guard yelled for help and emptied his revolver. The raider ran into the dark alley where he had tied his horse, thinking, *That bastard Phillips will be the one begging to die by morning . . : if he's still alive.*

The sound of women's high-pitched screams and men's curses filled the night air. ''The lieutenant's dead! Some breed gutted him,'' the guard yelled.

''Louie says Phillips nailed the bastard good before he died. He shouldn't get far,'' another cried.

Chase dragged himself onto the dun's back, glad of the big gelding's endurance. He had a long hard ride ahead of him—if he did not bleed to death like Phillips.

Stephanie was out gathering firewood when she and the other women with her heard the outcry. The few sentences of Cheyenne she had learned were insufficient to understand what was being said but she had picked up the words White Wolf. Anxiously she turned to Kit Fox and asked, ''What are they saying?''

Her friend's face suddenly bleached of its natural coppery hue. ''The White Wolf has returned and he is injured!''

Tossing down their bundles of wood, they ran toward the center of camp, soon spying Chase's big dun gelding walking slowly. His rider slumped across his neck, covered with blood, looking more dead than alive. As Chase began to slide from the dun's back, Stands Tall and Elk Bull reached up and lifted him down, then, each taking an arm, they half carried, half dragged him inside Stands Tall's lodge.

Stephanie stood frozen with shock. He could die in this savage wilderness! She had always known, from the time he left her in Boston, that his life with the Cheyenne would be dangerous. Learning about his dual identity and the raids had increased her awareness a hundredfold but somehow the image of him lying bloody and cold, shot dead, had never been real before. It was now. She worked her way through the murmuring crowd toward the lodge, never even thinking about what his death would mean to a white captive left alone among hostile Indians hundreds of miles from civilization. This was Chase, the only man she had ever loved, even if it was a forbidden love. *He cannot die!*

Elk Bull stood guarding the door and upon seeing her approach, he braced his feet apart and crossed his arms, a formidable warrior whose impassive face revealed nothing. It was apparent he would not let her pass.

"Please. You must let me help. I'm a nurse—a healer." She reached frantically through her limited vocabulary in his language and came up with the words, "medicine woman," pressing her fist to her chest to emphasize the point.

The big man remained unmoved but from inside Stands Tall heard her plea and pulled open the skin covering. Elk Bull stood aside then and she entered the dim interior. Red Bead and the shaman Sitting Medicine worked over Chase's unconscious body. He was breathing shallowly as his great-aunt cut away the bloodied shirt from his injured shoulder.

Stephanie knelt beside the old woman while Sitting Medicine chanted, keeping a watchful eye on the white captive. "He's lost a lot of blood. It's a wonder he made it back here."

"He rode from Fort Laramie," Red Bead said matter-of-factly.

"That must be over two hundred miles," Stephanie whispered, looking at the waxy pallor beneath his bronzed skin.

Red Bead instructed Stephanie, "Go and gather more red dock and make a paste. I do not have enough here. I have shown you how. It dries in the winter sun, growing along the river's edge."

Stephanie knew the plant helped clot the blood when poulticed over a wound. She ran from the lodge to the river and did as she was bidden, returning quickly as images of Chase's blood-soaked clothing flashed in her mind. As she reentered the lodge with the medicine, Chase's eyes fluttered open and focused on her, pain and fever clouded, yet flickering with recognition. *Stevie.* Had he said her name aloud? She was not certain if his lips moved but she felt the jolt of communication deep in her heart.

"Send her away. She disturbs the Spirits," Sitting Medicine said to Red Bead in Cheyenne.

But before the old woman could reply, Chase's hand reached out and clutched Stephanie's as she knelt at his side. She stroked the long black hair from his fevered brow, caressing his face. "Don't you dare die on me, Chase Remington. I won't let you. Your people need you." *I need you!*

Red Bead turned to Sitting Medicine. "I think the Spirits are content," she said simply.

"It is his white blood, then, that wins him in the end. I can do nothing for a white man." The fat old man stood up. Gathering his robes regally around him, he stalked from the lodge.

Stephanie did not require fluency to understand the gist of the exchange. "We must save him, Red Bead," she whispered. The old woman merely grunted, then continued cleaning the wound. When she made ready to apply the poultice, Stephanie asked, "Has the bullet come out the back?"

"It is still inside," Red Bead replied. "We can do nothing for that."

"He will die of blood poisoning or infection if we don't take it out."

"He has lost much blood already. He can not lose more," the old woman said, but she looked at Stephanie with a measuring gaze as if trying to decide what she should do.

"I've seen white doctors remove bullets from soldiers . . . I can do it," she added after a moment's hesitation.

Red Bead knew most warriors shot by the Long Knives died if the bullets remained inside. She, too, hesitated for a bit, then nodded. "You will need a knife."

Stephanie took the slender boning knife the old woman offered her and laid it in the fire with trembling hands. She had assisted post surgeons several times when soldiers were brought in with gunshot wounds. Although the skill levels among army physicians were not particularly high in spite of their medical degrees, they had ether and scalpels. Could she do as she had said? If this were any man but Chase she would not find it half so daunting. Yet he would surely die if she did not try . . . but he might also die because she did. What would be her fate if the Cheyenne believed she had killed her captor? Stephanie realized that it did not matter. If Chase died, her life meant nothing at all to her. Willing herself to stop shaking, she picked up the blade, now sterilized by the flames. "Be ready with the poultice to stop the bleeding as soon as I get out the bullet," she said to Red Bead.

"He will need chickada to help him sleep and feverweed to rub over his body to bring out the sweats," Red Bead said late that night. Both women were bone weary. After digging out the ugly lump of lead, Stephanie had been terrified that the ordeal would kill him. He had awakened at the first probe of her knife but clenched his teeth after looking at her and saying, "Do it."

She had. Midway he had passed out and then the blood from her probing had welled out in a frightening amount. Calmly Red Bead had poulticed the clean wound and the red dock did stop the flow after a few moments—the longest of Stephanie's life. They watched over him until past moonset when the fever came on and he began to thrash and moan.

The old woman dug into the big buckskin sack holding her various medicines and retrieved several items. First she steeped an infusion from chickada leaves and stems and spooned it between Chase's lips as Stephanie held his head. When the restless tossing abated a bit Red Bead nodded in satisfaction.

Stephanie was unfamiliar with feverweed and watched as the old woman mixed the herb with sweet grass, then soaked it in a bowl of water. "Rub it on his skin—all over," she said, pulling away the covers in the warm lodge. When she began unfastening the fly of his pants, Stephanie swallowed nervously. "All over?" she echoed.

"All over," Red Bead replied with a hint of a smile, as she pulled the pants off, leaving Chase lying naked on the pallet. The old woman took a fistful of the herbal concoction and began to massage it up one arm. Hesitantly Stephanie did the same for his other arm, beginning with his long elegant fingers. How beautiful his hands were. She remembered how they had felt caressing her body, cradling her face as he kissed her. Thoughts like that were dangerous. She suppressed them. Just as they worked their way to his chest, Red Bead stopped. "You see how it is done. Now finish it. Then repeat each time he grows hotter until fever breaks. I am tired and must sleep." With that announcement, she stood up and slipped through the door, leaving the white woman alone with Chase.

Unable to stop herself, Stephanie looked down at his body. Once when she was half-frozen and semiconscious, helpless, he had looked on her naked body, touching it intimately, warming her to save her life. Now she must save his life. Had he looked at her, studied her flesh the way she longed to feast her eyes on his? Had she been as beautiful to him as he was to her?

"Stop it," she commanded herself, taking a fresh handful of the sopping herbs and plopping it on his chest. Doggedly she set to work, trying not to think about what she was doing as her hands rubbed gently downward, following the arrow descent of hair across his hard belly which pointed to the heavy patch at the juncture of his thighs where his sex lay. Avoiding that forbidden territory, she began to work on his legs beginning with his feet, moving upward. When she reached the same inevitable destination a few moments later, she paused. Surely Red Bead did not mean *there*!

All over echoed in her mind.

All over it would be. Easier said than done. For all the nursing she had done, never had she handled a man—any man, much less this one—so intimately. In the post hospitals the soldiers were always covered below the waist and male orderlies took care of their personal needs. She gathered her courage and continued, working gingerly around his genitals with the cool wet grasses. When his staff swelled a bit and twitched reflexively, she jumped back. Then realizing he was unconscious, she resumed her ministrations. She was merely curious about how male anatomy worked, she told herself, in spite of the heat flaming in her cheeks. In three years of marriage, she had never once looked upon Hugh's naked body—and never wanted to. But this was different . . . this was Chase.

Chase, who is deathly ill, she reminded herself as she began to dry off his fevered body. He was burning up, his skin dry to her touch. She started to spread the buffalo robe over him, then realized it was far too heavy. The lodge fire burned brightly, warming the tightly knit interior which held chill late autumn winds at bay. She needed something lighter with which to cover him. Then an inspiration struck her.

In moments she had returned clutching a bundle of soft black and white cloth—the dress and petticoats she'd worn when he kidnapped her. Washed and folded away these past months, the impractical garments would now serve a useful purpose. Of course she had to cut open the gathered waistbands on the skirt and voluminous slips but in a few moments she had a soft, lightweight bedsheet of sorts. Spreading it over him, she marveled at all the yards and yards of cloth she had worn in white civilization. "No wonder I was always so hot in summer," she murmured as she smoothed the covering.

Stephanie drowsed by the fire, checking him every quarter hour or so. She repeated the massage with the feverweed twice more but saw no improvement. Stands Tall entered the lodge just as she completed a treatment. She was embarrassed at the intimacy of the act and quickly covered Chase's naked body.

"Is he any better?" his uncle asked.

"No . . . but no worse either. If only I could get the fever to break," she said in despair.

Stands Tall knelt by Chase's side and turned his troubled gaze to the woman. "You love him."

A denial sprang to her lips but she did not voice it. "It does not matter what I feel. I am married to another."

"Perhaps," was his enigmatic reply. "I will watch now while you sleep a little." He sat back, indicating she should take the other pallet, which she belatedly realized was his. This lodge belonged to him, yet he had left her to tend

Chase and gone elsewhere, probably to the lodge she shared with Red Bead.

Stephanie would have protested but knew there was nothing she could do. A few hours of sleep would not hurt Chase and would make her a better nurse. She did as he said. Near dawn Chase began to thrash and toss restlessly, awakening her from the exhausted slumber into which she'd fallen. His teeth chattered as chills wracked his body.

"I will summon Red Bead. Do what you can for him," Stands Tall said as Stephanie quickly moved to Chase's side and replaced the light covers with the buffalo robe. She nodded to Stands Tall and he left. The only remedy at hand was the feverweed but surely it would not serve while chills gripped him. She leaned over him, willing her body's warmth to touch him, cupping his face in her hands, letting her warm breath touch it.

Red Bead entered and silently witnessed the gesture. As she walked closer, Stephanie became aware of her and pulled away. "What should we do? He has chills now," she said to the old woman.

"Wash with feverweed one more time, then lie with him," Red Bead replied calmly, pulling down the blanket and setting to work.

"Lie with him?" Stephanie's voice sounded as if she'd swallowed a burr.

"Body heat," was the laconic reply as she finished with the feverweed.

Stephanie hesitated for only a moment and then started to lie down beside Chase.

"Take off dress."

Startled, the white woman looked up at Red Bead. "My dress?" Now she sounded as if she had swallowed two burrs. "No! I can't . . . It would be . . . wrong . . . bad."

The old woman snorted impatiently. "Stephanie"—the name came out "Sta-fan-nee"—"are you weak here?" She patted the side of her head. "Doeskin gives no heat. Flesh to flesh gives heat."

Stephanie glanced at the unconscious Chase and then back to his aunt. "You don't understand . . ."

Red Bead made a chopping motion with her open hand, cutting off the explanation. "I understand. Hear me. Among the People you are the White Wolf's captive so there is no wrong. Among the whites, this man is . . . a patient, a sick one. He will not even know you warm him. No wrong. He needs the heat of your flesh to call his spirit back to his body. Call him back to us, Sta-fan-nee."

Stephanie swallowed, then quickly slipped out of her tunic and slid beside Chase on the pallet, pulling the robe over them. She lay on his left side, careful not to touch his injured right shoulder.

The old woman watched as his fevered thrashing subsided. "It will be good," she murmured to herself as she left the lodge with a smile on her face.

Alone with Chase, her naked body pressed to his, Stephanie whispered softly, "Now who's the liar? The Cheyenne *do* torture their captives."

Chase awakened slowly to the dull throbbing ache in his shoulder. He tried to move, then felt the softness of a woman's body. Without turning his head he knew. Stevie. Even without her apple blossom perfume she possessed an essence all her own. The covers provided a warm cocoon with her snuggled closely against him. A strand of long bronze hair feathered across his cheek. In spite of the weakness of fever and the pain of his wound, he felt a sense of contentment the like of which he could not recall. He remembered her with the knife, digging Hugh's bullet from him, hesitant and pale but her hand steady. She had more grit than any woman he had ever known . . . even his mother. Nothing, not even a demented sadist like Phillips, had been able to break her. Turning his head against the luxuriant curtain of her hair, he drifted back to sleep.

Stephanie blinked her eyes, suddenly awake in Chase's lodge, lying with her body fused intimately to his. Carefully she moved away from him, sliding from beneath the robes and pulling on her tunic. Only when she had removed her body from such intimate proximity to his did she reach out and touch his forehead. A light film of moisture dampened it but his skin felt almost normal. The feverweed and her body heat had worked! She began to gather up the bowls and utensils when she felt his eyes on her. Slowly, her hands stilled and her lashes fluttered up as she looked at him. "Your fever's broken." It seemed an idiotic statement but was the first thing that popped into her head.

"I'm afraid I stink of sweat . . . and that it's rubbed off on you." He enjoyed watching her blush. "In spite of months working in the sun your complexion still gives you away," he said in a husky voice.

"I . . . I must summon Stands Tall and Red Bead. They'll want to know you're going to be all right." She leaped up to get away from him.

"Wait, Stevie, please." He saw her hesitate but then she turned back to him. "I thank you for saving my life."

"I would've done the same for any injured man."

"Even sleeping naked beside him?"

That old teasing light was back in his eyes, the same way it had been in Boston. She found herself returning his smile. "You did the same for me. I owed you."

"All I did was warm you, not dig a bullet from your shoulder."

"I was terrified, Chase. You lost so much blood. I thought I'd killed you at first. How did it happen—who shot you?"

His expression sobered and a wary look came into his eyes. How could he make her understand? Damn, no matter if Phillips was her husband, she was better off with him dead. "It was Hugh Phillips."

She felt everything go black and the ground began to spin for a moment. Taking a deep breath she asked, "Did you kill him?"

"Yes . . . with my knife."

She knew he'd dressed as a tame Indian and ridden into a fort or a town to spy. "You didn't encounter Hugh on a raid, or by chance, did you?"

He met her level gaze openly. "No: I intended to kill him—but not for the reason you think," he added as she hugged herself and started to turn away. "He was a rabid wolf, Stevie, hunting down every small band he could find, attacking them as they slept, butchering women and children. Even Custer never pursued a mad vendetta like that. It had to stop.''

"And you were the one to stop him.'' Her eyes stung with tears. "He'd been searching for me, hadn't he, Chase?"

He could not deny it. "Yes—to kill you. You must know that.''

"But I never . . .'' Her voice faded. Hugh would never have believed that she'd remained untouched. After all, hadn't all the officers' wives assured her it was their duty to take their own lives rather than fall into the hands of savages? Just living with the Cheyenne had contaminated her. She would be an embarrassment to him, a humiliating object of pity, another reason for him to be denied promotion. "Yes, he probably would want me dead,'' she said, her voice beyond sadness, sapped of all emotion. She turned away and opened the tent flap.

"Stevie, you're better off without him.''

Her eyes were glacial when she looked back over her shoulder. "Do you expect me to thank you for killing my husband for me?''

"I didn't kill him for you. I would have done it anyway, dammit.''

"How can I believe you? Even if I could, how can that make it right? He was my husband and you took his life. Dead as much as alive, he'll always be between us, Chase.'' She stepped through the opening, leaving him alone in the lodge. He did not try to stop her this time.

Over the following weeks Chase mended swiftly. Stephanie avoided him as much as possible, spending her days with Kit Fox and the other unmarried young women. As her command of the language improved a bit she approached Crow Woman who allowed her to share in caring for Smooth Stone and Tiny Dancer. Among the Cheyenne, watching over children was always a communal responsibility. Her love of the children and her willingness to learn and work with the other women earned her the trust of many of the villagers. If everyone wondered why the White Wolf did not take her to his blankets or at least use her body as his slave, no one was impolite enough to speak of it in front of her.

As soon as he was strong enough, Chase joined the other men in their duties around the camp, repairing war weapons, standing sentry duty and overseeing the training of the young boys as warriors. One morning he took Smooth Stone, along with several other little boys, to practice snaring rabbits.

"This is how you set the snare." He showed them, holding up the little rawhide loop with its slip knot. "Be certain you conceal it carefully, just so, but not so much that it won't slide fast enough when your quarry is ready to be snagged." The lessons continued as each boy took his turn fastening the snare and finding a spot on a rabbit run in which to conceal it. As Chase watched, giving encouragement, Smooth Stone sat down beside him, glum and silent. "What is wrong, little brother?"

"You and Stephanie never speak anymore," he said in serviceable Cheyenne. "My sister says she is very sad. Why do you not take her to your blankets?"

A grimly ironic smile touched Chase's lips. *The very question I've been asking myself.* "It is difficult to explain white people's ways to a Cheyenne," he said carefully.

"She is very beautiful, even if she is a white woman . . . and you, too, have white blood so that should not matter," the boy persisted.

"It is not her blood—or mine that is the problem, Smooth Stone. I killed her husband and she cannot forgive me."

"But everyone says he was an evil man. Surely she did not love him."

"No, she did not . . . but he was her husband and that makes her feel all the more guilty for his death. It is very complicated."

The boy sighed. "She should not be angry with you. Maybe if you brought her presents she would be happy and forgive you," Smooth Stone ventured hopefully.

Chase ruffled his shiny black hair and smiled sadly. He would never have a son of his own. The Remington blood would die out with his generation. Perhaps this was the way the Powers intended for things to be. "I will think on what you have said, Smooth Stone," he replied gravely.

From the hillside across the creek, Stephanie watched Chase with the boys. *What a good father he would make.*

Kit Fox observed where her friend's eyes strayed and she smiled. "Blue Eagle and I are to wed at the Freezing Moon. There would be great rejoicing among our people if you and the White Wolf were to wed also."

What could she say? That Chase was a murderer? Or that she was so riven with guilt she could not sleep at night for loving him instead of mourning Hugh?

"Yesterday I overheard Stands Tall and Red Bead talking," Smooth Stone confided to his sister a few days later. "They say the White Wolf will soon be strong enough to leave the winter stronghold and go raiding again."

"If only we could do something to make him and Stephanie join their lives before he has gone," Tiny Dancer said.

"That is what his aunt and uncle said, too," he replied with excitement. But then he added glumly, "They decided it was up to the Powers to decide if their fates are truly to be one."

"Then we can do nothing." She sighed, clutching the doll Stephanie had made her.

"I have a plan," her brother ventured, then proceeded to tell her about it.

A few days later the first snowfall of the winter occurred, turning the rich golds, browns and reds of autumn color to dazzling white. By afternoon the sun shone brightly and the children all ran to the hillside with their sledges made of buffalo ribs, eager to slide on the fresh snow before it melted away. Both Chase and Stephanie joined the crowd of adults watching the little ones' antics, but among dozens of spectators, they managed to stay well clear of each other. They both had their eyes riveted on the two Crow children as they slid down the hill repeatedly, shrieking and giggling.

"Come, watch me, White Wolf!" Smooth Stone yelled at his hero. He then picked up the sledge and ran toward another slope some distance away where the ground was not so smooth and open. Tiny Dancer, who left her brother and ran breathlessly into Stephanie's arms, distracted her as Chase followed her brother. Then she tugged on Stephanie's hand. "Come, Smooth Stone has found a new place to sail our sledge." With that she dashed off.

Smiling, Stephanie sprinted behind her. Not until she walked clear of a copse of snow-laden yellow pines did she spy Chase watching the children climb aboard their sledge and take off. She stood back silently.

Suddenly the sledge veered into a bank of snow-laden hawthorn and tipped over. A loud wail echoed up the hill. Chase skidded down the slope from one direction while Stephanie came running from the other. They nearly collided as they reached the bushes. Chase knelt down and pulled Tiny Dancer from beneath the overturned little sledge. She ran into Stephanie's arms, saying, "That was such fun!"

"Then why did you cry out?" Stephanie asked suspiciously.

The little girl looked abashedly over to her brother, who was tugging his sledge from the bushes as Chase watched. "I was excited," she replied.

"Now we will go for another ride," Smooth Stone said, seizing his sister's hand. The conspirators dashed off, pulling the sledge behind them, leaving Chase and Stephanie standing in the shelter of the tall pines, alone.

She stood, unable to tear her eyes from him. He looked like a dark sentinel against the whiteness, dressed with rich wolfskins thrown across one broad shoulder. Light flecks of snow sparkled like diamond dust in his raven hair. His eyes glittered like his namesake's as they swept hungrily over her. She tried to break the spell. "That was a dangerous thing for them to do."

"I'll speak with Smooth Stone. I rather imagine he was the instigator," he replied.

"He meant well," she said awkwardly, knowing she should turn and leave him at once. But she did not.

He drank in her loveliness. Her face was framed by a soft doeskin hood trimmed with beaver. Even swathed in heavy winter clothes, he could scent the female heat of her. She was as no other woman to him. "They want us to come together. You are my captive. No one understands why I do not take you. It must be my white blood," he added with a bitter smile.

When he raised one hand and brushed a bit of snow from her cheek, she closed her eyes in agony. "Don't . . . please." And still she did not walk away. Her conscience screamed for her to do it, but her heart refused.

He lowered his hand, still standing close to her. Their breaths mingled, tiny puffs of white, like clouds colliding and merging in the crisp, bright air. "I'm leaving with my warriors tomorrow," he said at length.

"Kit Fox and Blue Eagle are to be wed in less than a month. Will he return in time?" She could have bitten her tongue. She should not have spoken of weddings.

"I'll bring Blue Eagle back in plenty of time." He hesitated, then said, "I still want you, Stevie. Nothing will ever change that."

"You've changed that," she said flatly. "Where do you go tomorrow? Off to burn and loot some more, to kill more soldiers?"

He felt her words like a lash tearing into his flesh. Pain and anger rose in equal portions as he fought the urge to take her in his arms and shake her . . . but he knew if he did he'd soon be ravishing her instead. "You've seen what those soldiers do—don't deny it. They're killing these people!" He flung out his hand toward the circle of lodges nestled in the valley below. "Every year game is scarcer, slaughtered wantonly by whites who leave the meat to rot on the earth. Every year we die of smallpox and diphtheria, measles and cholera—all gifts of the white man.

"While I was in Fort Laramie I learned Custer's old

friend Zachariah Chandler is the new interior secretary. You know what that means for the treaty lands guaranteed us on the High Plains. Grant will let Sheridan unleash Crook and Custer on us come spring. What do you expect us to do, Stevie? Throw down our weapons, trudge onto those reservations and wait to die?''

She knew all he said was true. In her years on military posts she'd seen the brutal and even illegal way the army often handled the ''bloodthirsty savages.'' In her months with the Cheyenne she'd come to see them as human beings, with a society that was compassionate and good, possessing laws and morals more uniformly obeyed than any white civilization's. Rubbing her temples, she shook her head, confused and torn, not knowing any answer. ''I don't want these people to die but I can't stop what's happening and neither can you. I can't help it that I'm white . . . and neither can you!'' She turned and ran through the blinding brightness of the snow, leaving him alone to ponder her enigmatic words.

The next morning Chase, mounted on Thunderbolt, rode out at daybreak with his warriors all barbarously painted for war. No one knew when they would return. It was rumored they were after a supply train bound for the Black Hills gold camps.

Stephanie worked inside the warm lodge she shared with Red Bead. ''I would tell you a story,'' the old woman said, never breaking her steady rhythm, pounding a smooth rock to crush dried medicinal herbs.

Stephanie nodded, expecting to hear some tale about Sweet Medicine, the great Cheyenne prophet who had given them their laws and customs. She continued her struggle to master the intricacies of beadwork on the dress she was making.

''Did you ever meet the mother of the White Wolf in your city?''

The question startled her and she stabbed the needle into her finger. Sucking on it, she shook her head. ''No. Anthea Remington was . . . very ill after she returned to Boston.''

"Here she was called Freedom Woman." Red Bead smiled, something she rarely did. "She came as a captive, like you, taken by my nephew, Vanishing Grass, from a wagon train bound for Oregon. She had a white husband but he was killed during the raid. I do not think he was kind to her."

Stephanie felt her heart begin skipping beats. Why was the old woman telling her this? Was it true? She laid down her dress and waited politely in the Cheyenne manner for Red Bead to continue her tale as she wished.

"Vanishing Grass fell in love with her, for she was courageous and very beautiful with hair yellow as the summer sun at noon. She had married the white man only to escape her family. She came to approve our ways and was adopted into the tribe. Anthea Remington chose the name Freedom Woman, saying at last she had a life where she was free—a true home here in our land. That was when my nephew offered to take her to his blankets as wife. She saw it as an honor for she knew he could have taken her as a slave. She came to love him very much and she bore him a son."

"Chase," Stephanie said softly.

"He was called Chase the Wind then, a boy who was always getting into trouble ... like Smooth Stone. They were happy until the Long Knives came riding into our winter camp when he was six years old. We did not know to hide in the mountains then as we do now. We were camped by what the white men now call the Republican River. The buffalo ran as a solid black wall for miles then, but the soldiers would not let us hunt. They said we must come to their fort and let the White Father in Washington feed us. When our leaders refused to move, they burned our lodges and killed our warriors. Vanishing Grass died valiantly and Stands Tall was gravely injured. We were forced to march many miles in the cold. There was little food. When her son grew ill, Freedom Woman revealed to the soldiers at the fort that she was white."

"To save him."

Red Bead nodded. "We never saw them again until he returned as a youth of fourteen summers. He had left his mother in your city and fled in search of us. His heart was troubled but he never spoke of it. Or of her. He became a brave warrior in the seasons he spent with Black Kettle's band, for that was where we fled when Stands Tall led us from Fort Riley to the Arkansas River country.''

"And they recaptured him when Custer attacked at Washita.''

"They carried him away in chains, screaming that he would die a Cheyenne rather than live with his white family ever again. The soldiers did not listen.''

"He agreed to live with the Remingtons to protect his mother.'' Red Bead grunted in acknowledgment and Stephanie was not certain if the old woman already knew this or merely surmised it. "He attended a great school and learned many good things about his mother's people.''

"He learned about you,'' Red Bead said shrewdly.

Stephanie felt her cheeks heat. "We had been friends as children. Our families pledged us to marry, but then his mother died . . .''

The old woman could sense the bleakness in her voice. "And he left you to return here.''

"To become a famous warrior among the Cheyenne.''

"You think so? It is true the name of the White Wolf is spoken around the campfires of our people, even among our cousins the Lakota and Arapaho. But many do not trust his white blood. You have seen it with Pony Whipper and some of his Crazy Dogs. But in the high councils when all the great chiefs gather for the summer hunts, he is allowed to speak and they listen . . . yet they do not always heed, even though he has undergone the great vision quest of the Sun Dance.''

Stephanie shuddered, remembering the deep scars on his chest, hardly able to imagine what drove these people to seek out such pain. But she could imagine what caused Chase to do it. "He underwent the test to prove he belonged, didn't he?''

"For one so young, you are wise . . . at times.'' Another fleeting smile touched Red Bead's lips.

*   *   *

At last the Department of the Platte had recognized his accomplishments enough to give him his captaincy, even if he did have to nearly die to get it. Hugh Phillips leaned back in the rickety chair behind his cluttered desk. He was the newly appointed commandant of Fort Steele.

Although he despised this harsh primitive land where the whites lived little better than the savages, here lay his opportunity to seize glory. While George Custer played at being a Wall Street tycoon back East, General Terry considered other officers to lead the campaigns in the Department of Dakota. Phillips would not let slip his golden opportunity here in Wyoming. Before he was done cutting a swathe through the high plains tribes, old Phil Sheridan himself would sit up and take notice.

But right now he had to prepare for the Washington bigwig who was coming through on an inspection tour. It would never hurt to have the ear of a United States senator with direct access to President Grant. He yelled for his sergeant to come in and straighten up. As he stood up, a dull ache gripped his abdomen for a moment, a grim reminder of his encounter with that breed who had nearly gutted him back at Laramie.

What the hell had brought that thrice-cursed breed to attempt to assassinate him after so long? He rubbed the scar on his cheek, remembering that day when the bastard had escaped. "This time you weren't so lucky, I bet," he muttered to himself as he walked out the door. He'd put a bullet in the savage's chest, so he couldn't have gotten far. However, they'd never found his body or recovered his horse. But everyone had written him off after the knife wound and he had recovered. What if the breed was equally lucky?

The disturbing thought, one which had plagued him all during the past months of his recuperation, was put behind when he heard the whistle of a locomotive. The four-ten train had arrived. He checked his uniform with its new captain's bars once again in the mirror, slicking back his hair, then placing his hat on his head. He was ready to meet the senator from Massachusetts.

Burke Remington stepped off the train onto the wooden

platform of the tiny Union Pacific railroad depot alongside the fort. The vast open sweep of grassland plains was filled with sagebrush and saltweed bushes. *Desolate*, he thought to himself, like all this endless godforsaken country. But the monotony was broken by tall stands of cottonwoods and willows along the banks of the North Platte, their branches leafless and stark against a leaden sky. The only hint of green was a small smattering of fir and pines dotting the riverbanks and growing here and there around the meager frame buildings comprising the fort and the town beside it.

A contingent of officers stood on the opposite end of the platform. The tall, hard looking captain must be Phillips, the new post commander. Putting on his best politician's smile, Burke waited for him to approach, his hand outstretched in greeting. He and the young captain had a great deal to discuss.

Once the formalities were taken care of and his entourage offered serviceable quarters in which to freshen up, Remington asked to see Phillips in his office.

Closing the door on his sergeant, Hugh studied the barrel-chested man with the iron gray hair and cold blue eyes. He had an aristocrat's face, handsome and utterly ruthless. Idly the officer wondered if Stephanie's ill-fated half-breed lover had resembled his uncle. Not likely. "You had something urgent you wanted to discuss privately before the tour of our facilities, Senator?" he asked, offering Remington a seat.

The big man sat down on the old monstrosity of a horsehair sofa and leaned back. In his expensive custom-tailored gray wool suit, he looked as out of place on the rough frontier outpost as a thoroughbred on an alkali flat. Burke extracted an expensive Cuban cigar from a gold case and offered one to Hugh, who accepted the unheard of luxury with a thin smile. *Damned rich bastard throwing his weight around*. He lit the senator's cigar, then his own and waited patiently as Remington blew out a cloud of fragrant smoke. His calm facade was shattered when Burke spoke.

"I assume you still want to kill that renegade raider

White Wolf. I have some information that will help you.''

Phillips leaned across his desk. ''I've chased him from the Dakotas to the Arkansas River. What could you possibly know about a renegade horse Indian?''

''He's my nephew,'' Burke said in a cold clipped voice.

17

It was the month of the Freezing Moon and time for the marriage of Kit Fox and Blue Eagle. Stephanie had observed Granite Arm and the other women of the family constructing a small lodge situated near that of the bride's family. All the requisite gifts of horses, robes, jewelry and other items had been exchanged for the bride price and dowry. As soon as Blue Eagle returned from the raid, they would be wed.

Kit Fox's love was one of the White Wolf's warriors. They left shortly after Stephanie's last disturbing confrontation with Chase. She overheard whispers among the women that the raiders were going to attack an army supply train bound for Fort Fetterman from the railhead to the south and were expected to burn out a number of relay stations en route as well as destroy telegraph lines, a continual harassment which greatly slowed army pursuit of fleeing Indians.

Stephanie's Cheyenne had become fluent enough to understand the crier as his voice sounded across the camp late one afternoon. The raiders had returned. Putting down the adz with which she was scraping a deer hide, she followed the excited crowd gathering in the center of the village to watch the victorious warriors parade in triumph. Her steps were leaden with dread. She was drawn against her will to the sounds of jubilation echoing across the valley, not wishing to participate, yet powerless to stop herself from hungering to see that he was alive and unharmed—just to gaze upon him once more.

He rode at the head of the procession with his war lance held upright, bedecked with eagle feathers. His body was shielded against the fierce winter winds by a rich robe of wolf skins thrown carelessly across his shoulders. He sat Thunderbolt like a conqueror returning in triumph, back ramrod straight, head arrogantly high. His face was painted with jagged vermilion and white lines, giving it a hard alien appearance, like a drama mask . . . symbolizing what? His red and white halves brought together in this barbaric ritual?

He looked savage and deadly and foreign—and yet she felt a flame lick deep inside her belly as her breath expelled a small puff of white in the frozen air. She trembled, unable to tear her eyes away from his fearful beauty, drawn irresistibly to move closer. Only by sheer force of will did she halt at the edge of the crowd.

No one in the chaotic camp saw the lone Aricara scout concealed in a dense snow-laden copse of cedars high on the farthest ridge near the hidden entrance to the valley. Bloody Hand was one of the most skilled scouts ever employed by the army, but he could not credit his tracking skills for locating the winter camp of this small band of Cheyenne.

He had crossed paths with the returning warriors by accident and knew by their war paint and loot that they had just completed a raid. Although he did not know who they were, he thought it prudent to follow them to their village and report the location of another band of renegades to Captain Ansil at Fort Fetterman. They were well concealed in this valley. No army scouts would ever have found the camp by searching. Now all he had to do was get out of the Big Horns alive so he could lead the army back.

Of course that would not be until the spring thaw. Chances were this place would be empty by the time the soldiers could bestir themselves to ride here. But then again, sometimes a band would return early from the summer hunt to a favorite hiding place. They might just round up these stragglers before another winter season. With stealth born of years of experience, Bloody Hand slipped past the sentries and made his way out of the valley. He had a long cold ride ahead of him and no time to lose before the next snowstorm hit.

Chase's eyes swept the camp as he rode in, searching for the glitter of bronze hair. Then he saw her standing proud and alone, a tall slender woman swathed in heavy robes. Their eyes met and his chest tightened as he felt his breath leave him in a searing rush. Deliberately he made his way toward her, guiding the big black with subtle knee pressure through the laughing, talking people who would share in the bounty from the raid.

The warriors led strings of army mounts laden with sacks of flour, cornmeal, sugar and rice, hogsheads of molasses, bolts of cloth and assorted hardware and tools, even tinned foodstuffs. The Indians used their tomahawks to chop open the cans, exclaiming at the vegetables, meats or fruits they found inside as they devoured them and shared with others around them. Some of the women began unwrapping bolts of bright calico and heavy wool while others, usually older and more practical, examined hatchets and hoes.

Across the crowd Stephanie stood motionless, waiting as Chase approached. Thunderbolt stopped directly in front of her and he vaulted down the fluid, graceful way he always did. He could see the accusation in her eyes but there was more, the same unbanked fire, the hunger that gnawed at him.

"Have you missed me, Stevie?"

His voice was a taunting purr but behind the teasing she could feel his desire, potent as raw whiskey and twice as dangerous. *Don't give in.* "What I've missed is civilization, where men don't smear their faces with war paint and go on looting rampages." She was rewarded with a brief flicker of anger in his glittering black eyes but then he lowered his eyelids and a fathomless darkness filled them.

"Civilized men may not paint their faces, but they do loot. They've stolen all our land," he said coldly.

"Return me to Rawlins, Chase. If you could get all this booty through the passes, you can take me home."

"Home?" He arched his eyebrows mockingly, smothering the flames that still burned unquenchably. "You never considered those army posts home any more than you did Josiah Summerfield's mansion."

She blanched. "How did you know?" As soon as she blurted out the words, she looked away, horrified. She had never told him about her father's final betrayal. He knew only that Josiah was dead, not that he'd left his only child penniless.

Chase studied her, puzzled and surprised by the vehemence of her reaction. "I've known you since you were a child, Stevie. He wasn't much of a father . . . any more than Hugh was much of a husband."

He does not know the rest, she thought in relief. She did not need his pity added to all the other emotions swirling around them. "That can never change the fact of either relationship, can it?" she asked rhetorically.

"Some relationships can never be erased," he replied, pausing, "no matter how much we might wish it."

"White Wolf! You have returned with a great victory just as I knew you would!" Smooth Stone hurled himself across the clearing and skidded excitedly to a halt before Chase, who knelt and picked him up.

"Yes, I've returned with some things for you and your sister, and for my captive," he said, daring Stephanie. "Come see." He turned to the group of army horses, some of which remained laden with captured goods.

"It's cold outside. I'm going in by the fire," Stephanie said as he stared at her. She turned her back on him and the boy and walked away.

Stephanie was delighted when Kit Fox asked her to help prepare for the marriage festivities. Although Granite Arm received Stephanie with genuine friendship, the white woman had to brave the harsh stares of some of the other women who still viewed her as an outsider. Three other young women from the band along with Stephanie accompanied Kit Fox to the sweat lodge. They spent a long cleansing period in the thick steam created by throwing buckets of cold water over red-hot rocks in a tightly sealed teepee. As the women sat cross-legged, rubbing their perspiration-soaked bodies with dried sweet grass, they discussed Kit Fox's new life as a married woman. By now Stephanie had become inured to the casual nudity among the women, even if she was not completely comfortable with it. But as the only woman who had known a husband, she was very uncomfortable with their topic of conversation.

"I saw my brother's manroot once when he was bathing. Judging by the size of what lies in Blue Eagle's breechclout, his must be even larger," Green Grass said in awe as the others giggled.

"Do you think it will hurt when he mounts me?" Kit Fox asked, worrying her lower lip with small white teeth.

"My mother explained to me that it should not if a man is considerate," Swan Flower replied, sensing her friend's maidenly nervousness.

The three young Cheyenne were all virgins but living in a society where sex was a part of nature, they discussed the topic freely. Stephanie could feel their eyes on her. She obviously had experience none of them possessed. But Hugh had not been considerate—if that was what was needed to keep a bridal night from being both painful and humiliating. What could she say? "I was married for three years . . ." she began hesitantly. "There was a little discomfort the first time but then it no longer hurt. I think you will not have the problem I did. White women are taught nothing of what to expect on their wedding nights."

"Not even by their mothers or other female relatives?" Green Grass asked, amazed.

Stephanie shook her head. "It is not considered . . . proper." She groped for a way to explain Victorian propriety to these children of nature and found no adequate vocabulary in her limited Cheyenne—or even in English.

Swan Flower snorted. "Then that is why you did not enjoy it."

Kit Fox looked at Stephanie with an unspoken question in her eyes. She had seen the way her friend returned Chase's ardor and knew Stephanie had desired his touch although not her own husband's. "I hope I will enjoy what passes between me and Blue Eagle this night,'' was all she said.

The young women left the sweat lodge bundled in heavy robes and raced the short distance from the teepee to the bubbling hot springs sheltered from the cold by a curving rock ledge overhanging one of the pools. They shed their robes, shrieking when the icy cold air hit them, then dived into the steamy waters.

Stephanie floated in the warm water, letting its lapping bubbles smooth the tension from her body. There were small pleasures such as the sweat lodges and mineral pools that compensated a great deal for the grueling labor of everyday survival. These people lived close to the earth, in a rhythm with nature that she often envied.

Could you live as Freedom Woman had? Stephanie ignored the niggling voice. She did not belong here. Chase had killed her husband—and even if he had not, this way of life, these people were doomed. Soon this destructive and hopeless war against the whites would end in defeat. The Cheyenne and their allies would all be sent to reservations. Once her identity was discovered, she would never be allowed to remain with them. But what a lovely fantasy it was if only so many things did not conspire to destroy it. A chorus of gasps from the other women brought her abruptly from her troubling reverie.

''It is time and the family of Blue Eagle awaits you. Go now,'' Chase said to the women submerged in the pool. When he turned away to allow them to emerge and cover themselves with the robes, he added, ''You stay here, Stevie.''

She was across the pool and now he stood between her and the Cheyenne women who unquestioningly slipped quietly away. Kit Fox gave her friend a tremulous smile before following the others, as if saying, *Here is your heart.*

Suddenly Stephanie felt cold as the warm waters lapped around her. Careful to remain submerged up to her shoulders, she asked, ''What do you want, Chase?''

He arched his eyebrows and smiled at her but there was no mirth in his glittering black eyes. ''Poached white woman would be nice,'' he countered. But he did not remove his clothes. Rather, he took a seat on a rock beside the edge of the water, studying her as she treaded water, taking care not to reveal her breasts. Her hair spread out behind her, floating like a mantle of bronze silk.

"The walnut stain's worn off,'' he said at length. "You're pale as cream again.''

"Red Bead said there was no need here in winter camp,'' she replied, finding her throat and mouth gone suddenly dry in spite of the steamy air.

He watched her lick her lips, moistening them furtively as she sank lower in the water. "You'll turn to a prune if you don't get out—or else get overheated and I'll have to dive in and pull you out.'' He held up her robe for her, waiting patiently.

Stephanie hesitated, then steeled her courage and swam across the pool. She was his captive and if he decided to force the issue, she could not stop him. Cowering in the water would solve nothing. In spite of his comments, he seemed to have something weighing on his mind and needed to talk. She stepped dripping from the water and he enveloped her in the robe. As soon as she felt his arms around her, she clutched the robe and stepped away, then huddled on a rock facing him and began to wring out her sopping hair as he, too, took a seat.

Finally he spoke. "I learned a number of things while my warriors were raiding. General Terry is mounting a spring campaign for the Yellowstone basin. He's going to turn Custer loose on us. Crook's already preparing to march out of Fetterman, but the winter storms should force him to retreat until at least April.''

"So what you're saying is that the army is going to surround the last of the Indian treaty territory and attack from all sides. It's hopeless, Chase,'' she said with a catch in her voice. "You can't escape.''

"For certain I won't.'' He pulled a paper from inside his robe and unrolled it, holding it out for her to see. On it was a drawing of his face, so perfect a likeness she gasped.

"Yes, it's taken from an old photograph made during my days in Boston," he said bitterly.

A five-thousand-dollar reward was proclaimed below the picture—along with the words: "The White Wolf is also known as Chase Remington, a half-breed Cheyenne renegade."

"How could anyone know?" she asked.

"I also learned that Burke Remington came out west on a little junket this past fall. Inspecting the army's preparedness for the great winter campaigns against us. At least that was the official reason for his trip. But I know he's had agents trying to find me ever since I left Boston. I imagine he finally got a bit impatient. Maybe the old man's near death and he's worried he'll be cut out of the inheritance entirely unless he can prove I'm dead."

Stephanie digested this, knowing Burke Remington had tried unsuccessfully to have Chase murdered once already. But his next words stunned her.

"Hugh is alive, Stevie. I didn't kill him." He handed her the wanted poster. Now that her hands had dried, she took it, trembling so badly the paper shook. In small print in the right corner was Captain Hugh Phillips's signature as adjutant of Fort Steele.

"I don't understand," she said numbly. She should rejoice yet she could not. Stephanie did not wish for his death, especially not at the hands of the man she had loved in her husband's stead, yet she wanted with her whole heart to be free of Hugh.

"Burke and your dear husband are working together now," Chase said, breaking into her thoughts. "While searching for me, my uncle's agents apparently ran across your name, which Burke had no doubt supplied them in the hopes you could lead him to me. It didn't take him long to put two and two together when you were abducted by an Indian."

A shiver of fear snaked down her spine. She had heard the cold ruthlessness in the senator's voice that night at the Cabots' and she knew firsthand how obsessed Hugh was.

The thought of the two of them together was daunting indeed.

Chase studied her in the waning light. The air was cold in spite of the underground heat and shelter of the cliff. "You have good reason to be frightened. The Remington wealth is a formidable goad combined with your husband's vendetta against me. Now he knows I'm the one who marked him as well as the one who ruined his wife."

She was not surprised to learn it was Chase who had put the scar on Hugh's cheek. "You have not 'ruined' me yet, Chase," she said, trying to read what he was thinking. It was not difficult.

He stared at her hungrily, as if he could see through the heavy buffalo robe to her naked flesh. "I've finally admitted to myself why I brought you here, Stevie," he said at length.

She pulled the robe more protectively around herself, unable to frame a reply as he knelt in front of her and reached out, taking a long silky strand of her water-darkened hair. He raised it to his lips, then tugged gently on it, pulling her head lower, her lips nearer his own. The steam from the hot pool surrounded them in billowing wispy clouds. Water lapped softly as a lover's moan while he ran his other hand along the planes of her face, tracing the delicate symmetry of brow, temple, cheekbone and jawline. Then his fingertips found her lips, which were moist and trembling.

Kneeling on the soft earth in front of her, he breathed her name and drew her down into his embrace. When his lips touched hers, she reached out blindly, cupping his beard-stubbled jaw in her hand while he slipped an arm beneath the robe to press her firmly against his body. She felt the sleek soft glide of the wolf pelts against her bare breasts and the tips instantly hardened into aching nubby points. As he deepened the kiss, their arms entwined, loosening her robe, which slipped with a heavy *whoosh* around her legs.

Icy air pricked her back and buttocks, which were alternately scalded by the fiery heat of his fingers skimming along her pale skin. She reacted at once, pressing her hands against his chest. Her fingers sank into the wolf pelts as she broke away from him and seized her fallen robe. She held it in front of her like a shield, shivering and breathless. "No, Chase." Her voice was hoarse, soft with despair.

"Whether or not you lie with me, Phillips will never accept you back."

"But I would know what we had done and my conscience is the only thing I have to live by, Chase." When she pulled her robe around her and stood up, he did not try to stop her from leaving.

Everyone in the village turned out to celebrate with the families of Blue Eagle and Kit Fox. As was the custom, the bride was dressed in her special finery, made by Blue Eagle's mother, a bleached white doeskin dress with long double fringe, decorated with elk teeth and beads. She wore large silver hoops in her ears, a beaten copper necklace and bracelets and her hair was plaited in two heavy gleaming braids which were coiled at the sides of her head with beautiful white beaded ornaments worked into them. She was mounted on a sleek white mare, led by her brother Plenty Horses with Granite Arm walking proudly at her daughter's side. They approached the new lodge where Blue Eagle and his family stood waiting and the public presentment was made.

The look exchanged between the young warrior and the lovely maiden was achingly tender as he led her inside the lodge they would share. As everyone around them laughed and talked, eager for the feasting to begin, Stephanie stood to one side with several of Kit Fox's other friends. When she looked across the path the lovers had just taken, her eyes met with Chase's. The raw sensual hunger in their black depths sent a jolt of fire coursing through her veins.

She stood frozen, terrified of the answering emotion his naked vulnerability brought forth, unable to break eye contact. The crowd of people around them seemed to vanish as if they were the only two on earth, male and female, made for each other. Her heart hammered in her breast as she hugged herself protectively. Every instinct she possessed screamed at her, urging her to dash the few steps into his arms. But she could not.

Tears stung her eyes as the hopelessness of their situation washed over her. Chase slowly walked up to her and stood a respectable distance away, only reaching out one hand to trace the silvery trickle of a teardrop down her cheek. "I'm sorry, Stevie," he said simply, not knowing what else he could do, how he could explain his feelings to her—feelings he himself did not fully comprehend.

"Why? Why did you leave me behind in Boston? If only you'd come to me first, asked me to go west with you."

"And live in danger, poverty, moving from town to town while I searched for my family?"

"Do you think my life as the wife of an ambitious junior officer has been easy? I've spent years in far less comfortable surroundings than these." She gestured to the circle of buffalo hide lodges, drawn tight against the winter's chill. "I've lived with spiders and snakes and alkali dust so thick it frosted the window glass—when we were lucky enough to have window glass. I've moved half a dozen times from post to post, been threatened by hostile Indians, drunken miners and cutthroat outlaws. I've learned to survive, Chase . . . but I had to do it without you."

"I couldn't have asked you to chance this sort of life—to live with the Cheyenne," he replied defensively.

"Now is a hell of a time to think of that, isn't it?" she snapped. Anger began to purge the crushing weight of her melancholy longing. "Red Bead thinks I'm managing passably well."

He smiled sadly. "You are. Perhaps that's why I finally admitted to myself that I still needed you. I do need you, Stevie."

She shook her head, backing away from him. "It's too late, Chase. Please, don't do this . . . if ever you loved me, on the honor of that love, don't ask me to come to you." *For I cannot say no.*

This time it was Chase who turned and walked away, leaving her standing alone with the distant sounds of reveling from the marriage feast echoing around her. The thought of food sickened her. Stephanie turned and walked into her lodge to think . . . and to plan.

The fire in his lodge burned low as Chase sat alone staring into the glowing red embers, trying to see the future. What should he do about Stevie? Desire for her had become a constant ache, not only tightening his groin but his heart as well. *I love her. I still love her.*

He always had, even though he had not really known it back in Boston. She was right. He should never have left her behind to fall prey to the likes of Hugh Phillips. Now they were both trapped by her marriage vows to the butchering bastard. If he had killed Phillips, the murder would have stood between them, but with him alive, her rigid sense of civilized morality kept her bound to a man who had brought her pain and shame.

Although she was too proud to admit it to him, Chase was certain she knew about Hugh's predilection for cheap whores. Besides which, he was a vicious drunk. The thought of him raising a hand to her while in his cups was enough to turn Chase's blood to ice.

If she were Cheyenne, there would be no question of her divorcing such a husband. But Stephanie was white, Boston bred of stern Congregationalist stock where the scandal of divorce was an unthinkable sin and vows, no matter how cruelly betrayed by a spouse, could never be revoked. In so many ways Chase felt the Cheyenne way was far superior. White customs were often foolish, sometimes destructive.

"I have chosen one path, she another," he murmured into the dying embers. As the night wore on the flickering light gave him no answers. Sounds from the feasting died away gradually. Kit Fox and Blue Eagle slept in one another's arms this night.

Chase had been alone since childhood when his father died and his mother sold her soul to save his life. For a brief while when he rejoined Black Kettle's band as a youth, he had hoped for a woman and children, a place to belong. But that had been wrenched away from him at

Washita. After that, in so-called civilization and even here with his people, he had resigned himself never to take a wife.

Stevie had turned his world upside-down. He had no doubt that she desired him as he did her. If he came to her he could take her . . . for a night. But in the morning she would look on him with reproach and scourge him with silent guilt. "The Powers must not have fated us to be together," he whispered, reaching for his sleeping robes.

He rolled down into the thick pallet of furs and stared out the small smoke hole at the apex of the lodge. Stars winked down on him offering what comfort they could. Sleep would not come. Then the sound of footsteps on crunching snow and a discreet cough broke the silence outside the lodge. Chase recognized Stands Tall's voice and wondered why his uncle had returned so late, for he had said he would spend the night with Elk Bull's family.

"You may enter, Stands Tall," he called out in greeting, glad of the company.

"You are certain I do not disturb you," the older man said before lifting the flap.

"I am alone," he replied wryly.

With a grunt of acceptance, Stands Tall slipped inside. At once his eyes swept the area. "Then she is not with you, your bronze-haired woman."

A swift frisson of unease snaked down Chase's spine. "Why would she be here? She has refused me and I would not force her."

"She is nowhere in the camp. When all the feasting was done Red Bead could not find her. She has searched every lodge. A pony is missing, some food and a rifle, too."

Chase cursed beneath his breath as he began to dress. This was what he had feared ever since he brought her to his people—that she would try to escape and wander off into danger. After they reached the safety and isolation of the winter camp and she seemed to adapt to the life here, he had begun to relax his vigilance. Stupid of him! "She can't have gotten far. There is a moon tonight. I'll bring her back," he said, reaching for the Winchester that was always close at hand.

"It is calm now but Red Bead says a storm gathers in the mountains to the west. It will come upon us before morning," Stands Tall replied gravely.

Chase's heart froze. Red Bead had never been mistaken about the weather and Stephanie was out in the wilds of the Big Horns alone, at the mercy of the savage wilderness!

18

The snow was growing deeper, hurled by winds that howled like a berserk banshee. Stephanie had lost all sense of direction after the snowfall began. At first the gentle flakes had just covered the old snow, obscuring the packed-down trail the warriors had made entering the valley. Looking at the pass ahead, illuminated by a patch of faint starlight, she had held to her course. But when the snow thickened and the winds picked up, the world around her quickly turned into a swirling white vortex sucking her deeper and deeper into its freezing maw.

She had brought along a flint and a bit of dry punk with which to start a fire but she could find no shelter, much less enough wood to stoke the flames into life-giving warmth. In spite of the sturdy buckskins and heavy buffalo robes she wore, her freezing limbs began to grow numb. She knew she would soon topple from her horse. Then as abruptly as it had begun the blizzard stopped.

Stars once more illuminated a fairy landscape of tall cedars and pines jutting skyward, set against the steep walls of the majestic canyon, their black-green arms laden with snow. Somehow her horse had made its way to the opening of the pass. Before her stretched a vast series of lower foothills crisscrossed by hundreds of narrow ravines, wild rocky country covered with dense stands of evergreen and dried mountain grasses, mantled in white with dark patches of bare earth where the winds had randomly swept it clean of snow.

As if the banshee wielded a broom, she thought with whimsical humor. From here on how could she choose a course? She had no idea of the tortuous route the Cheyenne had taken into this wild high elevation. This country was the most awe inspiringly beautiful and desolately isolated she had yet encountered in her extensive western travels. The better plan now was to camp and keep from freezing to death. Once she lost all sensation in her hands, she would be doomed to die alone in this wilderness, her bones left for scavengers to pick.

Hugh would not mourn her. Would Chase? She knew he would be killingly angry when he learned of her escape. Would it not have been better to give in to him than to take this desperate gamble? She forced the useless thought away and scanned the area for a likely place to build a fire. A small clearing swept clean of snow lay at the side of the steep mountain wall to her right. She turned the weary horse in that direction.

Within half an hour she had scavenged enough wood for a small fire and sat watching it blaze to life on the frozen ground, grateful for the survival skills so hard won in her months with the Cheyenne. She took a bundle of food from the pack she had hastily gathered, and began to chew on a frozen strip of buffalo jerky. Gradually it softened in her mouth and the smoky flavor made her stomach growl in anticipation. After only a few bites she grew too tired to chew more and dug for a bit of Red Bead's soft pemmican. It, too, was hard and icy. Placing it near the fire, she gathered her buffalo robe around her and rolled up in it, curling around the feeble warmth emitted by the low flames.

Half-frozen, physically and emotionally exhausted as she was, sleep claimed her all too quickly. Then came the dreams, of Chase and Hugh with the reverend thundering denunciations in the background as the two men fought over her. Chase's grandfather called her the Whore of Babylon and the malevolent figure of Burke Remington stood at his father's side smiling chillingly. As she sank deeper into frozen lethargy, the images faded, replaced by a frighteningly alien scene.

Two huge wolves, one iron gray, the other a blinding pure white, lunged at each other, snarling with hate so palpable it crackled. They tore at each other, backed off and circled, then went for each other's throats again, and yet again, until both were bloodied and panting. She was hovering above them, a disembodied observer to the contest, yet her breathing quickened with fear every time the white wolf received another wound.

The gray began to tire at last and the white, growing red with blood now, made one final desperate leap. As they went down, rolling on the earth, a scream ripped from her throat and suddenly she was no longer watching from above. She was in their midst, feeling the feral heat, smelling the metallic stench of blood. The white's powerful jaws suddenly found an opening and clamped on the gray's throat. She heard the sound of bones snapping as the victor shook its victim, breaking its neck and ripping out its throat.

Then suddenly the white wolf released its foe and turned to look at her with glittering black eyes . . . Chase's eyes. She knelt, arms outstretched, waiting for him to come to her but he did not. Instead he turned and bounded away, vanishing in the thick mountain timber. She scrambled to her feet and ran after him, crying out his name over and over. . . .

Chase looked at the faint pink line on the eastern horizon where the sun was trying to climb over the jagged peaks of the Big Horns and invade the corduroy-ribbed interior. He reined in the big dun gelding and scanned the world of white below him.

"How the hell did she make it through the pass?" His voice echoed in the cold still air. The storm should have stopped her. As he'd ridden through it he had prayed every prayer he knew, to the Powers of his people, even to the Christian God. Chase had never been able to believe in the stern and wrathful deity of Jeremiah Remington. The mystic sense of unity between man and nature linked together by forces of creation in Cheyenne myth far better suited him. Yet in his desperation to save Stephanie, he was willing to plead for all the help he could get, white or red.

After several hours, he had fully expected to find her

frozen body lying beside the horse she'd stolen. But he had not. With no trail to follow he had begun cutting circles until the sudden blizzard abated. By luck he'd come across the trail a little over an hour ago, clear of the pass, heading south toward the middle fork of the Powder River. But the wind-driven snow had obliterated it before he could catch up to her.

If she died out here, he had killed her surely as putting a knife in her heart. He had no excuse for kidnapping her. The rash selfish act had endangered his people and now might cost Stevie's life. The latter hurt him more deeply than the former, and guilt over that fact added to the gnawing despair in his soul. As he had ridden through the freezing black night he had castigated himself ceaselessly for the love he could not kill, the love that would not die with her but lived on as long as he did.

"What a bleak and lonely mission you've charged me with, Mother," he murmured, "trying to save our people even when I know their way of life is ending, when I wish only to die."

He leaned forward, looking out across the vast undulations of mountains and valleys spread before him in the dim light, praying for some trace of her. Then he saw it, a faint wisp of smoke against the bluffs. Was it a trick of the air at sunrise? He murmured a prayer to the Everywhere Spirit and kicked the dun into a gallop. When he saw the small figure huddled beneath the mound of robes, lying so still beside the faint embers of the smoldering fire, his heart twisted with dread.

"Stevie!" He leaped from his horse and ran to her, cradling her in his arms. She lay cold and unresponsive. Frantically he buried his face against her neck and felt the faintest hum of a pulse. She was alive but almost frozen. Frantically he chaffed her hands and face, breathing his warm breath against her cold cheeks and fingers. She stirred and murmured something drowsy and incoherent, then drifted into unconsciousness again.

Chase could see this exposed place would offer no shelter if another storm blew up. Looking at the western sky, he knew that was a distinct possibility. He gathered her in his arms and kicked out the small fire, grateful at least that she had been able to build it. Its warmth and signaling smoke had saved her life . . . or at least he prayed it had. Now that he'd found her, he could not chance leaving the sign for an enemy to follow.

"Can you hear me, Stevie? You have to wake up. Help me. You can't sleep or you'll never wake up again." The low urgency of his voice brought a faint murmur. He thought she whispered his name but could not be certain.

"I'm going to put you up on my horse. You have to hold on. Can you do it?"

Without waiting for her response, he lifted her across the dun's withers. Somehow although still semiconscious she hung on as he swung up behind her and rode up the sharp rise of the western mountain. *Please let my memory be good.* Then he saw the partially concealed opening of the cave. "Now if a bear hasn't decided to hibernate inside, I'll have you warm and dry in a few minutes, Stevie," he murmured to her as he carried her up to the opening.

Stephanie felt the prickle of pain in her face, hands and feet, like the sting of tiny needles at first, gradually building to a stark agony. It felt as if her bones were being smashed by a great mallet. She had been having nightmares about blood and death, wolves and Chase. Chase was here, holding her—or had she dreamed that, too? Her head was muzzy and her eyes refused to open, so heavy were the lids. Then she sensed his presence. He was touching her and she was naked beneath the covers. He must have removed her clothes and now he chaffed her arms and legs, moving over her body. His hands felt warm and strong. She opened her eyes and blinked. They were in a cave. The leap of firelight danced over the walls and gave off sensuous lovely heat, but not half so sensuous or lovely as his touch against her bare skin.

"Isn't this where we started?" she asked, light-headed, the words slurred.

His expression was tense. "You're awake at last. I've

been trying to revive you for half an hour. The fire's finally begun to warm the air.''

''It feels heavenly. Where are we?''

''Not far from where I found you. I remembered this cave, which fortunately wasn't occupied. We had to have shelter before the next storm blows in.'' As he spoke he continued massaging her cold limbs. He could feel her shivering in spite of the warmth provided by the extra furs and robes he'd brought along. She was practically buried in them and still he could not break the chills gripping her.

He cursed beneath his breath as he pulled off his wet buckskins and climbed under the robe. Pulling her against him, he placed her between the heat of his body and that of the fire. ''Damn you for running away, Stevie. What the hell made you think you could find your way through hundreds of miles of mountain wilderness in the dead of winter?''

His soft breath against the sensitive skin of her neck set off alarm bells in her head, breaking through the comforting lethargy her brush with freezing had wrought. The crisp abrasion of his body hair rubbed against her delicate skin, tickling, enticing. In spite of his angry accusations, she could feel the pressure of his erection against her buttocks. She was back to full consciousness now, growing warm— altogether too warm!

''I wasn't certain I could find my way out . . . but I had to try, Chase.'' She felt utterly vulnerable—not only to him as they lay naked beneath the covers, but to herself, to the cravings of her hungry young body which had known lust but never love. If he took her now she could not lie to herself. It would not be rape. She ached to turn into his arms and beg him to hold her, to love her.

He could feel the awakening awareness in her body and the answering leap of his own flesh which he could not have subdued even if he wished it. Chase admitted to himself that he did not wish it. He sighed into the silk of her hair, dyed a rich dark hue by the firelight, the color of winter molasses. His fingers stroked the gleaming masses and her tense shoulder beneath. "I want you, Stevie . . . and you want me," he murmured.

"That's why I tried to escape, Chase. This is wrong."

"Maybe it is—by your laws—but not by mine."

"That's right. I'm merely a slave, yours to do with as you wish."

The words stung. "You know better, Stevie. You ran because you knew I wouldn't have to force you the way a warrior takes a captive." He turned her on her back and raised his body above hers, pressing her into the soft furs. His mouth came down in a fierce, life-affirming kiss as he moved his lips over hers, waiting for her to open to him, his tongue teasing along the seam until she complied. Then he probed the delicate recesses, tasting, savoring, letting the bittersweet memories of all their impassioned kisses of so long ago replay in his mind.

Groaning, Chase buried his fingers in her hair, holding her face framed between his hands. He continued to savage her mouth, his body growing taut as a bowstring at full draw, ready to release the power of an arrow. His back arched up and his hips ground into hers in an uncontrollable surge of long-denied passion.

Stephanie was lost in the hot rich passion of the kiss. For her, too, it evoked wondrous memories of a far happier time so long ago. But when he arched his back and bucked his hips, the power of his hard phallus scalded her. She felt her hands embracing his flexing shoulders and knew she was about to press her nails into the bunched muscles and urge him to drive deep inside her.

"No!" She quickly lowered her arms and pressed them against the hard slab of his chest, trying to push him away as she turned her head, crying angrily, "You really are the white wolf in that dream—ripping the gray one limb from limb. You take what you want no matter who you hurt!"

Chase froze. He stared down at her, his eyes wide with incredulity. All the air seemed to leave his lungs, searing them. "What do you know of a white wolf fighting a gray?"

As he pulled away from her in shock, the hoarseness of

his voice startled her. She turned her head and looked into his eyes, which burned like two black coals. The flickering firelight cast his harshly beautiful features in shadows, giving them a satanic intensity.

"I—I had a nightmare back there, when I fell asleep in the snow," she began, uncertain of how to explain what was more hidden than revealed, an intangible figment of her mind as it prepared to die, obscured like wisps of cloud scudding across the moon.

He sat up beside her, pulling one robe about his body and offering her another. Disconcerted by her nakedness, she seized it and wrapped it tightly around herself, scooting as far away from him as she could on the narrow confines of the pallet.

"Tell me about this dream."

His manner set her teeth on edge yet beneath the arrogant command she sensed confusion, even a strange desperation. "It's hazy now." She rubbed her eyes and rested her head in her hands for a moment, trying to gather her scattered thoughts. "There were two wolves, huge and fierce looking, one pure white." She paused to steal a look at him. His eyes were hooded now, glittering obsidian slits fixed intently on her. "The . . . the other was iron gray. They circled each other, then lunged, attacking with such savage violence it was incredible."

He let her describe the dream sequence in a terse, halting narration, interjecting a few questions, asking her to dredge up more detail. When she reached the part where she recognized the wolf as him and followed after him, crying out his name, he felt the final shock of recognition. "How can you know these things?"

Frightened by his intensity, she replied, "I don't know anything. It was only a nightmare."

"What you've just described so precisely is my medicine dream."

Her eyes widened and she blanched. While living with the Cheyenne she had learned a great deal about their customs and beliefs. She had even dared to ask Red Bead once about the scars on his chest. "The vision you received during the Sun Dance?"

He nodded, looking at her strangely, with a trepidation bordering on fear. "When I left you in Boston it was the hardest thing I'd ever done in my life . . . until I met you again in Rawlins and brought you to my people. I'd always told myself that you could never belong here. You weren't destined to share my life because you were white." A soft wistfulness wreathed his face. "Perhaps I was wrong. The Powers, for their own mysterious reasons, have cast our fates together." Rising to his knees in front of her, he extended his hand, palm up.

Now it was Chase who looked utterly vulnerable. *He's afraid.* She was frightened, too, as she reached out and placed her soft pale hand in his much larger dark one. "I violate every ideal by which I've lived . . . yet I can do nothing else but come to you," she said softly as he drew her up into his arms.

He dropped his robe and started to slip hers from her shoulders. She flinched. At once his hands grew still as he murmured into her ear, "What's wrong, Stevie?"

"I've never . . . that is . . . it's daylight and . . ."

"Phillips acted the gentleman and spared your sensibilities? He never undressed you?"

Unable to speak she shook her head, her hair shielding her face as she hung her head down.

Chase felt the anger churn deep inside of him, thinking of the perfunctory and cold way his beautifully passionate Stevie had been initiated into the marriage bed. He would make amends. Tipping her chin up with one hand, he held her close with his other splayed across the small of her back. Her cheeks were flushed and her lashes fanned down on them like sable brushes. He kissed the tip of her nose, her eyelids, temples, the soft indentations at the edges of her mouth, murmuring, "Proper Eastern gentlemen don't know how to make love to a woman. Don't ever be ashamed of your passions, Stevie. They're a gift of the most special kind, meant to be shared between a man and a woman."

Hugh had always made her feel cold and inept in bed, accused her of driving him to seek other women. She felt so uncertain, so insecure, yet the sweetness of Chase's kisses and the seductive purr of his voice made her bold enough to ask, "What if I don't please you? What if—"

"What if a starving man would not want food?" he crooned, smiling into her hair as his fingers began to massage her back and shoulders very gently through the heavy fur. "I've already seen all there is to see of your beautiful body . . . and what I saw I liked very, very much, remember? And you've just recently seen all of me, even if I was too feverish to enjoy it at the time."

She could feel Chase's body heat through her heavy robe, feel the magic of his hands as they slowly worked their way around the barrier of fur and began to caress her hips, gliding around to the ripe slim curves of her buttocks. He kneaded them, sending exquisite ripples of pleasure coursing through her, pressing her lower body against his. All the while he continued to rain soft delicate kisses across her face, down to the wildly beating pulse at the base of her throat.

She threw back her head, clinging to his shoulders, baring her neck to his lips. A hot, dizzying flush spread across her like a blanket of fire, sending her blood racing madly through her veins. She was so warm, burning up. A small incoherent cry escaped her lips as she felt the robe slip from her body. Chase enveloped her in his arms then and centered his mouth on hers for a deep dizzying kiss. Her lips, already parted, accepted the invasion of his tongue, feeling small frissons of delight as its tip probed hers, sweeping around her teeth, darting and teasing until she grew bold enough to answer in kind.

When he felt her response, it was all he could do not to press her down onto the furs and plunge into her. Schooling himself to go slow, Chase let her explore his mouth timidly at first, encouraging and coaxing her to greater boldness, until their exchange grew fierce and breathless. Tearing his lips from hers, he trailed soft nips and brushing caresses down her throat to her collarbone, then lower, taking her breasts in his hands as she knelt before him. Reverently he raised the small perfect globes, letting his thumbs graze and tease the nipples, which at the first touch of his hands had hardened into tight little rosettes of palest pink.

The touch of his hands on her breasts, raising them, cupping them and caressing their fiery ache, was scalding in intensity. But then he took one nipple in his mouth and tugged on it. What had been a tingling ache suddenly blossomed into an intense throbbing deep in the core of her body. She arched her back, pulling his head closer as he switched from one breast to the other, repeating the breathless magic. Her fingers worked their way deep into the coarse shiny thickness of his night black hair, holding him to her as she repeated his name over and over, like a litany.

Chase raised his head at last from the feast of her breasts, his fingers splayed around her rib cage. He looked up into her flushed face and met her eyes, heavy lidded and dilated with passion now. "Lie back," he commanded softly, helping her to stretch out on the pallet of fur on which they knelt. The rosy glow of firelight gilded her creamy flesh, so pale in contrast to the coppery darkness of his hands moving over it. He let one hand slide slowly from the soft mound of her breast over the hollow indentation of her slender waist, then skim across the concave silk of her belly.

"You are even more incredibly lovely than I remembered," he said raggedly, staring down at her.

Stephanie could suddenly see that long-ago day when they were in the hunting lodge and he had stood over her naked body, appraising it with frank male desire. What a different course both of their lives would have taken if he had not pulled away from her then, if he had made love to her. Her eyes locked with his as if he, too, were recalling that fateful day. "I only wish . . . I . . ."

"Shh . . . this was always fated to be. We just didn't know it then. But now we do." He took her hand and brought it to his lips, planting soft wet kisses on her palm and fingertips, then pressed it to his chest where his heart slammed hard and furious as a war drum.

Her fingers burrowed into the thick pelt of black hair. She thrilled at the racing of his heart, knowing it beat so for her. Then her hand felt the heavy ridge of the Sun Dance scar, alien and forbidding, yet as much a part of Chase as the dream which sprung from it—a dream she had mysteriously shared. She placed a soft kiss on the scar, then on the other one opposite it, unable to imagine the agony he must have endured to belong with the Cheyenne. "I belong only to you," she whispered.

"I've waited all my life to hear you say that," he replied, trembling with relief that she could accept who and what he was.

Stephanie marveled at the differences in their bodies, his dark, hard and sinewy, with crisp beguiling patterns of hair on his chest, arms and legs. She pressed her mouth to the muscled wall of his chest, letting the crisp tickle of hair brush her face as her lips sought the hardened coppery coin of a flat male nipple. Small white teeth nipped at it and he cried out in pleasure. She repeated the caress on the other one, nuzzling his chest and murmuring, "I love the feel of this."

He smiled, twining her warm bronze hair in his fingers as he said, "I always hated having a hairy body—a reminder of my Remington blood . . . white blood, but now I'm glad if it pleases you."

When she raised her head from his chest, he lowered his and kissed her once more, moving his body across hers. One long powerful leg pressed her into the pallet as he insinuated it between her thighs, spreading them. Willingly she let her legs slide apart, opening for him. His hand moved down, sweeping over her hip, then across her belly to reach the soft dark curls at her mound. When he massaged it she moaned into his mouth. The feel of his hand on her there sent a raw jolt of need through her. The low insistent ache deep in her belly had been growing with every love word, each caress. She felt her hips arch up, her pelvis tilt against the massaging of his hand. *Yes, do it now. Touch me!*

He moved deeper, his fingers brushing the soft wet petals

of her sex, finding her ready for him. Still he did not give in to the ache in his groin. To plunge in now would be disaster for he would surely spill his seed before he could bring her with him. She writhed restlessly beneath the soft massage of his hand.

"You want this . . . even though you don't know yet what it is," he murmured against her throat, kissing the racing pulse there, then moving lower, taking time to lavish more caresses on her breasts.

The faint scratch of his whiskers against her sensitive nipple made her keen her pleasure in a high soft wail. She stroked his cheeks and jawline, urging him on as he suckled her, then at last abandoned her breasts, moving lower to dip the tip of his tongue into her navel and swirl it around. She felt that tightening ache squeeze even tighter. His strange words of a moment before flitted through her mind. Yes, she wanted him to complete the act, to plunge into her, deep inside and join his flesh with hers. What then?

What more could there be? Before she had felt nothing but tight dry pain, and she had always been glad it was mercifully over quickly. But now she desired this joining— this man—so intensely she wanted it never to end. When his fingers found the small mysterious bud of her passion and glided ever so softly over it, she gasped, nearly fainting with the sudden, utterly unexpected pleasure.

She was like a watch spring, wound so tightly now that she was ready to burst. Chase could feel the delicate quivering of her sweet feminine flesh, smell the heady musk of her newly awakened passion. He sensed she had never before felt this gift he would give her. As he continued stroking her with his hand, he lowered his head, finally nestling it between her thighs.

Stephanie was so intent on the breathless, delicious waves of sensation sweeping over her that she did not realize his intent until she felt the heat of his mouth replace his hand. She should have been shocked! Appalled! She should have withdrawn, but instead she arched against the hot insistence of his lips and tongue, moving on her swollen aching flesh as it blazed to even greater life. All conscious thought slipped away as she felt herself spiraling down, down, deeper and deeper into the whirlpool of pleasure, drowning in a vortex which began to build toward a culmination—something she must have even though she did not understand it, could never imagine it.

But she craved it with such a fierce intensity she squeezed her eyes tightly closed and felt her whole body focus on the center of her femininity and the incredible pain-pleasure Chase was giving her. Suddenly the crest swept over her and she screamed out his name. Wave after wave of contractions suffused her body, radiating outward like ripples widening on a pool of water.

When she stiffened and cried his name, Chase raised his head, feasting his eyes on her loveliness as the rosy flush of climax painted her pale skin. He moved up, cradling her in his arms, kissing her breasts and throat, her fluttering eyelids and then centering on the lushness of her parted lips. All the while his hand continued to massage her mound as the contractions slowly ebbed. When she opened her eyes and looked into his face with total surprise and love it made his heart stop beating. And he knew this was what he had waited for all of his life.

"Stevie," he murmured.

Stephanie studied his passion-glazed eyes, heavy lidded, glittering with triumph for the pleasure he had just brought her, a gift truly beyond price. Yet even as she caressed his beloved face, she could sense the tightly coiled tension in his body and feel the hard insistent pressure of his staff pressing into her belly.

Her hand sought it and closed over the velvety length. He gasped when she did so, crying out raggedly in his need. "Come into me, Chase," she whispered softly, opening her body to him, glorying in the hunger on his face. He was utterly vulnerable now in spite of the way he pinned her wrists over her head. Chase raised his body above her, poised to take possession as she had invited him to do.

As he probed at her, gliding the thick dark head of his staff in the wetness of her petals, his eyes never left hers.

"Look at me, Stevie, while I come into you," he said, repeating her words.

She complied, arching to take the teasing pressure of his staff deeper, drawing him into the wet heat of her sheath. With a muffled oath he sank deep, burying himself fully. She was so soft yet so incredibly tight, surrounding him with her satiny flesh. He closed his eyes and poised very still inside of her, afraid to move, not only for fear of spilling himself too soon, but also to savor this moment, this joining. "At last, at last," he whispered through clenched teeth.

Stephanie looked up at the tense beauty of his face, feeling the power of his body as he filled her, stretching her, pinioning her to the furs beneath her with raw male power. She expected pain, but there was only a sense of wonder at the slick glide of his flesh inside her—and at his sudden stillness. She could see sweat break out on his brow as his eyes closed and his lips drew back in a feral grimace. The tendons stood out in his neck as he threw back his head. His expression could have indicated pain, yet she sensed it did not. She freed one hand from his grasp and reached up to caress his cheek tenderly. Then his eyes opened and he looked down at her. All breath left her body when she saw the raw need in his eyes, an openness of the very soul which she knew must be reflected in her own eyes. "I love you, Chase," she said, undulating her hips without realizing she had done so.

He let out an oath that was an endearment and held on to his control as he said, "I love you, Stevie." Then he gave in to the power of their passion, beginning to stroke now, slowly, letting every subtle, delicate nuance of possessing her steal over his senses, praising her with his body as he did with words. "You're so slick and tight, so perfectly formed to fit me."

Stephanie felt an answering awakening in her satiated flesh. Slow, delicate sensations began to radiate through her with each thrust of his phallus. He moved so slowly, carefully as if she were fragile as a flower. But she was made of sturdier stuff. Her young body, so long denied the satisfaction of this act, craved it fiercely. She locked her legs around his hips and met each thrust, urging him on, harder, faster, more . . . more.

Chase felt her nails dig into his back as her hips fitted themselves in perfect sync to his, glorying in each thrust. Her body silently begged for more and he answered her plea, moving with greater power and swiftness, carrying her along with him to the brink, then waiting, exerting every ounce of control he possessed until he felt her plunging over the abyss into the fire. Her eyes flew open and she cried out, arching up to meet him as the culmination began. Only then did he let his own body swell and pulse deep, deep within her, shuddering with every thrust, spilling his seed high against her womb in hard, long thrusts that utterly drained him.

Feeling him join her as his whole body stiffened, going utterly taut, brought her another surge of joy, newer and stranger yet than the last time. When he collapsed on top of her, he did not pull away as she expected. Instead he cradled her in his arms and held her, kissing her cheeks and eyes, her lips, then burying his face in her hair. Stephanie stroked his shiny black hair as the tears began, seeping from beneath the thickness of her lashes, trailing in silvery rivulets down her cheeks.

19

Chase raised his head, sensing her disquiet. Seeing the tears, he felt a pang deep in his chest. Wiping the trail of tears from her cheeks with the pads of his thumbs, he said, "Please don't be sorry, Stevie." He knew there was a plea in his voice but could not help it.

She shook her head, taking his hand in hers and tasting the saltiness of her tears on his fingers as she kissed them. "No, Chase, I'm not sorry for what we shared. How could I regret anything that beautiful?"

"Then why . . . ?" He cupped her face in his hand, looking deeply into her glittering amber eyes.

"Don't you see, I gave to Hugh what belonged to you. The first time for me was meant to be shared with the man who loved me—who I loved."

"The loss of that—the pain and deprivation you suffered—were my fault, not yours, Stevie. I left you to Phillips and I'll never forgive myself for it."

She reached up and touched his face, memorizing every harshly beautiful contour, reveling in the rasp of his beard, the sensuous curve of his elegantly sculpted lips, all the while drowning in the fathomless ebony glow of his eyes. "I can no longer blame you for leaving when you did, Chase . . . but I wanted to be a virgin when I came to you and—"

"You were! In every way that counts, you truly were." He paused for a moment and then laughed with pure joy. "And I guess in a strange way so was I. I've never known this sense of peace . . . of completeness."

"I never could have imagined what it would be like, Chase. Back in Boston women always spoke in hushed whispers of marital duties, a subject of some distaste to most of them apparently, although being young and unwed, no one ever explained why to me.'' A wry smile twisted her lips. ''At least with Hugh my expectations were not high so they weren't dashed.''

The thought of that obsessive madman touching her made his guts clench. Chase vowed that Hugh Phillips never would again. ''In the spring I'll have to return you to civilization.'' He forestalled her protest, rushing on to say, ''It's not safe with my people. If we're caught, the army will ride in and slaughter the women and children just to get to the men.''

She wanted to deny it but knew from the straggling bloody survivors often herded into the army posts en route to reservations that what he said was all too true. ''I would scarcely be safe with Hugh. You said yourself, after this he would never want me. I'd only be an embarrassment to him, to his career. I'll take my chances with Red Bead and the others. Kit Fox is the first true friend I've ever had and I couldn't bear to leave the children.'' *I couldn't bear to leave you.*

He could hear the yearning in her voice and wished with all his heart that they could spend their lives together but he knew the dream was impossible. ''We'll stay together as long as we can,'' he equivocated, pulling her into his arms, ''but you must promise me one thing.''

''What, Chase?'' she asked, guardedly.

''If the worst should happen—if I were to die—I want you to go home to Boston and sue Phillips for a divorce. I don't give a damn about Christian morality or what society says. It's madness to remain tied to a man like him. I know he would rather see you dead than alive. You'll have your father's money and if there was one thing I learned living as a Remington, it's that enough money excuses all manner of sins, even bastardy and bad blood.''

She had told him of Josiah's death but not her resultant penury. Before she had refused to subject herself to his pity. And now, could she hold onto him if it meant filling him with guilt for leaving her destitute and at Hugh's mercy?

No, she could never reveal her father's final betrayal. She would take each day they had together as a precious gift. Their love would be as endless as the High Plains sky, no matter that fate might ultimately separate them. "I can't think of leaving you now," she pleaded.

"Please, Stevie. I couldn't bear to think of him touching you again. Promise me you'll divorce him," he implored.

His anguish was so great she would have agreed to anything. "I promise, Chase," she replied gravely. Far better he believe that she possessed the money to secure a divorce, for if he knew that she did not, he would set out once again to kill Hugh. No matter what her husband's crimes, she did not want his blood on Chase's hands.

He studied her expression intently, then nodded, releasing a pent-up sigh. "Good. I'm glad that's settled. Now," he said, his voice growing low and seductive, "it's snowing again and we can go nowhere until it clears . . . so . . ."

"So . . . ?" she echoed, snuggling into his embrace as he rained soft kisses on her face, then moved down her body. This time she wantonly reveled in her nakedness, seeing in his eyes that she was indeed beautiful to him.

They returned to the village two days later to much rejoicing, for everyone had given them up for dead during the fierce blizzard—everyone except for Red Bead who had walked up to them and nodded her usual terse greeting, then turned to Stands Tall. The warrior and his aunt exchanged glances in silent understanding. That night Stands Tall moved his belongings into Red Bead's lodge, leaving Stephanie alone with Chase in his lodge.

The following morning the air was crystalline bright, a blinding azure that seemed to stretch forever, reflecting the brilliant glistening white of the new-fallen snow which had left a deep heavy mantle across the valley as well as the mountains. When Stephanie emerged from the lodge to go for fresh water, Kit Fox joined her, smiling a cheerful hello. Stephanie felt a surge of happiness at seeing her friend, whose cheeks bore the radiant glow of a woman in love. *Do I look the same way?* "Marriage agrees with you, my friend," she said, practicing her halting Cheyenne.

Kit Fox smiled more broadly and nodded. "Yes, it is good . . . and for you, also, I think."

"You're altogether too perceptive," Stephanie replied, switching back to English. "But I am not a bride."

Kit Fox could see Stephanie's cheeks flush and knew she was uncomfortable, yet there were words that should be spoken between them. "According to the custom of my people, you are."

"Remember that I already have a husband," Stephanie replied too sharply.

"But he is not here and you have chosen the White Wolf," Kit Fox replied with irrefutable logic.

"There is no such easy divorce among my people."

Kit Fox took her hand as they knelt by the icy river, unfrozen only because of the warm water pouring into it from the underground hot springs. "You are not among white people now but here with us. My heart is glad that you are my friend and I wish only your happiness. Will you live as one of us . . . for as long as the Powers permit you to remain here?"

"Someday I must leave," Stephanie said with genuine regret in her voice.

"Until then?" Kit Fox prompted.

"What would you have me do?"

Now the Cheyenne smiled. "I will speak with the lodge maker, Antelope Woman. She will direct us—Swan Flower, Green Grass and me. We will build your lodge. A woman must have a lodge of her own—and a bride price must be offered and gifts given to the White Wolf's family."

"But I have no family here," Stephanie sputtered, flustered by her friend's contagious excitement. This was getting out of hand. Such a ritual would not make her Chase's wife. Yet one look at Kit Fox's face told her it would be best to consent. Perhaps if they followed his people's customs, he might keep her with him longer. The thought of living with Hugh was unbearable and she had no means of doing what Chase asked of her if he returned her to civilization.

"I will speak with my mother. She will know what to do. Perhaps my family will adopt you as daughter and we will be sisters."

Stephanie smiled and felt the sting of tears in her eyes. "I would like that, Kit Fox. I would like that very much!"

The two women hugged on the snow-covered riverbank, then filled their buckets with water and returned to camp.

Their new lodge was tight and warm, secure against the night's howling wind. They had finished making love, then dozed for a bit, but he had awakened to stare into the glowing embers, unable to return to sleep. Sensing his restive mood, Stephanie, too, had awakened to his troubled gaze fixed on her. "You do not truly feel we are married, do you?" Chase said.

Shoving the heavy mantle of hair from her bare shoulders, she sat up in his arms and replied, "You paid a high bride price for me and my dowry was most generous," referring to the requisite exchange of gifts made between Kit Fox's brother Plenty Horses and Stands Tall.

"That isn't what I asked," he said softly, letting his fingers comb through her shimmering hair. "Phillips will always be there, won't he?"

"I love you, Chase, not him."

"And you feel guilty about it."

She could not deny the fact. "When Pony Whipper said I would bring death to your people and denounced me in front of the camp, I knew there were others who agreed but were too polite to say it. Hugh is not all that stands between us."

"Pony Whipper has taken his troublemakers and ridden off to join another Crazy Dog band in Montana. Most of my people accept you as my woman, but you won't believe you're my wife until you're able to marry me under white man's law."

There was no condemnation in his voice, only a sadness and an acceptance that made her heart ache. "We have now, Chase. For now, we are husband and wife." She gestured around them to the beautifully fitted out lodge, and touched her heart, then pressed her hand to his. "This is a gift, even more precious because it may not last. I want to grow to be a part of you, of your people, to live their way and forget everything else—for as long as we are given."

Chase sat up and reached inside his storage bin for a tiny pouch. It was covered with exquisite beadwork, the sort used to hold a sacred medicine bundle. He loosened the thin buckskin cord holding the bag closed and drew out something that glinted in the flickering firelight, a gold locket. It was small and heart shaped with delicate scroll-work on the front forming the initials *A.R.* As she watched curiously, he flicked it open revealing two faded pictures, one of a youth with solemn dark eyes, the other of a young woman little older than the boy. "This is one of the few things I've kept with me from the past."

"It's your mother's, isn't it, and the boy with her is you." She knew the delicate golden haired girl was Anthea.

He stared at the pictures a moment, saying, "She had the one of me taken when I came home from boarding school, our fourth Christmas in Boston." He closed the locket and replaced it in the beautiful medicine pouch, then reverently slipped it over her head. She pressed it between her breasts to her heart. "Consider this my wedding pledge to you. Be happy as she was while you're here. For as long as the Powers grant us."

Stephanie felt the sting of tears and clutched the pouch in her hand, holding it to her beating heart. "I will wear it always."

Chase nodded gravely, knowing that in the spring he must take her to safety. Perhaps the knowledge that he could not keep her even though she belonged heart and soul to him and he to her was why he deviled them by bringing up Phillips. "For as long as the Powers grant us," she repeated softly, as he cupped her face in his hands and lowered his mouth to meet hers.

And so they passed the winter, Chase hunting with the warriors and Stephanie performing simple camp chores with the women. Each night they made love in the warmth and security of their lodge while the snow deepened, isolating them from the outside world. All too soon the sun began its arching rise across the vault of sky, raising temperatures and threatening to end their idyll.

Yet another threat arrived in camp with the clearing of the pass. Pony Whipper and three of his Crazy Dogs returned bringing news of more disasters for the Cheyenne and their allies. In spite of Crook's failure to round up the Sioux still roaming freely across the treaty lands of Dakota and Montana, Sheridan was sending Terry and the hated Long Hair, Custer, marching against them as soon as the weather cleared enough for the railroad to move men and supplies. Game on the open plains had been scarce and the winter storms fierce. Many bands of Sioux, Arapaho and Cheyenne were starving and some had already turned themselves in to the agency men in exchange for blankets and the meager rations provided by the White Father.

A great battle between the Blue Coats and the plains tribes was in the offing. Pony Whipper was eager for the fight, and at night he found many willing listeners around the campfires who would join him. The village hummed with a keen edge of repressed excitement. Would the White Wolf lead his raiders against their enemies? Or had his white wife suborned his loyalty to the Cheyenne?

Before the confrontation between Chase and his old rival came to a head, another more immediate and terrible disaster struck—smallpox. Chase had brought serum for his people but many, fearing the white man's bad medicine, had refused to be inoculated. Stephanie, Kit Fox and Red Bead, along with many other of the women who were immunized, nursed the sick, making them as comfortable as they could. Almost all who contracted the dread sores died, including Crow Woman.

Stephanie left the lodge after covering the kindly woman's body in preparation for burial. Her husband had died the preceding day. Now it was her sad task to tell Smooth Stone and Tiny Dancer that they had once again become orphans. As soon as she saw the expression on their faces, she realized they knew. Kneeling, she opened her arms to them and they flew to her, throwing their arms around her neck and holding on tightly. Smooth Stone struggled to be stoic as the warriors he emulated and idolized but his small body trembled. A thin trickle of tears seeped from Tiny Dancer's eyes but she did not make a sound. The children's silence was somehow more poignant than loud crying.

"You'll come to live with us. The White Wolf will be proud to claim you as his own . . . and so will I if you will accept a white woman as your mother," she said, holding a child in each arm as they huddled together outside the death lodge.

Smooth Stone's head jerked up and fierce little black eyes held her pale gold ones. "Of course we will. Are you not Eyes Like Sun, wife to the White Wolf?"

"I have loved you ever since you brought us to the Cheyenne," Tiny Dancer said shyly.

"Come then, it is all settled. I will take you to our lodge while Crow Woman is prepared for burial."

"You take them nowhere, White Eyes." Pony Whipper stood glaring down at them with hate etched in every line of his face.

"We belong to the White Wolf," Smooth Stone said defiantly, taking a step forward to stand protectively in front of Stephanie and his sister.

"This is not the time or place for us to settle our differences, Pony Whipper." Chase walked up behind the big man, who spun around angrily.

"It is not you, White Wolf, who I quarrel with but your woman. She has brought this pestilence among us. It is a spider people's disease that kills the Cheyenne—from her." His finger stabbed at Stephanie as if it were a dagger. "She is bad medicine."

"Eyes Like Sun is a healer who nursed the sick along with Red Bead and the other women. It is true the red spots are a white man's sickness but she has lived with us, isolated here in the stronghold for many months. She could not have brought the contagion down on us. It was you and your men who sojourned among the reservation Indians outside the forts, you carried the disease to us. Crazy Fox, one of your followers, was the first to show the red spots.''

''You lie! The guilt is hers!''

Chase's face remained impassive yet the tensing of his body revealed his fury—a cold deadly wrath that boded ill for Pony Whipper. Hearing the strident voices of the two old foes, a crowd had gathered. Watching from the sidelines, Stands Tall stepped forward. ''What my brother's son says is wise. This is a time of mourning. It is not fitting for you to accuse him or his woman of anything. We must bury the dead.''

''What of Crow Woman's children? It is not fitting they be given to a White Eyes,'' Pony Whipper sneered, daring to insult not only Stephanie but Chase's white blood as well.

Stands Tall stiffened and a low murmuring went up through the crowd. The Crazy Dog was treading on thin ice indeed to challenge the White Wolf's entire family. Before either Chase or his uncle could reply, Elk Bull moved in front of Pony Whipper. ''Your words are intended to provoke bloodshed and we have seen enough of death. Go now and leave this matter rest, else I shall see that you are the one who *is* pony whipped.''

At the old man's words and the threat of being whipped and stripped of all his possessions, the young warrior's eyes blazed with fury but he said nothing, only clenched his fists and held his body rigidly in check. Then he spun around and stalked away but not before he fixed Stephanie with a look of such naked loathing that she felt it like a physical blow.

Holding the children at her sides, she whispered to Chase, ''He'll never forget what I did to him the day he attacked Kit Fox.''

''He's a dangerous enemy,'' Chase said grimly. ''I will speak with Plenty Horses about watching out for you whenever I'm away from camp. He may not like me but he pledged his honor when his family adopted you. As your foster brother he cannot let Pony Whipper harm you without losing face.''

"I was never certain why he agreed to accept me. He hates whites almost as much as Pony Whipper."

Chase smiled. "You obviously don't realize the power Cheyenne women wield over their men. Granite Arm is no one to cross. When she learned about his role in Pony Whipper's attack on Kit Fox, you can bet she made her son pay."

"She has been kind to me since her daughter's affections turned to Blue Eagle, but I never realized she could intimidate her son as she did me."

"You still have much to learn of Cheyenne life," he said dryly, then turned his attention to the children, who had stood silently through the ugly confrontation between the adults. Hoisting Tiny Dancer up in one arm, he nodded to Smooth Stone. "Come, let us see to moving your belongings into our lodge."

"Will we be a family then?" Tiny Dancer asked timidly.

"Yes, we will be a family," he replied as his eyes locked with Stephanie's.

The evening was chill but the wind had died down, leaving the camp in a pristine white stillness that seemed magical. Chase and Stephanie quietly slipped from their lodge and walked to the hot springs. Their footsteps crunched softly in the powdery dry snow as the soft glowing lights from the fires faded in the darkness. Tiny Dancer and Smooth Stone were sound asleep in their lodge.

Although it was the natural Indian custom for parents to make love in the confines of small teepees while their offspring slept, Chase knew Stephanie would be uncomfortable doing so. When he had whispered that they might take an evening swim in the hot water, she accepted at once, grateful for his sensitivity to her feelings.

Those feelings remained as confused as ever, a peculiar mixture of love and guilt driven by an undeniable passion. He had awakened the inner fires of her soul. She could never seem to get enough of the touching and caressing, the soaring physical release and utter repletion that came to her each time they made love. She couldn't imagine not lying beside Chase Remington every night for the rest of her life.

When they reached the steep overhanging shelf of rocks that shielded the hot pools from the winter's chill, he took her in his arms, sliding his hands inside her heavy robe. Beneath it she wore nothing. When his cold hands made contact with her warm flesh, she gasped. "Your hands are like ice!" She made no attempt to pull away.

"And your body is warm from the inner fire. Warm me with your beautiful heat, Stevie," he murmured.

"I love this quiet time of night, when we're all alone," she said as her hands pulled open his robe, eagerly caressing his chest, gliding around his neck and pulling his head down to hers for a series of swift breathless kisses.

Soon the cold was forgotten as they let the robes fall at their feet, standing in the chill dark, fused hip to hip, arms and legs entwined as the kiss deepened. His tongue plunged into her mouth in a series of rhythmic strokes as their lower bodies kept time. She met each thrust, sucking on his tongue until he groaned deep in his throat. Then she rubbed hungrily on his lips, letting her tongue dart inside his mouth in the delicate little dips and glides that she had learned made him wild.

"You're getting all together too good at this," he murmured into her mouth before savaging it with another fierce, hard kiss.

"Surely, you're not complaining. After all . . . you taught me," she said when there was breath enough to whisper.

Feeling the smooth skin of her back roughen with goose bumps in spite of the heavy mantle of her hair, he scooped her into his arms and waded into the steamy bubbling water. When the lapping ripples touched her bottom, she squeaked in delight, then sank into the heavenly warmth. She held fast with her arms around his neck when he released her, letting her slide down the length of his body.

Stephanie could feel the hardness of his erection, hotter even than the water swirling around them. She wriggled her belly against the probing shaft and felt him tense. His passionate, almost desperate sensitivity to her body's slightest touch gave her a sense of power beyond anything she could ever have imagined before. This virile man, sophisticated and savage, desired her above all women. All of her life Stephanie had felt inadequate and unlovable, never more so than when Hugh had bedded her. Her first husband had used her but this one, whom she wed in a primitive pagan manner, truly loved her.

"I've always wanted to bring you here to make love in these waters . . . I've fantasized about it," he growled, cupping her soft rounded buttocks and pressing her hard against him.

She pulled away and looked into his face, unable to see more than a shadowy outline and the glow of his eyes in the pale reflection of starlight on snow. "Have you brought other women here?" Although her tone was light, it was underlaid with anxiety. Then she could see the white gleam of his smile.

"No one . . . ever . . . you're jealous . . . and you have no reason, Stevie. But I like it anyway," he added, punctuating the words with soft wet licks and nips along her throat. He tangled his fingers in the long heavy fall of her hair, pulling back her head for greater access, then moved lower to where the water lapped at the tips of her high firm breasts. He took one in his hand and cupped it, watching the nipple harden to a stiff nubby peak, which he bit just hard enough to elicit a moan of pleasure from her. When he suckled it, she buried her fingers in his long shaggy hair, pressing his head closer while her legs scissored around his hips.

"Guide me home, darling," he murmured as he took her other breast into his mouth, leaning back against the rocky wall of a ledge on the cliff.

Her hand slid over the sleek wet muscles of his shoulder, then down his chest, lower, reaching between their bodies to grasp his hard straining staff, knowing the instant she touched it he would cry out with the ecstasy of her touch, and he did. She squeezed and stroked, reveling in her power over him for a moment, watching his eyes close and the tendons in his jaw and neck stand out. But the aching pulse at the center of her body could not long be denied. Guiding the ruby tip to the opening, she tightened her legs around him and rode down on it, impaling herself as the hot bubbling water rushed around them.

Chase stretched his arms out on the rock ledge behind him, bracing his feet wide apart and arching his hips to thrust deep within her. He could feel the tight hot sheath of her body wrap around him as if never to let go. He wished they could remain joined like this forever, but in a moment the fierce mating urge overpowered both of them. He withdrew a fractional bit and she rolled her hips, digging her nails into his shoulders.

The frenzy began building slowly as he thrust and withdrew to thrust again while she cradled him between her thighs, holding on to him, moving with him in perfect sync, raising up, rolling down. Their breath came out in short, sharp little gasps, the vapor puffs of it mingling with the steam from the pool. Every movement elicited an ever-increasing urgency.

The hot lapping water added to Stephanie's desperate need to experience that final culmination. It laved her body, surrounding her with soft wisps of steam. The wet slickness of her own natural lubrication was intensified by the heat surrounding them. She could feel the crest approach, now so achingly, beautifully familiar to her, an exquisite place of utter abandon, so mind robbingly pleasurable that it was almost painful. And yet she craved it, striving for it with Valkyrie-like ferocity, riding him as he did her.

When at last the climax rushed over her senses, she tightened her thighs to slow and prolong the moment, looking at the shadowed outline of Chase's face in the dim light of the rising moon, waiting for him to join her.

Chase was on fire. Making love to Stephanie in the hot pool was even better than he had fantasized and he had done that in most vivid detail. Her lithe young body was incredibly buoyant in the water, moving with fierce liquid grace. The bubbly current of the mineral spring teased against his testicles each time he thrust and withdrew from the slick wet heaven of her body. When he felt the first swift unmistakable contractions of her sheath around his shaft, he threw back his head and gave in to the pure animal satiation, spilling his seed deep within her.

His staff swelled and pulsed, adding to the incredible intensity of her release. She watched him arching up with every powerful muscle of his body as he gave in to the glory of completion. *As if he's offering himself to me like some splendid savage god.* The thought flashed through her mind as she felt herself filled with him, so deeply a part of him and he of her that she could not tell where one flesh ended and the other began.

When the trembling finally subsided, Chase wrapped his arms around her, holding their bodies still joined intimately together while he stroked the wet silk of her hair, flowing down her back. He buried his face at her neck and felt her arms tighten around his shoulders. They stood locked together for moments, or it could have been longer. Finally, he raised his head and their eyes met.

"Even my most fanciful and lascivious daydreams about this moment pale in comparison to the real thing," he said hoarsely.

She framed his face with her hands, feeling the raspy tickle of his beard. "You need a shave," she murmured with a smile.

"I didn't hear you complaining earlier."

"I'm not complaining now. I love to feel your whiskers. I'll never forget the first time I watched you shave after you'd taken me captive. My toes curled inside my shoes. It was the most disturbingly sensuous thing I'd ever imagined."

He took one of her hands in his and kissed the palm. "I never liked having to shave. It always reminds me of . . ."

"Of your white blood. Red Bead explained to me how difficult it was for you to gain acceptance among the People because of it."

"They would have accepted me if I'd been able to remain with them instead of living in eastern cities for so many years. The very education that's enabled me to outsmart our enemies makes me suspect in the eyes of my own kind.''

There was an edge of bitter irony in his voice. Stephanie felt a sudden chill in spite of the warm steamy water surrounding them. ''And am I your kind—or one of the enemy, Chase?''

He met her eyes steadily, willing her to understand. ''I can never be white again and you can never give up the values and beliefs you were raised to hold dear. Yet we love each other in spite of it all. That has to be enough, Stevie.''

She nodded in acceptance, wrapping her arms around his neck. ''It will be enough, Chase.'' *Any part of you I can hold for as long as I keep you, I will settle for.*

Chase left her floating in the water as the moon gilded her long sleek limbs in silvery splendor. He dried himself and slipped into the clothes he had brought with him. It was his turn to stand sentry duty at full moonrise. When he had disappeared through the snow-laden branches of the spruces she pondered the bittersweet enigma of their relationship. Red Bead and Kit Fox, even Stands Tall had come to approve of her. She had become Eyes Like Sun, adopted into their way of life and she had won the love of Smooth Stone and Tiny Dancer. Everyone she cared about here had accepted her. Everyone but Chase. Even though she shared his sacred medicine dream, she would always be in some measure the enemy to him. Was it perhaps because he himself was so tormented by his white half?

Stephanie had loved Chase Remington since childhood, loved him with all her heart and now with her newly awakened woman's body. She had abandoned civilization and betrayed her marriage vows simply to be with him. It was too beautiful and too volatile to last. All she could do was to savor each poignant moment of this time together and not dwell on the uncertain future.

After the White Wolf's footfalls had faded into the distance, Pony Whipper peered through the cover of the trees at the white woman luxuriating in the water. He had always found her delicate bones and pale skin unattractive, yet watching her with her half-blooded lover had elicited a surprising surge of lust in his loins. He had followed them, intent on taking his revenge against them both by killing her. Now he decided he would taste of her flesh first.

❦ *20* ❧

Stephanie climbed out of the water, shivering as the cold curled in tendrils through the steamy air, raising chill bumps on her skin. She wrapped her robe around herself, feeling an eerie premonition that something was amiss. She hurried to retrieve her comb and a few other items she had left on a nearby rock, but before she reached it the sharp sting of cold steel pressed against her throat.

"Do not make a sound or your blood will pollute the bathing pools," Pony Whipper said in a low growl.

His speech was guttural and she could not understand all the words, but she certainly devined his intentions quickly enough. With one hand he held the blade perilously close to the artery pulsing at the side of her throat, while the other began pulling the robe from her shoulder. *Anything but this*, her mind screamed as his hand found her breast and painfully tweaked her nipple. She bit her lip to keep from crying out in pain, certain that he would revel in her fear.

"Kit Fox was right. You do possess no more honor than a coyote, Pony Whipper," she hissed in Cheyenne.

The blade dug in a bit more but he said nothing, only laughed as he began to force her down to the frozen earth. She tried desperately to think. How could she get free of the knife long enough for a good blood-curdling scream and a chance to seize a weapon of some sort? Such would be no easy matter for he wasted no time, pushing her roughly onto her robe, which had fallen to the ground. He came down on top of her, his face a lust-crazed mask, twisted in hatred. Stephanie lay passively beneath him as he knelt straddling her, the knife still at her throat. He began to tear at his breechclout.

It would all be done in another moment. Twisting her head to one side, she jackknifed upward, raising her right knee to smash it into his crotch, but the blow only grazed his inner thigh. At once he grunted in outrage and raised the handle of the knife, smashing it into the side of her head. Everything went red, then black in front of her eyes, but she screamed before another blow knocked her unconscious.

Pony Whipper had made a tactical blunder. He had started his attack before his real enemy was out of earshot. Chase heard the sounds of scuffling before Stephanie's cry. A red haze enveloped him when he burst into the clearing and saw Pony Whipper with Stephanie pinned naked beneath him. Seeing the knife in his enemy's hand, Chase moved silently across the distance separating them and lunged at Pony Whipper, knocking him away from Stephanie's unconscious body. The two men rolled in the snow, both struggling for control of Pony Whipper's blade.

The Crazy Dog came up on top, pressing the knife down toward Chase's chest as he snarled, ''And now you die with the thought that I shall use your pale skinny woman until she begs for death. Then I shall answer her pleas. It will take her a long time to die.'' His hand quivered as he pressed down with renewed force.

''You boast of what you will never accomplish,'' Chase rasped, as sweat beaded his brow in spite of the cold night air. His foe, too, was slick with perspiration as the deadly wrestling contest continued.

For a moment it seemed as if Chase's arm would give way and the knife plunge into his heart but at the last second, when all Pony Whipper's consciousness was focused on driving home his weapon, Chase brought up his leg and slammed it into his foe's side. They rolled again, kicking and thrashing. Pony Whipper tried to smash Chase's head into a large outcropping of rock but failed.

At length they reached the edge of the water. The heat of the springs kept the snow at bay and the ground was moss covered and slick. The slightly sulfurous smell of the water mingled with the metallic odor of blood as both men bled freely from superficial nicks received wrestling over the blade. As blood and sweat poured down Pony Whipper's arm, Chase's grip slipped, freeing the Crazy Dog's knife. Pony Whipper jumped up with a grunt of triumph and plunged it down, but Chase rolled to the side.

The blade sank deep into the soft earth. Before Pony Whipper could free it and raise it again, Chase rolled up on his knees and drove his fist into his adversary's ribs, knocking the wind from him. Pony Whipper emitted a loud grunt but held tightly to his knife. Chase struck again, this time a powerful blow to Pony Whipper's jaw. The crack of bone splintered sickeningly as the big Crazy Dog's head snapped backward.

Yet he still clutched the knife even as his body was spun completely around. He landed facedown in the shallow water with a loud splash and remained motionless. Then a slow seepage of red began to darken the bubbling surface. Crawling on his knees, winded and gulping air, Chase struggled to turn Pony Whipper's body over. The knife blade was lodged firmly in his chest. Pony Whipper had died by his own hand, on the point of his blade.

Chase released him and rose, with Stephanie's name on his lips. Then he saw Plenty Horses at the edge of the trees, obviously winded from his run from camp. Without a word, Chase strode over to his wife and covered her bare body with the robe, cradling her in his arms as he examined the wound on her head.

"Stevie?"

She stirred and her eyes blinked. Then she moaned and reached up to him, holding tightly to his arm.

Plenty Horses approached them. "I followed Pony Whipper when I learned from Strikes Back that he boasted he would rid our people of the white witch. They were up late smoking and telling tales with the other members of our society when he said this thing. No one else believed him . . . or cared if he did it," Plenty Horses added reluctantly.

"The Crazy Dogs despise me for my white blood. Killing my wife would be revenge because I am allowed to lead raids and sit in the councils of the elders."

"I see the evidence of the dishonorable thing Pony Whipper tried to do and I witnessed the way he died. You will not suffer banishment for his death."

"I thank you for that, Plenty Horses," Chase replied gravely, knowing that testifying for a half-blood against a member of his own warrior society was an act of great courage.

Plenty Horses smiled. "It is the least I can do for both my sisters. Kit Fox told me of how Pony Whipper was brought down by our foster sister when he attempted to dishonor her."

As Stephanie stirred in his arms, Chase looked down on her tenderly. "She has great courage but it earned her Pony Whipper's deadly enmity," he said, stroking her cheek. "Warrior Woman," he crooned with a smile.

The rest of the winter passed in relative peace. Secure in their mountain hideaway, Elk Bull's band hunted deer and small game and prepared their weapons for the day the pass would clear and they could once again venture out onto the open plains. True to his word, Plenty Horses had borne witness to the shameful attack Pony Whipper had made on the White Wolf's wife. Since the Crazy Dog had died by his own knife, the usual sentence of banishment had not been leveled against Chase. For a brief while, he and Stephanie, along with Smooth Stone and Tiny Dancer, lived as a family, laughing, loving and sharing in the life of the village.

But all too soon the first warm winds of spring arrived and Stephanie knew her love would once again ride off to war against the white man. As soon as it was possible for a lone horseman to slip through the pass and ride clear of the Bighorns, Chase donned his tame Indian clothes and prepared to depart, leaving Stephanie to cry silent acid tears in their lodge.

"Please don't do this, Chase," she had implored.

"We've been happy here with the children—safe. You could be killed out there."

"Or I could kill some of them. That will always bother you, won't it?" he replied angrily, strapping a dirty bedroll on the back of the dun's saddle. "Who knows, I might even get it right and finish Phillips this time."

Stephanie felt his words like a blow. "I said I would divorce him," she replied coldly. "You need not murder him to keep him from reclaiming me . . . if he even wanted me."

"He wants your money. He'd kill you to get it." He dropped his hands to his sides and stood, looking at her, not wanting to leave it this way between them. *If I had an ounce of sense, I'd take her out with me and leave her safe with de Boef.*

She almost told him Hugh already had her money but she still possessed some shred of pride. No matter how they quarreled over his vendetta against the whites, he still loved her. She could not bear to see that love turn to pity. If they had to part—and she forced herself to admit it could happen—she would walk away with her head held high, leaving him to regret that he had chosen revenge over love. She would never attempt to hold him because he felt sorry for a penniless and abandoned army wife.

Grabbing the saddle horn, Chase swung effortlessly up on the dun. As he settled into the unaccustomed saddle he almost kicked the horse into a trot, but some irresistible impulse made him pause an instant as his eyes locked with hers. She stood defiantly, dressed in an old doeskin tunic with her hair plaited down her back. Working outdoors in the clear winter sunlight had given her face a golden tint and tiny amber freckles dusted her nose and cheekbones. She was so lovely it made his breath catch in his throat. Without thinking, he reached down and scooped her up in a fierce embrace, pressing her against his side with one arm while the other tilted her stubborn chin up so his lips could claim hers in a fierce kiss.

At first Stephanie pressed her palms angrily against his shoulders, feeling the steely bulge of muscles beneath the greasy shirt. His beard rasped on her delicate skin as long shaggy black hair danced across her face. He smelled of horse and old leather and she could not have loved him more. When his tongue rimmed the seam of her lips demanding entry, she opened to his kiss, raising her fingertips to skim across his unshaven face. Then she buried her fists in his hair, pulling him closer yet.

The children watched solemnly from the door of the lodge, overhearing the tense exchange before the White Wolf swept Eyes Like Sun into his arms. Neither understood the reasons for the infrequent fights their adoptive parents had, but when she wrapped her arms about his neck and returned his kiss, they smiled at one another. Things would be as they had been before once the White Wolf returned from his mysterious mission in the white world.

Chase did not return until the snows had almost melted and May was perfumed with fresh pine and wildflowers. The mountains were warmed by sunlight. The small band of Elk Bull grew restless and eager to rejoin their Cheyenne brothers and Lakota cousins in the great summer hunts. But the news the White Wolf bore made them wary. While they remained hidden securely in their valley this past March, General Crook had led his Blue Coats on a desperate winter campaign out of Fort Fetterman, riding up along the twisting path of the Tongue River, only two days from their stronghold. Fortunately Crook had been deterred by the fury of late winter blizzards and did not venture into the mountains, but now Long Hair, the feared and hated George Armstrong Custer, headed a great invasion force out of Fort Lincoln in Dakota Territory. Along with General Terry and Colonel Gibbons, he was ordered by the White Father in Washington to round up all the Indians along the Upper Yellowstone. That great river and its numerous tributaries comprised the hunting grounds guaranteed to the Horse Indians by the Treaty of Fort Laramie back in 1868 ''for as long as the buffalo should run.''

Of course, the army, along with the railroad, the miners and the buffalo hunters, were making sure that would not be long by decimating the great herds with systematic ruthlessness. Nevertheless, the time was ripe for another hunt and tens of thousands of the great shaggy beasts still populated the vast open reaches of the river valleys. Elk Bull's warriors were eager to race across the plains in pursuit of them. That night the leaders sat in council to hear all the White Wolf had learned.

"If we leave the mountains, I think it would be best to join Sitting Bull's Lakota to the northeast in the Powder River country," Chase said. "The Hunkpapa have drawn thousands to them—all the other tribes of the Teton Nation—Oglala, Sans Arc, Blackfoot, Brule, Miniconjou. And also our cousins the Arapaho and many other bands of Cheyenne."

"All are angry because the White Father has said it is all right for his settlers to seize our Sacred Hills and drive peaceful hunters from the land pledged to us in treaty," Stands Tall stated, wanting everyone in the council to understand the extent of the danger they would face when they left the sanctuary of the mountains.

"Why do they not put all the Indians on wheels? Then they could move us about as they please," Elk Bull said sourly to a chorus of angry agreement.

Chase briefly explained about the army units which would shortly be placed in the field against the various tribes. He ached to join the war parties already making their medicine to attack the hated Blue Coats, especially Custer. Nothing would have given him greater pleasure than to kill the fabled Long Hair—except to kill Hugh Phillips, the butcher of Wyoming Territory. But he could do neither, he reminded himself, for this band depended on him for its safety. He had a family now. First he must think of Stephanie, Smooth Stone and Tiny Dancer.

"We have supplied our Lakota brothers with many good Henry and Winchester rifles. Now they are nearly five thousand strong and growing every week as more people come to join them for the hunt. By summer they will number twice that. The Long Hair and other soldiers will chase the war parties but even Custer would not be so foolish as to attack the main encampment. If you choose to go, it is to that place I say we should travel. I will offer more presents to Sitting Bull from my stockpile of repeating rifles.''

Discussion ensued as each warrior with martial experience spoke his piece, as was the Cheyenne way. Finally a consensus was reached. They would join the summer camp of Sitting Bull. The great Lakota leader had never bowed to government dictates nor taken agency handouts. He steadfastly eschewed any contact with the whites, leading his people to live by the buffalo hunt on the open plains as they had for hundreds of years.

That night it was moonrise before Chase returned to their lodge. Smooth Stone and Tiny Dancer had been allowed to remain awake to greet their foster father. Stephanie stirred a steaming pot of stew, fragrant with chunks of mountain sheep and wild onions. During her years in the West she had become a competent cook, learning from the strikers on the army posts. Now she had mastered cooking over an open campfire under even more primitive conditions.

The sudden draft of cool air as he opened the tent flap alerted Stephanie to Chase's entry. He stood in the flickering firelight, so tall and dangerous looking, still dressed in the guise of half-breed drifter, hair unbound, beard bristling and clothes greasy and rumpled. An arsenal of weapons surrounded him, Winchester in his right hand, Navy Colt on one hip and a wicked Bowie knife on the other. A beaded Osage necklace hung around his neck where the open lacings of the worn buckskin shirt revealed a thick patch of black hair but concealed the telltale Sun Dance scars.

Stephanie knew they were there. How often in the nights they'd shared had she stroked them and touched her mouth to the ridged scars, signs of his savagery. She stood up, moistening her lips nervously. She had allowed them to part in anger, then worried herself sick that he would die alone in some dirty army outpost or wild frontier boomtown. The urge to throw herself into his arms and hold him almost overpowered her, yet she forced herself to wait, to gauge his feelings for her now that he had moved among his white enemies.

When Chase stepped inside the lodge, the sleepy-eyed children's faces lit up as they launched themselves at him, circling the fire pit to run into his arms. He knelt, hugging them both, then lifted one in each arm. All the while his eyes never left Stephanie's. She stood rooted to the ground, nervously clutching a bone spoon in her hand. He had felt her visual inspection the instant she became aware of his presence. He looked dirty and mean, contaminated by the dregs of white society with whom he had consorted. He'd ridden hard after leaving Bismarck, eager to return to her. Was she repelled by the stink of his unwashed clothes and body?

"You look very domestic, Stevie. That stew smells wonderful," he said. *I missed you so much I couldn't think of anything else.*

"You must be hungry." She knelt down by the bubbling pot and began to dish up a bowl for him as Smooth Stone and Tiny Dancer chattered about what they had done while he was gone, interspersed with questions about what he had seen on his long journey.

When he squatted down by the fire and accepted the food their fingers brushed. He felt scorched by the light touch and heard her sharp intake of breath. She looked away, chewing on her lip, and began to fuss with her cooking utensils. So, she was not put off by his rough looking appearance. Then the insidious thought occurred—at least as Asa Grant he looked part white, but here in camp he looked wholly Cheyenne. There was no use pursuing that thought. He began to wolf down the savory stew.

"What did the council decide?" she asked at length after instructing the children to return to their pallets and go to sleep.

"We begin packing up to leave the mountains at first light."

"You don't think it's safe, do you?"

He shrugged. "What place is safe anymore? We're being hunted down and exterminated just like the buffalo."

"But if we stayed here, the army could never find us."

"That's not an option. My people are horsemen used to

living freely on the plains. We can't live indefinitely on deer and smaller game. We need the buffalo for its hides, bones and sinews as well as its meat. And we need to mix with other bands. You know about our laws against marriage within the same clans. We've always been part of a great nation among other allied nations.''

Stephanie had learned from Red Bead, Kit Fox and others about the complex clan system of the Cheyenne, as well as the interrelated tribal councils of the whole nation that met each summer during the great hunts. The Cheyenne, like their Arapaho and Lakota brethren, were a corporate society. ''Where are we going?''

''To join Sitting Bull. If there's safety in numbers, the Cheyenne should survive surrounded by seven or eight thousand Lakota and their allies.''

She noticed he said ''the Cheyenne.'' Did that mean she was not going with them? Was he going to take her back to civilization? ''Chase . . .'' Her words faded away as he raised his head and studied her with glittering black eyes. ''I—I'd best begin gathering our belongings for the long trip,'' she said, refusing to even think of the plea she had been unable to voice.

He set aside his empty stew bowl and walked over to the storage packs, extracting clean soft buckskin clothing. Then he turned to her and extended his hand across the glowing coals of the fire. ''Before you start packing, there are a few wifely duties that I require, Stevie . . . beginning with a bath,'' he said, grinning wolfishly.

Remembering all the times they had made love in the steamy waters, she felt her belly clench and a deep tingling ache build between her thighs. Her cheeks flamed and her breath caught. *Am I so obvious?* Trembling, she clasped his hand and he pulled her into his arms. Together they glanced down at Smooth Stone and Tiny Dancer, now sound asleep beneath their robes, then slipped silently from the lodge into the warm spring night, headed to the beckoning seclusion of the hot springs.

*　　*　　*

The journey down from the mountains took them over a week, burdened as they were with old people and children. They followed the ridge above the swollen rushing waters of the Little Bighorn. Chase, along with several other warriors, scouted ahead and quickly located the still massing summer camp of Sitting Bull on the lower end of the river, which the Indians called the Greasy Grass. Finally the weary caravan of Cheyenne entered the long narrow valley and looked down on the most enormous encampment of Indians any had ever seen. The northernmost end of the long meandering lines of teepees were clustered just below the mouth of Sundance Creek, which flowed into the Greasy Grass. These were the lodges of the great Sitting Bull and his Hunkpapa. The other Teton groups were sprawled for over three miles downstream along the western bank of the river.

On the high bluffs at the edge of the valley, Elk Bull's band paused, looking down at the river below them, ice cold, brimming with the melted snows of the mountains from which they had come. Dense thickets of cottonwood trees rustled in the warm June breeze, clustered here and there along the banks, offering shade to many of the lodges. To the west side of the valley a series of low grassy hills undulated with pony herds grazing on the lush early summer grasses. There were thousands of lodges and countless more horses swarming across the level elevated benches in the west.

Stephanie reined in the small paint mare Chase had given her and sat uncomfortably on her wooden saddle, gazing down in awe on the encampment below. "It's incredible. The lodges stretch on for miles and the horses . . ." Her voice trailed away in incredulity.

Chase's eyes narrowed, studying the lay of the land. "They've chosen a good campsite considering the size of the group. The need for game for the stew pots, not to mention grass for the horses, will be huge. They've already moved several times since the convergence began in May."

"Do you think General Crook will attack?" she asked

worriedly, thinking more of her friends and family among the Cheyenne than of the soldiers.

"After the trouncing the Lakota gave him on the Rosebud last week, I doubt it. He was in full retreat last our scouts heard. But that still leaves Gibbon, Terry and Custer. It's Custer I'd worry about," he added grimly.

"Only a madman would attack a village of this size without half a dozen regiments," Stephanie said.

"From what the other scouts and I have learned, Terry's whole command is only around a thousand men and poorly armed except for the Gatling gun battery, which they'll never be able to move in this rugged terrain. Still, if Terry turns Custer loose, sooner or later there'll be trouble."

"Is—is there any chance Hugh's command from Fort Steele will be involved in this campaign?" she asked hesitantly. The matter had been preying on her mind ever since the band's scouts had brought word about the soldiers from Fort Lincoln and Fort Fetterman taking the field.

Chase looked over at her with an unreadable expression on his face but before he could frame a reply Plenty Horses approached them, smiling broadly. "What do you wait for? Our Lakota brothers send their greetings and a site for our camp has already been selected to the south."

Smooth Stone, who had been sharing a pony with another older boy, waved as they rode down the hill. Tiny Dancer, eager to be with Stephanie when they entered the new camp, jumped from the travois on which she had ridden with several other little girls. "May I ride with you, Eyes Like Sun?" she asked excitedly.

Smiling, Stephanie reached down and snatched the slender little body up onto the front of the saddle. "You must eat more. You still weigh next to nothing."

Silently the cavalcade made its way down into the valley of the Greasy Grass where they hoped to find safety and companionship after the long winter's isolation. By that evening the newest Cheyenne arrivals had set up their lodges beside those of the other bands and the sounds of a great celebration could be heard up and down the vast camp.

Elk Bull, Chase and the other leaders from their group were feted by their fellow tribesmen. Feasting and dancing went on far into the night. Stephanie took the children and returned to their lodge early, too weary from the journey and her own emotional turmoil to rest well. What would happen this summer? Would the army attack the warriors out on the hunt, forcing the tribes from this, the last open land on which they could roam freely? Would Hugh somehow find out she was here and attempt to rescue her—or if Chase was right—kill her?

Most of all she worried that Chase would send her away. Especially now since she had become certain she carried his child. Since his return to their mountain stronghold, she had been almost positive but told no one, not even her best friend, Kit Fox. Red Bead may have suspected but the enigmatic old woman did not speak of it. Stephanie did not know what to do. As the baby's father, Chase had the right to know, yet their tribal marriage was a fragile thing and the shadow of her white husband still hovered over them.

She did not want to bind Chase to her with a child any more than she wanted to use her penury as leverage against being returned to civilization. A part of her still abhorred the idea of raising their child—a child that would be three-quarters white—in the harsh and dangerous world of Horse Indians. Would she end up like Anthea, forced to leave the reservation in order to save her child's life after Chase had been killed? But the hope that Chase would ever leave the Cheyenne to settle down and live as a white man was a slim one indeed. With his family's wealth behind them, securing her divorce from Hugh would be possible. Had she the right to ask him?

Does he love me enough to become Chase Remington again, no longer the White Wolf? With that troubling question haunting her, Stephanie drifted off into a restless sleep. When she awakened the following morning, Chase was gone. He had come to their lodge late and drawn her into his embrace, holding her as they slept, naked flesh pressed to naked flesh. But first he had quietly made love to her, stroking her breasts and belly beneath the robes, then sliding into the welcoming warmth of her body from behind. Without the need for words they had lain together like two spoons when it was complete, silently reveling in the exquisite joy of simply being together.

She felt the furs beside her, still warm with his body heat. *Tell him. Tell him today.* She stretched and smiled, sliding her tunic over her head as she looked at the children asleep across the floor. *Perhaps I shall*, she thought as she threw off her covers and put on her moccasins and reached for the water bucket.

When Stephanie walked outside the hazy morning fog was just beginning to lift, revealing that she had overslept considerably. Being pregnant was beginning to take a toll on her energy reserves. All she wanted to do here of late was sleep. Waving to Red Bead, whose lodge stood next to theirs, she began to walk toward the rushing hum of the river when suddenly a warrior came splashing across the water, riding hell-bent into the center of the Cheyenne camp, yelling excitedly and waving his rifle in the air. Her heart froze as she mentally translated his cries into English.

"The Blue Coats are attacking!"

⁂ *21* ⁂

Stephanie dropped her water bucket and dashed back to her lodge. Everywhere around her chaos erupted as mothers called out for their children and babies wailed in fright. Young children stood by, their eyes round with fear. Two girls began gathering the smaller children together in a protective huddle while the boys looked to their elder brothers, hoping for the chance to use their toy weapons. Men rushed into their lodges in search of their bows and guns, shouting orders to their families.

Stephanie reached Red Bead, who remained calm amid the pandemonium, calling out for several boys to put down their small game bows and enter their lodges. Disappointed, they obeyed. "What are we to do?" Stephanie asked the older woman.

Before Red Bead could reply, Chase galloped into the center of the circle of lodges and leaped from Thunderbolt's back. He had with him half a dozen of the horses from their herd including the big dun. "Where are the children?" he demanded.

"Still asleep—or at least they were," Stephanie replied.

"Get them up and pack some food and water quickly. I've brought horses. Can you handle the dun?"

"Yes, but—"

"Our scouts say the soldiers will be here soon," he interrupted her. "I want you well out of the line of fire by then."

Red Bead nodded, checking the position of the sun in the hazy sky. "Plenty time." She entered her lodge and quickly set to work.

Stephanie did not budge. "How many soldiers are there?

Surely their leader can't hope to attack a camp of this size unless he has several thousand men.''

"We don't know their strength yet or even who it is— could be Crook or Terry, but I'd bet it's Custer, riding hell-bent through fog all morning with no advance reconnaissance to tell him how badly outnumbered he'll be.''

Icy fingers of dread squeezed her heart. ''What are you going to do, Chase?'' *He'll have to fight.*

"See you to safety, then join my uncle and the rest of our warriors. Because he has a son old enough to fight with us, Elk Bull will be in charge of protecting the Cheyenne women and children. Come, there's no time to waste.'' He took her arm to urge her into their lodge.

Stephanie pressed her hand on his naked chest, stopping him. "Chase, they could kill you.''

He stroked her cheek and held her, realizing that she did truly love him even though he was going into battle against her own kind. Oblivious of all else but each other, they stood with their eyes locked as frightened people cried out and ran around them. "I don't plan to die today,'' he said simply. "Now, let's get Smooth Stone and Tiny Dancer. I want to be certain you're well away from the fighting. The soldiers will come from across the river. Elk Bull wants the women to camp on the benchlands far to the west, out of harm's way.''

They entered the lodge where the children were awake, sitting wide-eyed on their pallets. At a glance it was obvious that they were badly frightened. They had already suffered so many tragic losses in their brief lifetimes. Stephanie prayed there would be no more this day. "You must pack your things quickly. We are moving west to the benchlands with the other families,'' she said calmly.

Tiny Dancer ran to her but Smooth Stone looked at Chase expectantly. "I heard the crier say Blue Coats were attacking.''

"They're on their way, yes,'' Chase replied.

"I will fight them beside you. You will be proud of me,'' the boy said boldly, reaching for his small bow and quiver.

"Listen well, Smooth Stone, for I give you a very important duty.'' At once the child paused and looked up at him. ''You must protect your sister and foster mother and Aunt Red Bead. Some warriors must see that they get safely to the benchlands. Will you do this thing for me?''

The boy swallowed manfully, disappointed that he could not join the battle with his hero but not surprised for he knew he was yet small and unproven. He had been entrusted with the women of their family. That was an honor for which he would endeavor to be worthy. ''I will do as you say,'' he replied solemnly.

Chase hugged the boy. ''I am proud of you, Smooth Stone.'' Then he took Tiny Dancer from Stephanie's arms and held her for a moment to calm her trembling. Setting her down he said, ''It will be all right. Gather your belongings and do as your foster mother says.'' She nodded gravely.

Stephanie and Chase looked at each other as the children obediently began to pick up their simple possessions. ''I must go. You know what to do. Elk Bull and some of the other older warriors are waiting at the edge of camp.''

''We'll hurry, Chase.'' There was so much she longed to say but she could not find the words. Now was not the time, but when would be? ''Keep safe, my love. We'll be waiting. I love you, Chase.''

He pulled her into his arms for a swift kiss, just as the sharp crack of rifle fire echoed up the valley from the south. At once he released her. ''They're coming at the Cheyenne camp first! No time to waste,'' he said, scooping up Tiny Dancer and thrusting her into Stephanie's arms as the child clutched her doll tightly to her chest.

Smooth Stone led them out of the lodge, looking over his shoulder to be certain Stephanie followed. Chase lifted the boy onto a small pinto, then handed Tiny Dancer up. Red Bead, laden with two large packs, emerged from her lodge. Chase took the items from his aunt and helped her onto a gentle old mare, then handed her one of the packs. Stephanie waited beside the dun, holding the reins of the spare horses. There had been no time to pack their belongings. She had heard stories around the forts about whole villages set to the torch. Visions of the charred ruins of a whole winter's hard work flashed before her eyes. *It isn't fair!*

Chase lifted her onto the dun and handed her the pack. "At least you'll have food and water," he said simply. "Now go." His eyes met Smooth Stone's and the boy nodded, kicking the pinto into a trot. Chase watched as they rode over to where Elk Bull and a number of the older warriors were assembling the women and children.

Not everyone was proceeding with the evacuation in an orderly fashion. Women still raced about calling for missing children, most probably boys who were too young to fight yet did not believe they were. Some frightened girls ran squealing up the open valley floor to the north headed toward the Sans Arc teepees. Everywhere horses were churning up thick dust as youths rode in with their family mounts and women began to load the ponies with belongings. Dogs barked excitedly, adding to the melee. The shouts of angry warriors blended with the wails of babies. Ominously the sharp report of distant gunfire and the loud yips of embattled Cheyenne and Lakota rolled up the valley floor.

Once his family was safely en route across the valley, Chase turned Thunderbolt to the south, headed toward the battle. By the time he arrived the warriors had driven the attacking soldiers from their horses. The Blue Coats were dug in along the river in a dense stand of timber from which they fired desultory shots. The warriors, too, had mostly dismounted and were returning fire from behind rocks and bushes. There seemed to be more than ample defenders to keep the troops pinned down.

Judging from the number of rounds fired, there could surely be no more than a couple of hundred soldiers in the trees. Where were the rest? Remembering Custer's tactics at Washita, splitting his command and attacking from several sides at once, Chase grew worried. Then he saw the rising plumes of dust to the east, northerly along the steep ridge across the river which was rent by two deep ravines. It would take only moments for soldiers to pour out of them and across the shallow ford in the river.

The nearest of all the combined camps was that of the Cheyenne, most of whom were engaged in fighting the entrenched soldiers to the south. Turning Thunderbolt around, he headed back up the valley toward the Lakota camp where the chiefs readied their men. If this was Custer, Chase had learned a thing or two about how they must fight the Long Hair. As he urged the big black forward, he prayed not all of General Terry's forces were converging on them, especially any coming from the west where the noncombatants had sought sanctuary. But he knew blue-bellies never considered the old, the women or the children exempt from slaughter.

When he reached the central Lakota camp, which was scattered several miles along the twisting riverbank, he saw the same pandemonium he'd witnessed earlier with the Cheyenne. Wasting no time, he searched for the young war chiefs among Sitting Bull's men. The great leader, like Elk Bull, had sons to fight for his family and he was in charge of evacuation. Spying Gall, one of the most influential chiefs, Chase headed toward the Lakota, a man who had listened with respect when he spoke in council.

"My warriors bring word of many more Long Knives beyond the ridge," Gall said without preamble, pointing to the east. "What of those who attacked from the south?"

"They are being held down but I fear many more come from the east. They will ride through the coulee there."

Gall nodded. "My warriors ready themselves to stop that. I have already sent some down to the edge of the water to lie in wait in the bushes."

"What of Crazy Horse?" Chase knew the young war chief mistrusted him because of his white blood, yet Crazy Horse was the most brilliant tactician among all the Lakota.

"He gathers his warriors to the north of here. There are many of them and they can strike quickly wherever they are needed. He has said to tell you he is grateful for the many-bullet rifles you brought us. Now more than ever they will be needed."

Chase had brought Henry and Winchester repeaters as gifts from his band. The loot had been taken from raids on stages and supply trains last summer. "I am only glad my brothers have the weapons this day," he replied. "I think these Blue Coats are led by the Long Hair, Custer. He would split his command this way. We must learn how many soldiers he has and where he has sent them. If they ride down on us from the north or worst of all, the west, our women and children will be in terrible danger."

"Come. You should tell this thing to Crazy Horse and see what he will do. I will lead my warriors across the river to the coulee and stop the Blue Coats there."

Chase nodded, knowing he would stand a better chance of having the Lakota war chief listen because of his gifts than he would have before last night. Just then the sound of a bugle blowing a charge rolled across the open river. Gall yelled for his warriors to follow him and vaulted onto his horse. Quickly the dust churned up from hundreds of ponies filled the air as the Hunkpapa charged toward the river with his warriors. Several groups of men, some of them Cheyenne from his band, were returning from the south where the first attackers had been repulsed and pinned down. Recognizing Blue Eagle and Plenty Horses, Chase called out to them. They quickly rode over to him.

"I need you to scout around the western perimeter of the valley and look for soldiers."

"Many are coming from the east," Blue Eagle said.

"We have already driven back those who attacked our camp. They run like scalded dogs," Plenty Horses added scornfully.

"They probably did not expect so many of us, or that we would be so well armed," Chase replied, running his hand along the barrel of his Winchester. "I go to speak with Crazy Horse, but we must know if the Long Hair has split his command again and plans to attack from the west."

"The Long Hair!" Plenty Horses said excitedly. "What an honor to count coup on that one."

"Is it truly him?" Blue Eagle asked, looking across the benchland worriedly to where Kit Fox and the other women were waiting.

"I cannot be certain, but this is the way he fights. There may be others with him—General Terry, perhaps even Crook."

"The Lakota defeated Crook on the Rosebud," Plenty Horses scoffed.

"I will search to the southwest," Blue Eagle replied, looking at his brother-in-law.

"I will ride to the northwest," Plenty Horses replied although it was clear he itched to join the fight which had just begun in earnest across the river.

Chase nodded in satisfaction. "If you see soldiers, ride at once to Crazy Horse. He has the best trained and most numerous of the Lakota warriors."

They split up and each rode hard. Satisfied that his kinsmen would sound the alert if the worst befell, Chase kneed Thunderbolt, guiding him through the melee of people toward Crazy Horse's camp. Some warriors still adorned themselves for battle while others rushed back for fresh horses. Women returned to seize more belongings left behind in the first dash to get the children to safety. In a few moments he spied the great war chief, mounted on a splendid piebald stallion, and made his way toward him.

Crazy Horse was a young man with fiercely imposing features. Although not particularly tall by Cheyenne standards, he sat his horse with arrogant grace, calling out commands with the cool aplomb of a West Point veteran. His keen brown eyes were set deep in a wide flat face with high cheekbones and surprisingly well-defined eyebrows below a shallow forehead. His heavy hair was stretched tightly from a center part into two thick braids adorned with eagle feathers. A deeply grooved mouth with wide thin lips set in a flat line gave his face a perpetually austere appearance. He inclined his head to Chase when the Cheyenne reined in beside him.

Chase quickly outlined his fears and explained about the two scouts he'd sent to the western rim of the valley.

Crazy Horse took it all in, weighing the White Wolf's words. Then the slightest hint of a smile touched his mouth. "I, too, am going to attack from behind." He pointed northward to a shallow ford in the river across to the east where the steep bluffs sloped off. "We will go around the hills and circle the Blue Coats." He made a sweeping motion, curving his arm in an arc. "No one will escape. My scouts have seen them and they number many less than us, but no one could see if the Long Hair leads them. I hope he does."

"Custer's luck may finally have run out," Chase said.

"It would be just for the betrayal of your people on the Sweetwater," Crazy Horse replied.

"I was at Washita the year before and swore vengeance against him."

"Then join us now and count coup on him if he is their leader."

Grimly Chase cast an anxious glance across the valley. "I thank you for the honor, but I must be certain there is no menace yet to strike from the west. Then I will join Gall at the coulee. We will hold them on the east side of the river."

"It is good." Crazy Horse called up his warriors and they rode north across the river, leaving behind a great swirling cloud of dust.

Chase turned Thunderbolt about and rode toward the heavy firing coming from the deeply gouged ravines across the river. The bluebellies had been driven back, their charge through the coulee quickly broken. What fools to blunder onto a camp of this size. Surely there was no way they could rout the Indians. Chase prayed he was right as he stared into the smoke and dust of the battle. Within a short while Plenty Horses and Blue Eagle returned with welcome news. There were no soldiers to the west. The vast open grasslands stretching above the benches were calm with not so much as a puff of dust to indicate a lone horseman.

The three warriors rode toward Gall's men to join in the bitter contest. On impulse, Chase leaned over to Plenty Horses and spoke. "If I should perish this day, I would ask a great favor. Take my wife, your foster sister, to the Frenchman who sometimes trades among us. Gaston de Boef will see she is returned safely to her people."

"It will be as my brother asks," Plenty Horses replied gravely.

Stephanie could hear the guns, so many rifle and pistol shots they merged at times like distant thunder echoing across the Valley of the Greasy Grass. Some of the women, upon hearing that the soldiers were being defeated, rode boldly across the river to watch the men, cheering them on with high, excited trills.

"I wish to see this great victory, Eyes Like Sun. It will be safe for us to return," Smooth Stone cajoled.

Shuddering, she could imagine the carnage that must be taking place in the rough terrain across the river. "No, Smooth Stone, we will remain here. I do not wish to see anyone killed."

He studied her, puzzled at her vehemence. "Is that because you are still loyal to the White Eyes?" he asked without rancor.

"I cannot change what I am," she said, suddenly feeling incredibly sad and bone weary. She wanted nothing so much as to lie down and sleep until the killing was over. But she could not sleep or even close her eyes. *My first responsibility is to the children,* she reminded herself. In her heart she knew what she would see every night hereafter—Chase, the White Wolf, dressed like the other savage warriors, riding off to kill or be killed. Soldiers, possibly even men she knew, were dying at that very moment, as were these people who had become family to her. What cruel fate had asked her to choose between them? *I choose Chase, every time. Please, don't let him die!* she prayed silently, holding tightly to Tiny Dancer, who had wrapped her arms around her foster mother's neck trying to console her.

"It's all right, Eyes Like Sun. Our warriors are defeating the invaders. Soon there will be a great victory dance," the little girl said in Cheyenne. Stephanie did not reply, only stroked the child's shiny hair and held her.

Red Bead, unperturbed by all the commotion, set about making camp. To occupy Smooth Stone and keep him from trouble she had him prepare a fire. She dragged out the large cookpot she had rescued, along with the makings for some stew. Soon she had Stephanie and Tiny Dancer enlisted in helping her, but as the white woman worked, her eyes kept returning again and again to the smoke and dust rising in the distance.

Chase, what will happen to us now?

The sun was at its full summer zenith. Chase reckoned the date to be late in June although he had no way to accurately count the days. Waves of blistering heat pounded down on him as he rode through the scene of carnage, intensifying his building sense of horror. In the past five years he had seen bloody battlefields, but nothing ever of this magnitude. Although the victorious Lakota and Cheyenne did not know it, they had utterly annihilated the command of George Armstrong Custer, the infamous Long Hair. Chase recognized what remained of the regimental flags and other insignia.

The battlefield stretched nearly three miles across the ridges and ravines of the Valley of the Greasy Grass. Everywhere bodies lay sprawled grotesquely in death, some scalped of their hair, others of their beards. Paper money, bright green against the brown dusty earth, fluttered in the wind, tossed away by the Indians, who saw no value in the 7th's last payroll. Rather they took the gaudy uniforms of the officers, proudly donning jackets with gold braid and trousers with yellow stripes, even though the tall Horse Indian's arms and legs were usually too long for the clothes to fit. A group gathered around a stripped soldier, marveling at the large eagle tattooed across his chest, never having seen "war paint" on a white man before.

The 7th's horses were rounded up. The saddles would be given to the women and old men. Cartridge belts and guns were also sought-after prizes as were tobacco and coffee. Here and there other items were taken, the whiskey flasks being especially popular with some of the young warriors. Field glasses were another valuable prize, but pocket watches and compasses frightened the Indians. One youth pulled a ticking watch from the pocket of a soldier and held it to his ear, exclaiming, "It is alive!" Then he tossed it away, fearful of the White Eyes medicine.

Chase could only guess how many soldiers had died in the senseless attack but the numbers were staggering—probably several hundred. He had seen Custer's body, shot in both head and heart, lying up on the ridge surrounded by his troops. The blaze in those zealous pale blue eyes had been extinguished forever, yet Chase found no comfort in the sight. The Indians had not recognized the Long Hair for he had cut his hair before this campaign. Chase did not tell anyone who he was. What use was there now? The greatest tragedy of the day was not Custer's death, but the death it would bring to the Lakota and Cheyenne. The 7th Cavalry's destruction would be enough to bring white vengeance down on the victors who had paid a high price already. Dozens of Lakota and Cheyenne had perished. Now their women came to claim the bodies, slashing their arms in mourning as the slain warriors were carried away for burial. He knew by nightfall the sky would blaze brightly as the lodges and possessions of the dead were burned.

There would be no celebration after such a costly battle, but Chase knew his people had no idea what this unexpected victory would cost them. He did. Generals Terry and Crook would not be all that far behind Custer. Once Sheridan learned of the death of his favorite young officer, he would move heaven and earth to destroy those who had killed him. There would be no place on earth they could hide.

I must get Stevie out of here before it's too late.

He had put off the melancholy thought during the hours the battle had raged, fighting with Gall's Lakota in the narrow ravine where soldiers fired down on them from the heights until the numerically superior Indians climbed around and encircled them. If not for the repeating rifles he had brought in such numbers, the bluebellies might yet have cut through and ridden across the valley to destroy their families. As it was, a small force of troopers—the first to attack the Cheyenne from the south—still held out in the timber, having been reinforced later in the course of the battle. Once Custer's main force was destroyed, Chase had wished to fight no more. Some Indians continued to keep the troopers pinned down and had run off all their horses but would wait to rush them until their ammunition ran out. Enough warriors had already died this day.

Chase knew what he must do. Bruised and scraped from climbing around in the rocks, and bloody from several small bullet nicks, he turned his mount westward to collect his family. En route he passed through the center of the huge encampment, now deserted save for those preparing to burn the possessions of their dead. Some Lakota erected burial scaffolds as was their custom while the Cheyenne gouged out troughs in the sides of the steep bluffs and interred the bodies, covering them with rocks.

Everywhere wails of mourning filled the air but the sound of strident voices arguing in Lakota and Cheyenne caught Chase's attention near the Sans Arc teepees. An old man stood with quiet dignity as a group of Lakota warriors surrounded him menacingly, accusing him of helping the Blue Coats.

"I am Cheyenne," he replied, pounding his fist against his chest. "I do not ride with White Eyes soldiers."

He spoke in Cheyenne and the Lakota did not understand him; neither did he understand their language. The confrontation was getting ugly as the small group of Cheyenne warriors shielding the women and children who had come with them gathered in a circle ready to defend themselves. Recognizing their leader, Chase dismounted and stepped to the front of the crowd.

"This is Little Wolf of the Cheyenne, blood brother of my father and my uncle. He is a man of honor," Chase said in Lakota, then looked into the seamed face of the old warrior whose black eyes lit with recognition. "Chase the Wind, now grown to be the great White Wolf. My band sings stories of your bold deeds which match those of your father, Vanishing Grass." He clasped Chase's arms.

"It has been too long a time since last I saw Little Wolf," Chase replied, returning the embrace.

"You were a young warrior then, when the buffalo blackened the plains of the Arkansas River. Now we live on the white man's handouts at the reservation," Little Wolf said sadly. "That is where we have come from."

Seeing that the White Wolf would vouch for the new arrivals, the Lakota braves made them welcome. Afterward, Little Wolf took Chase aside and said, "You have saved my band this day. I am forever in your debt."

"There is a favor I would ask which would more than repay it," Chase replied. "You know the Blue Coats will pursue us mercilessly after what has taken place here." The old man nodded in agreement. "If the worst should happen to my band, I ask you to care for those who survive. My uncle Stands Tall will bring you our aunt Red Bead who is full of years and two young children whom I have adopted."

"It shall be as the White Wolf wishes, but let us not dwell on the future which is in the hands of the Everywhere Spirit. I would see my old friend Stands Tall if he yet lives."

Chase took Little Wolf and his people and headed for their new camp. Stands Tall was having a few minor injuries tended by Red Bead while the children watched gravely. Observing the bodies of dead warriors being prepared for burial all around them was another grim experience for Smooth Stone and Tiny Dancer, who had already seen too much of death. Stephanie stood off to one side, isolated in the midst of this grief. Chase watched his uncle greet Little Wolf and make him welcome. Then he walked up to her and took her hand. It was ice-cold in spite of the warm evening. "Come with me. We must speak," he said, pulling her away from Red Bead's cookfire.

They wended their way through the makeshift open camp. No one had put up the lodges taken down after the battle. Family possessions were packed up with only a few simple cooking utensils and basic foodstuffs left out. Many made their pallets out in the open and some erected brushy arbors for the night's shelter. No one knew how long they dared remain in the Valley of the Greasy Grass.

Stephanie followed him, still numb with fright. Stands Tall had returned over an hour earlier, saying that Chase was alive. She had kept a vigil as more and more dead warriors were brought from the battlefields by their families, wondering if she, too, would have slashed her arms and legs to show her grief if he had been among the dead. But then he had come riding in, smeared with blood and dust, alien and deadly looking, a half-naked savage with feathers in his long braided hair.

She had started to run to him but something stopped her—not the newcomers whom he escorted to their fire but something in his manner. There was none of the triumphant blood lust that had so horrified her when he had returned to the stronghold from successful raids. Rather, he looked as bone weary as she felt. A cool dark distance seemed to separate him from her even when he took her hand. As soon as they reached the edge of the camp, he relinquished his grip, expecting her to follow him over the slight rise where a small copse of gooseberry bushes allowed them some privacy to speak.

She stopped when he did, feeling a chill of premonition as he turned to her in the twilight. The bleakness in his eyes robbed her of breath, yet there was also such stinging bitterness in the set of his lips that she dared not offer comfort. What was there to say? His people had killed hundreds of soldiers. The desultory firing from the small remnants in the timber to the south only served as a reminder. She hugged herself and waited for him to speak.

"I'm returning you to civilization," he began without preamble. He'd spent hours hardening his heart, assuring himself that there was no other way. Yet just the sight of her standing alone so slender and lovely in her doeskin tunic had nearly cost him his resolve. He thought of her as his wife. But that was in the Cheyenne manner. In white society she would be legally bound to Hugh Phillips. Surely she would not return to him. Chase prayed it was so, but could not ask now, for to do so would reveal the depth of his pain, the irrevocable loss he suffered in sending her back to safety.

Stephanie could read nothing behind his terse statement. The message did not surprise her but the cold, clipped way he spoke did. "Why, Chase? Why now after all we've been through?"

"The army won't take a defeat of this magnitude lying down. That was Custer's Seventh we wiped out on that ridge." She gasped in shock but said nothing as he went on relentlessly. "The army will come after us with everything Phil Sheridan can muster."

"But the children—they'll need me to—"

"They're Cheyenne now. You're white. They'll have Red Bead and Stands Tall to look after them while I fight. And I will fight your Blue Coats, Stephanie . . . and I will die, sooner or later. There's no future for us." As if to punctuate his words another burst of gunfire erupted from the timber.

"I have no future without you, Chase. Don't send me away. I've made a life here—or at least I've tried to. We have been a family, the only family I've ever known. Please—"

"Cheyenne women don't beg," he said coldly, turning away from her before he did something foolish, something he would regret.

Stephanie stared at his back, bare and bronzed, the hard muscles moving fluidly as he stiffened his spine and crossed his arms over his chest. His hair hung past his shoulder blades in a thick plait woven with eagle feathers. She ached to reach out and touch his barbaric splendor. She had lain with this man and even now carried his child in her womb. And like the enigma he had always been, he turned away from her.

Cheyenne women don't beg. She would not tell him about the babe. Somehow she would protect her mixed blood child in white society. He would never know he was a father, for if that was the only thing to bind them together, the child would suffer as much as they would. "I love you, Chase. You told me you loved me. Did you lie?"

Her voice was soft yet it cut like a knife. He felt the agony of it twist deep in his gut, almost unmanning him and he clenched his jaw until the tendons in his neck stood out. "No, I did not lie. But it's over now. My people mourn their dead. Tomorrow they'll pack up and scatter to the four winds with the bluebellies in pursuit. Custer's ghost already mocks us. In death he'll achieve what he couldn't in life—the utter destruction of the Cheyenne and Lakota."

She felt the bitterness that radiated from every fiber of his being sting her like a desert sandstorm. "And so it's over, just like that," she said hollowly. Could he blame her for the inevitability of history? Just because she was white? Or because she had first married one of those hated "bluebellies" who would hound his people to their deaths? Looking into his face she saw implacable resolution. Whatever his reasons, there would be no changing them.

Perhaps he was doing this because he loved her. That would hurt most of all. Unwilling to examine the unbearably painful thought, she simply turned and walked back to camp, her footfalls keeping cadence with the sounds of a wailing mourning chant.

Leaving the children had been the hardest part, Stephanie thought as they rode south toward the source of the Little Bighorn River, the name the white men gave to the Greasy Grass. Chase had informed her they would leave while the children were still sleeping. Smooth Stone would have borne his hurt stoically but Tiny Dancer would have cried and begged her to stay with them. Perhaps it was best to make the break clean. They would be assimilated into the communal life of the band, under Stands Tall's protection. Red Bead and Kit Fox would give them a mother's tender love in her absence.

Stands Tall and Elk Bull would soon lead the people back to the mountain stronghold. Perhaps they would escape the terrible retribution to come. Even if they did, the price would be dear for they would be only a small group living without the buffalo which had provided sustenance to their kind for generations. Their tribal way of life, with its rich ceremonies and rituals, would be lost, eradicated along with the rest of the free roaming Cheyenne and the buffalo themselves.

Stephanie would never again see Smooth Stone and Tiny Dancer or Kit Fox her friend and dour old Red Bead whose wry insights had often sustained her over the past months. With each plodding step of the horses, she was leaving so many loved ones behind. To keep the grief from overwhelming her, she turned over in her mind what she would do once back in civilization.

Chase had informed her only that he was delivering her to some mountain man, a French renegade who traded with the Indians. Gaston de Boef would see that she was returned to Rawlins where she could catch the Union Pacific back east. They shared the implicit assumption that she would not return to Hugh Phillips. As if she dared, carrying an Indian baby. She had never been able to conceive Hugh's child and he'd accused her of barrenness. She had believed him. Now her fertility was yet another reason for him to hate her. Surviving an Indian captivity was an unpardonable enough sin. He would have been humiliated to accept back such tarnished goods, even if she were not pregnant. Chase was right that Hugh would kill her before he'd take her back. She shivered just thinking about it.

Chase had given her some money taken from a stagecoach raid last winter, enough to see her back to Boston. But what then? The Summerfield wealth was Hugh's now. Once her past and her condition were known, none of her distant relations or former friends would take her in. Last night as she lay alone on her pallet staring at the endless starry vault of Montana sky, she had vacillated. Should she tell Chase she was destitute? Did she owe it to their unborn child to swallow her pride?

But it was not pride which ultimately held her silent. She had listened to others around their campfire talking in hushed voices during the night. Each band of Cheyenne and Sioux would leave separately the following day, for scouts had already reported more soldiers at the mouth of the Little Bighorn. As soon as he rid himself of his white wife, the White Wolf would join a select group of warriors skirmishing with the soldiers, buying the rest time to scatter. Elk Bull's band would return to the mountains and wait for him there.

The Cheyenne needed Chase. He had thrown in his lot with them since childhood and all the years sojourned among whites meant nothing when compared to his loyalty to his father's people. He lived a dangerous life which all too soon would be over. Chase Remington was destined to die by a bullet or a noose and there was nothing she could do to save him.

Stephanie had lain awake thinking about the Freedom Woman whose liberation had, in the final analysis, been so ephemeral. At least Anthea had been given seven years, not just seven months with the man she loved. In the end, to save her child's life she had sacrificed herself by returning to the scorn and humiliation of Boston, returning to the Remington family she and her son despised. But if the old reverend had cared enough about preserving the family name to make Chase his heir in spite of his tainted blood, Stephanie knew what she would do. She would go to Reverend Remington and tell him she was carrying his great-grandchild. Surely he would take her in, for she carried the small gold locket with Anthea's picture which Chase had given her at their Cheyenne marriage.

Jeremiah could do what she could not—secure the freedom and safety of her child from Hugh Phillips. After that it would be up to her to protect it from the rapacity of Burke Remington. Her resolve made, she rode toward the railhead and tried not to think of what might have been.

They stopped that night at the edge of the mountains amid the splendor of spruce and aspen in a narrow ravine where a small stream ran swift and icy from the melt off of snow. The air was warm and redolent with the scents of wild grasses and summer flowers. As night fell, the sky overhead became an endless canopy of stars, winking down their cold brilliant light.

Stephanie sat beside the campfire unconscious of the beauty of her surroundings, tending a pair of freshly killed rabbits spitted on the flames. She was too numb to think as her eyes followed Chase while he cared for their horses. He looked completely Indian now, dressed in breechclout and moccasins, his skin rippling with muscles and shimmering bronze in the firelight. There was such savage grace in every movement he made that she could not break the spell holding her in thrall as she watched him.

All at once Chase turned and their eyes met. And held. The dun snorted softly as he dropped the hackamore onto the grass and walked slowly toward Stephanie. Her legs trembled as she stood up, waiting for him to touch her. There was at once a defiance and an acceptance in her stiffened spine and highly held chin. Her eyes never wavered under his compelling glittering gaze.

"One last time, Chase." She mouthed the words softly as her arms reached out and pulled him into her embrace.

He did not answer with words but his lips came down over hers, ending the need for speech. She returned the voracious kiss with a feral savagery equal to his own. Questing deep inside each other's mouths, their tongues dueled until they grew breathless and desperate. She dug her fingers into his scalp, combing through his hair until his braid came unfastened and the thick night-dark curtain obscured his face. His arms pressed her tightly to his chest and his hips rocked against hers insistently. Her own rolled up in reply as he cupped a breast with one hand, sending a spiraling ache from her nipple down into the deepest recesses of her belly.

Slowly they sank onto their knees in the soft grass. He lifted the fringed edge of her tunic, pulling it swiftly up and over her head. She was naked beneath, as was the custom of Cheyenne women. But she was not Cheyenne. Her body, lush yet delicate, bloomed milky pale where the sun had not touched it. His hands were dark against the satiny whiteness of her breasts, lifting the full soft mounds to his lips, suckling on one pink tip, then the other. She arched into his caresses, all the while her fingers tugged at his breechclout until it came unfastened. When she grasped the hard pulsing staff in her hand, he let out a ragged cry of pleasure.

"I ache to bury it deep inside of you," he said, pushing her toward the ground.

But Stephanie surprised him, pressing her palms against his chest until it was he who lay down on his back beside the fire, looking up at her. She sat back on her heels and shook the long shimmering cascade of bronze hair away from her face. All the while her eyes looked down on him, devouring every long-limbed powerfully muscled inch of his naked flesh. Then she straddled his hips and positioned herself above his straining phallus. Slowly she impaled herself on it as he watched.

Chase's hands bit into the curve of her hips and moved around to her buttocks, cupping them and kneading the soft flesh, lifting her as she rode him. Stephanie moved slowly and deliberately, setting an even rhythm to make their joining last as long as possible. Leaning forward she touched the washboard hardness of his belly, then moved her hands higher into the thick black hair on his chest, digging her fingertips into the pelt, then feeling the jagged edges of his Sun Dance scars. The muscles of his chest bunched as his hips kept pace with hers.

She could feel his heart slamming against her palm as she slowly lowered her head to his chest. Her long hair spilled over him, curtaining them from the dull glow of the firelight, the soft ends feathering against his skin in light wispy caresses that he thought would drive him mad. Her mouth made contact with his hot skin. He could feel his chest heave and tremble as she began to press kisses on his scars. When she opened her lips and traced the thick ridges with her tongue, he moaned her name and tangled his fists in the bronze sheen of her hair, pulling her closer, closer.

This was her Indian lover, scarred in a pagan ritual. This was the father of her unborn child, the only man she could ever love. Stephanie gloried in these scars for they had given him his vision and she was part of it, even sharing the dream with him. That and the child they had made would bind their spirits together long after they would be separated. She kissed the rough knotted tissue, pressing tongue and lips to it, laving it as he groaned deep in his throat, a guttural cry of pleasure and longing. Her scalp stung from the tug of his hands in her hair but she felt no pain.

Of their own volition, Stephanie's hips began to increase their tempo, taking him deep inside of her, then rising high, only to plunge once more. Chase kept sync with her, thrusting up on each downstroke. What had begun slowly now built to a desperately sought climax. He pulled on her hair until her head raised up to meet his and his lips could claim hers in another devouring kiss. When he felt the satiny flexing of her sheath and heard her low mewling cries deep in his mouth, he let go, swelling and pulsing his life-bringing fluids deep inside of her.

Stephanie held onto him, riding out the maelstrom of anguished pleasure that filled her mind as well as her body. His heart slammed furiously against her palms as they crested together. The hot spurt of his seed sent her spiraling yet higher until the sky and all the stars dissolved and the earth beneath them melted away. They were the White Wolf and Eyes Like Sun, all there was in the universe at that moment, two lovers alone and utterly at peace in the warm sweet wash of satiation. But that peace was fleeting.

Stephanie collapsed on top of him, pressing her face to his chest, feeling the roughness of scar tissue against the smoothness of her cheek. She felt his arms around her, one hand splayed across the small of her back while the other reached up to brush the heavy curtain of hair away from her face.

"I will always remember this," she murmured against his chest, letting the tears seep from beneath her lashes to touch his hot skin.

"Don't, Stevie, don't speak, don't cry," he replied softly as he stroked her hair. *How can I give her up? She is my life.* His vengeance against Phillips, his warrior's honor, even the Cheyenne themselves meant nothing compared to his love for her. And he had told her that was over. Such a paltry lie. Yet it was a lie he must live with until he died. For if he did not she would die with him and he could not bear that.

So they held each other in the stillness of the night as a coyote howled on the distant plain and an owl hooted softly from the overhanging limbs of an aspen tree. After a while, their bodies still joined, Chase rolled them over and they made love again. Alternately through the night they slept and loved as if racing against the sun.

But the sun did rise. Stephanie awakened to find Chase already up, saddling her mare as his big dun watched placidly. He was dressed in buckskin leggings but still bare chested. His hair hung loose, falling across his shoulders as he walked over and stirred the fire where another freshly killed pair of rabbits were roasting. Feeling her eyes on him, he turned his head and grinned. Absurdly after what they had done all night, she felt the urge to blush and cover herself. There had always been a magical newness about loving Chase Remington, from the first moment he'd kissed her so long ago in Boston.

"We let the ones last night burn up so I snared us more. Hungry?"

His eyes taunted her. "Starved," she replied, reaching for her tunic, which lay discarded hastily beside their pallet.

They ate in silence, then shared the simple tasks of breaking camp and mounted up, heading relentlessly south, to civilization.

"I hate this place! The dust is thick enough to choke the horses and the mosquitoes could carry away a large dog!" Sabrina Remington slammed the lid of her traveling trunk with an oath and glared at her husband across the austere room in the Brunswick Hotel. "Why did you insist on dragging me into this hellish wasteland?"

Burke studied her with a detached air from across the room where he stood sipping from a glass of brandy. "You're not exactly trustworthy, left to your own devices in Boston, much less Washington, while I'm traveling west on senatorial business."

"Why, Burke, whatever—"

He cut off her indignant protest with a sharp bark of laughter, harsh and ugly. Then he fixed her with cold blue eyes. "The 'whatever,' as we both perfectly well know, is that damned Nevada congressman you've been fucking."

Sabrina's porcelain complexion mottled red with temper. "That's a vulgar and disgusting thing to say! Rory Madigan and I are merely social acquaintances. He's very wealthy and moves in our circles even if he is a Democrat."

"He's a crass Irish immigrant who managed to strike it rich. Just the sort of pretty face you've always fancied. If I weren't already assured of your barrenness, I'd have killed you long ago, Sabrina my pet, before I let you saddle me with a bastard from one of your indiscretions."

Her face quickly lost its rosy tint as the implication of his remarks sunk in. "Have we come here because of Chase, Burke?"

"Of course. We have to verify that our beloved nephew has finally been laid to his well-deserved rest," he replied with false geniality.

"You don't need me to prove Chase is dead. I know you've hired men to track him down and kill him for the reward money you've secretly put up through various merchants." In spite of her precarious position, she could not resist the hint of snideness in her voice.

His icy blue gaze riveted on her. "You fucked him. That, I'm afraid, I shall never forgive—a dirty, filthy savage. You'll recall it was at the time you began your dalliance with Chase that I quit your bed permanently. I can stomach a great many things, even an Irishman, but the leavings of a red Indian are beyond the pale."

"You've scarcely noticed whether I was dead or alive since you married me, much less cared to bed me. All I ever was to you was a social ornament, a hostess for your political friends."

"And a splendid ornament you have been," he purred, moving across the threadbare carpet to where she stood beside a hideous gargoyle of a settee. When he touched one bouncing inky curl, she flinched in distaste. "But you've grown indiscreet. I can no longer trust you to your own devices when I leave the capital. I will not have the political harpies gossiping behind my back, making me a laughing-stock—an older man with a beautiful younger wife who's cuckolding him. Bad enough when it was the Indian but then he broke it off." He smiled chillingly. "Imagine that, a savage with more conscience than the flower of Virginia aristocracy."

"Is that the real reason you're so obsessed with killing Chase?"

He studied her as if she were a butterfly pinned on a velvet board. "My reasons are my own and you do not signify in the slightest. Although I daresay if Jeremiah did succeed in making our nephew his sole heir after I die, you'd be rather put out. I doubt he'd be so foolish as to marry an older woman.''

She instinctively raised her hand to slap him but he caught her wrist in a bone-crushing grip. ''Ooh! You're hurting me, Burke. Let go!'' she wailed, rubbing her arm when he flung it away as if it were a viper.

Disgusted with his faithless whore of a wife, Remington turned and walked to the window. The streets of Rawlins were thick with dust. If the pewter gray clouds gathering in the northwest were any indication, a torrential rainstorm would soon reduce that dust to knee-deep mud. God, how he hated Wyoming! He hated the whole windswept barren starkness that was the West with its bitter searing cold and intense blazing heat, its endless sky that stretched in every direction, limitless, soulless, empty. It frightened him with its immensity. But this was where Chase had fled and he must follow to see that Anthea's bastard died.

He took another pull on the brandy in his glass. It was early, only four or so, but it had been a hellish trip and he needed the liquor, an indulgence Burke seldom allowed himself. ''We're having dinner with Major Phillips tonight. He indicated in his wire that he finally has some news regarding your Indian. It's about time he did something to earn the major's bars I secured for him.''

The way he said the words *your Indian* sent a shudder racing along her already overwrought nerves. ''Why have you really brought me to Wyoming, Burke?''

The cold dread in her voice amused him. Feeling expansive, he polished off the brandy and turned to her. ''Why do you think, Sabrina?'' A slight smile touched his lips but not his eyes.

She swallowed nervously, instinctively knowing after all the years she'd been married to Burke Remington, that showing fear would set him upon her like a hound on a hare. ''I wonder if you think you can arrange an unfortunate accident for me out here in this heathen wilderness, so far away from the protection of my family. It won't work. Papá would find out. He's always hated you.''

''Yes, he has. If it weren't for all those dirty Yankee

dollars I've lavished on his vaunted Virginia heritage, he'd have lost Sugar Pines and he can't get that unstuck from his craw, can he? But he's still beholden to me and he damn well knows it." He reached out and caressed the swell of her breast, then moved his hand up to lift her chin. "If I were to return East prostrate with grief over your death at the hands of marauding savages, he'd never guess—or even if he did, he'd keep quiet."

He let the words sink in, watching her try to hide the cringing fear licking like flames behind her eyes. "But perhaps it won't be necessary. If you promise to amend your ways. Madigan's returned to Nevada. I hear he doesn't plan to seek reelection. If you don't take another lover . . ."

She did not trust Burke but had little choice. He was a United States senator and his family had President Grant's ear. The only one who'd ever defied and eluded him was Chase. *Chase!* She seized upon the idea greedily. If anyone had more cause than she to hate Burke, it was his nephew. They were natural allies. And when he won the war with her husband, Chase Remington would be a very, very rich man. She felt certain Chase would turn the tables and kill Burke. If she could just stay alive till then.

"Very well, Burke. I shall be a model of decorum," she said smoothly, willing her hands not to tremble as she poured herself a generous libation from Burke's brandy bottle on the table. "Now, tell me about this cavalry officer you've kept in touch with over the winter . . ."

Hugh Phillips raised his field glasses and scanned the dense pines and firs towering on the steep cliff sides all around him. "Damned if I don't think we've lost them," he said to the Arikira scout.

Bloody Hand's impassive face looked up and his keen black eyes scanned the rugged mountains surrounding them. "There," he said, pointing to a particularly dense stand of white fir. "That is way to stronghold. In not many miles, there be Cheyenne, watching."

"Sentries, yes," Phillips murmured, considering. This could be a trap. His forces were well armed and prepared.

After word of the Custer massacre reached the shocked and stunned army posts across the High Plains, every company of men that could be mustered was put on alert for hostiles. The destruction of the 7th Cavalry provided Phillips the perfect excuse to requisition additional supplies for a campaign which would finally end the career of the infamous White Wolf.

After receiving word from his agents, Senator Burke Remington had arranged the transfer of Bloody Hand to Fort Steele from Fort Fetterman last fall. The Arikira brought news about a well-hidden encampment of Cheyenne whose war leader matched the description of Chase Remington, the man he now knew was the White Wolf. The nagging suspicion had grown then that it was the half-breed who had kidnapped his wife. Or Stephanie had gone willingly with the man she had planned to marry so long ago. The thought of such a betrayal had eaten at his guts like an ulcer all through the endless winter months as he sat in the fort, helplessly snowbound.

Now Hugh and Bloody Hand had prepared a trap for the White Wolf in his own lair. Knowing Sitting Bull's huge summer hunting encampment would scatter to the four winds, Hugh counted on the White Wolf's band running to ground in this hidden stronghold where he had vanished without a trace during the past years of feckless pursuit. This time things would be different, he thought with grim determination as he gave the signal for the other scouts under Bloody Hand to scale the steep cliffs and kill the sentries. Then the cavalry could surprise the savages and sweep down, exterminating the whole bloody village like so much vermin.

Vermin, that's what they were. Led by an arrogant savage who dared put his hands on a white woman, the wife of an army officer. Remington would pay for that offense before he died. The shock had been great when Burke had shown him Chase's photograph. He'd immediately recognized the breed who'd given him the scar on his cheek. He was stunned again to learn that the same breed had been the one he'd captured at Washita, a seventeen-year-old boy who he had dragged back to civilization, screaming curses in some heathen tongue. Well, if Remington had sworn revenge, so had he—for the scar and for the humiliation of Stephanie.

Now he knew why she had never fallen under his spell, why she'd been so cold in his bed, the prissy Boston bluestocking. All along she had harbored a secret tendresse for that damned mongrel who'd jilted her! Hugh smiled to himself, thinking of the pleasure he'd take in killing her and capturing her savage lover. Of course it would be considered an accident when she was shot in the chaos of battle. Lots of Indian women and children got in the way of stray bullets or the occasional overzealous saber thrust. A pity.

All his fellow officers and their wives would commiserate with him, relieved that they'd never have to face his ruined wife. He had her money and at last he would be free of the stain she'd placed on his honor. After destroying the White Wolf, he would be written up in the Eastern press as a tragic hero, avenging Custer and his own poor unfortunate wife, both victims of the savages. At the signal from Bloody Hand, he gave the order for his men to follow him through the narrow twisting canyon entrance.

Deep in the hidden valley, Chase sat staring into the fire, deep in melancholy thought. The look on Stephanie's face when he left her with Gaston de Boef would remain with him until he died. She had not begged him. They had ridden to de Boef's cabin on the Sweetwater, stopping to camp every night under the glittering canopy of stars . . . and to make fierce desperate love. Each morning they had arisen and resumed the journey in silence. There was nothing left to say.

Did she hate him? Chase honestly didn't know. He had kidnapped her, ruining the life she had tried so hard to build as an officer's wife, then given her a home and family here with his people only to wrench that away, too. At least she would be free of Phillips's debased touch. Chase hoped she was grateful for that, if nothing else.

"The other warriors wish to know when we will ride,

my brother," Plenty Horses said, interrupting the White Wolf's reverie. Since he'd returned without his white wife, the fearsome raider had been heavy of heart.

"Tell them to prepare. I will say my farewells to Stands Tall and Red Bead," Chase replied, eager to leave the safety of their hideaway and once more engage the soldiers in combat. His carefully trained and well-armed raiders could score hit-and-run victories over the ponderously moving columns of Blue Coats now taking the field against the victors of the Greasy Grass, buying time for their brothers and Lakota cousins. But Chase knew how it would ultimately end. He only prayed this small band would remain safe during the holocaust to come. If only Stands Tall and Red Bead and the children lived, he would be glad to die. If only Stephanie lived . . .

From the cover of dense pine and fir to the east, Phillips studied the peaceful village below, waiting for his men to get into position. Even though they had been forced to abandon their mounts and come through the steep twisting entrance to the valley afoot, he could see his soldiers outnumbered the Indians two to one and only a relatively small percentage were armed warriors. The rest were women, children and old people.

In spite of the difficult terrain, Hugh divided his command as Custer had done at Washita. On his signal, they would sweep down from the cover on the mountainside. Attacking from four directions, the soldiers would cut a swift brutal swath through the scattered skin lodges of the savages who now went about their morning chores, blissfully unaware of the fate that awaited them. In spite of the cool early morning air at the high elevation, sweat dampened his back and armpits. The sour smell of it filled his nostrils, metallic, fearful. He had waited so long for this moment that his guts clenched with the wanting of it—to savor the triumph of seeing that brown-haired slut lying dead at his feet. He only regretted he would have to kill her quickly and make it appear an accident. Regardless of how she died, he'd not be merciful with Remington. On the other hand, the savages often killed their white captives when they were attacked rather than be forced to give them up. That would solve his problem even more neatly. *But I want to see her face as I pull the trigger myself.*

"All men in place," Bloody Hand said in a low rumble.

Hugh raised his pistol and fired twice in rapid succession. Then all hell broke loose.

Chase heard the shots from inside his lodge, immediately followed by the cries of Blue Coats pouring into their valley. *How have they found us?* Seizing his rifle and cartridge belt he scarcely had time to consider the thought as a volley of rifle fire erupted and several women fell to the ground, one with a cradleboard strapped to her back, another shielding a small girl with her own body. People screamed, rushing for cover, women grabbing their children, old men searching frantically for their weapons.

A few of his warriors were already armed and returning fire. Chase quickly took charge, directing them to pin down the soldiers coming across the river, but no more than they'd slowed the advance, withering fire erupted at their back as more bluebellies raced into the opposite side of the camp, setting fire to the lodges. Soon the air was black with smoke and filled with the screams of humans and horses.

Just like Washita! If he hadn't seen Custer dead on the Greasy Grass, Chase would have sworn he was attacking them now. But there had been another with the Long Hair that day, a young lieutenant who no longer rode with Custer's 7th. Phillips! Gaston de Boef was supposed to have taken Stephanie into Rawlins to catch a train east. Could she have gone to Fort Steele instead?

No! I don't believe it, he thought as he fired at the soldiers and yelled orders to his men. But they were hopelessly outnumbered with women and children in the line of their fire. The older men like his uncle and Elk Bull were leading as many as possible to the dubious safety of the dense aspen thickets to the south of the village, but Chase could see that it was hopeless. At least his men were well armed. They would go down fighting and take as many of the bluebellies

with them as they could. He looked around him searching
for Phillips. The last thing he asked of life on this earth
was to see Stephanie's brutal husband die.

Hugh hacked his way into another lodge where a pair of
little girls cowered. Snarling in frustration that Stephanie
was not there, he yelled for the corporal to put it to the
torch and moved on to the next. She had to be here! All
the while he searched, he watched for the renegade. Would
Remington keep her with him? Then he saw Chase leading
a group of warriors who were standing off C Company's
frontal assault. He could worry about dispatching Stephanie
later. Now he would deal with the White Wolf at last.

He signaled his men to surround the small force, calling
in the last of the soldiers still in hiding to the north. As
they opened fire, Phillips heard a war cry behind him and
whirled about. An old man charged him with a lance.
Hugh's Colt was empty so he raised his saber and hacked
at the lance, easily breaking it. The next swing of the saber
cut deep into the old man's neck and he went down, only
to be replaced by another warrior, this one younger and not
out of ammunition. Phillips swung his saber toward the
raised Winchester, knocking it aside, then brought the blade
back, biting into the warrior's arm before he could regain
his balance. The final blow was swift and merciless and the
warrior fell dead at his feet.

• The battle din began to die down. Reports of rifle fire
dwindled to a few staccato bursts and the fierce war cries
of the Cheyenne grew mute, replaced by low keening from
the women. He climbed over the bodies around him and
continued his search for Chase and Stephanie. After he'd
searched the last lodge left standing, he was satisfied she
was not hiding in the village. The women and children who
had tried to escape into the marsh grass were being herded
back into camp by a group of his men. He quickly scanned
them, relieved that his wife was not among them.

Had she burned to death in one of the fired lodges—or
had she never reached their hidden village? Had Remington
not been the one to capture her after all? Somehow he

doubted that. He turned his attention to the prisoners, hoping that the White Wolf had not been granted a merciful death.

His face split into a coldly beatific smile when two of his men approached him dragging the unconscious body of a Cheyenne brave by his long hair. It was Remington and he was alive. . . .

ᥭᦉ *23* ᦉᥩ

Gaston de Boef did not like civilization. As a fourteen-year-old boy he'd run away from the noisome filth of a Quebec slum to the pristine beauty of the great North American wilderness and never looked back. He spoke a dozen Indian languages and had three wives, an Ojibway back in Minnesota, a Shoshone in Colorado and a Cheyenne in Montana Territory. As the whim struck him, he'd left each one to strike out for new adventure. Adventure did not include towns—at least not any longer than it took to buy a bottle and skedaddle back to his cabin on the Sweetwater.

The breed's woman was trouble. He'd known it the moment he laid eyes on her, with all that rich shiny hair and golden eyes, dressed up like a squaw. But the White Wolf had paid him well and he knew he could never renege on his promise to bring her safely to the railhead in Rawlins. Simple enough, all he had to do was see that she got on the next train east as soon as they reached the big cluster of frame buildings sprawled along the south side of Front Street.

But something just didn't feel right. He scratched his scraggly beard and peered ahead toward the helter-skelter buildings of Rawlins strung alongside the Union Pacific railroad tracks. Ever since word of Custer's defeat had reached the army posts and towns in Wyoming Territory, everyone was on edge. A man like him with a foot in both worlds could find himself in a lot of trouble if anyone connected him with the missing wife of a soldier.

"You are about changed, *hein*?" he asked, wondering what was taking Stephanie Phillips so long to shed her doeskin tunic and don the familiar trappings of a white female.

"I'm sorry, Mr. de Boef," she replied from behind the shelter of a juniper as she finished with the seemingly endless buttons down the front of the dress he'd bought her in Granger's General Merchandise. "I'm a little out of practice with corsets and petticoats." Not to mention how the pointy-toed shoes pinched her feet! He had purchased the cheap ready-made apparel and the shoes per her instructions regarding size, but it was still guesswork on both their parts. The green checked dress hung loosely on her while the shoes were too small. Or perhaps not. She may simply have grown used to the comfort of moccasins.

Putting aside her supple, beautiful leather tunic and donning white woman's layers and layers of clothing had been far more difficult than she ever could have imagined. Every corset lacing, hook and button distanced her further and further from Chase. He had left her in de Boef's care two days ago and ridden off without a backward glance. He'd said no good-bye, just looked at her with those hooded black eyes, then kicked his horse into a wild gallop and thundered away. The image of his half-naked body astride that big dun gelding would remain with her the rest of her life. He was of one world, she of another.

Stephanie smoothed her hair as best as she could, studying her appearance in the cracked mirror the Frenchman had brought her. In spite of the months outdoors, her face looked pale and wan. Did she look like a white captive returned from the Indians? Or simply some sodbuster's wife bound east to visit kinfolk? She prayed the latter. Her worst fear was to have someone in Rawlins recognize Captain Phillips's missing wife before she could make good her escape on the eastbound train. God only knew what Hugh would do if he found her. Shuddering, she emerged from the screen of the junipers, reminding herself that Hugh was most probably out in the field chasing hostiles or ensconced at Fort Steele a dozen miles away.

"I'm ready now. Do you have the train ticket, Mr. de Boef?"

"*Oui*. The agent said she leaves the Rawlins station at ten past three," de Boef replied, handing her the ticket he'd purchased while in town buying her proper clothes. She looked a great deal better in the squaw clothes than the ill-fitting white woman's fixings, but either way, the breed had fine taste in women. Stephanie Phillips was a real beauty, even if she was desperately unhappy without her renegade lover. He had observed their final terse exchange and the way she watched as the White Wolf rode away. She was married to an officer but she loved the breed, he'd bet a good bottle of whiskey on it. Shrugging, he assisted her awkwardly onto the back of his patient old mule Sarie, then led the animal slowly down the trail into Rawlins.

Stephanie stared at the stark countryside without really seeing it. Once she'd thought the jagged rock formations thrusting up from the earth in sedimented layers were desolate, the tall stands of fir and aspen intimidating, the sheer immensity of the sky unimaginable. Now this wild land no longer daunted her. The High Plains had become her home for a brief and beautiful period in her life. *Wherever Chase is, that is home.*

When they reached the edge of town, the wiry little mountain man scanned the expanse of railroad tracks skirting Front Street. "That big wooden building there, she is the Union Pacific guest house and eating place. You can rest inside until the train comes."

To carry me back to Boston. Nodding, Stephanie slid from the back of the tired old mule and gave her greasy looking escort a shaky smile. "You've been most kind, Mr. de Boef. I shall always be grateful."

"Only ride the train to safety and do not look back," he replied softly.

They exchanged a look of understanding and then she walked down the wide dusty street skirting the tracks. Faint music wafted on the sullen noon air from a string of saloons lining the south side of Front. The church bells of St. James tolled at the hour from Cedar Street, summoning the faithful away from temptations of the flesh. She saw the austere clapboard facade of the Rawlins House Hotel at the opposite end of the street, and remembered sneaking out of it at

midnight to follow Chase. That late-night encounter seemed
a lifetime ago now.

Clutching her ticket, she climbed a step onto the porch
of the Union Pacific way station and entered the large ed-
ifice which still smelled faintly of raw lumber and sawdust.
According to the clock on the wall, she had nearly an hour
until the train pulled in, plenty of time to go into the dining
room and order a meal, but the thought of food made her
stomach rebel. Trying to ignore the smell of greasy pork
and boiled coffee wafting out into the waiting room, she
took a seat on a high-backed wooden bench in a dimly lit
corner of the room, praying she did not look too conspic-
uous in her ill-fitting clothes. A woman alone traveling
without luggage was always suspect.

When she reached Julesburg she would get off long
enough to purchase the necessities to see her respectably
over the seventeen-hundred-mile journey back to Boston.
The thought of foggy gray skies and narrow, congested
streets filled her heart with near panic. There was no choice,
at least none for now. Perhaps in time if the old reverend
was kind, she could hope to bring her child back to his
birthright here in the West.

Nervously Stephanie looked around her, scanning the
people in the large waiting area. The usual number of tran-
sients—drummers with their sample cases, miners, gam-
blers, even a few fancy women—sat or paced about the
room. A couple of hard looking cattlemen bound for the
stockyards in Chicago discussed beef prices and a homesteader's harried wife shushed two squabbling children as
an infant dozed fitfully in her arms. No one recognized
Stephanie.

Smiling ruefully to herself, she realized Hugh would
scarcely have advertised the scandalous circumstances of
her disappearance by posting her photograph in public
places. As long as she did not run into any officers or their
ladies from Fort Steele, she should make it safely onto the
train. Folding her hands in her lap, she leaned back and
tried to relax. Soon her eyelids grew heavy in the stuffy
warm air and she dozed off.

The sounds of voices shouting excitedly awakened her. Blinking to orient herself, Stephanie looked nervously around and found the source of the noise. A burly clerk wearing a Union Pacific uniform was talking loudly to a crowd of people gathering around him at the front door.

"They got 'im, sure enough! After all this time, the murderin' Injun."

"You sure it's him?" a man in miner's clothes asked dubiously.

"I seen him with my own two eyes. He's a dirty breed. Major's draggin' him behind his horse, right up Cedar Street to the jail."

At that, several men scrambled out the door headed to the next block to see the show. Nearby, Stephanie overheard a drummer ask the clerk, "Can Phillips collect that five-thousand-dollar reward since he's in the army?"

Stephanie's heart began to thud as his companion commented, "Who cares? I'm just relieved to hear the White Wolf's raiding days are over. A body had to fear every time he rode the stage up to Deadwood."

Chase! Hugh had captured Chase! But how? Where? Surely not on his return to the stronghold or else they would have beaten her back to Rawlins. The clerk answered her frantic question and a painful vise squeezed her chest.

"The major rousted a whole nest of them bloody devils up in the Bighorns. Found 'em hidin' after they sneaked away from massacring General Custer. Sent most of the bucks to the happy hunting grounds 'n' the women and kids to the fort. Said he was usin' our jail to make sure the White Wolf's safe until he stands trial for his murderin' ways. I 'spect he'll end up dancin' at the end of a rope 'fore a trial."

Stephanie barely heard the last of the conversation as she darted across the crowded room and out the door. Directly in front of her railroad tracks crisscrossed, some leading to the big roundhouse a few hundred feet down the street. The main track began to hum as the three-ten train rumbled toward Rawlins, screeching as the brakeman slowed its headlong rush. Ignoring it, she scrambled across Front

Street, running in earnest now toward the sounds of an angry mob on Cedar.

The crowd lined the wide street as Chase was dragged through the thick choking dust, his bound wrists secured to a twelve-foot rawhide rope tied to Hugh's saddle horn. Chase's skin was smeared with his own blood and coated with dirt from frequent falls as he had run behind the horses during the long journey back to civilization. Finally this last day, injuries, fever and exhaustion had claimed him. He slipped into semiconsciousness, unable to jog behind the Blue Coats' horses any longer.

Stephanie caught a glimpse of him from between two buildings when Phillips reined in his horse in front of the jail, making a grandstand spectacle of his famous prisoner. Dear God, had Hugh killed him? Every nerve in her body cried out to run to her love and cradle his head in her lap, but she knew such a feckless gesture would not only be greeted with angry hostility by the crowd; it would also ruin Hugh's moment of triumph and turn his wrath on her. She had to think, to plan. There must be some way to free Chase. Perhaps she could wire Reverend Remington in Boston.

Enveloped in the crowd, Stephanie worked her way toward Chase, wanting to glimpse him and assure herself that he was indeed still alive. Suddenly as she slipped surreptitiously between two cowhands, a sharp gasp of recognition directly to her side caused her to turn her head and meet the startled eyes of Abigail Shaffer.

Her husband, a captain, was in command of Fort Steele in Hugh's absence, but young Lieutenant Grimes had been assigned to escort her into town. He, too, recognized their commander's missing wife at once.

"Stephanie, my dear," Abigail croaked, seizing hold of her arm with clawlike fingers. "However did you manage to escape? You poor, poor child." Her eyes swept over Stephanie's sun-darkened face and took in the cheap, hastily purchased dress.

When Stephanie tried to pull away, Abigail's grip only

tightened. Lieutenant Grimes took her other arm a bit more gently but none the less firmly.

"No reason to take fright, Mrs. Phillips. You're with friends now," he said soothingly, as if comforting a spooked horse.

"Please, let me go. I—I don't want Hugh to see me like this!" She struggled to keep the hysteria from her voice, but she knew the stark terror had to be welling in her eyes.

"The major's been searching for you since you were kidnapped, Mrs. Phillips, driving his men every day, even in the face of winter blizzards. Why he'll be thrilled to see you safe and sound," Grimes assured her.

One look into Abigail Shaffer's glittering eyes told a very different story. Hugh would be livid finding her alive and well. Every respectable white woman was supposed to kill herself rather than let the unspeakable happen. *She's looking at me to see if my mind's unhinged from my ordeal—or to see if I have some residual stain because a red man touched me.*

"Checking for lice, Abby?" She couldn't resist the biting words as Lieutenant Grimes propelled her through the crowd toward his commander.

Hugh was discussing his famous prisoner with several freight line and stagecoach owners while the Rawlins sheriff looked on glumly, sensing the ugliness of the crowd and fervently wishing he was back in Kansas.

"I'll expect you to keep the prisoner here while I inform Senator Remington. He was privy to our raid on the savages' hideout and is working closely with the Interior Department on this situation," Hugh said to the unhappy lawman. "You should only have to be responsible for one night. Then we'll—"

Lieutenant Grimes's voice cut into the conversation just as Hugh caught sight of Stephanie emerging from the crowd. He fell silent, poleaxed to see her alive and in Rawlins of all places. She was dressed in cheap clothing and her face was almost as brown as a squaw's. "If you'll excuse me, Sheriff, gentlemen," Phillips said abruptly to the men he'd been conferring with. "I must see to my wife."

He quickly interrupted Grimes before the young idiot made
the already untenable situation even worse by blurting out
the circumstances under which he'd located Stephanie.
"Take charge of the prisoner, Lieutenant," he ordered,
reaching out to Stephanie with mock tenderness.

Stephanie felt the bite of steel in his fingers when they
dug into the soft flesh on the underside of her arm, pulling
her toward him amid the whispers and gasps surrounding
them. Chase raised his head. Through fever-glazed eyes, he
saw Stephanie's tall slender form and unmistakable bronze
hair. She was in Hugh Phillips's arms. *No, it couldn't be!*

During the hellish days on the trail, beaten, kicked and
dragged, all Chase had been able to think of were his people. Red Bead had died, struck down by a Blue Coat bullet.
Kit Fox had remained with the children until Stands Tall
had been able to lead them through the aspen thickets
across the creek. Chase did not know if they had made it
to freedom or not. Some of Phillips's soldiers had been
ordered to stay behind and search for escapees, mostly
women and children. Many of his warriors were dead.
Some had been captured and bound just as he was, then
sent directly to the fort. Blue Eagle and Plenty Horses were
among them. Only the White Wolf himself merited this
exhibition in Rawlins. The rest of the village lay destroyed
in the impenetrable fastness of the Bighorns. How had Phillips found them? Could Stephanie have . . . ?

He refused to accept the horrifying idea. It was simply
more than he could comprehend. There must be some other
answer. Two of the soldiers grabbed him under his arms and
dragged him inside the ugly squat stone structure that
was the jail. Escaping from such a prison would not be
easy. At the moment he felt little inclination to care what
became of him as he was shoved into a hot filthy cell with
one tiny window. Everything he had ever loved had been
destroyed. There was nothing left to live for . . . until he
heard Burke Remington's voice.

Chase squatted on his haunches in the corner of the cell.
The sudden blind surge of hate pumped adrenaline past his

fevered exhaustion, fueling him with renewed energy. There was a reason to live—vengeance.

"Now you look just the way you should—a half-naked, dirty aborigine huddled cravenly in a prison cell, waiting for the hangman's noose to tighten around your neck." Burke's voice was rich with satisfaction as he inspected his nephew's battered and bloodied form. "As soon as I heard a savage had abducted your old flame, rather ironically Hugh Phillips's wife, I knew she was the key to capturing you."

Although his knees were like water and his head still spinning, Chase surged to his feet, standing straight. His eyes glared from behind the bars, locking with Burke's in a silent duel. He could feel his uncle's hate meet and clash with his own. He said nothing, only stared impassively, letting Burke do the talking.

"After all these years, all the botched attempts to kill you . . . at last you're mine, you red bastard. I told Phillips to bring you here. The good citizens of Rawlins are understandably upset about the massacre of Custer's Seventh Cavalry. Oh, by the way, Reno and Benteen and their companies held out on the Little Bighorn until Terry and Gibbon arrived, but that's little mollified civilians from Wichita to Wyoming. They're out for blood.

"And here we have the most infamous raider of our generation right in the Rawlins city jail. To cap off the matter, he's half-white, a real renegade. The perfect man to make an example of. If you entertain any hope of wiring Jeremiah, abandon it. My men are stirring up that lynch mob even now. I expect by midnight they'll be ready to string you up to the nearest tree . . . I make it that big cottonwood at the corner of Front and Third."

Chase knew Burke was baiting him, waiting for a response. As a boy he'd flown at his tormentor kicking, biting and punching and Burke had cuffed him away, amused by a boy's powerlessness. By the time he'd returned from the Cheyenne as a seventeen-year-old youth, those days were past. Their hatred had ripened into a more subtle thing after that. Denied all weapons and watched like a hawk at first,

Chase knew he would have to wait out his uncle. Keeping
his mother out of an asylum depended on his good behavior. A flat absence of reaction and sarcastic taunts became
new weapons in his arsenal as he bided his time until Freedom Woman was beyond Burke's reach. And now things
had gone full cycle. Once again he was as powerless as he
had been as a boy, caged behind bars like an animal.

"Gloat while you can, Burke. I *will* kill you before I
die." Having said that with quiet unshakable resolve, he let
the words have their effect on the gray-haired aristocrat
standing in front of him. Then Chase turned his back and
stared impassively out the window, dismissing Burke Remington as if the senator were a petitioner.

After Burke had left, Chase burned to know if Stevie had
actually betrayed him and his people, but he would never
ask. His uncle would revel in describing every detail—or
lying through his teeth even if she was innocent. He moved
around the small cell, studying the long narrow hall between the cubicles and the doors at either end, then settled
back in the corner again to wait until the sheriff or a deputy
appeared. There had to be a way out of here other than
being dragged by a lynch mob.

Down in the next block, Stephanie was ushered into the
same room in the Rawlins House Hotel that she had occupied the past fall on her fateful excursion with Emma
Boyer and Abigail Shaffer. Still numb from all the horrifying events of the past hour, she desperately wanted time
to sort out her chaotic thoughts and find some way to escape and send a wire. Jeremiah Remington was Chase's
last hope.

Hugh did not intend to leave her unattended for even a
moment. He had bidden Mrs. Shaffer good day in the
lobby, thanking her and Lieutenant Grimes profusely for
rescuing his poor abused wife, wandering unescorted
through the streets of Rawlins. He then ordered Grimes to
ride post haste to the fort and fetch her trunk, which had
remained unpacked since it had been returned to him after

her abduction. Once they reached the privacy of their room, his solicitude vanished abruptly.

Hugh raked her disgustedly with cold dark eyes. "You look like a sodbuster's wife with those ghastly clothes and sun-darkened skin. I'm surprised you weren't all tricked out in buckskins and beads after living with savages." He waited a beat as Stephanie remained silent, simply meeting his gaze without flinching. Her calm demeanor infuriated him and he ached to reach out and backhand the serenity from her face. But the situation was already bad enough. He must remain the long-suffering husband for now and not mark her. Perhaps there were other ways to crush her spirit. However, before he could begin she surprised him by breaking her silence.

"I never intended to embarrass you by coming back into your life, Hugh. I was going to get on that train east and never return. You could've told everyone I was dead if Abigail and Lieutenant Grimes hadn't dragged me to you. I know you despise me. I didn't do the honorable thing and take my own life after surviving an Indian captivity."

"I knew you went with Remington when his uncle came last fall and told me his nephew was the raider I'd been searching for. Imagine my added surprise to learn he was also the breed who gave me this." He touched the scar on his cheek. "Burke Remington has returned to Rawlins. He wants that bastard dead as much as I do . . . if that's possible."

"I'm not surprised, Hugh. Burke paid an assassin to kill Chase while we were still in Boston," she replied deliberately, refusing to give in to the panic clawing at her. "Chase knew Burke was behind the reward posters with the photograph circulating across the territories. I suspect he was also behind your receiving your major's bars so quickly."

Hugh's face reddened with rage and he raised his hand to strike her, then regained control of his emotions. "Burke went to the jail to see your breed lover. By now he knows that his dear uncle has men whipping up a lynch mob in the saloons along Front Street."

"You planned this together, you and Burke Remington,"
she accused. The certainty of Chase's death closed in on
her with crippling pain. *Be strong. You carry his child, the
only hope for the future.*

Hugh watched for some chink in her armor, some sign
that she was weakening. He wanted her to plead, cry, get
down on her knees and beg. By God, he would reduce her
to cowering, shivering terror so repugnant and uncontrollable that when she appeared to die by her own hand, everyone would accept it as a blessing and commiserate with
him, the noble suffering husband! She stood with her back
stiff and her chin, that irritatingly willful chin, held up
proudly. He walked around her, but she remained motionless, staring straight ahead. He had to rattle her somehow.

"What, nothing more to say, my dear? I can hardly let
you ride the rails east now, can I? After all, you are still
my responsibility, my *wife*." He accented the word as if it
were an epithet, hissing in her ear, as he raised his hand
and insinuated it along her throat, then down to the swell
of her breasts, straining against the weight of the shapeless
dress, which was too tight across the bust and hung loosely
around her waist. The slightest hint of repugnance seemed
to emanate from her when he cupped her breast, but she
did not flinch or draw away, just continued to stare straight
ahead.

She did ball her hands into tight little fists, almost hidden
in the folds of her skirt. That made him smile. "You always
were a cold stick in bed, Stephanie. Perhaps that was my
mistake. I shouldn't have allowed you the comfort of a bed!
Tell me, did lying in the dirt with a naked sweating savage
pumping over you make it better?"

"What made it good was love, Hugh. Something you
know nothing about," she replied quietly. He was going to
play this out until he got some perverse sort of satisfaction
from her. *Damned if I'll give it to him!*

"Love," he sneered. "I'd believe it if he were still a
Boston Brahmin, rich enough for one of the vaunted Sum-
merfields to marry. But he left that all behind, more the
fool he."

"You put a price on everything, Hugh. That's been your downfall all your life, cursing the Baltimore Phillips' decline in social position. You've become so obsessed with covering yourself in martial glory you've sacrificed your soul to achieve it . . . if you ever had one."

"I suppose that renegade killer has a soul? Or was it something as crass as his dark-skinned body that you craved? You broke your marriage vows for that buck!" Finally he struck a nerve. Her face flushed and the pulse at her throat sped up. "So, the truth at last. My prim little bluestocking lusted after that renegade. My mistake was believing you possessed ladylike sensibilities when all the while you had the morals of a scarlet poppy. Fitting since you seem to prefer *red* meat."

"You are a vile hypocrite who'd know a lot more about scarlet poppies than I would!" *Don't rise to the bait! Stay calm,* she admonished herself, but it was too late. A cruel twisted smile spread across his face.

"Jealous, my dear? Perhaps you'd like me to return my undivided attention to my husbandly duties." He reached up and seized hold of her hair, pulling the pins loose as his fingers dug into her scalp. His other hand squeezed her tender breast in a viselike grip.

Sensitized and swollen in pregnancy, the delicate tissue ached sharply. She bit down on her lip to keep from crying out. Sour with bile, his breath touched her face as he pulled her head closer. Stephanie fought the nausea beginning to churn in her stomach but made no attempt to fight him. *That's what he wants.*

When she still did not beg or struggle, his anger began to rise. He forced her to her knees, rasping out, "You think I'd take the leavings of that red-skinned bastard? Take my pleasure where he'd been! No, the cheapest whore in the lowliest crib is better than you now. But I'm going to teach you how your sort should behave."

He was breathing hard now as he reached down and grabbed her chin in his hand, forcing her to meet the insane glaze of his eyes. "Strip for me, whore. Do it! Take off your clothes. I'm certain you did it for your lover—you who were so modest your own husband had to slip between the sheets under cover of darkness to take you with your prissy little night rail buttoned up to the neck!''

"You don't want me, Hugh. You told me so. Why—"

"Now!" he cried, giving her a swift stinging blow across her cheek. "Remove every stitch or I'll rip those rags off myself. I spent a fortune dressing you in the best. No wife of mine will be seen in cheap calico."

He shoved her away and stood up, towering over her with his arms across his chest, waiting. Not patiently. If she refused, God only knew what he was capable of doing. And no one would interfere. After all, she was a pariah, a woman who'd lived among savages. The way that young lieutenant and Abigail Shaffer had treated her, they were certain she had been deranged by her captivity. Hugh could do whatever he pleased, say she'd gone berserk and attacked him. Who would believe her story? Slowly, she began to unfasten the buttons down the front of the shabby dress.

Hugh poured himself a generous slug of whiskey as he watched her slowly take off the ugly calico, then the petticoats. Her skin was sun darkened half the way up her arms and around her throat. "You look like a squaw," he sneered, polishing off the glass and refilling it. "Or some homesteader's daughter. Now, the corset and the rest of the underwear."

There was a dangerous glitter in his eyes. He had always been erratic and prone to violence when he drank. Stephanie looked around for some way to defend herself but the hotel room was bare, with not so much as a fireplace poker in the spartan sleeping chamber. The only weapon was the pistol at his waist. Somehow she would have to lure him into lowering his guard and seize the gun. Or outlast him and pray he drank himself stuporous and passed out, a feat he often performed in the past years of their marriage. She unlaced the corset and let it fall behind her, glad to have the freedom of movement in spite of the hot wash of shame that scalded her when he looked down at her.

''Stand up and pull off that tatty chemise and under-drawers.''

She got as far as removing the chemise, baring her breasts, but could not slip the drawers over her hips. ''Please, Hugh, don't make me do this.''

''Yes, beg! I love to hear you beg.'' He reached out suddenly and grasped one breast in his hand, threatening to punch her in the stomach with his other fist.

Stephanie paled, her arms flying protectively to her mid-section. Everything was revealed in her eyes in a split second. His snarling oath exploded as he backhanded her, knocking her against the bed. She fell onto the lumpy mattress.

His eyes took in the new fullness of her breasts with their aureoles enlarged and darkened. Her belly did not swell yet but soon it would—if she lived. ''You're breeding! Goddamn you, you carry an Indian bastard—that bastard's bastard! After all the times I bedded you, your protestations that you wanted children—I actually thought you were barren . . . and now *this*.''

The deliberate calm of his last words sent an icy prickle of pure terror racing along her spine. *Please God, no! Don't let him harm Chase's baby. This is all that's left of our love.* Stephanie sat up on the edge of the bed, waiting for an opening to go for his gun if he moved in to strike her another blow.

But he surprised her and turned away, walking back to the table to pour a second drink. He raised it in a mocking toast. ''To your delicate condition, dear wife . . . which will ensure that you do precisely as I tell you to . . . lest I decide to do the only just thing and remove that bastard from your belly.''

''I'll do what you want, Hugh,'' Stephanie said quietly. He was going to kill her. Perhaps she'd known that all along and only suppressed it to save her sanity. She had to stall for time, to find some way to save Chase's unborn child. *I will not let it end this way!*

''What an obedient wife you've suddenly become,'' he slurred. ''Grimes should be back with your clothes shortly.

Once you're dressed, we're going to take a little stroll under cover of darkness . . . down to the jail. You see, a couple of my handpicked men have bribed the sheriff's deputy to leave the White Wolf unattended for an hour or so. Mere hanging's too good for him.

"I want him to suffer the way I have first . . . and you will watch. No crying out, not a sign of sympathy. If you make one sound while my men and I deal out justice, I'll rip his bastard out of your belly in front of his eyes. He'd better believe you're enjoying my little amusement as much as I am. Is that quite clear, my dear wife?"

"Yes, Hugh. Quite clear."

A sharp rap sounded on the door, the lieutenant with her trunk. Phillips motioned for Stephanie to gather her strewn articles of clothing and step behind the dressing screen at the side of the room. She obeyed woodenly. There was no use appealing to Grimes. He would probably believe her deranged from her captivity, but even if he did think she was being mistreated, he would never disobey his commanding officer.

Dusk was falling as they walked the short distance from the hotel to the jail. Hugh had selected one of her best outfits, a deep green traveling suit of raw silk with a matching ostrich-plumed hat. They looked like an elegant young couple out for a pleasant evening's stroll, but people on the street recognized them at once. No one addressed them, however. Stephanie could sense their eyes following her and hear hushed whispers after they'd passed. Poor woman. Brave man. How terrible for him to have her return after what had happened. Two well-dressed women stared with open contempt and crossed the street to avoid contamination, as if surviving captivity were somehow *her* crime. Thelma Harris's words echoed in Stephanie's brain: *I, for one, would take my own life before I'd allow a filthy savage to touch me!*

What would the wife of Hugh's fellow officer think if she knew Stephanie had willingly given herself to one of those "sadistic miscreants" and would do anything to keep his child in her womb? What would any of the good people of Rawlins think? Her bitter reverie was interrupted when they reached the jail. Just as Hugh had said, the local officials had vacated the premises and left Sergeant Bedekker in charge, together with two enlisted men he had already dismissed. The fewer witnesses the better. Her stomach twisted as she felt Mikko Bedekker's hot yellow eyes on her. He licked his thick reddish lips in anticipation of the sport ahead. She had heard the sergeant had beaten a mule to death with a singletree because the poor dumb creature balked at being harnessed. His nasty leering face made her shiver and look away.

"Yer Injun's all tied up 'n' ready to go, Major, like a hog to slaughter," Bedekker said with obvious relish. He clutched a braided rawhide whip in one meaty paw, stroking it with the other as if it were a pet snake.

"Good. Shall we, my dear? And remember what I promised," he added in a whisper, ushering her through the door into the small cramped corridor of cells beyond. "I could turn you over to Mikko's tender mercies—I'm confident he could get rid of the 'cargo' you carry in your belly."

The area was dimly lit by flickering kerosene lanterns, one at each end of the hallway. Stephanie blinked trying to accustom her eyes to the poor light, searching for Chase in the shadows. There was only one other prisoner, apparently the town drunk, sleeping off a binge in the last cell. Then she found Chase, almost hidden in darkness. He was suspended against an outside wall, his shackled hands tied to a beam in the ceiling. Barely touching the ground, his feet were secured with leg irons. Blood and dirt matted his hair and covered his body, which was bruised and abraded from being dragged behind Phillips's horse. His leggings were torn and his moccasins in shreds. Although he was facing the wall, he turned his head slightly when Bedekker opened the cell door.

She could tell the instant Chase caught sight of her. His back stiffened and from beneath heavy lids his eyes bored into hers, glittering onyx in the darkness. Keeping his face an inscrutable mask, he said nothing, only waited to see what would happen next. Stephanie was relieved that he had not called out to her. She was uncertain that she could have kept from running to him and throwing her arms about him, sealing their doom and that of their child.

"You may proceed, Sergeant. My wife and I will observe." Hugh's voice was low, vibrating with excitement. Making a great show of courtesy, he took Stephanie's arm and escorted her closer.

Although they remained outside the bars, Stephanie could see the small tremors racking Chase's body in the cool evening air. His face and upper body were covered with a fine sheen of moisture. He was feverish and chilled and they were going to beat him! Merciful God, he could die by morning from the abuse they'd already inflicted upon him, even if they did not perform this barbaric torture. She willed herself to remain composed when Bedekker raised the short heavy whip and struck.

The sergeant plied the lash with savage ferocity. Each punishing blow left a heavy red welt across Chase's bare back. He made no sound as the rawhide ripped his flesh, but his body flinched in involuntary spasms. The only sound in the room was a steady, rhythmic *whump, whump, whump* . . .

Stephanie wanted nothing so much as to seize the cruel weapon and turn it on their tormentors, but fear for Chase's baby held her motionless. Hugh's long aristocratic fingers dug into her elbow like steel pins and his eyes moved from Chase to her, watching for the slightest betrayal of her agony. When Chase's body finally went slack and his head slumped forward in unconsciousness, Bedekker threw a bucket of ice-cold water in his face to revive him.

"If you kill him, the local authorities will be forced to ask questions," she dared to comment when Chase passed out the second time and the sergeant doused him again. She was careful to keep her voice coolly neutral. Hugh was so keenly excited by his grisly vengeance that she knew he might lose control completely and flog her lover to death.

"I doubt he'll be so obliging as to die. I've fought these red bastards for eight years now. They're tougher than mustangs. No, what's left of him will survive long enough to dance at the end of a rope before dawn."

As he came to, Chase heard their exchange through a

haze of pain and fever. His head throbbed incessantly, his arms felt as if they were being wrenched from their sockets and his back was on fire, yet he focused on Stephanie standing beside his hated enemy, the man in league with that abomination Burke Remington. Why would she betray the People? She had loved Red Bead and Stands Tall, Kit Fox and Granite Arm. Most of all she loved Smooth Stone and Tiny Dancer. She had loved him. Or had she? As the whip came down again and again, consciousness finally gave way to bottomless black oblivion and he welcomed it.

The next thing he remembered was the faint essence of a woman's perfume, not apple blossoms yet vaguely familiar. Soft coaxing hands wielding a cloth dripping with cool water and a frantic whispering voice brought him to full consciousness. He raised his head, blinking to clear his vision, then let out a hiss of pain when the cold rag was pressed against the raw flesh of his back.

"Chase, you have to wake up! Oh, damn, what will I do if he's killed you! There's a lynch mob forming down the street and you don't have much time."

Apparently they'd unshackled him after the beating and put him on a narrow cot. Forcing his eyes to focus, he peered into the darkness at the woman sitting on the edge of his bed. Long dark curls framed a small heart-shaped face and fell across the lush expanse of her bosom. "Sabrina? What the hell are you doing in Wyoming?" His voice sounded rusty and he coughed, sending renewed waves of agony rippling up and down his back.

"I'm here to save your life—if you'll get a move on!" she replied, her petulance overlaid with real fear.

He eased up into a sitting position. When the room finally ceased spinning, he said, "How do you figure to do that?"

"I've brought you some civilized clothing and there's a fresh horse out back." She shoved a bundle into his hands and he slipped the shirt on, wincing as it touched the raw oozing wounds on his back. She kept talking as he pulled off his shredded buckskins, slipped a pair of dark wool trousers over his bare legs and stood to button the fly. "After they finished beating you, the deputy came back. I bribed him to let you escape. He figures the sheriff's set him up to take the blame when the lynch mob gets hold of you. He left the keys on the desk and took the night train bound for San Francisco.''

When he finished dressing, he reached for the Army Colt and ammunition belt she had brought and strapped it around his hips. He could hear the distant rumble of angry voices. ''Burke's boys must be doing a good job getting the citizens worked up.'' He looked down at the woman's pale face, illuminated by the moonlight filtering in from the window. ''Why, Sabrina? What's in this for you to make you risk your neck?''

She stroked his whisker-roughened jaw. ''I'd like to say fond memories of old times but neither of us would believe it. I figure you're my best chance to stay alive, Chase. You see, I know you'll kill Burke for me.''

''That I will, Sabrina. That I will,'' he said softly as she arched up on tiptoe and pulled his head forward for a deep swift kiss. Then he walked unsteadily out of the cell and through the back door, vanishing into the darkness of the night.

As she emerged from the front door, Sabrina could hear the soft clop of his horse's hooves heading up Fifth Street. The torches of the mob were waving and bobbing in the darkness several blocks down Front and the angry cacophony of voices filled the night air. She pulled her cloak more tightly around her shoulders and turned the corner. By the time the word spread that the renegade was missing, she would be back in her room, safely nestled in her bed before Burke even thought to check on her.

Chase rode until sunrise, pushing the sturdy brown gelding Sabrina had given him almost as hard as he pushed his own feverish, exhausted body. Only the thought of vengeance kept him from slipping out of the saddle onto the hard dusty earth amid the rocks and sagebrush. When he stopped to rest his lathered mount, he found cheese and biscuits in the saddlebags, along with a vial of ointment for his injuries.

He washed and applied the medicine as best he could, then rested for a few hours in the shade of a large fir tree.

By midmorning he was back in the saddle. He figured the ride to Gaston de Boef's cabin on the Sweetwater would take him another day, if he pushed hard and his luck didn't run out. Of course, if Stephanie had betrayed the location of the stronghold, she would also be able to send the blue-bellies after the Frenchman, but he had nowhere else to go. Some instinct persuaded him to take the chance.

I'm a fool to believe in the possibility she's innocent.

Stephanie stared at the bed as if it were alive and ready to devour her. She stepped away from it and walked through the room like a somnambulist, touching her old things, a wicker basket of dried wildflowers, her sewing kit, a small velvet case with the jewelry Hugh had bought her over the years. Everything in her bedroom here at Fort Steele was in perfect order.

"Are you certain you don't want me to help you get ready for bed, dear?" Thelma McPherson asked in a kindly voice. The elderly woman was married to the post's master sergeant, Angus McPherson. Hugh had brought his wife back to Fort Steele after they left the jail, unwilling to chance her escaping on the train or creating an embarrassing scene in Rawlins. After all, he had accomplished what he set out to do in town. The rest was up to the ingenious Senator Burke Remington. When they arrived, it was nearly midnight. Still playing the solicitous husband, Hugh had summoned the sergeant's wife from bed to care for his "distraught" lady. Word of their unexpected return had spread and everyone on the post was whispering about her. Back in town the mob incited by Burke's men had most probably hanged Chase. But she could not let herself dwell on that.

Pressing her hand to her stomach she attempted a smile for Mrs. McPherson. "No, I'll be fine, thank you. It will seem a bit strange sleeping in a bed again after so many months on fur pallets." She saw the look of guarded sympathy in the older woman's eyes and forbore telling her she had no intention of lying down on the bed she had once shared with Hugh Phillips. She would rather sleep on jagged rocks in a snake pit!

"All right, dear. I'll be just down the hall if you need anything . . . anything at all. The corporal should be here with your bathwater in a few minutes. You're sure—"

"Yes. I'll manage just fine," Stephanie assured her, eager to have some privacy to gather her scattered thoughts. There had to be some way to escape before Hugh returned to kill her. She was certain he would not wait for the additional scandal of her pregnancy to get out. Both in town and here upon their arrival he had insinuated that her mind was afflicted. After all, how else could she have endured the unthinkable but for a descent into utter madness? She knew he planned to make her death seem some sort of macabre accident—or perhaps a suicide.

Since Chase was dead the thought of going on held no appeal, even without the specter of Hugh menacing her. But the baby she carried had become her reason to live. She would protect Chase's child at any cost. Their love may have been doomed, but their son or daughter would have a chance. She was positive Jeremiah Remington would move heaven and earth to reclaim the child of his heir. If only she could find a way to reach the old man.

A wire to Boston was the most immediate solution but it still presented several problems. Given the way Hugh had set people to watch her, getting to the telegraph room would be difficult enough. Convincing the operator to send it would be virtually impossible. And then there was always the danger that the old man would wire back to Burke, expecting his son to escort her home. A small bubble of hysteria welled up in her as Corporal Briggs knocked on the door with her bathwater.

Hugh had gone to his office, no doubt awaiting a wire from town announcing Chase's death. Then he would have to deal with the other warriors captured with Chase. She prayed Blue Eagle was among them, still alive, although certainly the army would hold some sort of kangaroo court and hang every able-bodied man left alive from the White

Wolf's stronghold. The rest, old people, women and children, would be shipped off to a reservation. Hopelessness filled her heart and tears burned her eyes as she thought of her children. Smooth Stone and Tiny Dancer had been orphaned once more. Stephanie prayed they would survive reservation life. If only there was some way she could rescue them.

"I can't even rescue myself," she murmured dejectedly. After bolting the door, she quickly stripped off her clothes and threw the expensive green traveling suit on the floor. Because it was a reminder of Hugh's hideously cruel games at the jail, she would never touch it again. The small beaded pouch with Anthea's locket inside still hung suspended between her breasts by its thin leather thong. Stephanie pulled it over her head and carefully laid it on the small table beside the tub, then climbed into the water. She took only long enough to bathe away the contamination she felt from this ghastly night, then dried off and donned a high-necked cotton night rail, carefully concealing the beloved keepsake from Chase beneath the neckline of the gown.

Tomorrow she would think of a way to contact Reverend Remington. Tonight she was so bone weary, physically and emotionally, that she swayed on her feet. Pray God Hugh stayed away until morning. With Mrs. McPherson just down the hall, she felt reasonably secure for the night. Hugh would not want to start more gossip by smashing down her door. To be on the safe side, she braced a chair beneath the heavy brass knob before making her pallet on the floor and sinking onto the hard boards. In moments she slipped into an exhausted sleep.

Across the compound in his office, Hugh sat with a half-empty bottle of whiskey on his desk. Holding the amber contents of his glass up to the lantern light, he studied it while his mind ran over various ways to kill his wife. An overpowering urge to beat her to death with his bare hands almost won out, but he realized that would lead to his own ruin. No, she must appear to die by her own hand.

"How to accomplish it?" he muttered. The deed must be done soon before anyone learned Stephanie had an Indian bastard in her belly. The thought that a filthy breed could set his seed in her while he had never been able to ate at Hugh's guts like a cancer. He took another swallow of whiskey. At least by now the bastard should be dead, dangling from a tree limb.

He still had the pleasant duty of executing the other bucks who rode with Remington. There would be some sort of perfunctory hearing first, but it was only a formality. Burke was handling the matter with the Interior Department. It should only take a week at best. Then he could order those savages to be marched onto the parade grounds and shot. "Some small consolation," he said, taking another drink of whiskey. Of course, not as much consolation as watching Bedekker flay Chase Remington's back raw, after he had dragged the breed behind his horse for three days. Hugh smiled and leaned back, putting his feet up on the edge of his desk, turning his thoughts again to how he would handle the disposition of his wife.

This pleasant divertissement was interrupted suddenly when the silence outside was broken by hoofbeats and the jangling of harness. It was past midnight. No one should be riding in or out of the fort at this hour. The only men authorized to move about now were the telegrapher and the guards on watch and they were afoot. Hugh swung his feet down and sat forward, reaching for the pistol at his side. Whoever had just arrived entered the headquarters building, storming toward his office.

Without bothering to knock, Burke Remington shoved the door open and stepped inside. "Your celebration is a bit premature," he said, scowling at the nearly empty whiskey bottle.

Phillips stood up, holstering his gun. Remington looked haggard, almost wild eyed, not at all the urbane Boston aristocrat. A feeling of uneasiness swept over Hugh. "What do you mean?"

"I mean my nephew's escaped from the Rawlins jail. Vanished into thin air without a trace. I've put that idiot of a sheriff to searching but I doubt he'll turn up anything. The deputy who was on duty's missing, too." Burke combed one well-manicured set of fingers through his thick gray hair and began to pace.

Hugh cursed and reached for the bottle once more. "Someone must've bribed the deputy, but who?" Instantly his thoughts flew to Stephanie: He grimaced as he swallowed the last of the whiskey, realizing she had not been alone for a moment.

"I don't know who freed him, but I have my suspicions," Burke replied ominously. "I'll deal with that matter in my own good time. Now the priority is finding Chase." Burke paused in his pacing and studied Phillips. The major's eyes were bloodshot and his uniform wrinkled. "You look like hell. The last thing I need now is for you to fall apart. I want that half-breed cur dead."

"Not as much as I do. My darling wife's carrying his bastard!" he blurted out before he could stop himself.

Remington blanched. "Why the hell didn't you tell me sooner! All I need is for that to get back to old Jeremiah."

"No chance. You can't imagine I'll let her live to disgrace me more than she has already. I was just planning her *suicide* when you walked in."

"No, wait. Let's not do anything too hasty. This may be just the bait we need to lure my bastard nephew under our guns. I understand that Indians are quite sentimental about their brats. I suspect Chase doesn't know he's to become a father or he would never have let Stephanie go." Burke stroked his jaw consideringly.

Phillips's face, already mottled from drink, grew even redder. "If you think I'll let a whisper of that get out and ruin me—"

"Obviously not among your soldiers," Burke said, dismissing the major's outrage. "Among the savages. Those men you have in the stockade—the bucks who probably raided with Chase ... . what if they learned that the White Wolf would soon have a cub? And that Stephanie was desperate to escape from her bluebelly husband?"

"I don't see how that will matter once I execute the bastards," Hugh snapped, not liking the turn the conversation had taken.

Burke sighed patiently, once more the smooth politician in control of the situation. "You won't shoot all of them. You will let one or two escape. They'll either lead us to Chase or Chase will come to us: We hold the key—Stephanie and the child."

What Remington said made sense but it rankled Phillips that anyone else, even the damned savages, would know about his disgrace. He cursed the whiskey that had loosened his tongue. If word ever got out among his men . . . He refused to even think about the subtle whispers and sly laughter at his expense. At length he said, "You don't realize how big this country is. Half the Department of the Platte spent over three years searching for that goddamned raider and came up empty. He managed to pillage right under our noses and slip past trap after trap."

"Then you didn't know who he was—and you didn't hold his woman and child hostage. Surely you can figure a way to lure him in so he can't escape . . ."

The following evening Mikko Bedekker and his corporal spread a rumor among the Cheyenne, laughingly reporting that the major's white wife was carrying a red baby in her belly. On guard duty, they pretended to be drunk and gossiped scurrilously in earshot of a number of women. They knew at least one could speak English, a pretty young thing named Kit Fox. Then Kit Fox and several other women were selected to serve food and tend injuries among the White Wolf's warriors being held in the stockade.

Blue Eagle and Plenty Horses listened intently as Kit Fox explained what she had heard from the drunken Blue Coats. "I fear her white husband will kill her and the child. She spoke little of this Hugh Phillips when she was with us, but I know he is an evil man."

Plenty Horses struck his fist impotently against the stone wall of their cell in frustration. "What can we do caged up, waiting for the Blue Coats to kill us?"

"If only you could escape," Kit Fox said fervently.

"If he was able, the White Wolf would come to free us but he was gravely hurt when Phillips took him away. I do not believe the White Eye soldiers will wait long to kill us,'' Blue Eagle replied in a stoic voice.

"But he himself escaped. The soldiers have said this. I have watched the guards. They are stupid and careless,'' Kit Fox said, fighting down the fear clawing at her. *My husband cannot die! My brother and sister cannot die!* "If they continue to let me bring you food, perhaps I can find a way to distract them. Green Grass will help me. She and Swan Flower can steal the keys to this locked up place while the guards drink whiskey in the evenings.''

"I have never heard of soldiers being allowed to get drunk on duty,'' Plenty Horses said suspiciously.

"I do not want you near the soldiers, Kit Fox,'' Blue Eagle said sternly. "It is too dangerous.''

"What is safe? Waiting like rabbits in the compound, surrounded by soldiers until they decide to herd us all to a reservation in the hot country where we will sicken and die? If you can escape and find the White Wolf, he will know what to do,'' Kit Fox argued.

"He has a hiding place with a white trapper, a Frenchman on the Sweetwater. I know where this Gaston de Boef can be found,'' Blue Eagle said in resignation. It was a slim chance, yet the only chance they might have.

The next night Kit Fox found the same guards on watch at the stockade. This night their drunkenness was no ruse. They had passed a bottle back and forth between them until the corporal passed out against the wall while the one called Bedekker studied the comely Cheyenne female with hooded eyes. The keys lay out on the table beside the empty whiskey bottle.

"You and me could have some fun if you want to,'' the sergeant ventured with a lopsided grin, stumbling to his feet, leaving the keys unattended. "Just leave that gruel for the bucks 'n' come out back,'' he wheedled. "I got lots of pretties,'' he added slyly, pulling a tangle of beaded necklaces from his pocket and holding them up in one meaty fist. He did not understand or approve orders which allowed cutthroat Indians to escape but at least the wench was mighty pretty for a redskin. She would be his payment for taking the risks in this crazy scheme of the major's.

Bobbing her head eagerly, Kit Fox put down the kettle of greasy tasteless stew and followed the big foul-smelling soldier outside into the darkness. *No matter what he does I will not cry out.* Her family would be free.

In moments Swan Flower had sneaked into the small room from down the hall and scooped up the keys to Blue Eagle and Plenty Horse's cell. If only she could free the rest, but they were far down at the opposite end of the stockade and there was no time.

"Where is Kit Fox?" Blue Eagle asked as soon as they were outside the cell.

"She went with the big soldier," Swan Flower replied unhappily.

Blue Eagle looked at his brother-in-law. "Go and search for horses. I will see to my wife, then we will meet you down by the riverbank in the cottonwoods."

The two men split up after relieving the unconscious guard of his carbine and pistol. Within the quarter hour Blue Eagle came loping down the riverbank to where his brother-in-law waited with several Cheyenne ponies.

"Where is Kit Fox?" her brother asked.

"I knocked the Blue Coat out before he could defile her, but she refused to come with me. She said we could ride faster without her and that she must remain behind to care for Smooth Stone and Tiny Dancer. We will go to the White Wolf. Surely he will know a way to free them all."

The two riders slipped silently through the trees and vanished into the moonlit night, unaware of the white men in the stockade who watched the scene through field glasses.

"This sure as hell better work, Remington," Phillips gritted out.

"I know that red savage. He'll come for his brat, believe me," Burke replied.

"It's a trap," Chase said flatly after crawling back from the edge of the escarpment that overlooked the railroad tracks below.

"I knew it must be so," Plenty Horses replied. "Our

escape from the drunken soldiers was too easy.''

''I still believe your woman carries your child,'' Blue Eagle said to his leader. ''Will you abandon her without learning the truth?''

''I asked Gaston if he saw her get on the train. He hadn't but she could've been waiting for it in Rawlins around the time Phillips dragged me in,'' Chase said grudgingly. ''The bastard could have captured her and forced her to do his bidding.'' The raw lacerations on his back still ached abominably although they were starting to heal thanks to the herbal poultices with which the Frenchman had treated his wounds. He had not told anyone about Stephanie watching with her white husband while he was beaten. The memory was even more painful than his injuries. ''I will find a way to reach her . . . but I don't know if she wants to be rescued,'' he added enigmatically.

''The White Eye soldier will kill her if we do not save her,'' Plenty Horses stated flatly and Blue Eagle chorused his agreement.

''Perhaps.'' Chase sighed. ''But I can't ask you to risk your lives for one woman when the rest of our band will need you. You must go search out Stands Tall on the reservation at Fort Fetterman. If our people have not already been sent there, they soon will be. The soldiers at the fort will see only two more starving Indians gone tame in return for rations. You two and my uncle can help what is left of our people slip away and join Little Wolf in the Tongue River basin. He has promised me he would help us.''

''What will you do?'' Plenty Horses asked shrewdly. ''Once you asked me to safeguard your wife if you were dead. What if the Blue Coats kill you?''

''I will do what must be done for my wife. Your first duty is to the Cheyenne. Go with my blessings, my brothers. Perhaps one day we will meet again.''

''If not here, then on the Hanging Road to the Sky,'' Blue Eagle replied gravely.

Chase watched his friends ride away, then turned his attention back to the cluster of buildings situated on the bend of the river. Stephanie waited down there—in fear of her life? Or in hopes of seeing him ride into Hugh Phillips's death trap?

∞ *25* ∞

After nearly two nerve-wracking weeks of being isolated
and guarded as if she were a dangerous convict or a lunatic,
Stephanie was happy to smell fresh air and feel the sun on
her face once more. She breathed deeply, grateful the nausea that had been plaguing her upon arising for over a
month had at last abated. She had no idea why Hugh had
invited her to ride with him today, but suspected that he
and Burke were plotting something together. She was
amazed he had not killed her yet.

Stephanie had made several abortive attempts to escape,
but the more she tried to slip past her guards, the more
certain everyone on the post became that she was deranged
and intended to harm herself. Visitors and guards alike
looked on her with pitying eyes. She knew they whispered
about her and "poor Major Phillips" when they left the
commandant's quarters. However did the loyal husband endure the tragedy of his wife being dishonored by savages?

How neatly her death would solve Hugh's problem and
complete his revenge. Chase had been lynched in Rawlins
and his warriors executed by a firing squad on the parade
grounds. As the shots rang out that awful morning, she had
squeezed her hands over her ears. At dinner the same evening, Hugh and Burke had eaten with relish as they discussed the executions, forcing her to sit at the table with
them and endure the verbal torture. She could not swallow
a bite as she thought of her friend Kit Fox, now widowed.
If Blue Eagle and Plenty Horses had survived the battle at
the stronghold, then both had surely died before that firing
squad.

Stephanie longed to talk with someone who understood

how she felt and accepted her in spite of the heinous sin of loving a half-breed renegade. The only one who would understand was Hannah, but Hugh had forbidden the Quaker to visit his wife. As the lieutenant escorted her to the main corral, her eyes swept furtively across the parade grounds searching for her friend's thin, gray-clad figure outside the infirmary. She knew Hannah would have tried to help the remaining people from Chase's band while they were held at the fort, but the survivors had now been sent to the military reservation at Fort Fetterman.

Stephanie prayed her family and friends among the Cheyenne had been spared. Would she ever learn their fate? She reached up and felt the small beaded pouch between her breasts, her keepsake from Chase, a legacy for the grandchild of Freedom Woman and Vanishing Grass.

Then she saw Hannah across the parade grounds, a tiny figure carrying a bundle of bed linens that seemed almost as big as she. The wind would carry away her words if she dared to call out a greeting—or an entreaty for help. Even if Hannah heard her plea, disobeying Hugh's orders would only result in her being evicted from the post. Hannah did too much good here for Stephanie to jeopardize the Quaker's work for her own selfish needs.

"Come on, Mrs. Phillips. You don't want to keep your husband waiting," the cherub-faced young officer said with false heartiness. The lieutenant obviously found escorting the major's tarnished wife a trying duty.

He's afraid I'm going to run screaming across the parade ground, rip off my clothes and climb the flag pole, she thought dismally, but said nothing.

Hugh waited at the corral with their horses. He smiled cordially. "Good morning, dear wife. I trust you're looking forward to our little outing?"

She was sick of oily civility. "Why do you want me to ride with you?" she asked flatly.

"I thought the fresh air and exercise would uplift your spirits. I've been most concerned about your despondency, Stephanie," he replied.

"I know how concerned you are. Shall we ride?" The

lieutenant saluted Hugh after assisting her to mount the cumbersome sidesaddle. Sergeant Bedekker was to accompany them at a discreet distance. As they trotted across the compound and left the fort, she gauged her horse's mettle. Did she stand a chance of outrunning them?

As if reading her mind, Hugh said, "I chose the mare because she's gentle, but I'm afraid she isn't very swift." His smile would have frozen whiskey.

She eyed him warily. "Do you plan to have Bedekker kill me?" she asked at length. "Or are you reserving that pleasure for yourself?"

He laughed mirthlessly. "Careful, my dear. If the good sergeant were to hear you, he would attest that you've indeed lost your mind."

"I doubt at this point you require the sergeant's testimony." She looked ahead toward the North Platte, a bright serpentine ribbon undulating beneath the brilliant azure sky. Cottonwoods and willows lined the banks in dense stands, many with low-hanging branches. She'd ridden here often when Hugh was first stationed at the post. Perhaps she could arrange a little accident for him. He rode close to her side and she observed the stock of his Springfield sticking out of the scabbard on his saddle. She would need to seize it when he went down if she was going to have some defense against Bedekker when he came to his superior's rescue. To save her baby she'd kill both men in a heartbeat.

As she and Phillips approached the cover of the trees, Stephanie was not the only person sizing up the possibility of disposing of the cavalrymen. From his hidden position on the escarpment to the west, Chase observed the three riders through a pair of field glasses. For over a week he had been watching the route of the patrols and sentries, studying every detail inside the compound. Locating the commandant's quarters and offices had been simple. He figured Stephanie was inside the two-story frame house on the west side of the parade grounds, but she never ventured outdoors.

Chase had enlisted de Boef to ride to the fort with a load of pelts to sell at the trading post. The Frenchman had listened to the gossip about the major's lady, who was confined to her house after a ghastly ordeal at the hands of savages. Everyone tsked sadly about her captivity but secretly relished what they imagined to be the gruesome details.

Armed with the information from de Boef, Chase watched for his chance. He suspected the story of Stephanie's pregnancy had been deliberately spread among his people, and his friends' escape from the stockade had been no accident. Was the pregnancy real or only a ploy to lure him into their trap? Whatever the cost, he had to know.

Chase studied the striking looking couple as they approached the cover of the trees. First he would have to dispose of the sergeant. Remembering his zest for plying the whip, Chase's lips thinned in a ruthless smile. He slid back from the edge of the escarpment and walked over to where he'd hidden his mount.

Leaping onto the horse, he worked his way down the steep slope. Phillips and the sergeant were alone, of that he was certain. He'd been watching the fort from the ridge since moonrise last night. "Keep on going just the way you are, you damned butcher, and we'll see who traps who," he murmured as Hugh and Stephanie skirted the trees at the riverbank.

Soon they passed into the cover of the trees where the sergeant would be obscured from the vision of the officer and his lady—if they chanced to look back. Slipping off his horse, Chase used the cover of the trees to race ahead of the sergeant. The soldier would have to die quickly and quietly. Knocking an arrow in the bow he carried, he aimed and let fly the deadly missile. A slight whirring noise was all Bedekker heard before he fell from the saddle with the arrow embedded in his throat. *So much for covering your back, Phillips*, Chase thought grimly as he slung the bow across his shoulder and began to stalk in earnest.

As soon as Stephanie saw the big willows she began to implement her plan. As far as she knew Hugh had never ridden beneath them so he wouldn't expect the low-hanging limb from one tree which was hidden by the densely leafed canopy of the tree in front of it. She would have to time this just right. It would be her last chance.

When they drew within a dozen yards of the willows, Stephanie leaned forward and kicked her mare into a gallop toward the curtain of leaves. When she reached the trees, she flattened herself against the mare's neck and wheeled her around after passing beneath a horizontal limb that was easily a foot in diameter. Hugh was right behind her, cursing as he yelled, "Don't be a fool, Stephanie. There's nowhere to run!"

He'd no more than uttered the words when his head slammed into the limb, knocking him from the saddle, unconscious. Stephanie lunged for the frightened horse's bridle as it shied. She screamed as a steely arm coiled suddenly around her from behind. Desperately she kicked and flailed until a familiar voice murmured in her ear, "Stop struggling, Stevie."

Stephanie froze. "Oh my God! They told me you were dead," she whispered, feeling him warm and solid against her. When he turned her to face him, for the first time in her life Stephanie almost fainted. Everything went black for an instant. She ached to hold him, to touch his beard-stubbled jaw. Tears swam in her eyes, blurring his face, but she could tell he was studying her, an intent and cold perusal. "What . . . how did you—"

"I escaped from the Rawlins jail after your major had his fun."

Your major. The words stung. "Chase, he forced me to watch them whip you. You can't think—can't believe . . ." With dawning horror she blinked back her tears and looked into his eyes.

He felt her shudder in revulsion, then go very still. "I don't know what to think, Stevie. We didn't exactly part on the best of terms. I no more than returned to the stronghold when Phillips and his butchers swept down on us, Custer style. No one's ever found that place. You were in town when they brought me in. I saw you and Phillips walk off arm in arm . . . then that night at the jail . . . what could I think?"

"You could have believed in me," she replied intensely as a bit of the old spirit reanimated her. "I don't know how Hugh found you but I do know how he forced me to endure that night in the jail."

"By threatening to kill you?"

Her eyes blazed like the sun now. "He planned to kill me no matter what I agreed to. I'm certain that's why he brought me out here today."

He searched her face . . . and believed her. "I may be a fool . . . but I couldn't leave you without being certain you were safe."

Stephanie could see the truth shining in his eyes and her heart surged with happiness. There was so much she longed to tell him and to ask him. "I love you more than life itself. Hugh threatened to kill our baby that night if I didn't do exactly what he said at the jail."

"Then it's true," he replied, cradling her in his arms. "Blue Eagle and Plenty Horses heard it from the soldiers—"

"They're alive, too?" she asked, incredulous with joy. "Hugh told me he'd executed all your warriors. And the children, Kit Fox, Red Bead and Stands Tall?"

His expression hardened thinking of the decimation of his band. "Red Bead is dead, killed by a Blue Coat. So is Elk Bull and the rest of my warriors. Stands Tall and Kit Fox got Smooth Stone, Tiny Dancer and most of the children to safety during the fighting, but Phillips rounded them all up afterward. They've been sent to the reservation at Fetterman. Blue Eagle and Plenty Horses went after them. With luck they may be able to slip away and reach Little Wolf's band. After that . . ."

"Oh, Chase, what can we do?" Her voice choked with tears. So many of her friends, her family, dead or living under terrible conditions that would break their spirit.

Chase raised his hand to wipe away her tears. "I don't know," he replied disconsolately. She reached up and embraced him but he flinched when her fingers dug into his shoulders. At once she realized what she had done. "Your back—it must still be terribly painful. I'm sorry. Oh, Chase, how did you endure such pain and . . ."

"He always was difficult to kill." Burke Remington stepped from behind the trunk of a huge willow that had concealed him. "Throw your knife and pistol on the ground or I'll kill Mrs. Phillips," he said as Chase attempted to shove Stephanie behind him, cursing his stupidity. He was certain Phillips and Burke had laid a trap but how had his uncle gotten here without his seeing him?

Burke gloated now as Chase tossed the Army Colt and the blade down. "I told your husband this would work. I knew he'd be watching, planning, but be unable to resist when he saw you. I slipped into the woods along the river at dusk last night before the moon came up, then slept until dawn. Living out of doors in tune with nature is greatly overrated . . . unless one is a savage such as you, dear nephew," he said, his geniality turning to deadly venom. Then he returned his attention to Stephanie. "You see, I've known this bastard since he was a sniveling brat . . . and now I hear you're about to bless the Remington name with yet another mongrel."

While Burke talked, Chase inched imperceptibly away from Stephanie, closer to his uncle, his mind racing for a way to distract him long enough to move into position. He had to bring down Burke before Hugh regained consciousness. "You've never gotten over the fact my mother loved another man—married him and bore him a son—my Cheyenne blood is the least of my sins in your eyes, *Uncle Burke*," he taunted, watching the tic in Remington's cheek, the fiery blaze ignite in those freezing blue eyes.

"The Remington heir, a half-breed bastard," Burke rasped. "Anthea never married that savage. She was raped."

"Yes, she was, Uncle, but not by my father. She loved Vanishing Grass. You raped her—you, the filthy pervert who was her brother!" By now, Chase was struggling to control his anger. He heard Stephanie's sharp intake of breath and saw Burke's complexion redden with rage.

"I loved her! I was the only one worthy, the only one—"

"It killed you, didn't it, when you couldn't have children with her—or Sabrina, or any other woman? But Anthea ran away from you and had a son with an Indian. A son who, in spite of his tainted blood, would inherit everything."

"I wanted heirs for the Remington name—but only with her. She was the only one . . . but she betrayed me and Jeremiah's God struck her down with madness."

"You drove her to madness the night her fourteen-year-old son saw you invade her bed. She couldn't live with the shame."

A feral grimace of triumph twisted Burke's face. "I wanted you to see who she really belonged to—me! Me!" he bellowed, raising the rifle.

Stephanie's scream rang out as he pulled the trigger. The bullet slammed into Chase, hitting him in his side when he dodged. He kept coming as Burke fired again. The shot slashed wickedly into Chase's leg when he struck the barrel, wrenching it from his uncle's hands. Locked in a primal embrace, they fell to the ground like two snarling wolves. Frantically Stephanie looked for a weapon. The red stains blossomed around Chase's side and down his leg. He couldn't hold out for long against Burke's maniacal strength, not shot twice! She saw Chase's discarded Colt lying on the ground and darted over to seize it but dared not fire for fear of hitting him. Dear God, this was Chase's vision, her dream! Chase was the white wolf and Burke the gray. It made a bizarre sort of sense now. Chase would win. He would kill Burke. *And then he would leave her.*

The combatants punched and gouged. Burke aimed his blows at Chase's bleeding side and kneed into his injured leg, eliciting grunts of agony from the younger man. Chase clenched his teeth against the pain and rolled with all his strength, pushing off on his good leg so that he came up on top of Burke. The older man was literally foaming at the mouth, fueled by an insane rage. "The Remington blood will out, eh, Burke?" Chase gasped as his fingers tightened on his uncle's throat. "You're the one who's mad—you always were!"

Stephanie stood with the gun raised and cocked, but it was unnecessary. Over Chase's labored breath she could hear the sickening crack of Burke Remington's neck snapping. She almost dropped the Colt to run to him when she caught a movement from the corner of her eye.

Hugh had regained consciousness. He was crouched, his pistol trained on Chase. "It's a good day to die, you red bastard."

"Only for you, Hugh." Her husband whirled to face down the barrel of the Colt. Startled and infuriated that his wife had drawn a bead on him, he aimed at her heart and pulled back the hammer, snarling, "I always planned to kill you."

A single shot rang out and Hugh fell backward with a look of amazement on his face. "I know," she replied quietly. He lay with his eyes staring sightlessly up at the willow branches overhead. Stephanie stared at the man she had married with such high hopes four years ago. She was not sad, only relieved that it was at long last over. Trembling, she dropped the weapon and rushed to Chase, who had crawled off Burke's body and knelt in a daze, his blood soaking into the ground around him.

Stephanie steeled herself to forget the ghastly deed she had just committed, letting the trained nurse in her take over. Seizing his knife, she began to slash the long train of her riding habit into makeshift wrappings to staunch the bleeding. "I have to get you to a doctor."

"Take me to Sabrina Remington at the Brunswick Hotel."

"Burke's wife?" Stephanie asked incredulously.

"She's the one who broke me out of jail," he said with a feral smile. "I have to tell her I kept my word. She'll be able to get a doctor quietly."

"But it's too far. You're bleeding," she protested.

"I've lived through worse for longer."

His speech was growing slurred. Stephanie knew the signs of shock. There was no choice. If they returned to the post, Chase would be arrested. So would she. After placing his Colt in his holster she gathered the reins of Hugh's gelding and slipped Burke's rifle in the scabbard. Then she helped Chase mount the cavalry horse. He hung onto the horse's mane as she climbed up behind him, baring her calves so she could ride astride.

Twilight was falling when the doctor finally finished stitching up Chase's wounds. White faced but steady, Stephanie assisted him with the ether as he probed the muscle of Chase's thigh to extract the bullet. The one in his side had passed clean through and was less serious than the leg injury which had missed an artery by a scant half inch. While they worked with the physician in his small cluttered surgery, Sabrina Remington paced nervously outside.

Sabrina had been relieved when she received Chase's blood-smeared message saying Burke was dead, although she was frightened to death about helping a shot-up renegade with a five-thousand-dollar price on his head. But she knew Burke had planned to have her killed—would have, too, if she had not persuaded his aide Stokley Aimes that she would be much more accommodating alive than dead. Stokley had read the note when she showed it to him, grinning boyishly at his own wisdom. He'd made the right choice. Now the rich widow would be grateful and generous.

A debt was a debt. Sabrina sent Stokley to help Stephanie bring Chase to Dr. Kandell's office. The old physician had a reputation for discretion, having tended numerous men considered on the periphery of the law. And he drank. That afternoon he had been mercifully sober when the senator's wife asked for his help, offering a very substantial payment in return for treating a shot-up half-breed "trader."

"How is he?" Sabrina asked when Stephanie emerged from the surgery into the dingy waiting room.

"He'll live, although he's lost so much blood the doctor considers it a miracle. He may walk with a limp the rest of his life from the leg wound. It nicked the femur, almost

punctured an artery.'' She shuddered with fear, thinking of
how close she'd come to losing him.

"You look pale. Here, you'd better sit down," Sabrina
said awkwardly, taking Stephanie's arm and guiding her to
one of the half-dozen battered wooden chairs scattered
around the room.

Stephanie sank onto it gratefully and smiled wanly at the
beautiful brunette who had proven such an unlikely ally.
"We owe you so much. If you hadn't helped us, Chase
would've died—or been recaptured. He told me how you
helped him escape from jail.''

Sabrina's blue eyes were cold and hard as sapphires in
contrast to her soft Southern drawl. "I owe him for killing
Burke . . . and other things.''

"You were lovers once, back in Boston, weren't you?"

Sabrina's full lips bowed up and a tinge of amusement
softened her expression as thoughts of her dead husband
faded. "It was a long time ago. No need to be jealous. He
was beautiful as sin even when he was a nineteen-year-old
boy. I was . . . a bit older, very unhappily married. I'll admit
I was put out when he was the one to end our little dalliance
but I'd done it as much to spite Burke as anything else.''
She shrugged dismissively, then chewed her lip. "Now
what are we going to do to get him away from the army?''

"He can't travel for some time, probably several
weeks," Stephanie replied. "I need someplace safe to hide
him while he mends.''

Sabrina chuckled. "I have just the thing—that nasty little
ranch Burke bought. It's just outside town, but I'm certain
that no one else—except for possibly Phillips—even knows
about the place. He had planned for me to have a riding
accident on it at some point, while he was here in town. I
managed to foil that little scheme," she added with a grin
of satisfaction. "Let me send for Stokley. He'll see to all
the details. Then I'm off to the bright lights of San Francisco with all Burke's lovely money to spend!''

Chase recuperated in the small ramshackle cabin by the
edge of the North Platte River. Although not at all the sort

of place a city-bred woman like its new owner would enjoy, it was nonetheless a comfortable haven for him and Stephanie.

"What are you doing out of bed? You're not supposed to walk by yourself. Dr. Kandell strictly ordered bed rest." Stephanie stood in the doorway of the cabin's main room with an armload of firewood, glaring at Chase as he limped across the bare creaky floorboards and eased himself gingerly onto the battered old horsehair sofa.

He stretched his aching leg out in front of him after setting aside his cane which doubled as an iron fire poker. "I'm sick of bed rest. I need to start moving around more. I don't like the looks of that foreman Burke hired. The longer I stay here, the more likely it is someone will discover you're holed up with a wanted man. My luck hiding out hasn't exactly been the best the last few months. Sabrina told me how I was followed back to the stronghold last fall. She overheard Hugh and Burke discussing what that Ree scout had found, planning it all. I'm so sorry I thought you could've betrayed the people you loved."

She touched his lips with her fingertips. "It's over now, Chase. We're safe. Hugh and Burke are dead. We can begin again." A guarded expression came over his face. She felt him tense and he looked away for an instant. Her heart stopped beating as she asked, "What do you plan to do when you can ride, Chase?" They had both skirted around the subject for the past two weeks while he mended. Sooner or later she had to face it if he planned to leave her again. *I won't let him do it!*

Chase looked at her, seeing the vulnerability, the longing in her eyes. He had hurt her painfully, accused her unjustly, been unable to protect her from the monster she'd married . . . all because he'd left her in the first place. "Life comes full circle, doesn't it, Stevie?" he asked with a bittersweet smile, reaching one hand out for her to join him on the sofa.

She took his hand and sat down beside him. "Will you just ride off again? Go searching for the rest of our band?"

He covered her small delicate hand with his larger dark

one and met her eyes. "You're carrying my child. I may be considered a bastard by white society's standards, but I won't let what happened to my mother happen to you. As soon as I can walk, we'll catch the cars heading east. We can be married in the territorial capital . . . then you can go back to Boston to have the baby—or wherever you want to live. With Phillips dead you're a wealthy woman even if you don't want to face old Jeremiah."

"And you'll just leave us? Not this time, Chase." She swallowed for courage, then played her ace. "I'm not wealthy. All my father's money went to Hugh. Now that he's dead it goes to his family. Josiah disinherited me for being born female."

He sat back, stunned by her announcement for a moment. Then he took her in his arms, wincing as the ache in his side twinged.

"Damn the old fool." He cursed Josiah Summerfield a thousand times more, thinking of how bitterly such a betrayal must have hurt his only child. "You never told me. At the stronghold when I made you promise to divorce Hugh, you knew you had no power to do it, yet you never said a word."

"I didn't want your pity, Chase," she said, pulling out of his embrace. "That's why I didn't tell you I was pregnant when you took me to de Boef. I wasn't going to keep you from your life with the Cheyenne because you felt sorry—or responsible for me."

"I love you! I don't pity you, dammit. But I can't go back east with you. I can't bear to look at the old man. I'll never be able to forgive what he let happen to my mother. I went to him, you know, told him the truth about his only son and heir. She was so ashamed she never dared. That's why she ran away to marry a white man she didn't love and join a wagon train bound for Oregon. But he wouldn't listen to me. Called me a spawn of the devil for inventing such monstrous lies."

Stephanie could feel his anguish. What tortured black secrets were hidden behind the wealth and glitter of the Remington name. "And so you ran away to find your father's people, a fourteen-year-old boy alone and so frightened.''

''I hated her then, even when they dragged me back three years later. But once I saw what she had suffered . . . hell, Stevie, she was a lot younger than fourteen when Burke started in on her . . .''

His voice choked with emotion as she held him. ''She knew you'd forgiven her when she died, that you loved her. There was nothing you could've done. It all began so long ago, before you were born.''

''I couldn't stop it but Jeremiah could have,'' Chase gritted out. ''He knew, the bastard. He *knew*!''

''Something that terrible . . . I imagine his mind just couldn't accept it, Chase. He'd lived by such high principles all his life and raised his son to behave the same way.''

''I don't ever want to see him again,''. he said flatly.

''But you'd send me to him, wouldn't you? You'd let our child grow up without a father. I'd planned to go to Jeremiah and beg help for his great-grandchild. I've been so careful with this,'' she said, taking the beaded pouch with Anthea's locket from beneath her blouse. ''It was my proof that I carried his heir. The idea seemed best at the time with Hugh still alive. But now everything's changed. You can't be the White Wolf any longer. The People are scattered onto reservations. That part of our lives is over, but we still have a future . . . and a baby who needs a father.''

She waited with suspended breath, watching him struggle with all the old demons of the past. He reached out and took her hands in his. ''Stevie . . .''

Stephanie would have given a decade off her life to have heard him finish what he planned to say but the sound of several riders approaching interrupted them. Chase tensed, then reached for the poker, struggling to his feet.

''Get me the rifle,'' he said, pointing to the loaded Winchester by the fireplace. ''Those riders came in way too fast for a social call.''

Stephanie dashed over and handed him the rifle as footsteps raced onto the porch. Before he could cock it the door crashed open. Half a dozen soldiers burst into the room with their Springfields leveled on him. "Drop it, breed," the lieutenant said.

Surrounded, with Stephanie in the line of fire, Chase had no choice but to comply.

"I tole you he wuz hidin' here. He's that Remington feller they call the White Wolf. When can I get my reward?" the foreman Sug Nelson asked eagerly.

"He's our escaped prisoner, all right," Lieutenant Grimes said. "Take him away. I'll see to Mrs. Phillips."

"No! Chase is ill. He can't be moved—he's been injured," Stephanie cried, throwing her arms around him.

Gently Chase disengaged from her embrace, giving her over into the young officer's care. "Go with him, Stevie. He'll see you get on a train to Boston, won't you, Lieutenant?"

Grimes's face was red with embarrassment as he watched Remington pry her arms from around his neck and urge her toward the soldiers. It was obvious that the major's widow loved the renegade. She'd probably even been with him when he killed her husband and the senator, although there was no evidence linking Chase to either death. The senator's foreman had drifted into the fort that morning and plunked down a wanted poster with the White Wolf's picture on it, saying he'd just learned about the reward and he knew where the half-breed was hiding.

Flustered by the woman's silent tears and the look of tender longing shared between her and the enigmatic renegade, Grimes said, "Yes, of course, I'll see that Mrs. Phillips is returned safely to the bosom of her family!"

Stephanie stood rigidly straight, certain she would shatter in a million pieces while Grimes stood deferentially at her side, watching his men drag Chase from the house and tie him on a horse. As befitted a Cheyenne warrior, he did not utter a sound in spite of the terrible pain from his injuries. She was a warrior's wife and must do the same. The tears poured like acid rain down her cheeks but she remained silent while the column rode off with their prisoner.

Grimes cleared his throat nervously. "Er, Mrs. Phillips—"

"I haven't been Hugh Phillips's wife for a very long time. Chase Remington is my husband," she said with quiet conviction.

26

The bosom of her family. Stephanie had no white family left. Certainly not the distant Summerfield cousins. Her Cheyenne family, who she loved so dearly, had been decimated and scattered to distant reservations. She prayed that Kit Fox would be able to care for Smooth Stone and Tiny Dancer. With Stands Tall to guide them and the protection of Blue Eagle and Plenty Horses, perhaps they would all one day escape captivity and return to freedom in the land of endless sky.

Feeling as much a prisoner as the Cheyenne, she blinked back tears as her hackney rattled over the narrow rain-washed streets of Beacon Hill toward the huge gray stone monolith. As a girl the mansion had always intimidated her. So had Jeremiah Remington. The massive austere house perfectly suited him. How ironic that he was the only family she had left—if he would consider her that. She was highly uncertain of her welcome. What if he refused to see her after she'd traveled over two thousand miles to confront him in person? Her mind simply shut down thinking about what would happen then.

Stephanie had sent numerous frantic wires to the reverend from Cheyenne, the territorial capital where the army had sent Chase for his mockery of a trial. None had been answered save for a terse statement from his secretary saying Reverend Remington was in mourning for the death of his son and had left Boston with instructions that no communications from anyone be forwarded until further notice. She knew he was well advanced in years and Burke's death, no matter that they had not been close, must have been a terrible blow. The bitter old man may have grieved himself to death without ever knowing Chase would give him another heir.

Dwelling on negative thoughts was useless. She assured herself that she would find him returned to Boston by this time or, failing that, be able to convince his officious secretary to relay her message to the reverend. She clutched the tiny pouch with Anthea's locket as if it were a talisman to ward off evil. Wearing it next to her heart certainly had provided comfort during the past nightmarish weeks.

At least Chase is not dead, she repeated like a mantra. The military tribunal had been presided over by an official from the Interior Department who ruled in favor of incarceration instead of a death sentence. "Relocation" was the euphemism he used at sentencing. Since she and Chase were not legally married, the army refused to allow her visitation privileges. That terrible day at Sabrina's ranch was the last time she had seen him.

The court had sentenced the infamous White Wolf to twenty years incarceration at Fort Marion, Florida, a terrible tropical pest hole outside St. Augustine. Dozens of leaders from various western tribes were being imprisoned there in the hope of breaking the spirit of Indian resistance. Stephanie had heard stories about the horrible old fortress, a cavernous moldy-stone facility built by the Spanish in the seventeenth century. Chase's bullet wounds were barely healing and his back was still a mass of raw tender muscle and skin. Inside a dark filthy cell in the humid Florida heat he could easily die of infection. She had to free him as quickly as possible. The Remington name and influence, which Chase had despised all of his life, was now his only hope of salvation . . . if Jeremiah Remington could be persuaded to exert it on behalf of his renegade grandson.

Stephanie had agonized over whether or not to tell the old man the terrible truth about Burke. Did he have any inkling his grandson had killed his son? Once she began to unravel the ugly mess there could be no half measures. She would have to confess everything. She could not imagine anyone being able to lie with Jeremiah's steely blue eyes impaling him. Burke had been able to do so when Chase

accused him. But then Burke had been a cold-blooded ruthless murderer, utterly insane. Stephanie shivered remembering that awful confrontation on the banks of the Platte.
Could Jeremiah Remington handle the whole truth?

The hackney pulled to a stop in front of the big house
and the driver opened the door. She stepped down and paid
him his fare. She had left her trunk at the railway depot,
not daring to presume she would be welcome. Her meager
funds were running low and she was uncertain where she
would go if she was turned away. Nausea churned in her
stomach as she walked up the steps and raised her hand to
the heavy brass knocker. The sound of it striking the massive oak door was like the peal of judgment day.

After she waited an interminable time in the muggy August heat, the door swung open and a small fastidious looking man dressed somberly in black stood unsmiling.
"Yes?" His well-turned white mustache covered the corners of his mouth making it appear perpetually turned
down. The wintry gray eyes inspecting her did not dispel
the effect at all.

Stephanie knew she looked frightful after the long, arduous railroad journey. Her hair was frizzing in Boston's
late summer humidity and her travel suit was dingy with
soot. Thank goodness her pregnancy was not visible yet,
but it soon would be. She must provide a home for her
baby at any cost. Swallowing for courage, she fixed the
butler with a firm look and addressed him with the imperious assurance of a Boston aristocrat. "I'm Stephanie
Summerfield and I'm here to see the Reverend Jeremiah
Remington." Without waiting for an invitation, she stepped
into the marble foyer.

"See here, Miss Summerfield, the reverend is still in
mourning and not receiving visitors except for close personal friends."

"I am a close personal friend of his grandson Chase. I
must—"

"What the dickens is going on down there, Thomas?"
Jeremiah's voice boomed from the landing.

"Some young woman, Reverend Remington, says she's a friend of your grandson."

"Chase?" Jeremiah walked down the steps surprisingly swiftly for a man of his years. He was still imposing with thick snowy hair and piercing blue eyes but his face looked haggard and his tall robust frame had grown thin, almost frail looking. He peered through the dim light of the foyer at Stephanie. "Miss Summerfield?" he asked incredulously.

"Yes, Reverend. Stephanie Summerfield. I'm here because of Chase."

The butler looked from the travel-stained young woman to the old man. Before he could say anything, his employer waved him away, saying, "Bring some fresh lemonade into my study, Thomas."

A small bit of relief energized her. At least she had gotten herself a hearing. She followed Jeremiah down the hall to a handsomely appointed room filled with books, most of them on religious subjects. He offered her a seat on a tufted back easy chair, then took a seat on the large leather sofa across the tea table from her.

"The last I recall, Miss Summerfield, you were going to Baltimore to marry a young army officer about four years ago."

She felt the heat stain her cheeks as she replied, "I did marry Hugh Phillips, but I'm widowed now." She thought it prudent not to mention that she was responsible for her state, at least not yet. "I went west with my husband back in 1872."

"And that's where you ran across my grandson again?" His eyes burned intently from deep, dark-ringed sockets. Chase had jilted her, causing quite a bit of scandal, yet she still seemed smitten with him. "I take it he must be in trouble."

"Chase is alive, Reverend . . . for now." She moistened her lips nervously, praying she could say the right words. "He's in prison in St. Augustine. I sent wires during his trial, appealing for your help, but you never received them.

A man named Bartley said you were away, in mourning . . .''

"You asked my help in keeping Chase from prison and that fool never told me?" His eyes blazed with a bit of the old hellfire spark she remembered. "I'll deal with Bartley," he added, dismissing the man. He leaned forward and asked, "How the devil did my scapegrace grandson end up in a Florida prison, not that I'm at all surprised? I always feared for his body as well as his soul."

Just then Thomas knocked and entered bearing a heavy silver tray laden with a pitcher of lemonade and two frosty glasses. The reverend harrumphed, waiting until they'd been served before motioning her to reply.

Stephanie tried as succinctly as possible to explain the tragic situation with Chase's people and his unorthodox means of helping them. It was difficult to determine how sympathetic Jeremiah was. Most people back east read the inflammatory one-sided accounts in the newspapers and simply assumed all Indians were savages preying on helpless whites.

". . . So you see, they put a five-thousand-dollar reward on his head and tracked him down. He'd been badly hurt—whipped by . . . by the soldiers, then shot twice. He was only beginning to mend when they dragged him off to stand trial. It was a travesty. I'm desperately afraid for him. Fort Marion has a dreadful reputation. You must use your influence to get him released—a pardon, anything." She looked at him with her heart in her eyes.

"You're in love with him, aren't you, child?"

"I always have been," she replied, holding her head up proudly.

"He deserted you, same as he did me. You ought to hate him."

"So should you but I believe you still love him, too."

"Boy never believed I did. I . . . I suppose I wasn't very good at showing it. He was wild and filled with strange heathen notions and I was a preacher puffed up with vanity, full of himself." He looked every one of his seventy-seven years at that moment. "I thought I'd never see him again. I imagine you thought the same?"

"Yes . . . or maybe I unconsciously hoped I would find him out west. Perhaps that's why I married Hugh when I did not love him," she confessed, admitting the truth to herself.

"Seems like you succeeded. You've apparently spent some time learning about those people he lived with."

"Chase kidnapped me when I recognized him in a small Wyoming town where he was gathering information for a raid." Now came the hardest part, telling him about their relationship, the Cheyenne marriage and the baby. She took several swallows of the lemonade to moisten her dry mouth, then plunged into the story of her months with the Cheyenne.

". . . He left me with the Frenchman, expecting I'd return to Boston where I'd be safe. I didn't tell him my father had given my inheritance to Hugh's family and I was penniless. I didn't tell him I was carrying his child either."

Jeremiah Remington blinked, poleaxed. Then to her utter relief he smiled and the look of anguish burning behind his eyes left for a moment. He stood up and walked around the table to her chair and took her hands in his. "My dear Stephanie, I arranged your betrothal to my grandson four years ago. At last I'll have the chance to marry you and that young rapscallion."

"First we'll have to get Chase out of prison," she said, smiling in spite of the lump in her throat.

Jeremiah's obvious delight over his great-grandchild dimmed for a moment. "Yes, I'll put my attorneys to investigating how we can free him. With the good Lord's help we'll have him home before his firstborn comes into the world."

He paced across the room to stand beside his desk, then turned to her and said, "Of course you will live here while I see to extricating Chase." It was not a request.

Stephanie fought a smile and replied gravely, "Of course, Reverend Remington."

His imperious expression vanished as he took a seat behind the massive oak desk. He extracted a small white leather volume from one of the drawers. At first Stephanie thought it was a Bible but something in his eyes when they met hers indicated this was not going to be a sermon. Then she saw the faint gold etching on the outside cover. It was a diary. He looked unsure of himself, suddenly old and oddly vulnerable. The pain in those fierce blue eyes held her spellbound. She waited for him to speak. When he began his ringing sonorous voice was hushed with bleakness.

"I found this only a few days before I received word that Burke was dead," he said, looking down at the well-worn volume. "I had finally worked up the courage to go through Anthea's personal belongings and dispose of them, a task I could not in conscience leave to servants. It was well hidden, no doubt to keep it secret from her brother. God forgive me, I might have killed him myself if he'd lived to return home." He shook his head, then looked up at her, his face haggard and pale, the only color in it those blue eyes, like Burke's, yet not alike. "Chase was the one who killed him, wasn't he?"

"Yes. Burke plotted with my husband to lay a trap to capture the White Wolf using me as bait. They intended to kill us both. Burke shot Chase twice before Chase got to him." She shuddered remembering the awful bloody reenactment of the medicine dream, then faced Jeremiah. He had a right to know it all. "The night of the Cabots' ball I overheard Burke paying an assassin to murder Chase. He's always wanted him dead. I assumed it was because he wanted your money for himself or because of the circumstances of Chase's birth." She met his eyes.

"My grandson tried to tell me about the monster my son was but I refused to believe him. I closed my mind to the truth." He ran his fingers through his hair and then cradled his head in his hands. "I look back on it all now, after reading Anthea's . . . my daughter's pleas." His voice broke. "She was a child and I was her father and I let this—this abomination happen!"

Stephanie went to him and placed her arms around his shoulders, something she was certain no one had ever dared to do before in his life. "You didn't know. Burke was cunning and devious . . . and quite mad."

"I was so busy setting other people's houses to right, castigating their sins that I failed to see the awful sin in my own house . . . or God help me I saw the truth and suppressed it, let my mind play tricks. I've dredged up every memory I have from their childhoods . . . and I just don't know. When my wife died, Anthea was only three, Burke ten. I grieved inwardly and let servants raise them. Perhaps if I'd paid attention then I could have saved them both. At least I should have saved her from him. I refused to listen to Chase when he appealed for me to help his mother. I think he blamed her as well as us and I have that on my conscience, too. That's when he ran away."

"He was only fourteen. By the time he was brought back he understood that she was a victim, only a child who couldn't stop Burke. She never asked for your help, did she?" Stephanie asked, already knowing the answer.

He shook his head. "She never accused her brother in words, but if I'd been a better father, if I'd been home with them instead of furthering my own career, I could have done something before it was too late. She married a German blacksmith's son when she was only seventeen just to escape."

"Perhaps it was destined to be that way. If she hadn't gone west she wouldn't have met Vanishing Grass and Chase might never have been born."

He reached up and patted her hand awkwardly. "You are a remarkable young woman. One of the few things I did right in my life was to approve his choice of you." She blinked at that but said nothing as he continued. "If only I had listened to Chase when he came to me on his mother's behalf . . . I could have saved you both so much suffering."

"He was a distraught boy then, always unhappy here in the East. I can understand why you couldn't accept his accusations. He intended to return to his father's people long before he learned about Anthea and Burke."

Jeremiah snorted. "He made it crystal clear that he hated my guts even before he learned to speak English."

"You're a great deal alike, you know."

The old man looked startled, then pleased, a bit of the anguish in his eyes replaced by something else. Wistfulness, perhaps? "Do you really think so? I can't wait to see the expression on his face when you tell him that!"

The months wore on yet all their attempts to free Chase from prison were frustrated. Even the wealth and prestige of the Remington name could not expedite the legal wrangling as Jeremiah's attorneys petitioned through the courts. Feelings against Indians had run high ever since the battle on the Little Bighorn. Custer, always a popular figure with the Eastern press, was now elevated to the status of a martyr, an image his widow, Libby, was highly successful in magnifying. Chase Remington, as the White Wolf, had been one of the participants in the battle—or massacre, depending on whose point of view. Indeed, one cynical newspaperman said that a "battle" was an occasion when the whites won, a "massacre" when the Indians did.

Stephanie testified before judges and congressional committees. Through their attorneys she sent dozens of sworn depositions explaining how the peaceful Indian camp had been attacked by the army, how the warriors were forced to defend their women and children, even that Chase was nowhere near Custer's last stand but engaged in fighting down in a coulee by the river when the Long Hair was being overwhelmed on a rise to the northeast, over a mile away. No one listened. Or if they did, they were afraid to move against the temper of the times. An appeal to President Grant failed. In spite of his political differences with Custer, as a career military man himself, Grant could never free an Indian who had challenged the army's right to pacify savages and place them on reservations.

Then in November the furor over the presidential election forced the nation's attention away from the Indian question. After much political maneuvering and chicanery the Hayes-Tilden controversy was settled in the Republican's favor and Rutherford B. Hayes became the nineteenth president. He would be inaugurated in March of 1877. Jeremiah, who had been a substantial contributor to Hayes's campaign, planned to travel to Washington for the ceremony, taking Stephanie and her baby with him. Surely such a personal appeal for a pardon would not be turned aside. In the meanwhile they waited and they prayed.

Stephanie wanted to go to St. Augustine herself to be certain the food and medicine intended for Chase actually reached him. However, Jeremiah persuaded her not to make the trip because of the danger to her unborn baby if she undertook such a long and arduous journey in the latter stages of her confinement. She wrote to Chase but her letters were unanswered. The only thing she did know for certain was that he was alive.

The same could not be said for his Cheyenne family. Desperate to find her adopted children, Stephanie had convinced Jeremiah to send agents to search the reservation outside Fetterman but Stands Tall, Kit Fox and the other survivors of the massacre at the stronghold seemed to have vanished from the face of the earth, taking Smooth Stone and Tiny Dancer with them. Chase had told her about Little Wolf's pledge to accept them into his band and prayed they were once more wintering somewhere in the isolated reaches of the Yellowstone country. But it was only a matter of time until all the Cheyenne were forced to join their brothers and their ancient enemies alike in the hot country to the south. She vowed to find the children and bring them to live with her before she let that happen.

Her life with Jeremiah was a pleasant surprise. The stern old clergyman had become much more of a father to her than her biological father had ever been. As a child, she had stood in terrified awe of Jeremiah Remington. Now she found his stern Puritanical zeal greatly softened by a new compassion born of great suffering. He still carried the guilt over Anthea and Chase. His daughter's forgiveness was beyond hope this side of the grave, but Chase's was not. Stephanie poured out her heart to her love in letters, telling him about the old man's kindness, his compassion and his profound regrets. With every stroke of the pen, her determination grew. Chase must see the changes in Jeremiah. He must forgive his grandfather.

"Perhaps he can't and that's why he refuses to answer my letters," she murmured, looking out at the thickening swirls of snow blocking the view through her window. The city had been blanketed by a foot of snow at Christmas and every few days in January brought another blizzard, each seemingly fiercer than the one before it. The one howling around the corners of the formidable Remington mansion now had begun hours earlier and showed no signs of abating.

Stephanie felt the baby kick and patted her distended abdomen, feeling a warm rush of love. How eagerly she awaited the birth. Suddenly the gentle kick, which she had grown used to over the months, became a long hard pull that seemed to wrap around her belly. She dropped her pen as the tightening intensified into a full-blown pain. The doctor had told her last week that she had several weeks to go yet. What if this meant something was wrong?

Trying not to panic, she took a deep breath when the contraction eased, then stood up and reached for the bell-pull, summoning her maid. By the time the cheerful little Irishwoman entered the room, another contraction had Stephanie doubled up on her knees beside the desk. Bridget's frantic cries brought more servants on the run. In moments they had Stephanie undressed and changed into a night rail, lying in her large four-poster bed. Outside snow and sleet drove against the window as the wind howled ominously.

"What do you mean he's not at home?" Jeremiah bellowed at his driver, who had been dispatched to fetch Dr. Jamison.

"His wife said he went to the hospital this morning, then sent word he'd be staying the night because of an outbreak of cholera," the snow-covered coachman replied through frozen lips. "I tried to get through to the hospital but the storm is that bad. I couldn't make it with the brougham, yer reverence, sir. Thought I'd give it a try on horseback soon as I can saddle one of the riding mounts."

Jeremiah stopped his agitated pacing long enough to look

at the man's frozen features. "Go to the kitchen, Jonathon, and have Mildred fix you some hot coffee. I'll send one of the stable boys."

Upstairs Stephanie lay smothered in pain, focused on the breathless agony that ebbed and flowed in waves. How many hours had passed? She was uncertain of time. It was dark outside and the storm had not abated. Jeremiah had come to sit with her, then left to check on the doctor while Bridget and the housekeeper, Mrs. Keenan, kept watch over her. The reverend had offered encouragement as best he could, and prayers. She knew he was worried about Dr. Jamison's tardiness, although he put on a brave front for her benefit. She was worried as well, even though she assured him the doctor had told her these things took many hours, especially with first babies.

But what if this isn't going right? her mind screamed at her. She was three weeks early. *Please, God, spare Chase's baby. He's suffered so many losses—Anthea, Vanishing Grass, Red Bead . . .*

Suddenly Stephanie became aware of a presence other than the two nervous women who fussed with the bed covers and urged her to lie still and wait for the doctor. She struggled up on her elbows, blinking her eyes as she stared at the foot of her bed.

"Lie back down, my dear," Mrs. Keenan said, pressing on Stephanie's shoulders.

Stephanie ignored her. The presence seemed to float, suspended in midair like bay fog, growing stronger now, materializing into sharper focus. Then another contraction seized her and she fell back with a gasp, arching helplessly as the crippling pain seared her.

Do not fight the pain, move with it. Let your body work for you. You must arise and walk until the little one drops. He will be a fine, strong baby just as his father was.

"Red Bead?" Stephanie croaked through cracked lips bitten bloody. She could make out the old crone's toothless smile wavering in front of her and recognized her raspy voice.

I assisted at the birth of Chase the Wind. How could I desert his son?

"You must save your strength, my dear," Mrs. Keenan said.

"Sure now 'n' don't be gettin' yerself all worked up," Bridget added.

They are blind, Red Bead said. *You must show these foolish ones what to do. They know nothing of birthing.*

When the contraction was at its lowest ebb, Stephanie took a deep breath and said, "I am not worked up, Bridget. I need to walk. It will help speed the birth." Without waiting for a reply, she swung her legs over the side of the bed and sat up. "Now, help me move," she commanded, feeling the pain begin to deepen once more.

"Ma'am, I really don't think—"

Stephanie ignored the older woman and seized hold of Bridget's hand saying, "Dr. Jamison told me this was what I should do." A prevarication but it stopped their protests.

Have them hold your arms so you can move with the pains.

Miraculously the contraction seemed to ease once she was in an upright position. A sense of acceptance and peace pervaded her body and soul. Red Bead was with her. All would be well. The Everywhere Spirit had heard her prayers. She ordered the servants to do as Red Bead had instructed her. They walked across the room, then into the long hallway where they encountered Jeremiah on his way back to sit with Stephanie.

He looked aghast. "What in heaven's name are you doing? Mrs. Keenan—"

"I told them I needed to walk, Jeremiah. It will help speed the birth," she assured him, taking his arm. "Come, help me. I think I feel another contraction starting up."

He blanched but did as she asked. "I sent Hiram to the hospital for Jamison. If he can't find the man, he's instructed to bring another physician."

Stephanie smiled through the pain, no longer stiffening rigidly, letting her body work with it. "Don't worry, Jer-

emiah. I'm going to be just fine and so is your great-
grandson.''

He looked at her oddly. ''So now you think it's a boy,
eh?''

''Now I know it is,'' she replied.

They walked the halls for several more hours. Jeremiah
expressed amazement that she could withstand the pain and
keep on moving. She assured him all was going according
to plan. Twice he left her with the women and went downstairs to check on the doctor's arrival. The storm had made
conditions virtually impassable on the streets of the city.
No one was venturing out into the thigh-high snow and
blinding winds. When the second stable boy failed to return, the old man was ready to ride out himself. Stephanie
convinced him that she needed him to stay with her.

''After all, Dr. Jamison explained to me precisely what
I was to do,'' she lied.

''I've never heard of such a way to give birth. What sort
of newfangled ideas do those Boston General doctors have
anyway?'' he groused.

Stephanie had to smile, thinking of the age-old ways of
Cheyenne women, but she said nothing.

When the contractions began to merge into one solid wall
of pain, Red Bead told her what to do next. *It is time for
the birth soon. You must send Grandfather away. His task
is complete. Yours has only begun.*

Stephanie grimaced, thinking of all the hours she had
already invested. ''Jeremiah, I think it's time for you to
leave us now,'' she said at the door to her room.

''I can't leave you alone,'' he protested. ''Where is that
damned doctor!''

''Mrs. Keenan and Bridget will help me. Everything will
be all right. Trust me.''

''I shall pray for you—and that great-grandson of mine,''
he said, squeezing her hand before he released it.

Stephanie went into her room with the women and closed
the door, waiting for Red Bead's instructions. *You must
squat down, like so and squeeze*. The apparition demon-
strated. It made sense, in an unorthodox way, to let gravity

work for her. Stephanie knew the women would be horrified. Just think, giving birth on the floor like a savage red Indian, especially considering who the baby's father was! But she convinced Mrs. Keenan by sheer force of will to spread a clean sheet on the rug while Bridget was sent downstairs for warm water, towels, a sharp knife, and a ball of string.

Your task has only begun. Supported by Mrs. Keenan, Stephanie braced herself and pushed as sweat began to pour down her body, soaking her hair and the night rail. Again. And again. "I . . . can . . . feel . . . him," she panted out shallowly between pushes.

A thousand miles away in the darkness and chill of a rainy Florida night Chase awakened to the sound of a woman's piercing scream. "Stevie!" He bolted upright in the dank little cell and rolled from his cot onto his feet. Slimy sand seeped between his toes but he was used to the persistent misery inside the ancient stone fortress. He paced over to the cell's one tiny window and looked out at the night sky.

"Stevie," he repeated, knowing he had not dreamed the cry. It was wrenching, primal. She was in terrible pain and he was a continent away, unable to help her. He clutched the bars and squeezed until his hands ached as the frustration of helplessness washed over him. This was the worst part of the rotting death of prison, not knowing the fate of the woman he loved. Her time was near now. What if . . . He closed his eyes and fought the welling despair. She could not die before he held her in his arms once more. He prayed to the Everywhere Spirit, he even prayed to Jeremiah's God.

Suddenly he heard a baby's thin shrill wail and felt Stevie's peace. Then the hollowness of fear left him, replaced by a deep sense of joy.

"He's a fine strapping lad, Mrs. Remington," Dr. Jamison said, shaking his head at the highly irregular way the baby had been born only moments before he arrived. He addressed her as the Reverend Remington's granddaughterin-law, believing, as did everyone else, that she and Chase had been married before his imprisonment. As he washed the infant in warm water, while Bridget assisted and Mrs. Keenan fussed getting Stephanie into a clean nightgown, the doctor asked, "What will you name him?"

Stephanie's smile was radiant as she accepted her newborn son and pressed him to her breast. "Jeremiah Chase Remington. Jeremy for short."

27

Stephanie looked at the huge pile of moldering stones with foreboding. Fort Marion was every bit as inhospitable and ominous as she had feared. The day was stifling with a hot salt-laden wind gusting erratically from the ocean. Billowy gray clouds promised a spring rainstorm within the hour. Casting an uncertain glance at the sky, she climbed out of the hackney she'd hired for the day and told the driver to wait. Her yellow lawn dress was wrinkled and she felt wilted in the humidity as she made her way up the crumbling steps toward the prison. Stephanie could feel a thin trickle of perspiration between her breasts.

She had left Jeremy at the hotel in St. Augustine with Bridget. There were things she and Chase must discuss before she would allow him to see his son. If she could keep her resolve. Over the years she'd shown amazingly little willpower where Chase Remington was concerned. Nervously she smoothed her skirts and stopped near the front gates of the fort. Heavy iron bars were set across its opening like ugly rusted teeth. How lightless and foul smelling the interior of the hellish place must be.

She had been instructed to wait here. Chase was to be released at noon. She had checked her watch before alighting from the hackney—eleven-thirty. But if there was any chance they'd let him out early she wanted to be here. After nearly a year of separation she was desperate to assure herself that he was all right. *That he still loved her.* The sun came out from behind the clouds, intensifying the cloying heat and she cursed herself for not bringing a parasol. Spying a cluster of cabbage palms she walked a few dozen feet and took what shelter they offered. Her eyes remained glued to the arched entrance of the fortress.

Time crawled by as slowly as the mosquito circling her wrist. She swatted it before it drew blood. Her watch read twelve noon. What was delaying them? What if Chase had been taken ill in the pestilent place since their last contact with the commandant? Foolishly she had insisted on leaving Jeremiah's attorney in town, wanting her reunion with Chase to be private. Now she was beginning to regret the decision as all sorts of awful possibilities flitted through her mind.

Then the whining screech of rusty metal grating against rusty metal filled the hushed stillness. She squinted against the merciless glare of the sun and saw a lone figure walk through the big arched entrance and pause as if momentarily stunned by the bright light after a long time without it. The gate clanged shut again and he stood staring directly at her, but he did not move.

"Chase!" Stephanie picked up her skirts and dashed toward him. Still he did not take a step, just continued staring at her with burning black eyes. He was thin to the point of emaciation with a gray pallor beneath his coppery skin, what was visible over the shaggy black beard that covered his lower face. His eyes were old. He wore a pair of light tan trousers, a white shirt and brown shoes, all cheap and ill-fitting. What had she expected—that he would still be dressed in breechclout and moccasins?

Stephanie slowed her headlong rush when he did not open his arms to her but remained motionless except for those restless eyes. The clothes hung on his big frame. She extended one hand, unable to stop herself from touching him. Her fingers dug into the coarse scratchy cotton of his shirt front, feeling the heat and muscle beneath. She was rewarded by the slam of his heartbeat against her palm. Her eyes studied him questioningly as she reached up and touched his hair, which was cut shorter to shoulder length.

Chase did not dare embrace her. She was a vision of paradise, smelling of apple blossoms, robed like sunshine, sweet and pure and beautiful. He would not sully her with his touch. "I should have known you were the one responsible for getting me free," he said at length.

"I didn't do it. Jeremiah did. He's moved heaven and earth for you, Chase."

He digested that, wondering if Jeremiah knew that he had killed Burke. Chase was not surprised that the old man would still try to claim him, but was grateful that he had taken in Stephanie and provided for her and the baby. The scent of her filled his nostrils, robbing him of coherent thought. His eyes strayed down the slender curves of her body, pausing at her breasts, now fuller. "The baby?"

"Your son is waiting for us back at the hotel. His name is Jeremy."

He released a pent-up breath he had been unaware he was holding as he watched her lips curve into a heart-stopping smile that lit up her eyes. *Eyes Like Sun.* "I was afraid . . ."

One day she would tell him about the birth and Red Bead, but not now. "They didn't give you my letters. I feared that had happened. No one was allowed in to see you. Oh, Chase," she said softly, pressing both hands against his chest, moving closer.

He held her at arm's length. "Please don't." She reacted as if he'd struck her, the light dying in her eyes. "Lice," he explained. "They don't allow much bathing. We're all dirty Indians anyway. I'm the only prisoner who required shaving. They had no provisions for it and weren't about to make accommodations for me. I don't want you to be contaminated by the filth of that place."

The grimness of his expression was softened by the hunger in his eyes and in his voice. With a sob she broke loose from his restraining grip and threw her arms around his neck. "I don't care! It'll hardly be the first time we've bathed together."

He could no more stop himself from holding her than he could block out the Florida sun with its glorious golden warmth beating cleanly on his skin. She was his sun, his light, his life. Her fingers dug into his filthy cropped hair, pulling his face to hers for a kiss that devoured them both.

Her hands moved everywhere, around his shoulders, down his arms, over his back. Chase simply held her pressed tightly to him, kissing her as if he could draw the sweet joy of life solely from her.

He was so thin! What hellish things had they done to him? Tears filled her eyes thinking about the months he had spent locked away from the sun, the fresh air and green earth that was life and breath for his people. "I'll make this up to you, everything, I swear it," she murmured between kisses.

"Stevie," he breathed in her name like a prayer, tasting the saltiness of her tears. He reached up to touch one silvered cheek, then stopped when he saw his begrimed fingers with their blackened broken nails. "I need a bath," he said, feeling the filth that penetrated him went far more than skin deep.

She could feel his subtle withdrawal and did not understand it. "Yes, of course. I have a hackney waiting to take us to the hotel. What did they do to you, Chase?" she asked as they walked to where the driver waited patiently on the dirt roadway.

As they climbed into the coach he shrugged. "What didn't they do? Prisons for whites are bad. For Indians, worse. I expected to die in some black dungeon."

"Surely you didn't think we'd give up, abandon you!"

He smiled at the indignance in her tone. "No, I didn't suppose you would."

"They wouldn't let me see you or testify at the trial and I couldn't reach Jeremiah until it was over. As soon as he knew, he set his attorneys to work. We've both written you so many times since they sent you here."

"I never received any mail. I imagine the commandant believed no dirty Indian could read."

"I was afraid of that. The election last fall finally gave us a chance after we had exhausted every avenue in the courts." At his puzzled look she realized he had no sense of how long he'd been in prison or that Grant was no longer president.

"You've been in prison for almost a year, Chase. There

was a presidential election last fall. Rutherford Hayes won. Jeremiah and I went to Washington to make a personal plea for you as soon as Hayes was inaugurated.''

''I'm surprised it worked.''

''Rutherford Hayes ran on a reform platform. Pardoning the grandson of such an illustrious man as the Reverend Jeremiah Remington was a good place to start. Of course, it didn't hurt our cause one bit that Jeremiah contributed very substantially to his campaign,'' she added with an impish grin.

''The army will take a long time to get over its defeat on the Greasy Grass no matter what any new politicians in Washington may do.''

She knew he was thinking about his family. ''I've tried to find Stands Tall and the children. They're not on the reservation.''

''If Little Wolf is still alive they're all right.''

When he offered nothing more on the subject, she wondered what he planned to do. ''Will you go searching for them?'' *Will you leave us again?*

''I don't know, Stevie. I never thought . . . hell, I figured to die in prison. Indians on the High Plains won't be allowed to run free either. They'll all end up penned somewhere,'' he added bitterly.

''Perhaps in the Yellowstone country?'' she ventured.

''Without the buffalo, they'll be forced to live on government handouts.''

''And you don't like handouts, do you, Chase? From the government or your grandfather.''

''Let's go to that hotel, Stevie,'' he said quietly, not replying to her remarks. He was too confused to argue, much less have any idea of what he wanted to do with the rest of his life. The only thing he was certain of was that he would not spend it dancing to Jeremiah Remington's tune.

They rode toward the city, the silence unbroken for several moments. Chase stared out the window at the flat sandy land and cloud-filled sky. ''I can feel the rain coming,'' he said, rubbing his thigh.

''Where Burke shot you?'' she asked, watching his hand.

He nodded. "Does the old man know I killed his son?" The question seemed to hang in the air. Why the hell had he brought it up?

"Yes. He guessed as much when I told him about your arrest. He doesn't blame you."

"Big of him," he replied, regretting bringing up the whole sorry mess. He tried to return his concentration to the scenery but he could feel her eyes on him as they sat side by side in the cramped coach.

What did I expect—that this would be easy? she reminded herself. He had good reasons for his bitterness, yet there were far more compelling reasons for him to forgive his grandfather. He'd been horribly abused in the prison. "You look starved," she blurted out hoarsely, fighting the urge to cry and throw herself into his arms again, but it would not be wise.

He grinned wolfishly. "Thanks. The food, what there was of it, wasn't exactly wholesome. Most of the prisoners have dysentery."

"I knew conditions were awful. That's why they wouldn't let me inside. We can do something to stop the abuse, Chase."

"We? As in the Remington we?"

"Are you questioning my right to your name?"

Poised stiffly on the edge of the seat, ready to shatter, she looked as if he'd struck her. And he supposed verbally he had. "I'm sorry, Stevie. I didn't mean that the way it sounded. I've dreamed of you all these endless months yet never believed I'd actually see you again. An hour ago the commandant summoned me to his office and told me I was being set free. Just like that. No explanation. I was given these elegant clothes to replace the vermin-infested rags I'd been wearing, then shoved out the gate. When I saw you standing there . . . I couldn't believe it." He could not keep from reaching out and touching her hand, just the lightest brushing of his fingertips.

"Was that why you didn't come to meet me?" she asked, raising her palm and pressing it to his lips.

"I'm still not sure this isn't a dream," he replied

hoarsely. "Hell, Stevie, it's going to take me a week to wash away the prison stink. I don't think I'll ever feel clean again."

She touched his lips to silence him, too overcome to speak herself. "Just hold me, Chase. For now it's enough."

She nestled her head against his chest and fitted her body to his side. Chase could do nothing but enfold her in his arms until they reached the small hotel on Charlotte Street. As she paid the coachman, he became aware that he had not a cent to his name, only the cheap clothes on his back. Everyone must know at a glance he was one of the Indian convicts from the prison. What must they make of a beautiful white lady bringing him into her quarters? At least no one commented or made any attempt to stop him from entering the cool high-ceilinged building made of natural coquina stone. Stephanie walked briskly to the desk and spoke with a clerk, whose eyes widened when he saw her "husband," but the man merely nodded to her request for lots of hot bathwater and extra linens.

In a surprisingly short time he was soaking in his second tub of water and contemplating the razor and scissors set out on the table beside the mirror. His first look at himself in nine months was not reassuring. Hell, he was haggard and pale as a tubercular patient and that was the good part. His eyes were cold and fathomless, filled with the horrors he'd seen and lived in that sinkhole. He looked like a hardened criminal, which in the eyes of the government he was—or had been until Stevie and Jeremiah got him pardoned.

What now, he wondered as he stepped out of the tub and reached for a towel. The door to the bedroom opened, and Stevie gasped softly. He turned to face her, holding the heavy towel in his hands.

"Your back . . . does it still hurt?" she asked. His skin was crisscrossed with jagged white welts.

"The scars are ugly but they healed before I was shipped here or I'd have surely died of blood poisoning."

She walked up to him and picked up one of the towels. "Let me dry your back," she said, moving around him.

Her eyes stung with tears as she remembered the brutal beating she'd been forced to watch.

"These are no badge of honor like the Sun Dance," he said as she began to gently massage the tension from his back with the towel. He dried off the rest of his body, reveling in the smell of fresh clean linen.

"It's over, Chase. I don't care that you're scarred, only that you're alive and free. I've brought some clothes . . . from Boston. I think they should still fit . . . a bit loosely." She pointed to the armoire against the wall. "Bridget pressed them when we unpacked yesterday."

He padded across the room on bare feet and opened the cabinet doors. Several of the summer suits he'd had custom-tailored during his student days hung neatly beside starched shirts and a navy silk dressing robe. He plucked the robe off its hanger and slid it on. "I'd better hack the bush off before I see my son."

"You just might frighten him at that, looking like one of those Spanish buccaneers."

He picked up the scissors. Peering into the mirror on the wall, he began cutting away as much as he could of the beard. "Tell me about Jeremy."

Watching his face begin to take shape once more, she found it difficult to concentrate. "He . . . he was born—"

"Late on January seventeenth. I asked the guard the date after I awoke hearing you scream, then a baby crying. Somehow I knew everything was all right."

Stephanie gasped. Her mind whirled thinking of Red Bead. "There was a terrible blizzard in Boston that night and the doctor couldn't get through." She told him the whole incredible story, including the comfort she received from Jeremiah's presence.

He sat, taking it all in, the scissors held motionless in his hand now. "Somehow there's a link between us that transcends the chasm between the worlds of red and white."

She nodded. "I know. Now we have to figure out where Jeremy will fit into these two worlds."

"That's not going to be easy," Chase said, working up

a lather over the remainder of his beard and picking up the razor.

"His full name is Jeremiah Chase Remington. He weighs fifteen pounds now, sleeps up to six hours between feedings and laughs all the time." She noted the razor had stilled when she mentioned Jeremy's name. "Yes, Chase, I named him after your grandfather as well as you."

"That's reasonably obvious," he replied darkly, resuming the steady even strokes with the blade. "Is that your way of throwing down the gauntlet to me?"

"I didn't intend for you to take it that way, but I do want you to talk with your grandfather. He's suffered, too, terribly and he's tried to make amends as best he can. He wants your forgiveness, Chase."

"Then he finally admits the truth about Burke?"

"Your mother kept a diary. He found it the week before Burke died." She let the words sink in as he wiped off his clean face with a towel, then hung his head. She could see his knuckles gripping the scarred edges of the dry sink. He was trembling.

He felt her soft hands on his back, her heat and sweetness penetrating the silk robe, reaching into the core of him. She had never left his heart. He could never let her. He turned and drew her into his arms, murmuring, "Stevie, you were the only thing that kept me from going insane in there. I need you like light and air—no, more."

Stephanie closed her eyes, glorying in his words, feeling the long-denied hunger in his touch. "I love you, Chase. I could never love another man."

He buried his fist in the mass of hair caught at her nape in a heavy chignon, working it loose from the pins until the bronze glitter cascaded around her shoulders. "Apple blossoms," he murmured, nuzzling her throat and trailing kisses around her ears, temples and eyelids, then touching his lips to hers, gently at first, tasting the edge of her mouth.

She was lost, desperate to hold him forever, to let the sweet harmony of the moment block out the world and all the problems in their future. But reality intruded with a sharp rap on the door.

"Mrs. Remington, Jeremy is fussing. It's past his feeding time." Bridget's voice sounded muffled by the heavy wooden door.

"Yes, I'll be right there," she replied as Chase released her. She took a breath to stop the room from spinning, then reached for his hand. "Come, I think it's long past time you met your son."

He followed her from his room through a sitting room and into another bedroom adjoining it. There in a wooden cradle placed near the bed a baby kicked energetically and fretted, gnawing on his small fist. A tall gangly looking young woman with the map of Ireland on her face gaped at him as if she expected to be scalped momentarily. He ignored her, fastening his attention on Jeremy as Stevie lifted him from his cradle, cooing to him in sibilant baby talk.

"It's all right, Bridget. Please go downstairs now and see about having some food sent up for us. Be certain to ask for extra portions for Mr. Remington," Stephanie instructed the maid, who eagerly scurried from the room. Holding their son, she turned to Chase and presented the baby to him. "Take him, he won't break."

A feeling of wonder filled him as he looked down at the small squirming bundle who had begun to cry lustily now. A thick cap of straight black hair covered his head, but other than that there was little to betray his Cheyenne blood. Gingerly he took the infant in his hands, holding Jeremy up to his face.

"He's a fierce little warrior," he said as emotion welled up deep inside of him. Was this how Vanishing Grass had felt the first time he had held his son?

"Normally he's quite happy, except when I'm late feeding him," Stephanie said as she began to unfasten her bodice. Her fingers were clumsy as a sudden surge of nervousness overtook her. Would he watch them as Cheyenne men did their wives when they nursed their babies? What had seemed so natural then seemed somehow constrained now. But it was too late for second thoughts.

As Chase stood there holding his son, his mouth suddenly went dry and his heartbeat accelerated crazily when she pulled open the lacy chemise beneath her unbuttoned dress. Now he could see that her milky pale breasts were lushly full. She reached out for Jeremy and he gave him over, uncertain of what to do next. The baby greedily fastened onto her rosy nipple and his tiny fingers splayed on the side of her breast while his father stood transfixed.

Stephanie sat down on the bed and swung her legs up, then leaned back against the headboard, cradling Jeremy to her breast as he nursed with his usual vigor. "Come sit by us," she invited Chase, patting a place beside her on the bed. Slowly he walked over to her and took a seat.

"I've dreamed of this moment ever since I first learned I was pregnant," she said, extending her hand out to Chase. "The three of us, a family together at last."

Chase took her hand in his and pressed it to his lips. He stroked Jeremy's head softly, watching his tiny face, then looked up into Stevie's eyes. "I never even dared dream . . ."

By the time Jeremy was asleep Bridget had laid out their food on the verandah outside the sitting room. The heat of afternoon was held at bay by a heavy canvas awning while a soft breeze blew from the ocean. Chase pulled out her chair. "Mrs. Remington?" She smiled and took the seat as he joined her at the small table. "We need to do something about making that name official, I think."

"Jeremiah wants to perform the ceremony, Chase." She waited expectantly for his reaction, clutching her napkin with both hands in her lap.

"That would mean going back to Boston, wouldn't it?" His voice was wary but not hostile.

"I know you haven't had time to plan—to think about the future but—"

"You really don't play fair, you know. Once I saw him—saw you together, you know I could never give you up."

He sounded more desperate than angry in spite of the accusation. "I didn't plan it, Chase . . . it just . . . happened. But I did want you to want us."

"Enough to go back to Boston?"

"Even that. We don't have to live there, but you must see your grandfather before he dies."

"The old man's ill?" He looked up from the mouth-watering plate of fresh shrimp in spicy red sauce, his appetite suddenly fled.

"He hid it well, but after we returned from Washington he collapsed. Dr. Jamison told me he's had a bad heart for several years. We don't know how much time he has left. That's why he didn't travel with us."

How could he spurn the earnest entreaty in her eyes? "I'll go to Boston, Stevie. I can't make you any promise beyond that."

"That's enough—more than enough, Chase."

They finished the meal, Stephanie urging seconds on Chase, teasing about fattening him up. He ate heartily, the first wholesome food he'd seen since he was arrested back in Wyoming. Finally, he moved his plate aside and looked at her. She had been watching him through most of the meal, pushing a few shrimp and some fresh fruit about on her plate nervously.

He stood up and reached for her hand. "Come." She put her hand in his and followed him inside.

They walked into the big bedroom where he'd bathed earlier. The room had been tidied while they were gone. Chase led her to the bed but halted, remembering the tense coach ride into town. Cupping her chin in his hand, he looked into her eyes. "Do you want this, now . . . or do you want to wait until I marry you in the white man's way? I will wait, you know."

At first when he had emerged from the prison, bearded and sullen, she had not been sure—not because she loved him less, desired him less, but only because they had not talked about commitment for the future, about little Jeremy and old Jeremiah. "It's going to be all right, Chase . . . now will do just fine," she whispered, cupping her hand around his and tiptoeing up to kiss him as a deep feeling of peace and rightness settled over her. "Now and for the rest of our lives."

Her murmured words were muffled as their lips met eagerly, brushing and pressing, opening to let their tongues dance and glide, tasting the once again familiar essence of one another. He rained small wet nips and caresses along her jaw and down her throat as she clung to his shoulders, throwing back her head until the long heavy weight of her hair curtained the arm he held about her waist.

She felt his hands at the buttons of her gown and helped him, tugging eagerly until several ripped loose but neither of them cared. His hands peeled the sleeves from her slender pale arms. She shoved the dress down and unfastened the tape of her petticoats, letting the whole mass fall to the floor.

"I no longer wear corsets, a lesson someone taught me out west." Her lips bowed.

"A wise fellow." His mouth returned the smile as he reached up to cup her breasts in his hands. "My son is very lucky," Chase whispered reverently, lowering his head to ring one dark-tinged nipple with his tongue, wetting the sheer lace of her camisole. "So am I." He carefully pulled the dainty covering away and made love to her naked breasts.

Stephanie arched into his hands and mouth with a sharp gasp of pleasure, burying her fingers in his thick shaggy hair. Her breasts had been tender and incredibly sensitive ever since she'd become pregnant, even more so since she started nursing Jeremy, but nothing on earth felt as wonderful as this! She trembled and murmured his name over and over. When he had worked the camisole free, he tossed it aside, then began to unfasten her underdrawers and push them over her hips.

He knelt, pulling them down, all the while kissing a path to her belly while he cupped her derriere in his hands. "Your stomach's as flat as a schoolgirl," he said, burying his tongue in her navel.

"You should've seen me just before your son was born. I still have stretch marks."

He kissed the faint pinkish lines around her belly tenderly, as he pushed her underdrawers to her ankles where they joined the rest of her clothing. Then he stood up and scooped her into his arms, laying her on the bed. The frilly drawers still clung to her slippered feet. He tossed them away and sat down beside her to unlace her shoes. Stephanie watched his hands, then let her eyes travel up to his face. *Beautiful as sin*. That was what Sabrina had called him and for once in her life, she had been right. His profile was harshly chiseled, that unique blend of boldly savage majesty and elegantly aristocratic perfection. The rigors of prison had only intensified his dramatic appearance—his high cheekbones had been hollowed, his straight prominent nose made even bolder and his powerful jaw more strikingly male now that it was cleanly shaven. His expressive eyebrows rose like great black wings over those heavy lidded glittering black eyes, eyes which studied her intently. She could feel his gaze sweep up her body like a hot sultry breeze caressing her skin.

When their eyes met she reached up, letting her palms press into the thick black hair on his chest. Her fingertips dug in, feeling the familiar texture of him as his heartbeat comforted yet inflamed her. "Take off the robe," she commanded, pulling the belt with one hand, then shoving the silk away. "I want to see all of you again."

For the first time in his life, Chase felt a twinge of anxiety. "You didn't see it all while you were drying my back, Stevie. I don't look the way I used to."

"I don't care. Every inch of your body is beautiful to me." To prove it she sat up, pressing him down until he lay stretched out full-length for her inspection. She could count his ribs. The slabs of muscle across his chest, arms and legs had grown thinner but he was still a powerful man, lithe and long-limbed. Her fingers traced the new puckered lines at his side and the heavy ridge slashing like a lightning bolt down his thigh. How close Burke had come to killing him! She lowered her head and kissed the wounds, offering a silent prayer of thanks that he had survived.

Her hair brushed, then curtained his body as she caressed it. He filled his hands with the glorious silken mass as a shaft of sunlight from the window caught it, turning it to molten bronze. She slid up against him and he enfolded her in his arms. They lay side by side with her breasts pressed against his chest as he rolled on top of her and kissed her. He raised up over her and looked deep into her eyes. They shared an exchange of silent understanding as she opened her thighs and he slowly entered her body.

Stephanie locked her legs around his hips, arching up and urging his hardness deeper inside her. She was slick and tight in spite of having had a child. He moved slowly at first, careful not to hurt her, but she rolled her hips in that old familiar rhythm they had perfected together, eager with the same innocent abandon she had always brought to their lovemaking. The wonder of her amazed him once again as he increased the tempo, unable to resist her urgency.

After so long an abstinence, their hunger quickly flared into a white-hot frenzy, ending in a mutual blaze of glory. He could feel the tiny tremors of her orgasm build into intense contractions, milking him of his seed. She recognized through her haze of pleasure the swelling rigidity of his staff buried so deeply inside her, and knew the thrill of added pleasure when he pulsed high and hard into her womb.

Sweat slicked their bodies in the sultry ocean air as he collapsed on top of her. They both struggled for breath, murmuring love words and clinging to each other as if never to let go. Chase remained buried inside her, unwilling to break their joining. He raised his head and looked into her eyes. "I love you, Stevie, more than anything. I always have, even when I walked away. I'll never do that again."

"On your honor as a warrior?" she asked with a purring smile of utter contentment on her face.

"On my honor—witch," he said with a sharp intake of breath when she wriggled her hips and squeezed his phallus in her sheath. "So you want more . . ." he murmured.

"I'm as greedy as our son," she whispered, feeling him harden deep inside her.

This time they went slowly, savoring every nuance, prolonging the ascent to the pinnacle, making up for all the lost years and celebrating the many, many more which would come. When it was at last complete, they slept while the late afternoon sun filtered in the window, bathing them with golden light. Chase rolled over on his stomach with one arm stretched possessively across Stevie's waist.

She awakened first and sat up in the bed, holding his hand, watching him as he slept. The cruel disfigurement of his back no longer brought tears to her eyes. She accepted that it was a part of Chase just as his other scars were. When he stirred and rolled over to face her she smiled down at him.

"What were you thinking?" he asked, heavy lidded and drowsy with contentment.

"That you were mistaken to say these had no honor," she murmured, touching the welts on his back and thigh. "You received these for love of me and there is honor in that as well as in the Sun Dance."

He pressed her hands to his lips and kissed them. "You are right. What a fierce and wise Cheyenne wife you've made. But we must also be married in the eyes of white society and we will be."

"I want it for Jeremy's sake but I no longer need it for mine, Chase. I've had a lot of time to think since the day Hugh died. You were right. He was no longer my husband—you were. I didn't kill him to be free, only to save your life."

"More than my life . . . my soul," he replied, folding her into his arms.

They were fortunate to book passage on a coastal packet headed north in the morning. The journey was surprisingly calm considering the uncertain spring weather as they traveled past Cape Hatteras and into the North Atlantic. The nearer they drew to Boston, the more Chase brooded and the tension between them grew. Stephanie knew he was dreading his meeting with Jeremiah. He agreed to it only to please her. She prayed he would be able to see how bitterly his grandfather had suffered and how much the reverend loved him.

Spinning off that dilemma was another—where would they spend the rest of their lives? Stephanie knew Chase's heart and soul lay in the West. He saw the narrow, crowded streets of Eastern cities as little better than the Fort Marion prison. After her years out West she shared his love for the land and would gladly return to it but for Jeremiah. He needed them now and he had so little time left on this earth. Surely God, the Everywhere Spirit, would provide a way.

When they finally arrived at the Remington mansion, it looked no more hospitable to Chase than it had when he was a boy. Jeremy fussed as if he sensed his father's malaise.

Thomas opened the door, smiling with as much enthusiasm as the old sentinel ever exhibited. "Good day, Mrs. Remington. The reverend will be delighted to hear you've returned safely with the young master and his father." As Stephanie and Bridget stepped inside, Thomas nodded uneasily to Chase.

"How is he, Thomas?" Stephanie asked, worriedly.

"Dr. Jamison gave him something to ease the chest pains but he refuses to take it. Says it makes him sleep too much and with the little time he has left he has no intention of wasting it in that manner."

The faint hint of a smile brushed Chase's mouth. The old man was acting himself in spite of his illness. "Is he awake now?"

"Yes, sir. Against doctor's orders, he's down in his study writing sermon notes for the assistant minister, Reverend Downey," Thomas replied with punctilious formality. He had always treaded lightly around the master's wild young grandson.

Chase turned to Stephanie. "Why don't you take Jeremy upstairs and feed him? We'll need some time alone."

She studied his expression for a moment, trying to gauge it, offering her love in her eyes. "Very well. Only remember he's been ill . . ."

He kissed her on the cheek, then watched as she and the maid climbed the massive circular staircase. He wondered which room she had been given as he made his way down the hall to the old man's office. He started to walk in, then stopped. *I'm turning over a new leaf,* he reminded himself as he tapped on the door.

"I told you not to bother me until Steph—" Jeremiah looked up as his grandson pushed the door ajar and stepped inside. "You look like hell," he rasped, as his eyes devoured Chase from head to foot. Was there a suspicious film of moisture over them? He started to get up, then whitened in pain and fell back abruptly onto the chair behind the desk. Before Chase could cross the room to him he shook his head saying, "I'm all right."

"You don't look so hale and hearty yourself," Chase replied, studying the frail stooped shoulders and gnarled veiny hands. It was the old man's face that shocked him most—haggard, weary, frightened. Jeremiah Remington frightened? Once he would have scoffed and said impossible. Now he was not so sure. *He is at last really old.*

"Our sins catch up to all of us one way or the other, Chase. Take a seat . . . please," he added, softening his usual preemptory command.

Chase pulled a chair up to the side of the big desk as Jeremiah swiveled his chair around to face him. "So, she brought you back. I don't imagine you were eager to come."

Chase did not deny the statement. "She told me all you did to get me out of that hellish place. I owe you."

"No, son. I owe you . . . and your mother, a debt I can never repay. You told me the truth and like Pharaoh of old, I hardened my heart and refused to listen."

"Stevie told me you found her diary. I never knew about it."

"It stopped in 1849 . . . the year she ran away." He shook his head. "I would say I never knew the depths of Burke's sickness but perhaps I did and simply couldn't face what he was—what I'd allowed him to become."

"Burke was pure evil. Some men are just born that way. You didn't do it."

"He was my son and Anthea was my daughter. I was responsible for them, but when their mother died I grieved so bitterly I shut them out. I closed my heart to any more pain by burying myself in my work, telling myself it was the Lord's work.'' He sighed. ''The self-importance of that appalls me now. Stephanie believes I only understood what I'd done to you and your mother when I found the diary. But the years after she died and you left I thought about it a great deal. I prayed for her soul and yours. Mostly for yours since she's in the Lord's care now and I believe He will be merciful. I knew I'd driven you away and drove her to kill herself to set you free. Oh, at first I couldn't admit it but it was there all the same. Then I started to watch Burke, really watch him. One reason why I made you my heir and only left him a portion was to see how he'd accept it.''

''He tried to have me killed not long after your announcement.'' Chase saw the shudder pass through the old man.

''I never believed he'd risk that, but I did see his hatred and his greed. Could he have been depraved enough to have done what you said to your mother? The thought kept me awake many a night since she died. I lost her and you. I never had Burke in the first place. I know it's too late to ask your forgiveness, but I will ask you not to repeat my mistakes. The greatest responsibility a man has on this earth is to care for his children. I failed. You have a fine son. God willing, you and Stephanie will have many more children. Don't ever turn away from them in grief or anger or despair. Even though you disdain the Remington money, it has secured your freedom and it can help you build a new life for your family.''

''Are you still lobbying to have me take over Remington Enterprises?'' Chase asked without rancor.

Jeremiah shook his head. ''I know your place is in the West and so is Stephanie's. While you were growing up I tried to force you to be a Boston Remington. All we ever did was fight over that. I can't make you over and I don't have the right to try. Go home, Chase, but take your family with you this time.''

''I think I am home . . . for the first time, Grandfather.''

Chase's voice was hoarse with emotion, intensified by the sudden blaze of joy that flared to life in the old man's eyes when he at last called him by name. "I've listened, not only with my ears and eyes but with my heart as the Cheyenne taught me. Until now I never learned to do that with you."

"Until now I never said anything worth listening to," Jeremiah replied with a shaky laugh, wiping the tears from his eyes unabashedly now.

"Stevie convinced me that you'd changed and she was right."

"I told her she was a remarkable woman. You could have chosen none finer, son. Of course, I could take some of the credit. After all, I did arrange your betrothal. Would it be too late after all these years to ask if you'd let me marry the two of you?"

"I would like that very much—almost as much as Stevie."

Stephanie was waiting in the parlor when they at last emerged from Jeremiah's office. The two of them had been closeted inside for what seemed like hours. When she did not hear shouting or breaking glass, her hopes had grown. The moment they walked through the parlor door, she knew by the looks on their faces and the way Chase deferred to the old man that her prayers had been answered.

After a long winter of the soul, Chase and Jeremiah Remington had found their way back into the sun. With little Jeremy in her arms, she embraced them both.

ஒ *Epilogue* ஒ

The reverend married them the next day in a private ceremony in his office. Chase decided it was best that they remain in Boston while he sorted out his life. Little Jeremy was too young to make a cross-country trip and his grandfather was too ill to be left alone in the big empty house. Jeremy grew strong and sturdy surrounded by the love of his parents and great-grandfather. During their months in Boston, Chase studied the vast holdings of Remington Enterprises, knowing that he and his son would one day inherit the privileges and responsibilities of great wealth.

To Jeremiah's delight, Chase proved to be not only astute in the business world, but actually enjoyed the cutthroat competition with Gould, Fisk and Carnegie. It was easier than counting coup on Crow warriors, he told his grandfather. But in anticipation of the time they would return to the West, Chase carefully trained a factor who would manage the day-to-day operations in Boston.

An agent was dispatched to the Sweetwater in Wyoming to search out Gaston de Boef, who was found happily drunk in his cabin. The canny little Frenchman was willing to search for Little Wolf's band for a price. And after several months had elapsed, he wired that Chase's family was indeed with them. Smooth Stone and Tiny Dancer were well, for which Stephanie shed silent tears of gratitude. One day they would all be reunited.

That winter Jeremiah died peacefully in his sleep and was laid to rest alongside his beloved wife, Ada. In the spring, Chase, Stephanie and little Jeremy left Boston forever. Among the Remington interests was an import firm and bank in San Francisco. The beautiful city on the bay ost. Its location near the town of Rawlins was perfect for our story.

Fort Marion was, in fact, a seventeenth-century stone bastion used by the army to house Indian prisoners transported from the far west. The harsh and unsanitary conditions depicted are realistic. President Ulysses Grant and General Phil Sheridan have been portrayed as true to life as I could make them. The policies they implemented were intended to destroy the autonomy of the Horse Indians whose lands were coveted by railroad barons and gold seekers alike. Custer was one of their tools.

Few men in American history have generated the controversy that George Armstrong Custer did, then and now. Was he the gallant cavalier and fearless Indian fighter of Libby Custer's carefully crafted legend? Or the self-serving and dangerous glory seeker portrayed by revisionist historian Frederick F. Van de Water in *Glory Hunter*? I studied the firsthand opinion in *Wooden Leg, A Warrior Who Fought Custer*, recorded by Thomas B. Marquis, as well as the balanced and scholarly account of Robert M. Utley's *Cavalier In Buckskin*, together with Van de Water's work and Edgar Stewart's *Custer's Luck*. Both from a feeling for historical honesty, as well as the purposes of my story, I chose to portray Custer unsympathetically in *The Endless Sky*.

Further adding to the damning evidence against Custer was George Bent's eyewitness account of the unprovoked attack by Custer at Washita. Unluckily for "the boy general" (a breveted rank from Civil War days, he died a lieutenant colonel); at the Little Bighorn, Sitting Bull was a good bit better armed than Black Kettle had been. To make matters even worse for the Seventh Cavalry, Crazy Horse was, in fact, a tactical genius as I depict him in this book. My account of the actual fight is as authentic as I could make it, but I did take one liberty. Contrary to my rendition, sentries were posted outside the huge Indian camp. When the Seventh blundered onto them they were caught completely by surprise. Only sheer force of numbers and

would be their new home. En route they left the comfort of a private railcar to travel deep into the Yellowstone country with Gaston de Boef, who led them to Little Wolf's camp.

"It is good to have the White Wolf among us once more. I am only sorry I cannot offer better hospitality," Little Wolf said, gesturing to the tough stringy antelope roasting on the fire. The buffalo were gone and game was scarce. Soldier patrols came closer every day. Soon they would be forced to accept the charity of the White Father and live on a reservation. It was a bitter thing for the proud hunters of the High Plains.

"I owe you a great debt for taking in Stands Tall and my people," Chase replied as they sat at the fire.

His uncle nodded. "We had a long ride from Wyoming but our hearts were good for it."

From across the camp Stephanie, once more dressed in a soft doeskin tunic, watched her husband laugh and talk with the others. He was the White Wolf of old here, dressed in breechclout and leggings, her splendid savage lover.

"Your eyes betray you each time you look on him. It is well that you are married," Kit Fox said teasingly as she rocked little Jeremy.

Smooth Stone sat with his foster father at the men's fire, enjoying the great honor, while Tiny Dancer had scarcely left Stephanie's arms since they rode into camp that afternoon. When they left the Cheyenne, the children would go with them. Stephanie had asked her friend Kit Fox and her family to join them as well. "I don't see why you cannot come with us to California. There is rich land, game—"

"We must remain here," Kit Fox replied, shaking her head.

"But game is scarce and the army will find you one day soon."

"At least when that day comes, we will all be Cheyenne and we will go to the reservation together. Blue Eagle and I have spoken about your kind offer but you must understand what it means for us to be part of the People. Our ways are communal ways. We share in times of bounty and we share in times of scarcity. All that we have is that sharing. It defines us.''

Stephanie nodded, understanding. She must accept the way of the People even though she found it difficult. ''I shall miss you, my sister. Perhaps over the years we will visit your fires again.''

''Yes, and bring many more children back with you,'' Kit Fox replied. The two women exchanged conspiratorial smiles for they were both expecting babies at the end of autumn.

Late that night after a long talk with Stands Tall, Chase joined Stephanie outside the lodge that had been given to them during their visit. ''The children are all asleep,'' she whispered. ''It's such a lovely night. Let's walk out and enjoy it.''

He extended his hand to her and they strolled away from the flickering lights of the fire. A million stars blazed above them as they stood together on the hillside, looking down on the peaceful village.

''Their time is short,'' Chase said sadly. ''I still have my life, you, the children, a white world I can fit into . . . but they cannot.''

''Kit Fox tried to explain it to me. There is a joining from generation to generation, a sharing of all the good and the bad that gives their lives meaning. I think we've been given a most precious blessing, Chase—to stand with one foot in that world and one in the white world. I've felt Red Bead's spirit watching over us ever since the night Jeremy was born and now I feel Jeremiah's spirit, too, out here under God's starry heavens. It doesn't matter that we are far from Boston.''

''You are more Cheyenne than I am at times,'' he said fondly, drawing her closer, ''but I've felt them, too.''

Life would go on and the heritage of the past be preserved in their children and their children's children for many generations. A deep sense of peace stole over them as they stood together beneath the blazing canopy of the endless sky.

✍ Author's Note

What if there had been white witnesses to the battle o[f] Little Bighorn, witnesses who told a story far different [from] that in sensational Eastern newspapers? What if their [ac]count had been similar to that of the Indians whose ver[sion] was not told until well into the twentieth century? On [this] intriguing premise I spun the tale of Chase Remington a[nd] Stephanie Summerfield, star-crossed lovers living with t[he] Cheyenne during those fateful days in the summer of 187[6]. The Endless Sky is not the first Indian book my associat[e] Carol J. Reynard, and I have done, but is in many way[s] the darkest. As the old Cheyenne proverb on the frontis[piece] piece says, ''Only the stones remain on earth forever.''

After their Pyrrhic victory on the Greasy Grass, [the] Horse Indians' days of riding free on the plains were n[um]bered. Yet as any romantic spirit knows, the seeds of [hope] for tomorrow can be sewn in tragedy today. May C[hase] and Stephanie's story inspire you to believe that l[ove is] strong enough to overcome the darkness of such tra[gedy].

Much of our plot is based on fact, although w[e have] taken some liberties for which we ask your ind[ulgence.] Army life during this era was arduous for the sol[diers and] their wives. Using such excellent resources a[s] M. R. Roe's wonderful account, Army Letters fr[om an Of]ficer's Wife, I strove to construct Stephanie's t[ime at vari]ous frontier outposts as realistically as possib[le. Attitudes] toward Indians as well as the treatment of pris[oners were] true to the times. Robert W. Frazer's Fort[s of the West] provided me with authentic names for Hugh['s posts, but] I took the license of making Fort Fred Ste[ele in Wyoming] Territory a cavalry post although it was, in[fact,] the fact that Custer had split his command allowed the Lakota and Cheyenne to rally and strike back.

It is my opinion that a military officer who stumbled onto a camp of over eight thousand enemy with a force of less than one thousand soldiers richly deserved his fate, even though the hapless men under his command did not. The Lakota and Cheyenne paid the highest price of all—the loss of freedom, land and way of life for their entire nations.

The primary source for details of everyday life among the Cheyenne remains George Bird Grinnell's *The Cheyenne Indians*. George E. Hyde's biography, *Life of George Bent*, and Wooden Leg's accounts also furnished a rich store of interesting anecdotes from which I borrowed, as did the fascinating reminiscences in *Cheyenne Memories* by John Stands-in-Timber and Margot Liberty. The proud Cheyenne nation and its rich culture has been as decimated by white society as their sacred buffalo. Wooden Leg himself summed up the bittersweet dilemma of modern life for Native Americans most eloquently: "It is comfortable to live in peace on the reservation. It is pleasant to be situated where I can sleep soundly every night, without fear that my horses may be stolen or that myself or my friends may be crept upon and killed. But I like to think about the old times, when every man had to be brave . . ."

Shirl Henke
P.O. Box 72
Adrian, MI 49221

A stamped, self-addressed envelope is appreciated for replies to your correspondence.